Books by
D. M. Almond

Chronicles of Acadia

Book One: *Secrets of the Elders*

Book Two: *Land of the Giants*

Book Three: Necromancer's Curse

Other Works

A Dark Rising

The Life & Times of Kwado Vance, Troll

Secrets of the Elders

Chronicles of Acadia, Book 1

Written by D. M. Almond

The characters and events portrayed in this book are fictitious. Any similarity to real persons, living or dead, is coincidental and completely a byproduct of the reader's overactive imagination. Why are you reading this excerpt when you should be getting a snack to go with your book?

Chronicles of Acadia, Book 1: Secrets of the Elders

© D. M. Almond; 2014

All rights reserved.

No part of this book may be reproduced, or stored in a retrieval system, or transmitted in any form or means, electronic, mechanical, photocopying, recording, virtual reality, painting with meaning, emoticons, interpretive dance or otherwise, without express written permission from the author.

Back cover art: Victor A. Minguez

ISBN 978-1499618365

To Julie, my wife and everlasting muse.

Without you, none of this would be possible.

TABLE OF CONTENTS

Chapter 1..2
Chapter 2..8
Chapter 3..15
Chapter 4..22
Chapter 5..32
Chapter 6..43
Chapter 7..59
Chapter 8..67
Chapter 9..79
Chapter 10..90
Chapter 11..103
Chapter 12..114
Chapter 13..128
Chapter 14..144
Chapter 15..174
Chapter 16..185
Chapter 17..201
Chapter 18..212
Chapter 19..231
Chapter 20..256
Chapter 21..276
Chapter 22..284
Chapter 23..299
Epilogue 306
Acknowledgments..311

Chapter 1

"To world's end with glint and valor,

We were promised eternity.

Reaching further toward the heavens,

Until we fell from the stars alone and small."

Elder Morgana was going to miss the simplicity of these everyday chores. She had toiled tirelessly for the last week to put everything right and had gone through the log cabin with a fine-tooth comb. Every shelf had been dusted and each plate was washed at least twice. She had even made time to fold all the boy's clothes after they hung out to dry. Morgana ran a drying cloth over the keen edge of her chef's knife, savoring the feel of cold Falian steel through the fabric. It was so strange how time seemed to slow in moments like these, when the world suddenly flared out before you in sharp detail. She took a moment to relish that feeling, polishing the knife until she could see her reflection, and then set it down, exactly evenly placed with the three beside it on a towel by the washing sink.

She wiped her wrinkled hands on the apron hanging around her waist and hobbled slowly over to the cabins front door. The door clattered close behind her, jumping against the frame as it settled in. Smells of the bonfire tickled her nose, its flames already kicking up in the late afternoon breeze, which came from the Southern Pass and broke over the hills on the border of Riverbell. She stopped at the top of her steps and looked northward, to the Great Crystal floating high above the massive cavern they and everyone else in the kingdom of New Fal called home.

Secrets of the Elders

Facets of cerulean and topaz worked over the Crystal's gleaming surface, bathing New Fal in Baetylus' light. She found it funny how, no matter how many times she had gazed across the distance at the Crystal God, she never ceased to be in awe over his radiance. She had no sorrow in her heart today. Elder Morgana had lived a good life, a full life, and had no complaints or reservations that today would be the day she died.

Children were laughing, running around the bonfire playing tag, and the sound of it filled her heart with a warm content. Elder Morgana did not fear for herself today. Her chief concern was that her boys, Logan and Corbin, would be all right once she was gone. Corbin was a little less to trouble herself with. He had found a good partner in Elise Ivarone, who would be Morgana's spiritual successor as the village Elder, as had long ago been preordained. Elise did have her work cut out for her. Corbin was a great young man, but he could be a little pigheaded at times, and it would not hurt for Elise to give him a good kick in the rear from time to time. Overall though, he would be fine. *Corbin* had grown up to be a fine member of the village.

Logan on the other hand...now that boy made her worry. She knew in her heart he would manage, but the thought of him being left to his own devices gave her no end of discomfort. He was, in fact, the chief reason she had made sure the cabin was fully in order. Logan was twenty years old, but sometimes he acted as if he was still the little boy she had taken in fourteen years ago, after his birth mother passed away.

"Elder Morgana!" Samual, one of the village children, called gleefully as he ran up to her front porch with a pack of his friends in tow.

Morgana lifted her old brown dress over her ankles and made her way carefully down the three steps. *"No sense in spending my last day bedridden from a twisted ankle,"* she thought. The group of children surrounded her with giggles and smiles. Morgana ruffled Samual's bowl cut hair. "Aren't we looking mighty fine today?" she said, throwing them a wrinkled grin and appraising their neatly groomed clothes.

"Mamma said my dress is special 'cause it's a Culhada," Bethany said, with the pride of a four-year-old.

Samual scowled at her as only an older brother could, "You're so stupid. Your dress is *not* a Culhada...*today* is the Culhada."

"That's what I said," Bethany pouted.

"Now now Samual, you be nice to your sister," Morgana said, smirking at them with a twinkle in her eye.

"Sorry, Elder Morgana," Samual said with rosy cheeks as he stared at the ground.

"Elder Morgana, ma'am, can you tell us the story of the Founding?" one of the older boys, Clarence, spoke up. A chorus of delighted squeals rose as all the village children grew excited over the prospect.

"Perhaps later," she said. "You children run along and play now. Morgana has lots to do to prepare for tonight's festival."

Their laughter and eager faces turned bleak, as if she had just told the lot of them there would be no Culhada dinner. Their gloomy eyes and frowning faces pulled at Morgana's heartstrings and she shook her head with a laugh of defeat. "Oh, alright, drop the sad faces and I'll tell you the story."

The children rejoiced, ushering the old bent woman to her place in front of the fire. The women of Riverbell had done a grand job of getting the celebration fire kindled. They had dug out a trench and built the roasting pit wide and long, so that when the spoils of the hunt came back, they could be roasted. Morgana leaned on Samual, needing a little help to steady her old bones as she settled on the mat Elise had set up for her, so that she would not get dirt on her dress. She sighed once her body settled in a crisscross position then smacked her dry lips together. When her eyes caught on the small jug of wine to her left, she grinned, pouring a wooden mug full, and throwing a wink to Elise and Logan who sat across the fire from her.

She was not surprised to find at least half the villagers already sitting in rows around and behind the fire, eagerly awaiting her to begin her story. It was after all a tradition in Riverbell. Morgana took a deep draught of the wine, letting it warm her cheeks and wet her lips, and then she began.

Secrets of the Elders

"Hmm, it would seem that there were more than just the little ones that wanted to hear about the Founding, eh?" she said, pointing to no one in particular. More than one guilty laugh went up. Morgana did not mind. She loved these folk, every last silly one of them, and would do anything to keep them smiling for the rest of eternity. That was really the point of it all, wasn't it?

"To understand how the great oak grew so tall and majestic you must first understand its roots. The cavern of New Fal is blessed to have our Lord, the Great Crystal Baetylus, who watches over his flock with warm arms and guiding light. We are fortunate to have found this place in this time where we have erected our kingdom.

Nevertheless, it wasn't always luck which guided the human condition, was it? No, for we weren't always so enlightened...not back when we lived up above."

The villagers were hanging on her every word, staring over the flickering flames of the fire as if in a trance. Elder Morgana licked her lips and took them in for a moment, before continuing.

"During the last days of life on the surface of Acadia, it became clear that mankind was finally being punished for its vast sins. In the beginning of the Third Age, mankind took over, sprouting like a weed in the forest. In the first half of that Age, our ancestors conquered the land, setting all creatures of Acadia at their disposal, spreading like a cancer across the surface and violating the very laws of nature. In our lust for growth and consumption, rich living forests were stripped away, and the oceans desecrated. Valleys, once teeming with life, soon became nothing more than desolate wastelands as the greedy man devoured Acadia's natural resources.

And for what, so that his empires would grow stronger? As the nations of man grew on Acadia so did the lust for power, each country convinced that their way of being was the one and only true path. Some used the Gods as an excuse for their bloodlust, while others bent the will of their people under an iron fisted rule. Regardless of the reasons, by the time the final world war began, it was on the heels of decade upon decade of ravaging the planet and countless, meaningless battles.

Each empire raced for the next great technological tool of destruction they believed would give their military the final upper hand. Some of the more barbaric even placed their children into military camps, raising them in the art of warfare. Hand to hand, these young warriors fought with the precision and deadliness of a knife in the dark. It did not take long before swords and rifles were no longer enough to satiate man's growing darkness, and so they turned to science, twisting advancements in robotics toward military means. The unstoppable android soldier was created for the sole purpose of decimating the battlefield and ensuring victory under the flag of their kingdom.

Genetic experiments opened the door to countless possibilities. Unlocking never before seen potential, humans began training in the ability to enter each other's minds. Powers were tapped into that would harness the very ebb and flow of the universe around us. And so, Magic had come to our world.

Such a discovery, such a oneness with the universe, should have awakened a time of enlightenment, an age of peace. Mankind could have reached out to the Gods to seek wisdom and understanding. Instead, we forfeited that sacred potential in favor of blind obedience.

It was to be mankind's darkest hour.

Those great empires chose to use Magic and science to continue their struggle for domination, and so the wars raged on for decades more. No one was safe. At every turn there was death and deceit at hand. Our ancestors fought so long and filled themselves with so much hatred they could scarcely remember anything else.

Until one day, the ice giants came to Acadia.

No one knows where the jotnar first came from, but their invasion was swift and deadly. Like the hand of the Gods, they crashed upon the great empires, overwhelming all in their path and caring nothing for mankind's petty wars. The other races, tired of man's destruction, fell oh so eagerly behind the Jotnar, siding with the blue-skinned devils. Once that happened, it did not take long before our planet was forfeit to their might. In the last desperate hours, one of the greater empires set off their doomsday weapons in hopes of vanquishing the conquering horde, but instead, it was to be followed by every other country setting off their own in one fatal chain reaction of ultimate destruction. The surface was awash in the eternal flames.

It will take centuries to repent for the sins of our forefathers. Thankfully, there were some, like your ancestors, that had no part in those wars. These smaller lands of goodly folk were wise enough to seek survival inside our planet. Those pilgrims traveled for years in search of this sanctuary, moving deeper and deeper into the very core of Acadia. It was only here, in the kingdom of New Fal, under Baetylus' guiding light, that peace had finally been found. Moreover, it is here that we set ourselves on the path of righteousness, determined never again to repeat the sins of our past. It is this lesson that we humans must never forget.

That was two hundred and twenty-six years ago..."

Chapter 2

Under the waning light of dusk, Elder Morgana's words rang hollow in Logan Walker's ears as she retold the tale of the Founding. He did not understand why the villagers were huddled around the great fire, gobbling up her every word as if it were a revelation. This was the same story she told every year during the Culhada, a celebration of the Great Crystal's cycle of renewal, and it was a version of history that, even as a child, he could never seem to swallow. Today he was no longer a child, but a young man of twenty years, already almost halfway through his life. However, he still found that doubtful nagging feeling lingering in the back of his mind. Yet here he was stuck around that fire pit with his fellow villagers just the same.

The Culhada was a time for merry festivities, an occasion to share the traditions that made up their culture and celebrate the splendor of their god Baetylus. Every villager eagerly awaited the festival all year long. Days before the feast, the women of Riverbell would come together to prepare for it, baking all variety of delicacies; oversized pies filled with sweet snaps, honey baked berry fruits, cocoa paste, crescent cookies, and even candied grapes.

For weeks before, Logan could feel his stomach rumbling in anticipation, imagining all the delicious desserts awaiting him. As a boy, he had found himself at the end of Miss Greta's switch more times than he would like to recall for sneaking into the village pantry and stealing a nibble or two. He counted his blessings that they had no idea how few and far in between those times he was actually caught were. If they knew the truth of it, they would have strung him up by his toes years ago. Logan chuckled to himself at the thought. After all, he did pride himself for his devilish antics.

For instance, how much fun had it been to let a basket of mice out inside the village community pantry! He could barely contain his laughter at the shrieks below his hiding spot, while the women ran out half crazed and throwing aprons at the scrambling little rodents. Or how about the time he had filled the water barrels with dye, so everyone's teeth were stained green for a week. They always suspected him, of course, but never had a way of proving it. Logan sighed aloud, drawing a sharp look from Elise Ivarone, who was sitting by his side fervently listening to Elder Morgana's story, as if each word were from the mouth of Baetylus himself.

Logan gazed about the village square in boredom, praying for something to occupy his mind. He thought it was funny how they called it a square. It was really more of a circle, with low squat wooden cabins forming the perimeter. For him everything about Riverbell was boring. The houses were dull, the people were predictable, and everything was covered in a perpetual layer of dirt. Even their clothing was drab, rough wool breeches, beige tunics, and canvas loafers.

Looking up he wondered, not for the first time, what would happen if one of the hulking stalactites that hung high overhead, from the caverns ceiling, came crashing down into the square. Not that he wanted anyone to get hurt, it was a morbid curiosity to be sure, but he would never wish any of his fellow villagers any actual ill will.

But it would sure shake things up around here for a change...maybe add a little excitement to all this, he mused to himself.

"What kind of trouble are you thinking of getting yourself into now, Logan Walker?" Elise demanded poking his shoulder and speaking to him as if he were a child who had just been caught doing something naughty. The village women and children all around them were rising, brushing off their long thick woolen dresses, which mustered up a cloud of dust. He had been so caught up in his daydreams that he had not even realized Elder Morgana had finished her parable of their forefather's sins.

"Well, do you have wool stuck in your ears, or are you going to answer me?" Elise stood looking down at him with clear blue eyes, cocking her head to one side, thick blonde ringlets falling over her shoulders and hands resting on her hips. Her dress was surely one for the Culhada, with brightly embroidered roses stitched from the hem, working upward toward her slender waist.

"Surely I have not the slightest inkling of what you are referring to, *Madame*," Logan mocked, speaking in an uncharacteristically haughty

9

tone. Despite herself, Elise chuckled, and Logan reached out to have her help him to his feet.

"Don't you play the injured lamb with me, Logan. You may have spun your little tale with Elder Morgana and the hunters, but surely you don't think I'd fall for this nonsense?" Elise reprimanded, even though she still helped him to his feet.

Logan stood tall at five foot eight, almost a full foot over her, with broad shoulders and chiseled features. His eyes shone mischievous and emerald-green down at her, giving stark contrast to the walnut-colored mop of short-cropped hair atop his head. Elise thought he would truly be a handsome man one day, if only he took some care to groom himself up a bit more from time to time. Logan was nearly as large as his brother, Corbin, her fiancé, in build and capable of taking on most of the men his age in a grappling match for sure. She frowned slightly at the idea that all this muscle was to be wasted on Logan's silly pranks and loafing about.

Looking as if his pride may truly have been wounded, he said, "Now that is *not* fair, Lisie. You know I hurt myself pretty bad when I fell." He faked a pout, glancing at his left foot for sympathy.

"Well, if you weren't being a peeping little smurf it would never have happened in the first place, eh? Maybe then, instead of trying to spy on ladies in the nude, you could be out there doing your part in the great hunt," Elise scolded, though she knew each word fell on deaf ears. In fact, they both knew that he had zero interest in hunting. It was not that Logan could not hunt, because he happened to be very skilled at tracking and better than most with a bow. Elise had often overheard Rimball, the village trainer, lamenting the wasted potential of the boy with the men of Riverbell. However hard they pushed him though, Logan always claimed he was built more for life in a real city, like the capitol, filled with the hustle and bustle of society. Villages like this were no place for such laziness and vanity.

Riverbell was a close-knit community, where families worked hard to survive. Their goods came chiefly from farming and hunting the land, which produced bountiful crops and furs that they would trade with the capitol of Fal and nearby town of Dure. Once a year they would celebrate the great Culhada, a time when their god, the great floating Crystal Baetylus, at home high in the cavern above their heads, would snuff out his light for an entire day, regenerating for a new year. A month after this the city traders would come, bringing silks, chocolates, and ever precious oils for burning and energy; all the goods the village needed. When everyone else was hard at work, Logan was the one to be found daydreaming in the gardens. When he should have been working the fields, it was not uncommon to find him hidden away in the tall grass napping.

"Aww, come on Lisie, that's not what happened. I already told you, I thought I saw a sand snake going up the wall and wanted to catch it before any of the women were given a fright!" Logan said, though his blush belied a guilty conscience.

No one believed him about the snake. It began innocently enough, with him trying to catch the tiny serpent. Except the sneaky thing went slithering straight up the costume building exterior, forcing Logan to climb a stack of crates in his pursuit. Once he reached the windowsill, the snake slithered inside, and Logan found himself staring through the pane at three giggling women, naked from the waist up while they were trying on costumes for the upcoming celebration. How was he expected to look away from something like that?

When the crates gave way and fell out from under him, it was all he could do to hold onto the old window frame. When the women saw what they believed was a peeping tom they broke into shrieks. Logan quickly tried to explain about the snake, but then a popping sound of the wooden frame coming loose told him he was in real trouble. When he hit the ground, with crates all around him, he wanted only to run and hide, but the flames of pain shooting up his left leg would not allow for that.

It seemed that Elder Morgana decided his injury was punishment enough. She had said she knew her boy better than to think he would be peeping on women. However, she also forbade him from being a part of the upcoming hunt.

"If you know I wasn't being a pervert then why are you punishing me?" Logan asked, though he could care less about being left out of the hunt.

Elder Morgana had looked at him shrewdly, "What was the snake for?"

"Huh?"

"You say you were trying to catch a snake. What was it for?"

Logan grumbled. She had him there. Catching the snake to let it loose in the dining hall would have been a fun prank to play, and there was no use in trying to make something else up. Morgana would see right through it. So, in the end he wound up with a sprained ankle and a week off from village duties. In Logan's mind that was a great bargain to pay for a little embarrassment.

While the hunters were out providing for the feast, he was stuck back here with all the women and children. Logan actually felt that this was a reward. So much so, that he neglected telling anyone his ankle had gotten better three days before the celebration. Instead, he worked the limp with dramatic flair whenever anyone was watching.

Elise wagged her finger at him dangerously, "I have known you all your life, and I can see right through these childish games! I can tell when you're acting the part, which seems to be most of the time lately, so don't you try fooling me." Logan hid a smirk. He could see that glint in her eyes that told him she still secretly found his antics amusing. As children, Elise found herself laughing with him more than once at the trouble he so easily found himself in. Back then, she took almost as much pleasure in them as he did.

Holding his hands up in mock surrender, he said, "Okay...okay, you got me, I never fell from the window."

At this, Elise wrinkled her nose and boxed his ear. "Oh quiet! You *are* a wool headed mule after all.... If only you had your brother's integrity, then you wouldn't need to be sneaking peeks at women's underskirts."

Logan grunted at her reference to her relationship with his younger brother. The three of them had been inseparable friends as children, but in the last three years she and Corbin had become much more than that. He did not like to think about his brother holding Elise that way, it felt weird. Not that he held any resentment toward the couple; quite the contrary. Logan was very happy for them and thought they made a great pair. They made sense. He just did not like the reminder their coupling represented. The thought of having to settle down with one of the girls from the village terrified him, though he knew the women folk were cooking up plans to do just that.

Once Morgana and her flock of mother hens decided who was a good fit, meaning which girl would put up with his nonsense, there would be little he could do to avoid that fate. He knew in their eyes a good woman would take care of his mischievous nature and tame him into a respectable member of the village. Which was why Logan had every intention of leaving Riverbell this year, when the traders came after the festival. He had told no one, only hinting it to Corbin when they ate their meals. It was off to Malbec for him, to roam the city and start a life of adventure.

"Well here comes your Knight of Integrity now, *milady*," one of the village boys who had been eavesdropping teased, tugging at Elise's skirts. All eyes were already on the gates at the seven-foot wall of sharpened wooden stakes that encircled the small village, protecting it from the roaming beasts of New Fal.

Logan perked up to see the hunters returning through the gates, with all the women swarming around them in excitement. Elise grabbed him by the sleeve, happily running toward the hunters. His ankle only lightly throbbed making him a match for her speed. Year after year he had watched the men come back with their meager catches during the Culhada and never did he understand the need for all the fuss. Their bounty was rarely different from the regular hunts.

There was one festival where the game had been larger, back when his father was still alive and had helped four others take down a bull of enormous proportions. The beast had wandered into their territory, virtually stumbling across the hunters' path as they were tracking a wild boar. That Culhada feast was more than plentiful, and everyone swore it would be a wondrous year, filled with good fortune. Logan did not believe such rubbish. That was the same year he lost both of his parents.

Logan and Elise made their way through the gathering to watch as the men paraded into the village with their prizes. Some had nothing but a smile to offer, while others carried bags of tree squirrels for stews or cages of sand snakes for roasting. A few hunters had actually caught a baby boar, carrying it hung on a spear with prideful smiles.

Günter was walking by, with one such trophy, when Elise tackled her father, smothering him with hugs and kisses. "Now, now my little rose; careful you don't stain that pretty dress," he laughed jovially, hugging her back.

"Pa, where is Corbin?" Elise asked, eagerly searching the group for some sign. "I don't see him anywhere; did we miss him coming through?"

Günter gave one of his boisterous laughs, his large stomach bouncing. "That boy is something else! He said he was tracking the truffle thief, and nothing could get him off that trail. I expect he will probably keep on it until he gets the game. Don't fret though pumpkin; that Corbin can certainly take care of himself. I'm sure he'll be back soon enough." Elise pouted and crossed her arms as her father patted her cheek lovingly, while Logan looked out past the wall into the wilds.

"What can my little brother be up to out there all alone?" he thought to himself.

Chapter 3

Corbin Walker slithered across the rock, like a panther stalking its prey. His muscular arms and legs stretched wide with his stomach and bare chest pressed flat against the smooth cool surface of the rock as he waited. He had left his leather vest hanging in the branches above, before slipping down from his temporary perch in the tree, to tie his shoulder length raven-black hair behind his head. Gritting his teeth, the bones of his square jaw pulled against the smooth pale skin, as he scanned the area with probing blue-grey eyes.

Corbin had come out this cycle with one goal in mind, to hunt down the elusive wild boar that had been pillaging the villager's truffle supplies all year. The beast had so seldom been seen and had thus far proven to be most elusive, that his people thought it would be impossible to trap the swine. Some even considered it a phantom. The older hunters told him it was a waste of time to track the beast, unwilling to join in what they deemed a futile hunt, not when there was a festival waiting for them back in Riverbell.

When he caught scent of the boar, Corbin quickly found himself alone. He had tracked it all the way up the side of Mount Monkton, which climbed high in the air toward the massive cavern's ceiling, before deciding it was time to try and reverse roles so that the boar would be coming to him instead.

Knowing this region from his childhood explorations with his older brother, Logan, he quickly left the path and set out through the thick undergrowth and trees. Corbin scaled the nearby roots of a great ract tree as if he were bred for such climbs, carefully avoiding the notoriously sharp barbed branches. The gnarled trunk stretched high up toward the cavern ceiling and angled to bask in the light of the Great Crystal, feeding off its generously radiating energy. He did not need to go even a third of the way up before he found a large enough branch jutting over his attack point.

Swinging himself up to straddle the branch, Corbin made fast work of stripping down to necessity for his next move. He would need to be quick on his feet if the rumors of the boar's prowess were even half-true. Corbin found himself down to his breeches, tightly tied at the ankles around his boots. Strapped across his back was a spear that was taller than the length of his whole body by a solid foot. In his right hand, he gripped the hilt of his trusty curved dagger. Properly prepared, he slid down to the large rock jutting over where the slabs provided a natural barrier. This would be where he would trap the truffle thief.

After hours of anticipation, Corbin tensed his muscles, hearing a rustling sound. A large wet snout poked through the dense green foliage, sniffing the air for the truffles he had hidden at the base of the stone boundary. It felt the ground for enemy vibrations with tentacles that waved back and forth from between the curved tusks of its mouth. Adrenaline flooded his body, and he had to steady himself with the steely discipline of a hunter. His prey had finally arrived and there was no sense in scaring it off. Cautiously entering the clearing, the brown furry beast looked about once more for potential enemies before making a beeline for the tree.

No sooner did it step foot in the clearing, than Corbin was on the move. He lunged from his perch above the clearing, his legs snapped out into a straight line, twirling his body into a spinning arrow dive, with his blade held straight forward, aimed for the boar's skull. The sheer force of gravity alone should have provided sufficient strength to rip the blade clean through his prey's head.

But the beast was swifter than he could have believed. It shifted weight to its hindquarters and let a charged tentacle from its open jaws whip out, aiming for Corbin's chest. One touch from the tingling pod at its end could paralyze him, leaving his body exposed to its goring tusks. Barely shifting his descent in time, Corbin's weapon crossed his chest to deflect the dangerous tentacle, although not quickly enough to avoid the tip, which sent a pulse of energy rippling through the dagger into his fingertips. The blade slipped out of his grasp as a tingling numbness coursed through his knuckles and he found himself crashing into the side of the boar.

Hitting the ground in a tuck and roll maneuver, Corbin quickly sprang to his feet whipping his long spear out to defend himself. The boar was already circling him, its long snakelike tentacles waving ominously, protruding from just below its gaping maw. He knew he needed to disable its deadliest weapon, but the boar was shifting side to side so quickly there was no way he could get a clean hit

A grunt was all the warning Corbin had to get back. Reacting on pure instinct, he ran up the side of the stone column as the boar charged for the attack. He used his momentum to do a backflip over its body, swinging his spear down to pin it in place. Again, he was nearly too late as the tentacle wrapped itself around his spear in midair. However, this time the swine was the one surprised, as Corbin changed his trajectory and planted a boot hard into its ribs. The large creature let out a painful squeal as those bones snapped inward and it rolled over onto its side.

Ready to deliver the killing blow, Corbin hit the ground running. He cursed himself a fool for charging in overly eager as radiating pain flared up through his torso.

This boar has more wits than any animal has a right to, he thought.

The boar's tentacle had scored a solid hit to his ankle. Panic flashed through Corbin's mind as he fell to one knee, unable to feel the muscles in his left foot. He watched in agonizing horror as the boar was back on its feet and whipped its head sideways, knocking him backward into a nearby tree. With barely any time to react, Corbin wrenched his spear up into a nearby cluster of vines and pulled himself up into their thick net between trees.

Corbin had to wonder if he should have heeded Rimball's warning and steered clear of the truffle thief. His vision cleared slightly from the pain, but the boar was nowhere in sight. He wheezed as he untangled from the vines, dropping back to the ground. On his left was a dense expanse of brush, in front of him squirming on the ground lay the podlike tip of one of the boar's paralyzing tentacles. Corbin grinned wryly to himself at his dumb luck.

He dragged his numb, locked left foot in a circle while his lone arm still gracefully weaved the long spear in front of his path. A shift of light to the right gave away the beast's deadly charge. With a mastery built from years honing his skills, Corbin leapt straight up into the air as it stampeded by under him, squealing in outrage as if it knew this was the end, just before Corbin's spear shot down hard, sheering cleanly through the beast's neck. Gurgling blood, the boar rolled repeatedly, stuck in the momentum of its charge, slamming with a dim thud against the oversized stone barrier behind them.

Thank the All-Father, Corbin sighed in relief, crossing his heart as he looked to the Great Crystal in gratitude.

It took a good two hours before he regained enough feeling in his hand to retrieve his dagger from the brush and another still, before he could even begin to feel his foot enough to stand steady. Corbin took time gutting his prize, respecting the boar with an honorable offering of blood to Acadia's soil. The head he buried in a makeshift stone grave so that the Great Boar could return to the light of Baetylus above. Even a boar deserved respect for the warrior's spirit, giving it a proper burial.

The swine was so large that he had to tie many large, flat, tough roots and leaves from an eltin tree together, building a makeshift sled so he could drag the meat back to Riverbell. Corbin's hands were sore from all the work, and he decided it would be wise to take a short rest before setting off, especially since nightfall was rapidly approaching.

From his seat on the edge of the cliff, Corbin could see a far distance, revealing a good section of the cavern of New Fal. He gazed out across the landscape from that high vantage point on the mountainside. Close below him the land curved up and around the base of this behemoth of a stalagmite that was broken long ago from reaching up to the cavern's ceiling. The top of the cavern was so high Corbin barely believed it existed sometimes. There were a few times they had climbed the nearby Gratunmite Mountain, and actually seen the litter of purple stalactites hanging from the cavern ceiling. He was amazed at how barren that expanse was, and Logan had been deeply troubled by the prospect of one of the massive coney protrusions falling, crushing the valley below under their mighty weight.

The expanse of New Fal below him now was teeming with life from the lush woody forests, which spanned for miles, divided by long valleys and deep chasms that disappeared far into the bowels of Acadia. Faraway in the distance, he could see the glittering reflective surface of their god, the Great Crystal Baetylus, sparkling across the still waters of Lake Ul'toh.

Gazing out at all this beauty, his chest swelled with pride over today's hunt. With his catch, the Culhada feast would be grand this year, bringing much fortune to his people. He wished Logan could be here with him, like when they were kids, but just as quickly lamented the reality that he would not look at it the same way. Where Corbin saw beauty and wonder, Logan saw lack of excitement and boredom. Corbin just could not understand the divide that had grown between the two of them. Logan's only obsession of late was with the capitol city of Fal and nearby kingdom of Malbec. To Corbin both of those places represented the same sins that their forefathers had brought upon their race, forcing the pilgrimage to the core of Acadia in the first place.

Why can't he see how fortunate we are to live among all this grandeur, in the splendor of the All-Father's blessing? he wondered, shaking his head absently at the notion.

Corbin let those troubled thoughts slip away and focused his attention back on the Crystal floating far to the west. The Elders compared Baetylus to Themis, the daystar that rested in the heavens above the surface world. Corbin kneeled in prayer, offering thanks to the All-Father for providing everything below it with life. Without their god's radiant azure blue energy, which bathed the land, there would be no way to survive.

Soon the Crystal's light would go out, signaling the beginning of the Culhada. It was already dim enough that he could stare openly at Baetylus without wincing, so that Corbin could trace its long sharp edges with his finger in the air.

When they were children, he used to try to make pictures out of the things he and Elise saw when they stared at the Crystal during the Culhada. Perhaps out of nostalgia he found himself doing this again, forming the Great Boar in the air as if it were crashing toward him. Suddenly a spark of light flared in the heart of the bright Crystal, causing Corbin to flinch to the side, covering his stinging eyes.

"What was that?" he gasped. Another strange reflection of light in Corbin's peripheral vision caught his attention. Deep down in the valley something was moving, and it was large!

With his heart racing, Corbin jumped to his feet and whipped out his bi-vision scope. Holding the lenses to his eyes, the valley below magnified into view. With a flick of his thumb, he moved another lens in place, expanding his view further. He frantically searched for the source of the movement.

"Skex!" Corbin shouted in fear and disbelief.

The giant insects were not a common sight in the cavern of New Fal. About the size of a man, they looked like some sort of monstrously oversized flying scorpion, with translucent wings that resembled a dragonfly, and an armored black exoskeleton that was not easily penetrated. Their eyes glowed red and they had mouths lined with razor sharp teeth and filled with grotesque tentacles. It took three or four good men to take one down, when the rare occasion occurred that the beasts wandered near their village. It was the type of battle no hunter in his right mind relished and many had lost loved ones to the foul, carnivorous insects. Corbin had seen maybe two his entire life, but never together. He sucked in air realizing he was not breathing as he was in shock over the spectacle below.

There had to be hundreds of the flying monsters down in the valley, all traveling in a massive swarm unlike anything his people had ever known!

What could they be doing out here? he thought. When a flare of light rose from the center of his village, followed by another, each one bursting into a colorful glowing flower that trickled back down to the ground, it was as if the Crystal itself answered him.

"They've started the feast," he said, with an icy dread gripping his heart. Corbin watched in horror as a swarm of the skex broke off in a strange triangular formation, heading directly for his small village.

"*They're being attracted by the light from the fireworks!*" he thought.

A pit formed in Corbin's stomach, his mind not wanting to believe what his eyes were telling him. Tiny Riverbell did not stand a chance with its meager defenses against a group that large! Forgetting entirely about the boar's meat, Corbin jumped down to the lower path and raced down the stalagmite's edge. He knew he had to get to the village in time to warn the hunters. He had to warn Elise!

Chapter 4

Baetylus' Acadian form grew dim; it would soon gather its energy inside, creating two days of dim light followed by three days of total darkness across the kingdom of New Fal. The people of Riverbell were celebrating, singing songs of the Great Crystal's time of sleep. When their god's sojourn was over it would awaken to a brilliant glow of greens and blues, a multitude of colors dancing over the many facets of its keen edged surface, once again warming the land with the promise of a long growing season.

The feast had begun with much excitement all around. This year they had a rare treat, having fireworks imported from the nearby kingdom of Malbec. Elder Morgana blessed the plentiful bounty that was brought before her into the village circle, praising that the hunters had done extremely well this year securing enough food to last long through the time of darkness.

A flash of light billowing with smoke shot forth from the circle high overhead, teasing the villagers with a momentary pause before bursting into a brilliant crimson flower. The spectacle drew the usual oohs and ahs from the crowd. As the petals drifted back toward the ground and dissipated, it left behind a smoldering silhouette, replaced by another burst, this one bright purple outlined in soft yellow like a Lotus blossom.

The villagers were singing and dancing all around the bonfire as the Coilden Boys kicked into gear with their upbeat banjo and fiddle.

Logan was quickly swept away by his friends, forgetting to show any pretense of an injured foot. Elise threw her head up and laughed raucously, showing him she could care less, as they interlocked arms, merrily dancing in a circle, and trading off with those nearby.

"Looks like things are getting started, eh Buck?" Watt said, clapping his friend's shoulder, causing him to spit the ginger root he was chewing over the edge of the village guard tower. Staring down from the railing the two watchmen began tapping their feet to the rhythm of the music. It was not a great night for guard duty, but at least they had the best seats in the house.

"Aw shucks, Watt, I just can't wait to get down there and dance with Sally Mae tonight!" Buck whined as he tried to peer up around the thatched roof and get a glimpse of the firework display.

"Be shift change before we know it!" Watt said optimistically, expressing his enthusiasm by slapping a knee as his foot tapped in beat to the music. Buck took his friend's cue, jumping around and dancing a clumsy jig.

He was trying to stay in time to Jonny Coilden's drumming below, but one of the boys was throwing off the beat something fierce. Bouncing around in his jig, Buck spun to look down past the wall, back toward the village circle. He probably enjoyed music more than anything else in the world, taking whatever chance came his way to listen to the performers that came to the village. Last year he had even tried joining the Coilden boys, one of his favorite groups, but they turned him down, saying he was not good enough with an instrument just yet. Buck did not hold any grudge though. He knew there were no instruments he could play with the skill the Coilden boys possessed. However much he still needed to learn about playing the drums like Jonny Coilden, he *did* know what rhythm should sound like and these boys were throwing it off with an awful racket.

"What is it, Buck? Sally down there dancing with someone else?" Watt teased with a wink as he sipped his ale. Buck was only dimly aware of the question, scratching his head as he craned his neck to see what was going on. He could barely make out the high pitch of another instrument over the sudden cheering and was trying his darnedest to place the strange sound.

"That's odd, the longer I look over there the louder those boys are playing…and the worse it's getting." Buck brooded, more to himself than his friend.

"What did ye say?" Watt shouted, covering his ears. "I can't here you over that awful racket!"

By the time it struck Buck exactly where he had heard the awful sound before, it was already too late. He turned to shout a warning to

23

his friend, only to see a skex crashing into the tower. The insect's shiny plates of black armor reflected the fireworks above in a morbidly mesmerizing way, sparkling in stark contrast to the ravenous glowing in its red eyes.

There was not one thing Watt could have done to protect himself from the sword-like insect legs that skewered his body, splattering Buck from head to toe with the blood of his best mate. The horrified watchman never even had time to scream out the man's name as the entire rocking tower came crashing down, crushing a section of the wall beneath in a shower of stone and splintered wood.

The skex attack came on hard and fierce, with not a single warning. Even as the watchtower fell, more of the man-sized insects came zipping down into the dancing crowd, a flurry of buzzing wings and black claws. Logan knocked Elise forcefully to the ground, out of the way of a swooping attack. She hit the dirt so hard he worried he may have broken some of her bones. The monstrous creature did a mid-air turn, thinking to carry away the meddling man for a light snack instead. The skex was nothing if not surprised when Logan suddenly stopped short, spinning on the balls of his feet, and jumped out of its path, leaving it to crash headlong into the great bonfire behind where he had been standing. The burning creature let out an eerie screeching noise as its eyes melted.

Logan tried to make sense of what was happening, *Skex? Here in Riverbell? Why would they be this far to the north? And what in blazes are they doing traveling in a swarm?"* His mind raced to understand. The insects were normally lone hunters, and it was common knowledge that it was not in their nature to attack a town or village for food.

There was no time to ponder the implications of this further, not when his entire village was steeped in the throes of a vicious attack.

Some of the villagers had enough sense to run for any weapons they could find, but it was sheer chaos everywhere he looked. His people were being torn apart and mauled by the skex on the ground, while others were carried away into the air, their blood curdling screams echoing from the cavern ceiling above. Elise did not move from where Logan had thrown her, but he could see her flinch when a shattered corpse fell from the sky, thudding to the ground beside her.

He quickly unhooked a set of bolas from his belt; normally he would use the weapon to knock fruit loose from high branches or to stop a runaway goat from escaping the herd. However, at this moment he intended to use them to try to take down one of the vile skex. Spinning the cord like a lasso to his side, the weighted balls hummed through the air in a blurred circle, as he sought the nearest monster. One was coming down over to his left, chasing a screaming child. Without hesitation, Logan let the weapon fly. The momentum of the throw spun the balls in a perfect circle directly into the monster's fluttering wings, part of it cracking through the veins holding together the thin layer of translucent chitin material. As the broken wings bound together, the skex came crashing to the ground behind him.

Logan ran to retrieve the bolas, which rolled to the ground, sighting another of the creatures rapidly approaching. The eager monster swooped low for him, twitching rows of sword-like legs. In pure survival mode, he flattened out on the ground, feeling the hot breath from a chittering craw slide by, just barely grazing his back. His stomach lurched at the rotten stench the foul creature emitted.

No time for a weak stomach, he told himself, already back on his feet spinning the bolas and readying for the insect's return. The hairs on his neck rose, tickling across his skin, as a chirping sound demanded his immediate attention. Logan glanced fearfully over his shoulder, his eye twitching to see the fallen skex rise with its many red eyes glaring hatefully at him.

This was exactly why he hated hunting; the creatures of New Fal were never fair. Quickly making a choice between the incoming skex and the fallen one behind him, he let the spinning weapon fly. This time it wrapped tightly around the second insect's wings. He scrambled quickly across the dirt in a desperate attempt to escape the other charging beast. His toe hit a rock and Logan came tumbling down to the ground. The skex closed the gap between itself and the juicy morsel in a dead rush and Logan could do nothing more than scream in defiance, enraged at the beast, as he turned to face his death head on.

From over his shoulder, a solid beam of blue light lit the area and pierced the insect's armored face. Its crimson eyes bulged before popping with a loud crackling sound, spewing forth the skex's gelatinous cooked brain. Logan stared wide-eyed and slack-jawed, having never before seen the effects of a laser rifle up close and personal. In fact, as far as he or anyone else knew, the weapons had long since become a thing of lore, another technology lost to the ages. Yet here was Elder Morgana holding a large white laser rifle in her frail bony arms. The weapon looked two sizes larger than it was in the village leader's hands, but she wielded it as easily as if she were carrying nothing more than a bag of mushrooms. Elder Morgana would be damned if she was going to watch the boy she raised be murdered.

"Morgana, what in the nine blazes are you doing?" Logan shouted, scrambling to his feet and running over to her.

"Watch your mouth lad, or I'll have to wash it out for you when this is all over," she scolded, pointing the rifle at another of the insects and gritting her teeth. An arc of blue light flashed, and she blasted it from the sky.

The tide was turning now for the villagers, but so many were lying dead or in pieces that Logan did not know what more he could do without a weapon. Elise was on her feet again, gathering any children she could find, and herding them toward the village community hall. Four of the men folk surrounded the insect whose wings were bound by Logan's bolas, poking at it with spears. They pressed forward backing the thing up with thrashing pincers attempting to block their blows. The skex fell for their trap, walking right into the waiting swing of the blacksmith's sledgehammer, which crushed through its head.

All around Riverbell hunters had retrieved ranged weapons, firing off a barrage of arrows, bolts, and spears to fend off the remaining raiders. There was no rejoicing when the swarm of predators finally began to flee the village in search of easier prey elsewhere.

Their merry festival had turned into a bloody massacre, a flurry of death rained down on the village from above, leaving behind nothing but anguish and carnage. Logan spotted Corbin on the far side of the village, arriving amidst the chaos.

Elder Morgana was shouting orders to her people, holding the heavy rifle upright as easily as a toy slingshot, with the butt of it resting in the nook of her arm. She was completely oblivious to the incoming skex making a beeline for her exposed back. Logan screamed to warn her, running to push the old woman out of harm's way. For him it was as if time slowed to a crawl, moving in slow motion. He watched in horror as the monster swooped straight down. Talons tore right through her torso, stealing the village elder away into the air.

Logan howled, unable to form the words for what he was feeling. He was helpless to do anything more than watch as the woman who had raised him disappeared into the shadows reaches of the cavern ceiling. He flinched when the rifle went off, lighting up the stalactites around her and the skex. Elder Morgana had fought on, denying the monster its cruel feast. Charred pieces of the creature rained down hard as stones, clattering across the area circle along with Elder Morgana who landed heavily to the ground, bones shattering loudly.

Logan was quickly at her side, "Oh lord, Morgana, what have they done to you? You hang on, I'll go get help," Logan promised as tears blurred his eyesight. He knew in his heart that it was already too late; one look at morgana's broken body would tell anyone there was no hope.

"Silly boy, my sweet, sweet little Logan," she groaned, weakly stroking his cheek. "My time to join the All-Father's light is here now."

Logan rocked back and forth cupping her hand to his face and shaking his head in denial.

"Enough of that, young man. You calm yourself now and be brave like I taught you," she said, all the while trying to firm up her resolve. Her voice was so calm it shook him out of the mounting hysteria.

Logan wiped the tears away with flushed cheeks and tried to firm up his shoulders.

"That's my boy," she smiled at him before a flash of pain crossed her face. Blood began to run from the corner of her mouth and Logan whimpered.

"Morgana please...what should I do? What can I do?" he implored.

"Get yourself to Fal, they must be warned...ugh...t-the implica-ugh." The old woman convulsed in pain. Logan removed the rifle from across her chest, revealing the gruesomely twisted torso beneath. She had already lost so much blood. He did not even know that much could fit inside a person. It was thick and sticky and pooled all around. Elder Morgana suddenly gripped him hard by the collar. She pulled Logan close to her face, with an alarming amount of strength that no dying person had a right to possess.

"The council must be warned," she hissed, slapping the rare weapon into his hands as a whirring sound built up in her chest. Logan tried to make sense of it all, but she flung him back through the air away from her as if he weighed no more than a ragdoll, then rolled over onto her belly.

"Keep back you fool!" she screamed, as the high-pitched whirring grew louder, hurting his ears. All around the area people covered their ears as they frantically fled from the Elder. A massive explosion rocked the area, shaking the ground as fire billowed out from where Morgana's body had been. The force of it rolled Logan another two feet, leaving him face down in the dirt.

His world was ringing and blinding lights. Logan felt someone moving him from far away, down a long tight corridor. Their words were like a whisper and a roar at the same time. Rubbing his eyes, he tried to remember which way was up, reorienting himself in a double vision of Corbin, who was shouting for him to speak from somewhere just beyond that incessant ringing noise filling his skull.

Logan could see Elise had joined them, her eyes blood red from the dust of the explosion. She said something incomprehensible, and he thought it was time he took that nap now, as everything turned to black. Slumping back Logan's eyes rolled into the back of his head and his lids began fluttering. Elise snapped him out of the stupor with a desperate slap across his face, opening his eyes wide.

"*Owww*...what are you trying to do, take my nose off?" he yelped, fully aware of his surroundings once more.

Elise was so overwhelmed with relief that she let all the emotions she pent up during the wild attack out in one gushing wail and crashed into Corbin's arms. He did not look so well himself, on his knees in the dirt beside Logan, wearing a glassy shell-shocked expression. He was trying to take in the surreal scene of carnage, but the spectacle was more than anyone should be forced to bear in their lifetime.

"What are we going to do?" Elise sobbed.

"Um...well I...," Corbin began, gasping for air. Elder Morgana had always and ever been the one person everyone rallied behind in the village. Corbin realized he would need to be strong for their people and squared out his shoulders. "First, we should set up an area for the wounded, probably the community hall, then we should start getting a head count and moving the injured indoors. Also, I would send someone to get water. Then we can..."

"Morgana told me what needs getting done just before she...she...," Logan cut off, unable to process what he had witnessed.

"Exploded...," Elise finished for him, her lips still trembling.

"Yeah...*exploded*," Logan said, feeling the word on his tongue like a taste you could not place.

Corbin shook his head, denying the absurdity of such a claim. "Logan this is important, stay focused. What did Morgana say before she died?" he asked, grabbing Logan's shoulders and forcing him to look him in the eyes. Even though he had been drifting back into that dazed stupor, Logan shrugged him off, scowling.

"She didn't *die*. She was murdered by that disgusting creature," Logan said, bracing himself against his brother to rise with a grunt. "Morgana told me I have to get to the capitol and warn them right away."

Corbin tilted his head toward Logan, searching for something.

"Really? You think I would make that up just to go to the city at a time like this?" Logan snarled, rolling his eyes at his brother's silent accusation. He waved his free hand around at the villagers, who were running around trying to find their loved ones amidst the screaming and groaning.

Corbin thought little of his brother's willingness to do his part, but even Logan could not be so callous that he would ignore their people in this moment of need. "No," he admitted.

"If this is true, you will both need to leave at once," Elise said.

Some of the villagers were bracing Gunter and heading for the trio. Corbin ran out to meet them, offering his assistance.

"Elise, what do you want us to do?" one of the men named Rygor asked, bent under Gunter's ample weight. Her father was out of it, with blood flowing freely from a head wound that was staining his beard red.

"Oh pa...," she stroked his cheek, cupping a hand over her mouth. Logan feared she might pass out and he would scarcely blame her, seeing her father's wound. He reached out to support Rygor, as did Corbin.

"Madame Elise...please," Rygor urged, "we need to know what you want us to do." That was when it hit the three of them. Logan gazed over to his childhood friend, with her soot-covered curls and pale cheeks, and watched as the expression on her own face changed. She too was accepting this new reality. For all her life, Elder Morgana had been grooming Elise for this day that she never truly expected to come, the day she would become the village elder.

Elise pulled herself together, mustering up enough bravery to face this in her village's hour of need, and began reciting all of Corbin's ideas to Rygor and the other villagers around, who eagerly gobbled it up and began to assist. She left the brothers, moving through the crowd, shouting orders the way she knew Elder Morgana would have if she were still there with them. Within a short time, the village was returning to some semblance of order, the people all organized into tasks and duties to help their loved ones.

Corbin moved to assist his fiancée, but she turned, placing a gentle hand to his chest. "No, my love, you must get to Fal and warn the high council of the impending attack."

"But...there must be someone else who can go? My place is here by your side, helping our people," Corbin said, while Elise shook her head slowly with each word.

"There *is no one else*; you and Logan are the fastest runners in Riverbell. You want to help me? Then please do this *for* me... no not just that, do this for the people of New Fal," she said, appealing to his sense of honor. She could see in his expression that Corbin had given in and pulled her fiancé down to kiss him on the forehead.

Logan pulled Corbin back by the shoulder, after he and Elise broke their embrace. "We have to get on the road right away; there is no time to lose," he insisted, agreeing with Elise.

Corbin looked at a loss for words, feebly trying to counter the idea. "But you're too weak from the blast; you should stay here and recover."

Logan brushed off the notion, firmly shaking his head and looking Corbin straight in the eye. "Oh no you don't, I'm fine. It's just a little bump to the head." Without waiting for Corbin to follow, he turned to run toward their cabin for a quick scavenge of supplies.

Chapter 5

They had been running for three solid hours with no break. Logan's lungs burned raw, and his legs ached, but he felt that he could go a couple more hours yet, before needing to stop for a short rest. The mad dash through their cabin had gathered enough supplies to make a quick break for the road. Logan changed his tattered clothing, throwing on a plain loose-fitting tunic held down under brown suspenders that kept his plain looking baggy breeches up. He strapped his father's old revolver to his waist and holstered the laser rifle Elder Morgana had given him over a shoulder.

He regretted not owning any gloves but changed into his knee-high saddle leather hiking boots, so at least his feet would be somewhat protected. Corbin had not changed his clothing, but focused his time gathering dried meats and leftover crusty bread Morgana had baked earlier in the week. He divvied the rations up into backpacks for both of them with other basic supplies.

So far, the run had been easy going, and they were making steady progress. Logan could only hope they were moving swift enough to keep ahead of the skex. Corbin had told him of the sight he had seen from his hunting expedition, and he had no wish of crossing paths with even a fraction of that swarm.

Unfortunately, the pass ahead demanded they be overly cautious, and that meant slowing down. Up until now, they had been running through a narrow crevice in the flat rock floor, which marked an old trade route to the capitol of Fal. Ahead they could see the end of the path, where the rock abruptly disappeared, dipping down twenty feet or so, marking the beginning of a series of chasms where the land was ripped apart during a great quake from the time of Logan's infancy. It was the reason no one used this road anymore, even though it *was* the fastest route to the capitol. The council's highwaymen had built a new road on a more reliable pathway, but that would take too long to travel, and they sorely needed to buy any time they could if they wanted to get to Fal in time to warn of the incoming threat. Corbin skidded to an abrupt halt so fast that Logan almost ran right over him. Leaning on his spear to steady himself, Corbin gazed over the cliff's edge, deep down into the ravine.

"How far do you think you can jump?" Corbin asked him, tapping his thigh with the spear's hilt.

Logan tried to gauge the distance across the narrow chasm, "I'll make it across just fine," he replied, though the site made him feel uneasy. "Worry about yourself, big boy."

Corbin grumbled, annoyed at his brother's need to be trivial. "Well, I'm not sure *I can.*" he added, surprising Logan.

"Wow, finally something the pride of the village can't do?" Logan jested; regretting it when he noticed Corbin's pained expression. He felt like an idiot for not noticing the anguish Corbin was holding back over Morgana's death. Logan decided to ease off him a bit. "Relax, you've got this. Look," he said framing the ravine with his fingers held like a square, "it's no further across than the Witch's Elbow back home."

Corbin looked where his brother was referring to, picturing the river bend they used to hop across when they were children.

"Ready?" Logan asked. "Watch and learn…oh and follow." Logan took a couple steps back to get a running start and leapt right over the narrow chasm, landing deftly on the other side. He turned to beckon his brother across reassuring him it was no problem.

Corbin backed up further than Logan had, then sprang forward using his spear at the last second to pole vault across the distance with ease. He landed past Logan, wearing a weak smile, though his eyes never lost the look of deep anguish.

They moved from one jutting rocky outcrop along this side of the chasm to another, leaping across large gaps and small, scaling tall inclines and rugged stones. From rock face to the lips of stalagmite walls and back, the brothers rappelled in rapid succession, until they were pulling themselves up on the opposite bank of the shattered expanse. They skirted the perimeter for a short distance and came back to the old trade route. Logan gave one final look over his shoulder and a shiver ran down his spine, secretly relieved to be past the dangerous area. The thought of what might be at the bottom of those shadowy ravines, should they have slipped any step of the way, disturbed him more than a little.

"Come on Logan we have to hurry!" Corbin called back, darting up the path.

Oh sure, now that I talk him through moving across the chasm, he gets cocky again, Logan thought. If there was one thing, he never liked it was being bossed around. Corbin may have grown up in the villagers' eyes, but to Logan he was still just the little brat that followed him around pestering him all the time. If anyone was giving orders on this journey, it was going to be him, something he meant to establish quickly. "Keep your voice down, you grub-headed fool," Logan hissed, already caught up to his brother. "Or are you trying to bring every cougar in the area down on us?"

Corbin looked confused. "There aren't any cougars around these parts, are there? I thought they only stalked the jungles in Malbec?"

Logan did not miss a beat as he clapped the back of his brother's head. "Don't get smart with me; you know exactly what I meant." Corbin glowered, but did nothing to counter the discipline, silently rubbing his neck while running. "Either way you shouldn't be yelling like that around here," Logan said, hopping over the thick root of a tree, which had grown across the broken path. "Big shot hunter like yourself should know how exposed we are right now."

Corbin rolled his eyes at the petty insult. If Logan had a problem being told to catch up, maybe he should stop being lazy and causing trouble all the time. Corbin was not about to apologize for assuming he would lag behind, or let Logan make him feel bad for becoming a master of his discipline.

"We should stop for a short rest while we can," Corbin said.

Logan nodded, spying an area ahead where a goodly sized fallen stalagmite blocked their way. Without any hesitation and still running at full speed, they both jumped up and quickly scaled over the obstacle.

"This is as good a place as any," Logan said, as they came down the other side. He eyed the dry sticks littering the area and reached into his pack to pull out a pack of flint.

Secrets of the Elders

"We will not need a fire tonight," Corbin said, pointing at the flint. "Don't want to attract any undue attention, eh? Plus, we won't even be here long enough to warrant the work."

A man-sized gastropod stirred, hearing the thumping men enter its territory. The mammals sounded nice and heavy, good eating, enough even for it to share with its brothers and sisters in the area. Normally it would attack right away, but these creatures were quick on their feet. The oversized snail settled itself in to wait for the right opportunity to strike.

Logan plopped down, leaning against the outcropping of large stones that formed a perfect cozy nook. Ahead of them, the path continued through a dense copse of trees that would stretch on for about an hour, according to the map Gunter had given them. It was a slightly more unpredictable trek then they had been traveling, so the decision to stop and rest for a bit was wise. They would need all their wits about them to keep from falling into a predator's trap in those woods. Even with the Crystal only at half brilliance this area was dangerous enough, its light exposing them to any hungry beast around. However, the forest was even worse, its canopy blotting out most of the Crystal's light. They could only be grateful for the small amount of light they had left. Soon the Culhada would be in full swing, and the land would be as dark as the dangerous ravines they had passed.

Logan laid his small food pack on top of the nearest rock, which came up to just under his head. It was always a good idea to keep food off the ground, otherwise something might scurry away with it while they rested. He leaned back against the smooth rock face, which was strangely warm and comforting, and crossed his arms over his chest. Logan considered his brother for a moment, while Corbin unpacked his things, laying them neatly in a triangle formation in preparation for prayer.

His mind wandered to before they left Riverbell, when Corbin had spent a few minutes talking with Elise in private. He did not hear their full conversation but understood enough to know Elise was telling his little brother not to worry about her and to hurry back. Corbin knelt and bowed his forehead to the soil, facing in the direction of the Great Crystal.

"Why do you waste your time with that nonsense?" Logan snorted, referring to his devotion to the god, Baetylus.

Corbin scowled at his brother. "You should show respect to our All-Father, Logan. Even *you* are not above his radiance, no matter how much you laugh at the world he has provided us."

His words rolled off Logan like water over stone. He could care less about worshipping idols and wasting time with rituals. Where was this Baetylus when his mother was killed? Where was the All-Father earlier today when their village was torn asunder?

"Whatever you say little guy, just don't expect me to come over there bowing to the Crystal in the dirt with you." Logan said, rolling his eyes before sinking into his own thoughts, which quickly dwelled on their destination. Long had he dreamed of visiting the capitol city, wanting badly to see the intrigue of civilized society. The great palaces filled with lords and ladies in Fal kept him awake many a night in wonder when he was a child. Something funny occurred to him, and he was about to tease his prostrate brother again, when a sharp prick stabbed the back of his left hand.

For a moment Logan did not understand the sensation.

The rock behind him rumbled, rearing up to reveal the head of a giant land snail, or rather the rock itself *was the gastropod's protective shell!* Logan cursed himself for a fool, digging his heels into the dirt as the snail began trying to reel him in. It roared and contracted the long tongue-like radula that had a row of small teeth gripped around the flesh of his hand, which was only two feet away from a slavering maw.

With his free hand already gripping his knife, Logan stabbed at the extended fleshy radula to no avail. The teeth covering the tongue-like appendage were oozing in thick saliva that acted as a rock-hard coating to stop its prey from breaking free.

The giant snail had encountered prey like this before and it knew just how to handle them. It flexed the radula and roared again, bucking to swing Logan to the side, against the real boulders. As his body bounced off the hard surface, Logan went limp, the knife flying out of reach while he fought to regain his senses. The hungry snail took that opportunity to reel him in closer.

Corbin watched in horror as the sneaky creature quickly attacked his brother. Flipping his spear over his shoulder, he was already running into the fray. Snapping like a turtle, he burst forth lunging with the tip of the spear. The snail used Logan's body to attack Corbin and he had to shift his stance, rolling sideways before jumping back to his feet. In one fluid move, he used the spear to pole vault straight up into the air. The monster snail let out a high-pitched roar as Corbin came down, slicing his weapon through the thick meaty middle of its grasping tongue. White juices oozed forth in a stream of sour smelling blood across the dirt. The snail retracted the remnants of the appendage with a high-pitched mewling.

Logan himself let out a yelp, as the beast's severed tongue loosened around his wrist, the teeth popping free to reveal a swollen hand riddled with cuts. Flipping over onto his back, he lay propped on one elbow clutching his right wrist.

Corbin stood as a barrier between his older brother and the giant snail, protectively holding his spear at length to keep the beast at bay. The hungry gastropod backed ever so slightly away, never taking its eyestalks off his swaying movements. Another snail roared in the distance, close by up the rocky slope, responding to its sister's cry.

"We better get out of here before the bastard's friends come for dinner," Logan groaned, pulling himself to his feet despite the waves of pain in his hand. He knew if there were two in the area there were sure to be many more. While Corbin kept the beast hard pressed, stinging its soft flesh with his spear and dodging a lunge, Logan quickly gathered up his knife from the dirt.

"Corbin, we have to go *now*!" Logan hoarsely insisted, fighting the racking pain in his knuckles to pull Corbin by the shoulder toward the edge of forest.

"Perhaps I should finish this one first?" Corbin asked, threatening the creature as he stalked in to stab again.

Logan tried to shout a warning, but there was no time, and he found himself tackling Corbin to the side. The land snails had a sneaky defense if anyone came close enough, shooting highly toxic saliva from their mouth that, if it made contact, would melt their prey's flesh into the edible liquid they preferred feasting upon. It was a defense Logan had seen once before, but never wished to again. His body hit Corbin with enough force to send them both flying out of the way just in time, while simultaneously flicking his wrist toward the land snail. The gastropod's mewling turned to a death rattle, as his knife burrowed deeply into its face, just between the eyestalks.

The brothers lay there for a moment, thinking on what just happened, or nearly could have happened, while watching the giant land snail quiver in its death throes, futilely trying to retreat inside its shell. Again, the roar came from up the rocky slope, but this time a much closer answer rang out behind them, just down the side of the cliffs into the valley.

"I believe that was our last warning!" Logan scrambled to his feet, as Corbin quickly gathered their packs, and they fled into the forest.

Elise dropped the bloody cloth into a bucket of cold water again, swirling it around to get as much of the filth off as possible, before pulling it out and wringing the water over the pal. Her aching hands carefully worked back and forth, cleaning the long cuts running down farmer Benn's spine. His shirt had been torn to shreds when a skex had attacked him from behind, and they stripped the bloody rags off, laying the unconscious man face down on one of the wooden tables in the town hall to tend his wounds.

The long log cabin was filled to bursting with the groans and moaning of other wounded victims from the skex attack. As soon as Elise finished tending to one patient, another would be brought to her, in an almost infinite stream of her friends and family. Very few were able to make it out of the raid without being injured in some way. Though they all would equally share the psychological damage for years to come. She had been working non-stop since the Walker

Secrets of the Elders

brothers left the village to warn the capitol and it was starting to catch up on her body.

Elise's arms were sore, her fingers barely able to move anymore from hours of cleaning cuts and stitching wounds. She had no tears left to shed, her blue eyes stinging red and swollen, and her curly blonde hair was frayed, hanging wildly from a bun she had tied behind her head.

"Ahem, Madame Elise...," Rygor cleared his throat, startling her.

Elise turned around red-faced, "Oh...I did not hear you come up," she said, realizing she must have been nodding off while taking care of farmer Benn. "What is it Rygor, do you have a final count?"

The man solemnly nodded his head. "Yes Madame Elise...we are up to sixty-four wounded, seven of them minor injuries, but the other fifty-seven..."

That number loomed before her, sixty-four of her fellow villagers. "And how many are still missing?" she asked, afraid to hear the answer.

"We are still tallying it up Madame...but I can tell you it's not good." Rygor wrung his calloused hands together with a faraway expression creeping across his face.

Elder Morgana had been teaching her the ways of leadership since she was a mere babe, seeing some potential in her for greatness. She had been preparing Elise for this moment all her life. Surely, the village Elder had not anticipated a skex attack would be the catalyst to put her in the role of village leader, but everyone seemed to be falling right in step with it.

A stream of villagers had already come to Elise asking her what to do next or how to solve a medical predicament. When she was young, all she wanted to do was spend time with the Walker brothers, not knowing then that she would fall madly in love with one of them, but Elder Morgana, the boy's surrogate mother, had always told her she needed to focus on her studies so she could one day become a wise leader for Riverbell. At the time, she had scoffed at the notion, but after the disastrous events that had engulfed her peaceful farming village, Elise finally came to fully appreciate just what knowledge she possessed.

Firming up, Elise rubbed the weariness out of her eyes, willing herself to put on a show of strength for Rygor's benefit. "Now is not the time to dwell in sorrow, Rygor. Now is the time to help those that need us most and to keep our heads clear." She tried to sound confident and wise, through parched lips and the lump in her throat.

A light flickered in the man's eyes, and he began to nod. "Oh, I know… I know, don't you doubt it," he said, as if convincing himself and looking at her glazed eyes that wore puffy red bags under them, "It's just, I keep thinking about those monsters and it's got my blood freezing."

A flash of the horrible skex feasting on her friend Garrison, a young man her own age that they used to play hide-n-seek with when they were all children, ran across her mind's eye. The image of him screaming and clawing the ground while tentacles pulled the skin off his back in strips haunted her. Elise closed her eyes tight. "We mustn't dwell on such things," she said.

"You're right Madame, of course. I'll tell you one thing though, I certainly don't envy those poor wretches in Fal, they've no idea what Hel is about to rain down on them, do they?" he asked.

Elise dropped the cloth to her feet, the image of Garrison replaced by images of Corbin thrashing underneath the slavering insect.

"Would you get out of here and go do something useful?" Bertha snapped, moving away from the table beside them and clapping the side of Rygor's shoulder with the flat of her hand. "You've gone up and worried the poor lass."

Rygor rubbed the spot, ashamed that he had forgotten about Corbin racing to warn the capitol. Surely if and when the swarm arrived, he would be there to face them…if he even made it there in one piece. Rygor stumbled over an apology and quickly retreated down to the other side of the long log cabin, to tend what wounded he could help.

"Never you mind him sweet girl…he don't mean nothing by it, just being a stupid man that's all," Bertha comforted her, patting Elise's shoulder soothingly.

"Oh, I know he didn't mean nothing by it, just wasn't thinking before he spoke." Elise agreed, hiding the panic in her voice with a cough as she bent over to pick up the washcloth and place it back in the bucket. "Besides, even if he hadn't mentioned it, I still can't help but think about poor Corbin out there all alone." As she finished the thought, tears she could not believe were still in her, began to pour out of her eyes uncontrollably.

Bertha pulled her in, cradling Elise's head against her heavy bosom and stroking the young woman's hair. "Now now my dear, you know as well as anyone how capable that young man is. If there was ever a person could take care of himself, surely, it's Corbin Walker. And he ain't alone, why Logan is out there with him too."

Elise nodded her head, her sobs muffled under the large woman's embrace. Corbin was not only the finest hunter in Riverbell, but also one of its most skilled warriors. In fact, he was only matched in prowess by one other person, his older brother Logan. Except where Corbin spent years honing his skills under the disciplined tutelage of sensei Rimball, Logan seemed to be a natural talent, who possessed lightning-fast reflexes and brute strength to match even the finest fighters. Many in the village even claimed, if he had not turned his back on Rimball's teachings at a young age, Logan would have been even more adept at the techniques than his younger brother became. She knew the real problem facing them was not their ability to defend themselves, but their ability to get along for more than ten minutes at a time. It seemed the older the brothers grew; the more bitter and grouchy Logan became. It was heartbreaking to see the senseless rift that had grown between them.

Elise pulled herself back a step, gripping Bertha's arms and slowly nodding her head. The woman was right, and even if she was not, Elise *had* to have faith that the Walker brothers could make it to Fal in time to warn them before anymore senseless death occurred.

"Thank you, Bertha...sorry, I lost my head for a moment there."

Bertha scrunched her pudgy nose, "Oh darling it's nothing to apologize over. To think this is the way you would inherit the mantle of leadership...it's all almost too much to take."

Agreeing with the insanity of it all, Elise set the older woman to fetch clean water while she returned to tending farmer Benn's wounds, wrapping them with strips of cloth she had torn from a pile of old dresses they had stacked in the corner. Looking down the length of the cabin, she found the next villager in need of her assistance and wondered how many more were crammed into the nearby community hall. The image of Corbin being mauled by a skex assaulted her again. Clenching her eyes shut, Elise shook her head hard to ward off the visage *No more time for silly fears,* she thought, forcing herself to focus on the task at-hand.

Looking back at the rows of victims, she knew that attention was sorely needed, here and now. Yet, as Elise moved to help one of the men lift a wounded woman, so that they could stitch her ribs, she could not help but wonder where her fiancée was at that very moment and whether he was even still alive.

CHAPTER 6

Another hour passed without the Walker brothers slowing their pace, running as if the creatures were hot on their heels. The fact that they had not heard any calls from the giant gastropods in half that time did not curb their caution in the least. Based on what he knew of their insatiable appetites, Logan assumed the beasts were most likely feasting on their slain kindred. But why take chances?

Corbin had applied some ointment to Logan's knuckles, which quickly stemmed the bleeding from his swollen hand. Trying to flex the muscles in it gave little reaction, and it ached from the wrist down. If they did not get to the city soon, not only would it be too late to warn of the swarm, but also to get Logan to a healer in time to save his hand. He packed Logan's wounds with some chewed granch leaves, saying that they would help keep it sterile, and then wrapped some strips of cloth around them.

Logan was growing wearier by the second. Corbin outpaced him now by a good ten strides and he was rapidly losing more ground. Logan needed to stay focused on running and clear his mind of all else. The forest was getting sparser, letting in more light from the waning Crystal.

"It will be good to be out of these rotten woods," Logan said.

"The town is just ahead!" Corbin called back to keep him moving.

"Corbin...we cannot stop for too long. I have to get to a healer..." Logan moaned feverishly; waves of nausea had been washing over him for a while now. His younger brother stopped and waited for him to catch up. He grasped Logan's hand in his own, examining it with concern, then pulled the makeshift bandage tighter. Logan winced silently, refusing to let his brother see any sign of weakness.

"We *will* be there soon," Corbin said, patting his shoulder reassuringly. "Keep strong as long as you can, and I can carry you the rest of the way if need be." That earned him a scowl and Logan slapped his hand away, shocking him.

"I can run on my own, *Peck*." Logan said.

Corbin hated that nickname, they had read it in an old fantasy tale, and it always irked him to hear it. When they were children, Logan would call him *Peck* when he wanted Corbin to leave him alone. Corbin thought it was uncalled for. Did he really need to be so stubborn at a moment like this? He was only trying to help him after all.

"Fine then, rest for five and then we are on our way," Corbin replied curtly.

Logan ignored him, continuing along the path toward the cliffs, where a rope bridge extended across the wide valley below. It appeared to not have been used in many years, yet seemed to be sturdy enough to hold his weight.

Corbin shook his head at his brother's stubbornness; dropping down to pull a kala root. He quickly caught up and handed it over as a peace offering. He did not want to get into another petty argument when so much was at stake. Eating the root immediately invigorated Logan's body; clearing his mind from the fog of pain he had been mired under. It would not heal his hand, but sure did the trick to give him the necessary pick-me-up and would help get them to their destination three times faster than without.

The bridge did not sway even half as much as it looked like it might. It was very secure, and they were over it in no time, running back onto the stone walkway. Around the bend, they quickly came to the break steps that ran down the face of the cliff to the docks below.

As they neared the bottom, Corbin pointed excitedly across the lake at the ferry. "They're just leaving port now, we have to hurry and catch the boat!" he shouted, running faster down the steep stairs. Logan cursed, hopping off the last steps onto the wooden planks of the dock just as the harbormaster came hobbling out of a little building to the right.

"Garth, we must get on that ship!" Logan called out to the bald gnome, who visited Elder Morgana often. The old man laughed at Logan, pulling his pipe out of his mouth for a second to smack his lips.

"Come now boy, you know that's not possible," Garth replied calmly. "Now you go have yerself a seat like a good lad until she comes back this way. It'll be just under two hours, like clockwork."

"But Master Garth we need…," Logan began, sharply cut off by Garth's waving hand.

"Never you mind boy, I've heard it all before don't you be doubting it none. You heard me, now go have a seat!" His patience seemed to be stretched easily when it came to dealing with Logan. Possibly because he never got over the time Logan had put mealworms in the man's tea to embarrass him at Elder Morgana's birthday celebration. Corbin was not sure, but he thought he heard the harbormaster grumbling something about damned rotten troublemakers, before turning back toward his little seaside shack of an office.

Corbin quickly outflanked the old gnome, blocking his path. "Master Garth, please listen. The village has been attacked by a swarm of skex and Elder Morgana is…well…she's dead, Baetylus bless her soul." His voice cracked trying to spit out the words. The harbormaster's pipe hit the ground. "Those monsters are heading right toward Fal in a massive swarm come up from the southern expanse. We have to get on that boat and warn the Council of Twelve immediately."

The harbormaster wrung his hands for a moment, pondering what to do. He anxiously darted his eyes left and right as if the skex might already be there lurking in the shadows to capture him. "What in the Nine Worlds will we do?" Garth sputtered. "Once the ferries are set out there ain't no way of pulling them back!"

"Then all is lost," Corbin lamented, feeling the weight of it hit him square in the chest. "We failed."

Logan bit his thumbnail, searching his mind for an idea. This was not something they had foreseen. Apparently, the boat worked on a series of pulleys that were mechanically managed, so the vessel moved nonstop. Garth explained that the ferry operated through an extended power system, feeding off the magical energy of a very rare lightning stone. A massive coupling climbed up from the vessel to grip a beam overhead, suspended with hanging cables that affixed to the cavern ceiling. That beam powered the boat's movement with an electric current that ran from the magical artifact and around the hull of the ship, protecting it against the creatures below. If that power went out there would be little defense against the large squids that lived under the deeper oily black waters of Lake Ul'toh.

"Never say never, right?" Logan mumbled, a light growing in his eyes. "Garth, you have to turn off the power grid so we can swim to that ship!" he shouted, already heading for the generators. Garth had been nervously twiddling the tobacco pipe in his hands and now dropped it again at the outlandish suggestion.

"Listen lad, the two of you wouldn't last more than five minutes in that water before something ate you up like bait, and she's already a good ten minutes out as it is. Besides, you turn that power off, and we jeopardize the lives of every single man and woman aboard that vessel."

Corbin grabbed ahold of his brother's hand, stopping him from pulling the switch on the generator and earning himself a look that was so cold he did not even realize he let go again until the sound of the motor died down, opening the locked gates to the waterfront.

"We don't have a choice Corbin, either we make a break for it now, up there, or Fal is doomed," Logan said, pointing up the metal tower to the steel beam that guided the ferry. "With a little luck we can make it onto that ship before anything in the lake is the wiser and be on our way."

Corbin nodded. "You're right. It's either try this or watch as the swarm destroys the capitol," Corbin admitted, speaking more to himself than to Logan.

Garth came up behind them muttering to himself. "Damn it, fine. You kids get up on that platform and be ready for my signal. I'll take care of the lightning stone. You crazy Walker boys are going to need every second we can spare. Quick now, not a moment to lose...," he urged, shoving them toward the ladders that worked their way up the tower to the beams over the lake.

They scrambled up them in no time, Logan remarkably nimble considering he was unable to use his left hand, wrapping his forearm around every other wrung for support instead. Garth worked the control panel to open the cylindrical chamber and removed the lightning stone, tossing the hot thing from one gloved hand to the other.

Logan was just reaching the top when he set down the stone and hollered up to him. "You boys have exactly ten minutes to get across! Like it or not I'll not risk a moment past that, there's too many lives at stake down there. If you're not going to make it by then, you boys will just have to do your best to try and get a warning out to the ship." With that he disappeared back into the harbor shack. A long-fluted tube extended toward the water, shooting a series of bursting flares to warn the vessel that there was an emergency.

From the deck, the crew and traders stopped what they were doing to stare at the bright warning flashes. Captain Higgins started shouting commands to his crew to get to their defensive positions, wondering what the mad gnome back at the dock could be thinking. Had he finally lost what few wits he had left after all these years?

The vessel came to a screeching halt as the wheel settled in a shower of sparks across the bare metal of the beam above. The ship sunk heavier into the water, no longer buoyed by the electric current. Crew ran all around the deck, pulling passengers below, racing into positions around the perimeter, and pulling black steel lance batons into nervous hands.

There was no telling whether they would be attacked while the power was down. Captain Higgins wondered how long they had before the squids would be upon them, punching his hand down into the wooden rail outside his cabin in frustration. The wood splintered under his fist, strengthened by a lifetime of hard labor spent on the ferries.

"Captain, we're being attacked from above!" A frantic older sailor ran up to him, waving his finger at the steel beam overhead. Higgins brought his seeing glass up to his eye and focused the lens. There were men running toward them across the thin metal platform above! From this vantage point, he could see the renowned hunter Corbin Walker and his troublemaking brother, two lads he had seen plenty of times when he visited his cousin in Riverbell. Corbin was looking right at him, wildly waving his arms in the air and shouting something he could not make out over the frantic murmurs on deck.

"Fool, get back to your post. Those be no enemies, it's just the stupid Walker brothers!" he said, shoving the sailor to his post. What was going on here? *Why would Master Garth put all our lives in jeopardy for those two nitwits?*

Screams rose from the deck when the ship suddenly lurched up on one side violently. "Curses and damnation, the monsters are already attacking!" Higgins snarled.

Large barnacle encrusted purple tentacles slithered over the starboard side, feeling the area for food. They were met by the stabbing of electrified lances.

"That's it lads, don't ye be letting them gain hold of our ship! Hold that deck from the bastards and teach 'em what we're made of!" Higgins barked out orders to his men, knowing that if the large squids below got a firm enough hold of the ship, they would tear it to pieces within minutes. His sailors worked together to stab at the vile creature wherever it tried to gain hold of the boat.

Logan was worrying he would be sick, already dizzy from being up so high, when the vessel first rocked to the left below. He tried not looking down, flinging his arms about wildly to keep his balance which was hard with the fever that was settling over him. The kala root was wearing off and he felt nauseous.

The dizzying height only worked to slow them down, with Corbin focusing every step to be as accurate as possible while they worked their way across the beam with as much speed as they could muster. Master Garth had given them a window of only ten minutes to get across before he would switch on the power again and it had already been seven.

From their vantage point, the brothers could see the ship lurching to the opposite side; being pulled now in two different directions as another squid arrived for the feast. Logan screamed in rage as he helplessly watched the creature assaulting the vessel below, causing him to twist his ankle and lose his footing on the beam.

He desperately waved his arms out trying to regain his balance, as he fell off the precarious platform into the oily water below. Corbin grabbed the sleeve of Logan's shirt just in time, the weight of his brother almost tugging him off the beam as well. Working together, they managed to get Logan back up onto the thin platform, with only time for a look of gratitude before they headed off again.

The shipmaster bit his own fist watching the boys, pulling it away when he realized they were okay and cursing loudly to no one in particular. Darting his eyes between them and his sailors he was all sweat and desperation as a third squid joined in and began attacking the ship.

"Brolnan, help Tala over there!" Master Higgins roared to his shipmates, who were desperately defending the boat all around. Every man and woman, crew and passengers alike, was now fully engaged in battle against grasping tentacles all about the sides of the deck. It seemed each time they stabbed back a lashing tentacle, a new appendage appeared to take its place! Some of his men were screaming hysterically about the futility of trying to stop the squids from pulling the ship down. Higgins threw himself at the complaining sailors, rolling them to the deck, as a man-sized chunk of the side railing flew away in the aftermath of a smashing purple tentacle.

"Quite yer belly aching and get back at it!" Higgins shouted. Their distraction had almost cost the fools their lives. Chaos erupted as a fourth squid joined in the fray, seemingly sealing their doomed fate.

Corbin flung himself down onto the coupling that held the ship, twirling around its base, using his spear as a handle to fly down to the deck. He leapt off the last few feet of cabling, guiding the tip of his weapon right through a tentacle that reached for a woman who was distracted fighting another at her side.

The huge squid squirmed violently from the shorn tip of its tentacle, shaking the boat about and throwing sailors to the deck. As soon as Corbin's feet touched the deck, Harbormaster Garth shoved the lightning stone back inside the chamber, powering the generators back online. There was no sense waiting for Logan, only one needed to relay the message and with the ship in mortal danger there was no sense losing an innocent life, not over a fool boy with nothing better on his mind than bothering old men with his pranks.

Logan heard the motor spring back to life and ran on harder. His lungs were already set to burst, throbbing with each gasping breath. He had almost reached the coupling when he stopped dead, the sound of crackling energy racing across the beam behind him. Freezing he could see the burst of electricity as the lightning stone's energy coursed through the studded metal, the beam heating up under his boots as the deadly sparks headed his way.

"You said ten minutes," he gasped aloud. His shock turned to rage, and Logan shook his fist toward the dock, "You old goat! It was only some damned worms!" He screamed and threw himself off the beam in a half-suicidal attempt to escape the electric current. His hand caught the coupling of the ship, spinning his body around just like his little brother. Corbin watched in horror as Logan screamed in agony, the chain tearing the flesh from his already wounded hand.

The current licked his skin just as he let go, giving him an extra nudge and throwing him down from above. As the power surged around the hull of the vessel, it raised slightly on the current. Tentacles released the boat, quick to escape the stinging pain of the electricity.

The deck fell silent as the ship whirred back into motion across the water. Corbin was pulling his brother from a bushel of corn he had landed in when he realized all eyes were on them.

"Guess corn ain't that bad after all, eh Peck?" Logan mumbled in a daze. Corbin had never been happier to hear the nickname, grinning at his crazy brother. Both men quickly wiped the smiles off their faces however, when the shadow of Captain Higgins fell over them.

The man stood there clapping his fist into an open palm, with a look that could freeze lava. "Somebody better explain what in the blazes is happening around here!"

Lady Cassandra winced as the thorn pierced the skin of her thumb. Dropping her shears, she instinctively sucked on the digit, the salty copper flavor a reminder that she needed to be more careful. Her mind had drifted elsewhere today, while she worked the rooftop garden. Smelling the pungent, musky gardenia she had been clipping, she sighed contently. A little thorn-prick of blood was well worth the feeling of gratification these flowers brought to her.

"Hard at work again, I see?" Alain teased her in his jovial manner, walking onto the rooftop with Viktor in tow. She really must have been daydreaming not to have heard their coach arrive! Alain gave his wife a hearty hug and kissed her forehead tenderly, the bristles of his thick beard tickling her skin.

"Hello dear," she kissed him back lovingly on the cheek. After all these years together, her husband still made her smile every time he came into a room. "Good eve, Viktor," she said, shooting their friend a slight bow. "How was the council meeting today, boys?" A pet name she reserved especially for these two, even after over two hundred years of age. Alain grumbled, his thick red moustache twitching and walked over to pour himself some mulled wine.

"That good, huh?" Viktor raised a telling eyebrow to her. Their day must have been long and drawn out. "Who was it this time?" she inquired.

Alain handed his colleague a small glass then sat down in one of the wooden chairs, momentarily distracting himself in the scent of orange blossoms.

"Who else could it have been to get Alain so stirred up?" Viktor said. "He's still brooding over our last meeting of the day."

"Hmmm...the Magistrate poking the hornet's nest again?" Cassandra asked.

Alain grunted in response, with Viktor nodding beside him. "It was the whole Third District tirade all over again," Viktor explained, rolling his eyes.

"I swear that little rat has it in for us!" her husband growled. "After all we have done for him, every year he just grows more and more despicable."

Things must have turned ugly during deliberations for Alain to get this riled up. He was normally a calm, even-tempered man, one of the more rational members of the High Council. Moreover, for a group of Elders whose members had been presiding over Falian law, as richly interwoven as it had become, for ages now, that was saying something.

"And to make matters worse, Arch Councilor Zacharia excused that crooked bastard of standing testimony to the whole thing," Viktor said.

"Well then, if the high elder excused him then there must have been a good reason," Cassandra said. It was not like the man to act without due course after all.

Alain hopped to his feet, nudging Viktor to continue, and slammed his drink back.

"That *is* the odd part. There was no justification for it. Arch Councilor Zacharia called it a *fallacy in informal logic*, whatever that is supposed to mean." Viktor refilled their drinks, offering her an empty glass.

"No thank you, it's too early in the day for me to partake in libations." He chuckled at how formally she always held her demeanor. "And what that means is, basically, there was some flaw in the reasoning that renders the conclusion unpersuasive."

Alain laughed at his wife, as she was always one to take everything so literal. "Alright dear, no need to show off, we know what it meant. What good Viktor here means is that the reasoning *was* in fact, *not* flawed. We had a witness that was ready to testify against him, said he saw the magistrate accepting a bribe and everything," he explained.

The three of them stopped talking, each mulling over the futility of the situation. Viktor cleared his throat, uncomfortable with the silence. "What do you think Cass, how can we get this guy?" he asked. Alain leaned forward in his seat, eager to hear her potential solution.

"Ah, I see what you two are up to now," she said, winking one gray eye and playfully pointed at both men in turn. "Trying to rope me into council issues again, are you?"

"C'mon dear, you know how much we value your opinion. Instead of teasing us for hours and then giving in, can we just skip to the part where you give us advice?" Alain whined like a schoolboy. Except he was not a schoolboy, this was a respected member of the high council of Elders, a pillar of New Fal's community. Someone who gave everything he had to protect the civilization they had built here in Vanidriell, and she could not resist his endearing desperation.

"Alright, I'll consult on your case. Why don't you fill me in on the details tonight, so I have the full picture?" she said.

Viktor set down his glass and clapped his hands together. "Right then, I ought to be heading home, it's almost time for supper and we have some guests coming by."

"Helped your pal here get what he needs and you're pulling the old cut and run?" she teased, pecking Viktor on the cheek. As he slipped past the doorway, Alain came around to hug her from behind, his beard tickling the lobe of her ear. She reached back to stroke the thick mane as they rocked softly side to side.

"Looks like your best arrangements yet," he said, complimenting the decorative topiary she had been working on.

"Aw, thank you, I want to top last year's Culhada floral displays."

"Well, with what you have here it's sure to...ugh" Alain backed away gripping his temple, swaying slightly, clearly off balance. Deeply concerned Lady Cassandra steadied him; it was not like her husband to get tipsy off so few drinks.

"What is it dear, was it the wine?" she asked, trying to look him in the face.

Alain steadied himself, the moment of dizziness past. He wore a grim expression, staring out solemnly over the roof far to the south. His silence was unnerving as he contemplated the sudden surge of emotions that had rocked him.

"Something just happened to Elder Morgana...something awful." The implication of his words carried a heavy weight. Lady Cassandra grabbed his chin, forcing him to look down into her fearful eyes, the question written plainly across her face. Alain pulled his wife in to console her tightly against his broad chest.

"Is it...?" she asked fearing his answer.

53

"Elder Morgana is gone, my love," he groaned in despair, as the bloody thorned gardenia she had been clutching was caught up by a gentle breeze, drifting off over the rooftop.

Corbin started awake, violently slashing out to his left, catching his brother square in the jaw with a clenched fist.

"Ow, what in the Crystal has gotten into you?" Logan scowled at his little brother, gingerly rubbing his jaw.

Corbin's eyes were wide open and bloodshot. "I don't know, man I think I was having a terrible nightmare."

"Who ever heard of having a nightmare in the daytime? What the heck was it about?"

Corbin only answered with a shrug, the dream fading off into the foggy recesses of his mind. Every Culhada his dreams were plagued with horrible visions and though he wanted to tell his brother, they had more pressing problems to deal with at the moment.

"Hmm," Logan eyed him shrewdly.

"I said don't remember...the battle back in Riverbell, perhaps? I am sorry though, did I hurt you?" he asked with sincere concern.

The blow did throb, but Logan was too proud to ever admit it. He shook his head and turned to look out the window. Corbin followed his gaze, looking up the road through the carriage window they drove in as it sped across the rocky hill heading for the gates of Fal. The captain of the ship had seen to getting them his own carriage the second they were docked, abandoning the ship himself to travel with them. Captain Higgins whipped the horned red elks pulling the carriage, shouting at them to move faster. He had grumbled that the boys were too young to commandeer his ferry and carriage in the same day and said they needed a real man to do the job anyhow.

The capitol city came into view ahead, peeking over the treetops. Neither of them had seen the city with their own eyes before and they were instantly in awe by its grandeur. The place rose up, in tiered sections, carved directly from the cavern's mighty northern walls of ivory marble, reaching almost all the way to the ceiling of New Fal itself. Each section sat on a higher tier, in gradually smaller steps rounding out from the ground beneath. The walls were dotted with the city guard assigned to defending against any would-be predators. For a second Logan had to wonder if the city even needed the warning they had risked life and limb to deliver.

His concern was quickly put to bed as they made their way closer. He could see that the wall was indeed manned, but not by brave soldiers who were alert and prepared. Instead, the wall guards seemed to have two dispositions, one of being drunk and asleep, the other of being lost in some sort of celebration. He reasoned the men and women stationed along the perimeter were no doubt lax in their duties since there was realistically never a real threat coming from within the kingdom, and there were probably festivities of Culhada raging all over the city by now. It was most uncommon for insects to be in this part of the cavern anyway and even when it had happened, there had never been more than a single lost beast, which had strayed from the swarm.

"Logan, look at the city's defenses," Corbin said, referring to the gigantic artillery units mounted on either side of each level. Logan had heard that when the city was originally built by the first pilgrims, massive construction machina, which had long since been lost to the strains of time, were used to carve out the walls. When the building of the kingdom was completed, they had no more use for the machina and so they were disassembled, broken down to use their parts in constructing the giant man-operated crossbows Logan was drooling over.

"Captain, how will we alert the Elders once we arrive?" Corbin shouted through cupped hands above the racket of wheels grinding over the rocky path, coughing on the dusty cloud raised in its wake.

Higgins shot him a wild-eyed look over his shoulder. "Son, don't you worry about nothin'," he shouted, pulling hard on the reigns. Logan almost flew over the side of the carriage as it swerved around a sharp bend in the road. "We're headed straight to the Praetorian himself!" The captain pointed up the dirt road to the base of the city. White walls were all they could see going in either direction as they headed straight for the gates into Fal.

"What is a *praetorian*?" Logan asked his younger brother, trying to speak quietly and nudging him to get his attention.

"He is the captain of the city guard!" Corbin replied loudly. "He should have some sort of direct communication with the Elders!"

Since they had come over the hill, in plain view of the towers, Higgins had been blowing hard into his bullhorn, causing his cheeks to turn beat red. Not showing any signs of slowing as they came closer to the gates, the brothers feared he meant to carve a hole clean through the city walls with his vehicle. At the very last moment, they were only slightly relieved when he pulled hard on the reigns, spinning the carriage sideways to a dead stop. They were out of the vehicle in a dash, all three running like madmen for the gates.

The two soldiers standing guard looked extremely perplexed as to what the expectations of defending against raving lunatics were. In all fairness, at this point the captain did look like a wild man, with his red hair all frayed and spittle foaming at the corners of his mouth, clinging to his beard.

"Get the Praetorian, ye daft fools, we be under attack!" He shouted still running with his fist pumping in the air. One of the soldiers turned to run inside and alert the men, when he bounced off a giant of a man that had just walked out of the tower's double doors.

The Praetorian towered over Corbin, who in his own right was considered one of the tallest men in his village. The man did not wear his usual cloak and armor, which represented his status. He had clearly been in the middle of some *celebrating* instead and was clothed in long johns from the neck down.

"What is the meaning of this racket, Captain Higgins?" the Praetorian demanded, clearly in no need of cloaks or armor to fill his station.

Higgins was about to explain, when Corbin jumped in front of him to retell the tale. He explained everything, emphasizing the need for swift action. When he finished with the rushed story, the man looked

Secrets of the Elders

down at him, taking in all he had heard. "Hundreds of the foul beasts, you say?" he asked slowly.

"Yes sir, hundreds, though it only took twenty or so to wreak havoc on our village," Corbin replied.

The Praetorian took them all in under a withering gaze, measuring their worth before finally settling his eyes on Captain Higgins. "Bah, drunks, the whole lot of ye...out here wasting my time!" He spit on the ground at their feet and turned to leave. Logan glanced at the captain, who *did* look like he had been drinking, with his hair all disheveled and that crazed look in his eyes.

"Praetorian," Logan called, stopping the man and turning him about. "My brother speaks the truth you big oaf! We have run here nonstop for close to two nights now, risking life and limb to bring you this message in time!" Logan shouted at the barrel-chested man, pushing his face up as close as he could get, standing toe-to-toe with the hulking warrior. He jabbed his finger into the Praetorian's chest with each word, to accentuate his point. "Now get your ass moving and inform the Elders before it is too late!"

Perhaps it was the sheer audacity of this little man to approach Banner like this, something no man had dared in years, or perhaps it was the ring of truth in the little guy's words, backed by the cold resolve in his eyes. Either way, the Praetorian shifted his thinking and without a word, ran inside the great tower.

Logan stared helplessly after the man, at the empty doorway, which was now without guard. He wondered if at any moment the Praetorian would be running back out with an axe in his hand to cut him down. Instead, he heard the deafening sound of a horn booming from the top of the guard tower. It reverberated along the marble walls, echoing across the cavern as far as Riverbell, where Elise heard it with equal parts relief and dread, knowing the Walkers had made it and what they were surely soon to face.

No sooner had the alarm sounded than it was answered by responding horns blasting all along the wall, up and down the levels of the city. Soon all the towers blared their war sirens, causing Corbin to cover his ears from the deafening roar. With a sigh of relief, Logan slumped against the wall. He stumbled, realizing the captain was pulling his arm to lead him inside the city as soldiers all along the watchtower raced to their posts.

"Best to get on the other side lad, less we want to become pincushions?" he reasoned.

Shouting commands and quickly falling into defensive positions, the city guard leapt into action. Arrows were knocked and ready, aimed for the outside, and other four-man teams clambered into the massive crossbow ballistae units. Corbin turned to regard the road they had journeyed for the last several days. It seemed so serene and inviting. One would never guess that death was on its way through that quiet, rocky, forested landscape.

Somewhere under the blare of the city alarm, he could distantly hear Captain Higgins urgently calling to get inside before they sealed the gates. With one last look, Corbin bolted for the doors of the tower.

Chapter 7

Arch Councilor Zacharia was pondering some last-minute details sent up to him for the night's festivities in the Fourth level square, when he heard the clicking coming from his library. Curious, he stood, rounding his desk and entered the room. Books lined the walls from floor to ceiling neatly set in their shelves with masterful organization. Passing his leather armchairs, he flipped the hidden wall switch, opening a mechanism that was emitting the insistent clicking racket. Behind this panel hid a glass screen and several dials, he flipped one and the screen flared to life.

"Arch Councilor Zacharia," Magistrate Fafnir spoke to him from his office. "I have some *strange* news."

"I take it this is important enough to disturb my preparations for tonight's ceremonies?" Zacharia said, tapping his lips with a forefinger.

"Arch Councilor...," Fafnir paused, his face flickering in the static of the communications monitor, "there are a couple young men here from Riverbell. They are claiming the village was attacked by a swarm of skex, sir." Fafnir explained, deep lines of concern riddling his forehead. Zacharia furrowed his brow at this news. "Milord, they say th-the skex are on their way here in a mass horde!" the magistrate had trouble keeping the uncertainty out of his voice.

"Fafnir, sound the alarm immediately. Treat this as a very real threat, and may Baetylus save these Walker boys, if their tale proves to be false," Arch Councilor Zacharia commanded, not even waiting for the Magistrate to respond before flipping the switch to disconnect the line. Another flick of the dial opened the lines for all the Elder's quarters at once. He had to alert everyone.

Meanwhile, many miles down the wall below him, Magistrate Fafnir was calling all men to arms. He wondered fleetingly how the high councilor had known the names of the men at the gate when he himself had not known them. He told himself this was no time to ponder the strange ways of their leader, making his way to the armory where the Praetorian was already pulling a chitin-armored breastplate over his head. Now was the time to put to use the skills of his men, skills they had trained in all their lives, but never needed. He ordered the man to lead the walls' defense, as if such a command was necessary.

With grim determination, Praetorian Banner accepted the mantle, draping his heavy battle-axe over a shoulder and heading up to meet the enemy.

Through the still calm, Corbin could hear his heart beating, throbbing like a drum in his head. Every vein in his body twitched with anticipation, as he peered out over the wall, deep into the darkness. Every soldier in Fal was gathered on the walls and all there was to do now was wait.

Soon the Great Crystal would slink into its three-day slumber. They could only pray the initial attack came before that great event. Otherwise, the city would be hard pressed to defend against an enemy none could see. All around the landscape below had gone quiet an hour ago, bringing with it a cold sweat on the skin of all those men and women who waited with dread-filled hearts up and down the walls, on all levels of the city. Watchers peered out to the forest and canyons surrounding the capitol, searching with bi-scopes for some sign of the promised incoming threat. The cool night air was still, filled with the wafting aromas of food from the festivities that had come to a grinding halt once the war horns were blown. Inside Fal, citizens stood huddled together in their homes, fearing for what was coming next. Leaving the feasts behind, every able-bodied man and woman was ordered to the walls and other defensive towers built around the inner city.

Logan's stomach felt queasy, and he was gripping his bow so tightly that his wounded palm began to bleed again. He could not help but wonder if maybe this was all a huge mistake. What if the swarm had not actually been headed for the capitol after all? Why had they not struck yet, what were those monsters waiting for?

There was no way for him to know that the swarm had found a nest of antrocs and had stopped to feast upon them, or that through sheer dumb luck he and Corbin had narrowly missed crossing paths with the monsters when they skirted the ruined chasms. Maybe he should just go inside the city walls and leave all this defense nonsense to those more capable, like the Praetorian who was crouching to his left and growling. Logan could not think when the man had begun the noise but was sure it was a new event. He shot his brother a questioning look, but was ignored as Corbin was peering quite intently out over the wall. He scratched a tickle on his head with the tip of an arrow, searching the tree line for what could have them in such a trance.

Out into the darkness, Logan could see only the still trees with their leaves shivering in the cool breeze. The canyons were completely still, like a graveyard of departed monoliths, which had fallen in weird angles along the subterranean floor. Banner's growling rose an octave as the man tensed up, gritting his teeth with a chalky grating sound. High above the cavern their Great Crystal began its flickering indigo light, as it made ready to shut down, marking the beginning of the Culhada. In the flickering, slightly strobe lighting, Logan thought he saw something move below, in the trees. Craning his neck, he tried to focus, looking around all the shaking leaves on the forests edge, trying to get a grip on what he was seeing. He could not get a sense for it and nudged his brother's ribs with his elbow. He too was peering at the moving shadows, up on the tips of his toes to gaze over the wall's edge. Corbin did not respond. Refocusing his vision, Logan realized his mistake just as the Praetorian howled to his men.

"Ready your arms lads, here the bastards come!"

The *leaves* were not leaves at all, but hundreds and hundreds of swarming insects feasting on everything they found in their path among the trees.

No sooner had the realization hit him then the swarm burst forth from the forest with lustful fury. Corbin took a step back at the awful sight working his way behind his older brother, whose jaw hung slack while his eyes looked ready to bulge out of their sockets. Corbin was not sure if it was to snap his brother out of it or to pump himself up, either way he decided to give Logan a good hard slap to the back of his head. Logan's bow let loose a single stray arrow, which floundered straight up into the air and came back down between his legs.

"What in the...!" Logan scowled; the proclamation cut off by the first insect to reach their wall.

"Now lads, let's show them that Falians are no easy lunch!" Praetorian Banner howled, as he heaved his battle-axe through the air tearing into the skex torso.

There was no time to cheer Banner's kill as four more of the insects came buzzing over to their section. One man's gurgled screams were sickening, as an insect ripped its barbed tail into his spine, pulling the poor wretch howling into the night air. Another came plunging down at the large Praetorian, who pumped his arms at the beast, beckoning it to fight.

As it swooped past through the night air, Logan could smell the foul odor of the insect, like pond water rotting a corpse, and it gagged him. The thing pummeled the giant man to the smooth stone ground as it landed, with its side ramming into him. Logan let his first, second, and third arrow fly in rapid succession, quicker than most men would even be able to steady a single shot. The beast screeched as they ripped between the folds in its plated exoskeleton, exposing its left flank. Quickly the monster shifted its ravenous ire to the little man that had just stung it, flinging its tail at Banner as an afterthought. The Praetorian was just getting to his feet as the tail came at him and had to throw his body into a mad roll to dodge the deadly barbed stinger.

Skittering across the wall, the beast reached a pincer out hungrily for Logan, who let loose another arrow, which bounced harmlessly off the monster's clawed appendage. He considered making a run for it then and there, when something hit him squarely in the spine. Almost bowled over, he barely caught a glimpse of his brother jumping off his back, flying head over heel arcing through the air over the insect. In the flickering strobe light of the Crystal, Corbin looked like some sort of monster himself, slashing up and down into the beasts neck with his spear, wrenching guts all over his torso with a sick splattering while he pumped away like a demon. Logan thought that he would keep his complaint of being used as a launching pad to himself as he watched his brother dispatch the foul creature.

Behind the dying monster, the Praetorian and his men were working on another skex; this one slightly smaller than the first. Another screech resounded in the air and Logan let loose another volley of arrows, fatally wounding one of the monsters flying overhead. As it fell past, he saw that it was carrying the remains of a torn-up woman. He raced to the edge of the wall to watch the plummeting monstrosity with the soldier standing beside him. They could do little more than peer over the edge at the falling beast, helpless to save the woman.

One of the insects who had been skittering up the sheer face of the wall was just below them. It swung an oversized pincer up across where they stood. Logan reflexively grabbed the soldier beside him and flung them both backward, landing on his pack as the man fell next to him.

"That was a close one!" he shouted to the soldier, who would never hear him having had his head shorn cleanly from his shoulders.

Logan choked on his own vomit as the insect clambered over the side of the wall, claws whipping blindly ahead of it. He let an arrow fly from where he scrambled backward, with his back against the stone of the narrow wall space. It deflected harmlessly off the insect's defending claw. He let another off and it sank in deep near the skex's exposed rows of eyes, and chitinous pulsating tentacle lined mouth.

Corbin rushed in toward the skex side, tucking his legs tightly up under him, and leaping over a swinging claw. He landed squarely in front of the monster, jabbing his spear straight into its gullet, as Logan ripped through one of its eyeballs with another arrow.

Pulling back on the spear, it would not budge forcing Corbin to let it go, as the beast flailed furiously up and down in agony. The hunter in him quickly danced backward, never taking his eyes off the monster, which was futilely trying to grasp the protruding spear with its oversized claws.

Above them new screeching rang out, as two more of the insects rained down from the second level of the city. In the flickering light,

Logan could just make out a hysterical soldier caught in one of the beast's tails. Several men were running down the parapet toward them when the insects came in. Cursing to himself, Logan knew that he had to shift his attention away from his brother and the slavering monster half hanging over the wall, to the incoming threat.

He let burst a cacophony of arrows into the creatures' exposed underbellies before they even came close. The soldiers around him also let their weapons loose, spears and crossbow bolts raining through the air, plunging into the dangerous creatures. One of the skex must have realized there was easier prey elsewhere and shifted its flight back up to another level of the city. The other stubbornly hissed, its mouth quivering in hungry anticipation.

Weaponless now, Corbin was shifting back and forth in a mad dance of survival, dodging the wounded beast's grasping pincers. Working furiously, on pure instinct alone, he danced forward into an opening then rolled to the side and leapt away from a crashing claw, all the while waiting for an opening. The beast's tentacle lined mouth had begun working the spear out, pulsing purple flesh gripped tightly around the shaft of it, slowly wrenching the spearhead away.

At that moment Corbin spied his opportunity. Somersaulting through the air, he twisted into a dive, lightly tapping off the skex's waving claw to land back inside and grasp his spear firmly with both hands. He knew it would be futile to pull at the weapon with the tentacles wrapped around it, so instead he shoved forward, throwing all his weight into it, crunching the spear drove deeper through the beast's jaw. Then squatting, he wrenched with corded arms straight up into the air, ripping the spear cleanly through the monster's forehead. No death rattle emerged from the beast, as it grasped into the air for nothing, before slumping forward and almost bowling him over under its weight.

Logan had retreated amongst the soldiers as his quarry came in, the hazy blue strobe light of the Crystal dancing across its back. The group he was with pushed hard against the beast, stabbing it from all sides. Until the monster rolled off the edge of the wall, pulling large chunks of the parapet with it as it plummeted to its death. Another insect tried to flee the city walls, looking like a pincushion after its battle with the army above. Logan directed the men to attack, piercing the soft underbelly even further. That skex crashed dead on arrival following its brood down the side of the wall.

All along the wall, fighting was ceasing as the brave men and women pushed the enemy back away from their homeland. Those remaining members of the invading swarm were forced to retreat, back into the night. Cheers erupted at the victory.

"We did it!" Logan screamed, jumping up and down in celebration with the men and women around him. However, Banner walking by wearing a solemn look, silencing them. Glancing at Corbin, he motioned for him to follow over to the wall. The man was deep in concentration looking out into the night.

Logan felt confused, wondering why his brother wore an equally disturbing expression. "Take heart Corbin, we've won the day...victory is ours," he said, clapping Corbin's shoulder halfheartedly.

The Praetorian shook his head, "I'm afraid not, Logan. What we *have* won was no more than a minor victory. It would appear they were toying with us. Testing our mettle so to speak, the cunning beasts...," Banner growled under his breath.

"But...how could you possibly know that?" Logan said, waving his open hand at the dead skex littering the area. Corbin directed his attention to the tree line again, where the larger swarm waited at the edge of the forest. The valley below was still virtually teeming with their ranks. What they had faced was but a taste of the horde.

What in blazes are they be waiting for? Logan asked himself horrified.

As Logan was about to shake his head, they received their answer. Deep inside the city the cogs of the great temple wound into place, and the bells chimed announcing the new cycle had arrived. Overhead, high toward the ceiling of New Fal's cavern, the Great Crystal god Baetylus' pulsating indigo light flared blindingly, white hot, for only a moment, forcing everyone to shield their eyes against its brilliance. That light quickly faded, as a long-haloed shadow of darkness stretched in toward it, the Crystal's brilliance receding in the shadows wake back up to the ceiling where it floated. The halo surrounded it like a crown until finally it too was engulfed in darkness, leaving them all in the pitch-black.

The only lights that existed now were thousands of glowing red eyes, peering at the humans from beyond the city walls. Looking at them with an unmatched hunger and ferocity, even seeming to sparkle with malicious laughter, as the massive swarm closed in on the capitol.

"Baetylus help us all," Corbin moaned.

Chapter 8

Dull drums were beating back in the distance, while the dancing laughter of worms wriggling around through a torso played in Corbin's mind. He could sense himself slowly unwinding from the taut cord of death that wrapped around his neck. Choking on the clean air, desperately gasping to fill lungs too bruised to hold it in, he tried to shout his denial. The smoke flitted by Corbin's eyes as shadows danced past his vision. Through the thick fog in the distance, an emerald gleamed brilliantly, cutting into the pain like a knife of clarity. The Great Crystal's singing played in the back of his mind, clearing away the fog and instead filling the world with brilliant, blinding light quickly followed by nothing. Jerking his head up from the wet stone path, the dream slowly faded into the recesses of his mind.

Where am I? he thought in a panic, as he opened his eyes wider, thinking perhaps that would dispel the sheer nothingness that surrounded him. He tried to focus his vision in vain, futilely hoping to perceive something, anything at all in the pitch-black night. *How long have I been unconscious?* he wondered.

Twitching fingers groped along the floor beneath him, making their way up from his waist. Something must have hit him from behind, knocking him face down to the ground. With his breath no longer coming in such awful, ragged gasps, he pushed himself up to his knees. A flash of blinding light cut across his vision, the pain in his side ripping the air back out of his throat and dropping his body to the ground. The crunching of his teeth gritting together resounded like shards of broken ceramic being ground under heavy boots.

Great Crystal, what has happened to me? Corbin's mind raced to remember how he had gotten here.

Flashes of insects battling the Falians raced across his mind's eye, but they were only momentary glimpses, disappearing into the shadows as quickly as they formed. Shaking his head to deny the seeping frustration, he grunted with the effort of moving, deciding that it was more important to get to safety. Steadying his breath, he braced himself for the pain that was sure to come and tried to rise a second time. Much slower now, he pulled himself up to his knees, taking deep even breaths. Pain radiated upward like crawling snakes from the ribs on his left side, but he braced against it this time.

Where did my weapon go? he wondered, trying to peer into the murky shadows around his knees, hoping for some miracle to light up his spear. To the right side of his body, the shadows seemed more of a gray, than pitch. His eyes must be slowly adjusting to the lighting or lack thereof. Corbin leaned in toward the grayness, rubbing his aching palm against the cool damp rock wall that he found there.

At that moment, it was more inviting than a campfire. Probing fingers explored the marble wall with his right hand, until they fit snugly into a secure hold. He stopped for a moment, to catch his breath, and then pulled himself slowly to his feet. Those snakes started cruelly biting into his side again, with waves of nausea wracking his body and painful sparks dancing across his vision. Corbin damned the pain in his side, fighting on until he was leaning heavily against the wall.

There was no sense trying to figure out which way to go since leaning on his left side would not even be an option, and he had no intention of walking backward. Corbin figured his ribs must be broken. In this darkness, he would be completely defenseless with a such an injury if one of the skex came upon him.

What was that?

He had not realized he was already shuffling along, his whole body leaning into the wall, until his foot was stopped short by something on the ground. Not wanting to risk bending over, with the potential of never getting back up again, Corbin prodded the object with the toe of his boot. A dead man's arm slapped wetly, sliding freely across the ground. The whole thing had been severed, no doubt the work of a skex.

Distant shrieks rose into the night air as another monster was filling its abdomen with human meat. Corbin embraced the anger that wracked him, spurring his legs faster toward the path ahead.

Soon he came upon an area of the wall that glowed faintly luminescent in the shadows, casting a glow of green haze from a moss

Secrets of the Elders

the city had planted as *emergency lighting*. All around the floor of the area, Corbin spotted dead bodies, torn and mauled by the flesh-eating insects. He also eyed a sword one of the men had strapped to his waist. This would be worth the risk of bending over for, so he carefully made his way down to a crouch, racking his body with waves of pain. The weapon was much lighter than it appeared, its metal reflected in the pale green glow. Corbin balanced it in his hand, moving left to right, getting a feel for the weight of the new weapon.

With a little effort he set forth again, back into the engulfing shadows, with his pointer finger nervously tracing circles over the blade's hilt. Sounds of battle were echoing off the smooth marble walls. It was coming from ahead, but still, he could see nothing.

Is this how the roc-bats live in the valley? he wondered, thinking of the blind flying creatures who let out shrill screams, like banshees, to guide their flight.

Leaning against the wall, and taking the pressure off his ribs again, he cocked an ear to listen ahead. *It sounds like a drunken man is laughing just around the bend,* he thought. With renewed vigor Corbin set forth, still guided by the wall, an image of men celebrating their victory was playing in his mind fueled by the new sounds. More of the luminescent green light oozed into the shadows, where a laughing man was sitting propped against the wall ahead.

"Sir...where are the others?" he tentatively asked, speaking low in case there were skex in the area, and looking around into the dark for the man's companions.

Still laughing the man dreamily looked up, his unkempt brown beard dripping foamy spittle. The clouds parted in his eyes as the he focused on Corbin's face and his laughter cut short.

"I killed three of them, lad," he somberly explained.

"Three of who, do mean the skex? I don't understand...are you alone? Where are the other soldiers I heard a moment ago?" Corbin fired the questions out in rapid succession, never giving the man time to answer as he leaned down to a crouch beside him.

"Others? *I got three.* Killed the bastards before they got me," He directed Corbin's gaze to his hands, where they were clutched tightly around his large belly. For the first time since he woke, Corbin truly came out of his stupor and became fully aware of the world around him. The man was dripping blood from a deep gash that ran across his entire midsection. So much blood covered the ground that Corbin's boots were sticking in it, where the stuff pooled around his feet. The world lurched as his body rejected the contents of his stomach onto the man's legs. He quickly tried to wipe the vomit from his face and instead smeared some of the dying man's blood across his chin.

They were both in shock, staring at each other in silence. The man's eyes glazed over again, and bubbling laughter gurgled out of his throat. His hysteria began building in crescendo, to the point where Corbin was not even certain whether it was laughter or screaming. Knuckles white, he shoved his blade with a crunching sound up through the poor man's jaw and into his skull. He watched in sick horror as the old soldier was released from his agonizing drawn out death, until the madness faded from his eyes, drifting into peace, and then slowly pulled the blade out. He had never killed another man before. Even though he knew this was the right thing to do for the tortured soul, every nerve in his body grew cold and rigid at once. For the second time his stomach lurched forward, this time with nothing to give to the aching world.

Careful not to disturb the soldier's dead body, Corbin lifted the goggles from around his neck. It made him sick to know he needed to remain pragmatic. Despair aside, these would help him see in the pitch-black. The miners of Parian wore them when going into the deeper caves. With the set tightened around his head, he twisted a small dial on the strap, adjusting the emerald quartz lens and lighting up everything before him. At first, the area was framed in a grainy green glow, much like the moss, then everything sprang into life as all the other natural colors began seeping through the shadows. It felt like looking through a shaded screen at the world, nothing quite as brilliant or focused as normal light from the Crystal would provide. It wasn't the best, but Corbin would take this diluted view over what he had just stumbled through any day.

He wondered of the soldier had anything else useful and rummaged through the man's utility pouches until he found something. It was a small animal skin tube. Corbin sniffed around the opening.

Medi-gel! he thought, flipping the wax seal off with his thumb, as he hiked up the side of his torn shirt, revealing the long gash across his ribs that was caked with dried blood and dirt. He gingerly squeezed the tube, spreading the healing gel over his wound. A hiss escaped through gritted teeth, as the gash sizzled close, leaving a long rounded white hard nub across his skin. Finally, he began to feel some semblance of being balanced out again. Looking around him and the dead soldier he found nothing else along the wall. All about the city, he could hear the battle still raging.

On his feet again, Corbin started out at a steady pace, still leaning on the wall for support. It was not long before he realized the air fully filled his lungs once more, giving him renewed strength and clarity. The mining goggles functioned properly, bending the light with their special lens, revealing a good yard ahead of filtered view. To the right he found a steep stairwell cut into the wall leading up to the next level. Corbin fell into his hunter's crouch, sensing the need for caution as he climbed the steps. At the top of the stairwell, sounds of clashing steel and shouting came closer.

A large skex, with its back to him, stalked from left to right and then back again, staying just out of reach of its quarry. Three more of the monstrous insects surrounded a group of people fighting back, including his brother Logan, who was smack dab in the middle of it all!

Corbin quickly scanned the battle. Between himself and the nearest winged monster, sprawled across the ground lay the carcass of another skex, its head littered with arrows.

Logan must have dealt that on its deathblow, he thought. Torn pieces of several people littered the ground all around the grisly scene.

His brother must have lost his bow as he was now holding a metal staff that he used to parry, first the large insect in front of him and then the one to his back, barely keeping the beasts at bay. There were two people next to him, one on either side. The woman at Logan's right was a soldier by the looks of her. She was firing her pistol in between dodging the skex attacks. On his left was a citizen who must have been caught on the walls when the attack began. He was bleeding from a bad wound on the side of his head, holding a long spear, which he frantically waved about in the dark to keep the insects at bay. By Logan's feet laid Elder Morgana's laser rifle, but none of the trio could possibly see it in this pitch-blackness.

Crouching low to the ground, Corbin made a dash to the fallen insect, hiding behind the armored plates of its thorax. Peering around the side of the dead monster, he could make out his brother better. Logan took three steps forward, bringing the largest insect's snapping pincer in, then a backward dash with his staff slamming down on the claw and slapping it to the stone floor. The skex was enraged and brought its tail in hard, the stinger dripping with sticky poison. Though he was clearly exhausted, Logan was somehow ready for this, dodging quickly to the left and opening the way for the insect behind him to take its sisters barbed stinger squarely in one of its eyes. A high-pitched screech erupted from the thing's quivering maw and the two struggled to separate, flipping over on their sides besides the edge of the wall.

Just behind where the newly blinded insect had stalked from was one of the city's defense turrets. It was an enormous weapon, made to shoot down any monstrous insects, sauria-lizards, or even roc-bats, that came too close to the city's borders. It resembled one of Logan's small hand crossbows, but was as large as two riding elks side by side. The defensive unit had a giant stone seat that would house one city guard while another worked a hand crank, which they used to pivot left or right. Corbin felt an idea forming, noting there was still a handful of massive spears loaded into the side of the mechanism.

How many of these unfortunate souls would still be alive if they had only been able to see the turret in this darkness? he wondered.

Logan jabbed his staff hard into the side of another skex, as it batted the wounded man beside him back down to the ground. The soldier joined in, firing her gun and flinching as the bullets ricocheted off its armored skin.

"We need to get out of here while the other two are distracted!" Logan yelled to his companions, as they scrambled to help the man rise.

Corbin seized his opportunity while the skex were all fully distracted, flinging himself over the dead monster he had been using as cover, he made a beeline for the turret. Logan had just fallen onto his back, barely rolling away from the insect's tail, as it whipped across the air. As he hopped to his feet Corbin came running across his limited view, like a ghost emerging from the shadows.

"To the left, by your feet!" Corbin yelled.

One second, he was there, the next he was slipping back into the shadows, leaving Logan to ponder whether he had just seen a phantom or perhaps even a flickering piece of his imagination playing tricks on him. He judged the truth of it, when stooping down to blindly grope around his feet, his fingers found the cold metal of the laser rifle he had dropped.

Jumping into the seat of the turret, Corbin leaned far to the side and furiously worked the crank, spinning it hard with both hands. He moved the weapon in the wrong direction at first, then realizing his error reversed, to aim at the two skex struggling to break free of one another. Once they were in his line of sight, it almost seemed as if the larger skex sensed the danger.

Recognizing its vulnerability, the massive beast sheered the smaller one's head off, sacrificing its sister to save itself. The monster rumbled and chittered in defiance just as Corbin brought the weapon's sight downward, pointing it directly at its head. With a tight squeeze of the trigger, the spear shot out of the machine with a large snapping sound, shaking the floor, where it was securely bolted, and shoving him back hard against the seat. The barbed steel bored straight through the beast's compound eye, and deep into its body. Its insides sprayed out in a steady stream where the spear had pierced. Screeching, the dying skex took two staggering steps forward, before its face came down with a crunch into the ground.

At the same time, Logan aimed the laser rifle he had retrieved, his blood pumping hard with the elation of finally regaining some sort of advantage in this fight.

"Time to say bye bye," he snarled.

The remaining skex came on with a ferocity he could not have predicted, spurned by the death of its kin. Logan was forced to the ground as it rammed right into him. Far too fast for him to react the skex smashed one of its crab-like pincers down hard over his wounded hand, pinning him to the ground. The pain of shattered bones coursed through his body like an electric current

The only thing stopping the monster from goring him on the spot was the swift reaction of the soldier, who was back on her feet and running the civilian's spear in at the skex. Catching it right between its rows of armored plates, she bought them just enough of a distraction. Logan squirmed, frantically trying to break loose from the hulking monster's grip. His blood curdling scream made Corbin jump and his blood freeze, as he was watching his own prey fall from the edge of the parapet.

Corbin had to shield his eyes from a succession of bright flashes, followed by a series of loud screeching noises as the laser rifle blasted through the skex' armored hide. The beast fell dead on its side, freeing Logan from its grip. He dropped the rifle, numbly staring at what was left of his hand and roared in agony. Every finger was shorn down to the knuckle, leaving only a thumb, brokenly jutting at a weird angle from the crushed area of pulpy flesh where his hand used to be, as fountains of blood squirted from the mortal wound.

Corbin screamed for his brother, jumping down from the turret. Before he even made it to Logan's side, the soldier was there tying off his wrist with a makeshift tourniquet of cloth that she had quickly torn from her pant leg.

"Do you have any medi-gel?" Corbin asked, wishing he had not used the tube he found on his own wound. Thankfully, the woman was already squeezing some of the stuff onto the nubs of his brother's hand. Desperately grasping Logan's tunic, Corbin pulled him up to a sitting position, "Logan talk to me, stay with me!"

Logan looked at him with glassy eyes and smirked, "Those glasses look ridiculous, little bro."

The soldier began to chuckle, "Man, this guy is something else! If he hadn't shown up when he did, we would all be dead for sure." She said, shaking her head at the insanity of it all.

"We need to get my brother back inside the city, to see a healer!" Corbin said. He lifted Logan from under his shoulders while the soldier grabbed his ankles and together, they carried him just behind the defense spear, where she said there should be a doorway. The irony that they had been that close to salvation was not lost on Corbin, as they skirted the dead littering the area. The wounded man pushed open the door for them and once inside the corridor a soldier quickly brought them to the healer's barracks.

"You're damn lucky son," a soldier said, chewing on the butt of a cigar while a long gash on his arm was stitched up. "Not only to survive a fall like that, but then to find your brother on top of it all. Must have the gods looking after you to have that kind of fortune. You Walker boys are heroes, no doubt about that."

Corbin only dimly heard the man, sickly watching as the healers tried to save what was left of his brother's shattered hand. Without looking over at the soldier, he mumbled under his breath, "Right...real lucky."

At the apex of Fal, on the highest wall of the city, a metal banged opened. Out of the twelve levels of the capitol, only the top two had yet to be breached by the invading horde. The battle below was at somewhat of a standstill, as the swarm of carnivorous insects distracted itself to feast on their already captured prey. It was a short reprieve that the soldiers meant to take full advantage of, retreating into the city walls to regroup, and carrying whatever wounded they could to safety.

Some of the people out on the walls were still alive as the skex ripped them apart with hungry tentacles. Elder Alain looked down at the grisly scene of carnage from the top level, despair filling his heart to see the great massacre that had befallen his beloved homeland.

From the doorway, Lady Cassandra emerged, just catching up to her husband. She was breathing heavily from running, her white hair and ivory robes whipping around in the wind, as she made her way over to him.

"Alain, stop this madness at once!" she weakly demanded between gasps. The look he shot her said volumes and Cassandra felt as panicked as a trapped bee, shaking her head violently to deny what she knew he was about to do.

He regarded her for a moment and gripped his chest. The idea of losing her almost was too much for him to bear. Her heart surged with a fleeting hope that he had changed his mind.

"There is nothing else to it, my dear Cassandra. The day has come, and it must be done," somberly he stroked his massive, braided beard as he spoke. Before she could deny him again, he gently took her by the shoulders and pushed her back into the stairwell. "Now, get yourself back inside where it is safe, star of my stars."

Lady Cassandra lost herself in his eyes, unable to speak, silently imploring him not to leave her. Alain nodded sadly, hearing her voice in his mind and pulled her trembling body close to his, smelling her hair for the last time.

Without warning Alain abruptly spun around and slammed the stone door shut, locking her inside the stairwell. He turned his back on the woman he had loved for almost two centuries. Through his hard life she had meant everything to him.

All the happiness in the world could be found in that woman's smile, he thought to himself, fighting back the sorrow enveloping him, *but this must be done.* The finality of it all hit him as he made his way to the large dais set in the middle of the parapet. An enormous obsidian egg twice his height was cradled in its center.

Cassandra could hardly find the air to breathe; tears seemed to be flowing from every pore of her body as she choked down the aching in her chest. Alain had put in the code to seal the gate, leaving her trapped inside, feeling helpless in the face of his imminent sacrifice. He gave one last look at his wife, through the window of the stairwell, before flipping the switch to activate the powerful weapon.

The egg opened with a mechanical whir, revealing small steps leading inside the chamber. Once inside he stretched his arms out above his head, locking them into the harness, which automatically began the process. The whirring continued to build in its crescendo as hot metal coils sealed around his forearms and clamps clasped his legs firmly in place. His robes were tossed about as the air began to crackle with the building energy inside the egg. On the smooth outer surface colors ran in waves flowing brown to green then back to black again.

Alain's command had to be shouted to be heard over the ancient machine's deafening roar, the whirring sound now so loud it shattered his eardrums. Blood ran from his nose and ears. The air literally crackled, as whips of energy began lashing anything not bolted down off the platform.

Pieces of stone showered over the wall, raining down on the swarm below. Some of the skex stopped gorging on their meals, their frenzy interrupted by this new commotion.

"Farewell, my dear," Alain whispered. The roar of the machine was deafening now, as the countdown ended inside the weapon. Behind the sealed stone doors, Lady Cassandra's screams were lost under the cacophonous waves of energy, and she pounded hysterically on the window for her husband. In her mind, she could hear his screams as the obsidian egg tore his life essence apart converting it into raw energy.

Lost in the deepest anguish a human can experience, Cassandra slammed her forehead repeatedly against the door, as if that could silence his screams wracking her mind. She felt him erased from existence and her legs wobbled like jelly, spilling her to the floor in sobs.

The obsidian egg flared in a brilliant blue glow, all of Alain's essence melted into raw energy. A massive concussive force wracked the walls, as the egg fired long waves of blinding green plasma off its surface in all directions. The stuff was hotter than lava yet moved down the city walls like a tidal wave. Not an inch of the surface was left uncovered. Everything organic it touched upon melted under the sheer heat of the otherworldly ooze, absorbing into it and making the plasma stronger as it washed further down.

It was only an instant, a blinding hot minute, and the skex were burned away, along with all their victims' mutilated bodies. One blinding flash and the only thing left was a half circle at the city's base level, where the plasma had flowed into the grated moat built for just this contingency plan. A handful of the insects were all that remained in the air, fleeing from the site of their near genocide.

The battle was over, the city of Fal saved, and Lady Cassandra's husband was gone forever.

Chapter 9

"Stop that, Logan Walker, you fresh little devil!" Maggie lightly slapped his hand away, blushing as she playfully shooed him back, pawing her hand in the air.

"Well maybe not now then, Mag…," Logan said, noticing the more he smirked, the redder her cheeks became.

Covering her smile, she gave a couple more paws as she left the room. Not that it helped much. He could hear her giggling with the other healers, down the hallway, immediately after leaving.

Ah well, at least I tried, he thought, stretching his arms and legs out on the cot. All the strange medical equipment had been removed from his room now, leaving only the bare essentials behind. Logan sat up and looked around the room for where they had stored his boots. He could not expect to sneak out of the place without boots now, could he?

No, definitely not, he decided, shaking his head, while still wearing the smirk. Three days ago, he had been able to pry some information out of a porter. The man had been stopping in nightly to play a couple hands of cards with him, and until this point Logan had still been too weak to make any use of the info. However, today…today was different. He felt excellent, right back to his old self.

That thought stopped him short and he found himself staring where his hand had used to be. *Well, except for my new friend,* he thought. The healers had done their finest work to save his life and stop the bleeding, which the medi-gel only barely suppressed. They tied up the broken nubs and gashes of his hand quickly enough, but the appendage was ruined beyond repair, fingers and knuckles left back in the carnage of the battle somewhere on the wall.

Once they had finished, the Elder's personal bioengineers rapidly took over. They worked methodically to install a new hand, first melding his nervous system to the cybernetic circuitry, then the vessels, muscle, and ligaments were all replaced with hydraulic pistons and gears. The new hand was covered with a soft thin elastic coating. It looked metallic but felt slightly squishy. One of the older bioengineers boasted that the stuff was as strong as any steel blade, and more than an adequate reward from the Council of Twelve for his heroic deeds.

Logan wiggled the fingers of the mechanical miracle, delighting in the spectacle of hydraulic drives seamlessly responding to his nervous system. He was never one to dwell over the past, not since a tragedy of youth robbed him of feeling. Initially, he had been quite distressed to find out his natural born hand was gone, as was only natural. However, as the days passed, he realized his body was getting used to the new appendage and before he knew it, the new hand was something he was just accustomed to, functioning so naturally he began to forget it was even mechanical. He knew in his heart that he was more than fortunate to have received such an amazing gift.

"If only it wasn't so damned shiny though," he lamented again, this time out loud. He had tried to coax them into coating it with a dermal layer one of the nurses told him about, but the bioengineer said the High Council would not authorize any further expense. The work they had already done was rare enough, only given to him as a reward for saving the capitol with his warning, and it was not as if he had the funds to pay for such an expensive procedure on his own.

He pulled a small pouch of gold and silver pieces from behind his pillow on the bed and grinned wolfishly. He might not have enough to buy a dermal layer, but the winnings he had taken from the porter were more than enough for a little something he had cooked up. If he had to live with a mechanical hand, he planned on having some minor *adjustments* performed on it.

Logan peeked around the open doorway, looking up and down the corridor to see who was around. His smile widened to find that his boots were resting on a pad just outside in the hallway. Snatching them, he instantly went to work getting his things together, saving the new black leather gloves that some of the nurses had pitched in to buy him for last. Apparently, his ceaseless flirtations had paid off, though he would have preferred to have someone to share his time with. The gloves should disguise his hand just enough to blend in, as it was common knowledge that the young man who had saved the city now had a mechanical hand.

Another quick glance around the doorway into the corridor, to make sure no one was about, and Logan made a dash for the exit. If he did not take this opportunity, the chance might not come again, especially once his nagging little brother came to pick him up for their trip back to Riverbell.

The great marketplace of Fal was alive with sounds and smells on that fine afternoon. It had been a short trip from the healing center to the large bustling square for Logan. Again, he wondered why people had an obsession with calling such places a square. It was more of a winding labyrinth filled with shop stalls, all arranged at odd angles, set up in no perceptible pattern. As he came closer, the bustle of people ahead was almost dizzying, being the most people he had ever seen in one place. The square was just bursting with the people of Fal bustling about their daily routines. All about vendors were shouting their wares and every direction he looked customers and merchants were haggling over prices. The whole thing delighted him to no end.

Logan dove into the crowd, working his way through the bustling marketplace. Fires crackled as food carts cooked up their specialty dishes, made to order and guaranteed fresh. He marveled that only two short weeks ago this city was under a life-threatening attack. Logan deftly sauntered his way through the crowds, trying to blend in as best as possible and not be such an obvious country bumpkin.

Just when he began feeling comfortable with his city swagger, a lovely woman with thick black curls cut across his path. Their eyes locked for a moment, and he walked hard into a table of potatoes for sale. The vendor slapped the back of Logan's head with the frond of an ent tree, yelling about the mess he had made and demanding payment for the damaged vegetables, while the girl giggled to her friends about the silly young man. Logan tried to apologize, scrambling to pick up the mess, but the old woman just kept hitting him, until he finally gave up and escaped back into the crowd of benignly indifferent citizens.

He found it strange how no one seemed to pay any attention to each other. People were so unaware of their surroundings they were even bumping shoulders without a single word of apology. This was nothing like Riverbell. Just past a stand selling ceramic bowls and another vendor peddling playing cards, the crowd opened wide around a group of people dancing merrily in pairs. The band played on joyfully while couples twirled in circles, switching partners, dipping them and laughing raucously. Crowds of shoppers stopped to enjoy the spectacle, many clapping along with the music and rhythm of the musicians.

Some passers' by dropped coins into a donation box, which was guarded by a hawkish looking man who menacingly gripped a leather-laced club. He was watching this way and that, looking as if he dared someone to try to steal the money he was being paid to protect. Logan could not help but laugh at the merry spectacle, but when a young lass held out a hand for him to join in, he politely declined and moved on.

He came by a food cart that was swarming with hungry patrons waiting to have their orders taken. The stocky woman behind the counter was barking orders over her shoulder to the cooks.

Logan thought this was one lady who didn't need anyone guarding over her money. Shimmying in closer to see what was on the menu, he caught a mouth-watering smell wafting out of the oversized frying pans. The cooks were skillfully working to sauté hunks of meat, throwing strips of mushrooms and onions into a thick yellow curry. His stomach rumbled as his senses were assaulted by the exotic dish.

"What'll you have, son?" the large woman bullishly asked him.

"Ah, I wish I had time, food later, business first," Logan said, earning himself an eye roll. "Maybe you can help me? I'm looking for shop called the Grey Crow?"

"Look kid, if you're not buying then step out of the way," she said, waving on to another customer in line. The man behind him shoved past into the small space, knocking Logan rudely out of the way and already placing his order.

Logan decided he would need to learn to become more thick-skinned, if he was going to stay in Fal. Not one to dwell, he circled the tent, continuing his search. Todrick had given him directions to the Grey Crow as payment when he came up short on a bet. Despite the disorienting nature of the bustling marketplace, with a little prodding Logan wad able to reorient himself using Todrick's directions. The porter had warned him how easy it would be to get lost and had given a great piece of advice.

Keep your eyes on the tops of the buildings around you. Stalls move daily, making the markets unpredictable, but the buildings of Fal are carved from the great mountain itself, and they are not likely to be moving any time soon.

To the right he could see faded blue waves painted under the third story windows of what must be the public bathhouse. That was the direction to head so he made his way around another set of stalls, slipping between them to take a shortcut and get away from the swelling crowds. As he squeezed through them, he caught a glimpse inside one of the wider squared out tents. A group of citizens was gathered inside praying to the Great Crystal, Baetylus. On their knees in supplication, the men and women rocked back and forth moaning.

What rubbish, he thought, dismissing their faith for idiocy, before slipping down a narrow alleyway that led behind the bathhouse. He was surprised to see that even here tables were set up with merchants hocking wares.

A big-bellied man cut in front of his path, peddling beaded necklaces. "For your lady, a fine gift to be sure made from the-," he began.

Logan just kept walking, flicking the man's arm out of his face in annoyance. "No lady here, pal," he said, but the merchant was persistent and jumped back into his path.

"Then what about for the lady of the evening, my friend?" His large devious smile was ruined by rows of rotting teeth.

Logan just kept walking, without attempting to mask his contempt. Remembering the porter's directions, he veered right, where the alleyway split, stumbling across something quite unexpected in the fair city of Fal.

A makeshift table had been knocked over, blocking the narrow alley. It looked to be made of nothing more than a wooden slab that was set on top of some dirty old boxes. Small paper charm bracelets were scattered all across the dirt. The owner of the cheap merchandise appeared to be nothing more than a child; he could not be more than ten years old, Logan guessed. The boy was backed up against a wall, with three scruffy looking teenagers cornering him. Two of the ruffians wore bands of tan cloth around their right arms, while their leader wore a high collared jacket that covered the lower half of his face.

"Quit your lying, street-rat! Cough up the money what you owe us," The leader jammed a bony finger into the kid's chest, pushing him against the wall with every syllable.

"Owe you?" the boy said. "Um…b-but my m-mam needs the m-money." He looked like a cornered mouse about to be eaten.

The ringleader backhanded him hard, knocking the boy to the ground, while his lackeys cackled. "Don't act like ye don't know who this alley belongs to!" he spat, kicking the boy in the belly. When the boy began to cry the ringleader turned to laugh with his friends and adjusted his beret.

"Now be a good little rat and cough up the toll," he added, kicking the kid again for good measure.

Logan was already making his way around the table by the time the other two noticed him.

"Hey, fuck off, Sally!" one of the punks flexed.

Without even thinking, Logan backhanded the little prick, sending him flying into the alleyway wall from the jaw rattling impact of his new mechanical fist. The troublemaker's head smacked hard against the stone, knocking him out cold.

"Watch your mouth little guy. Didn't your momma ever tell you not to talk to strangers?" Logan taunted, and grimaced at the remaining pair.

"Hey…easy man…easy," the other lackey said holding his hands out for Logan to calm down. "This ain't got nothing to do with you. We just collectin' our dues for Old Roger is all."

The punk's nose made a crunching sound, like splintering wood, as Logan's fist shattered the cartilage inside. Blood splattered down the troublemaker's face, covering his leather vest.

"Is that right? Oh, *do* tell me more," Logan said, while the thug was clutching his broken nose and crying as blood gushed out from between his fingers.

As he taunted the thug, the ringleader howled into motion, lunging at him with a knife. Logan spun around, kicking the tabletop across the ground. The wooden slab skittered directly into the charging thief's path, knocking his legs out from under him. He let the knife slip from his grasp, flying into the air, as he tried to stop himself from falling face first into the soil. Logan caught him by the collar, tightly twisting the leather jerkin and cutting off the attacker's air.

"Tut tut," he said, wagging a finger inches from the trouble-makers face. "Now is that any way to treat a tourist?" Logan grinned, raising his other fist, readying to punch him in the face.

Unable to avoid the oncoming blow, the ringleader winced, gurgling incoherently for him to stop. Logan's eyes squinted and his face curled in disgust, looking down to see the punk had just pissed through his pants. Still scowling, Logan lowered his fist, and wrinkled his nose.

"Oh, you little coward, big enough to beat on this poor kid, but can't even take a punch like a man?"

The punk just whimpered, looking to his friend for support, but he was still so worked up trying to stop his nose bleeding that the thug probably had not even noticed what was happening. With a sigh of impatience, Logan gave two quick tugs, wrenching the wooden earrings from the ringleader's right ear. Then he let the punk go and slammed his left fist into his gut, knocking the air from his lungs and dropping him to his knees.

"Get out of here and go play in your sandbox, *Peck*," Logan said.

The bloody nosed thug was already helping their dazed companion up from where he was slumped against the wall. He eagerly nodded to Logan and scrambled down the alleyway. Just to give it good measure, Logan shoved the ringleader's behind with the heel of his boot.

Once he was satisfied that the thieves were leaving, he turned to check on the young boy they had been harassing. Several of the peddlers stood watching the commotion in awe. When Logan turned about, they began clapping and talking excitedly with one another, one man even walked up and thanked him, shoving a belt into his unsuspecting hands as a token of appreciation.

The boy sat on the ground gazing at Logan in wonder. To the kid, he was a hero of myth come back to life, like Great Ulysses overthrowing the world dragon. No one had ever stuck their neck out for anyone else in the alley markets. Logan walked over and knelt to the boy's level.

"You okay, kid?" he asked, his gusto replaced by genuine concern.

"I am now, mister! Wow you really gave it to the Drugenns!" The boy hopped to his feet in excitement, punching the air like a boxer.

"Why were those punks messing with you anyway?" Logan asked, as he helped set the boy's table back up.

"Oh, that's just the way it is around here, mister," the boy frowned. "My bracelets have been selling pretty good. They must have caught wind of it." He showed Logan two coppers as way of explanation.

They beat this poor kid over two coppers? he thought. "Well, they won't be bothering you again. Try and stay a little safer from now on, you hear?" Logan said, mussing the boy's hair before striding away.

"Sure thing, mister!" the boy called back, starry eyed. As soon as Logan walked away the boy was quickly surrounded by the older peddlers, all of them eager to recount the fight.

After a series of back-alley zigs and zags, Logan came to the inner city. He had heard of this part of Fal, and often wondered what it might look like in person. Up until now the city was made from stone buildings expertly carved into the very rock of the mountain that at one time made up this grand place. However, in the inner city he began to spot wooden buildings that had been erected in-between the older houses. As the population of Fal grew, so too did the need for additional housing.

It was in this part of the city that he found his destination. Though it was constructed of ashen wood, the shop looked as old as the caves of New Fal themselves. Its windows covered with solid sheets of soot and cobwebs. A worn sign hung loosely above the door proclaiming *The Grey Crow* then underneath in smaller letters *Oddities & Wonders*.

The shabby old building stood in stark contrast to the parlor next door, which had the sign of a buxom lass leaning back in a silhouette of red clinging to its facade. Instead of a proper door, or shutters, the parlor had red velvet curtains, which were swaying in the breeze. Out on the balcony upstairs, some city watchmen were laughing rowdily, their arms wrapped around the working women.

As Logan approached the storefront, one of the women next door called down to him. "You got the wrong door, sugah. The real experience is right here." She suggestively pointed down between her legs at the doorway directly below. Falling for her ruse Logan blushed, and a group of the women burst into laughter, coming together to taunt him with promises of what could be.

"Ye got that right, Veronica!" One of the watchmen drunkenly agreed, sloshing his beer over the edge of the balcony in his excitement. The man turned to wink at Logan then buried his face in her bosom. He had to admit to himself, the prospect was intriguing. He had never seen so many women ready and able. Riverbell had nothing even remotely like this bordello, not unless you counted Francine Erwil's place. She *was* considered the village tramp. A name she never deserved in Logan's opinion as he could not understand how sleeping with two men before settling down with her husband was any different than what most of the guys in the village did, but they were never called names for it.

Logan smirked and gave a slight bow. "Maybe later, fair ladies, but for now business is calling."

"Don't know what you're missing, lad!" One of the other city watchmen called down as Logan headed inside the shop.

The old wooden door slammed shut behind him, bouncing against the frame on springs that wore out ages ago. A little bell above the door clanged to announce his arrival, as if the slamming racket were not enough. The Grey Crow was nothing like Logan expected, with dusty tables and shelves overflowing with wares, literally crowding the room. There was not an empty spot among them, that he could see. The place was dimly lit by a single candle, glowing somewhere in the back of the cluttered storefront, its light dancing back and forth flickering across the ceiling. The shelves held so many interesting artifacts, most of them utterly foreign to him; like the large winding brass tube or the small carriage wheel that was coated in a blackish gray substance. Many empty oil lamps hung from the ceiling, some rusty, some polished to a sparkle fit for a queen, all with cobwebs. He had also never seen so many books in one place. The village only had around eighty and he had read them all cover to cover well before his fifteenth birthday.

Someone cleared their throat behind him, causing his heart to skip a beat.

"Ahem, what do ye want? We ain't open," the man said. Logan circled around to find a little gnome standing behind him. He could not imagine how the gnome had snuck up on him. The shopkeeper looking up at him could not have been more than four feet tall, wearing red suspenders over a white collared button up shirt, rolled neatly around the sleeves and tucked tidily into beige trousers. What little hair still remaining on the gnome's head was white as soap and seemed to glow in the light from the candle floating in the air above him. He adjusted tiny spectacles over his broad flat nose to get a better look at Logan, impatiently waiting for an answer.

"Uh...w-well...that is to say...," Logan stammered, still taking in the gnome, and wondering about his odd white patent leather shoes.

"Well? Out with-it son, I haven't got all day!" the gnome barked, wrinkling his bushy white moustache, then adding under his breath, "Very busy man I am, important things to do."

"My apologies, I guess I'm still a little jumpy after the surgery," Logan said, offering the mechanical hand as way of explanation.

Faster than he could blink, the gnome scurried closer and grabbed his hand. Flipping another lens in front of his spectacles, the shopkeeper studied the mechanical fingers intently. He scrutinized every angle of the thing, turning it this way and that, opening and closing the digits one by one, all the while muttering to himself, "I see, I see...oh yes, very nice design."

Beginning to feel like the prize ham at the picnic, Logan interjected, "Right then, if I'm not mistaken you *are* Mr. Beauford, correct?"

The old gnome eyed him, still turning his fingers. "Might be that I am, just as likely I ain't. Who are ye to be askin' then, eh?" he said.

"Todrick Thornhill told me you were the man to talk to about a little *upgrade*," Logan said, drawing out the word while he tried on his best carefree smile.

"Never heard of him," the gnome said.

"Oh?" Logan asked.

The little gnome grumbled and leaned back with arms folded over his chest, silently brooding. Logan pulled a pouch of coin from his pocket, which seemed to be all the credentials the shopkeeper needed. As it landed on the table, a couple gold shillings skittered out, lighting up the gnome's eyes. He looked to the stash then back up at Logan with a newfound smile that stretched ear to ear.

"Well, why didn't ye say so earlier lad! Oh, it's certainly great to have ye 'ere, it is. Why any friend o' Todd Thornybeak's a friend o' mine, I always say!" Mr. Beauford said, hopping up onto a chair to clap Logan on the shoulder. He hopped down and pulled Logan away from the table by his forearm, ushering him into the backroom... "C'mon then let's get to it! No time to be a wastin'!"

Chapter 10

"Now then, let's leave that to set for a bit before we finish the job," Beauford said as he pulled away the tiny precision torch from Logan's mechanical fingers, guiding his other hand to cover the spot with a dampened white cloth.

"Just keep pressure right there for a few and I'll go fix us some brew, eh?" Beauford said, slipping into the next room, out of sight.

Logan could hear the gnome opening cupboards, followed by the clanking of pans clapping together. Logan had been looking around the room while his hand had been modified, trying to keep his mind occupied. This room, like the many shelves and tables in the main storefront, had the most peculiar items for sale. There were small tin cylinders, sealed over the top with funny painted pictures of dancing animals; Mr. Beauford called them *"soda,"* glass picture frames with no pictures in them that he called the *"telie."* One shelf had rows of glass bottles filled with various liquids of all different colors. When Logan asked what they were called, the little gnome gruffed and grumbled for a moment then said, "What do I look like, a flippin' tour guide?"

Logan realized he had been asking the gnome one question after the other at that point, but he could not help chuckling at the shopkeeper's grumpy nature. Clinking sounds interrupted his train of thought as someone triggered the little bell above the storefront entrance and quite hurriedly made their way toward the back room.

Mr. Beauford popped his head around the corner of the kitchen. "Eh? See who that is, lad," he said, motioning to the doorway.

Logan was just about to get up when a teenage boy in a brown hooded tunic came huffing into the backroom. Looking surprised to see Logan sitting there, the kid stopped for a moment, then shrugged to himself.

"Have a hand delivery for you, Master Beauford," the boy called out, looking around the backroom for the gnome.

"Eh? No doubt ye do, lad," Beauford said over the sounds of running water. "I'll be right there in a jiffy, hang on to your whiskers already."

The boy smiled and nodded, as if Mr. Beauford could see him through the wall, then looked around the room while awkwardly shuffling his feet. He caught a glimpse of Logan's hand and perked up like a cat, leaning in toward him.

"You're that fella that came to save the capitol, aren't you?" he said, brimming with excitement.

Logan was confused by the delivery boy's words. He had never been known for being much more than the village trickster back home. The revelation that someone was actually looking to him in admiration made him squirm slightly in his seat.

"Aye, I guess that I am. The name's Logan Walker, what's yours?" he replied.

"Who...me? Aw, I ain't nobody special sir, just a simple mail porter. Name's Henri, sir." The boy said shyly shifting from foot to foot under Logan's stare.

"Seems like a good gig for a kid to have around the capitol." Logan said.

"Oh, it is, sir, it is. Helps put food on the table for my family plus I get to meet all sorts of interesting folk." Henri puffed his chest out, beaming with pride.

"You know Mr. Beauford pretty good then?" Logan asked. The boy shrugged noncommittally.

"Where does he get all this crazy stuff from?" Logan asked, cocking his head toward the nearest shelf of shiny stones.

"Well...uh...," Henri dropped his arms down to his sides, nervously looking over Logan's shoulder.

"From the surface," the gnome said, making him hop straight up from the seat with fright. The damned little man snuck up on him again, with nary a sound to announce his arrival. Beauford was standing right beside his chair. The delivery boy took that as his cue to spring into action, quickly moving to help Mr. Beauford with the tray he was carrying. A ceramic teapot clanked, as he pulled it out of the little man's hands and set it on the nearby table.

"Oh, wipe the skepticism from your face, boy, don't tell me ye still be believin' in those children's tales," Beauford said, waving away the notion as if it were the most ridiculous thing imaginable.

"I don't follow what you're trying to say, old timer," Logan said, which stopped Mr. Beauford dead in his tracks. When his eyes landed on Logan, they were cold as ice.

"Whoa…okay, down boy," Logan said with upraised hands. "No offense meant, it's just an expression. But I still don't follow; the surface of Acadia is a wasteland, scorched during the Jotnar Invasion. No one can travel up there and hope to survive. So where did you *really* get all this stuff?" he asked.

Beauford's eyes were as round as saucers, as he listened to Logan. He looked to Henri for confirmation that they just heard the same thing, then back at Logan and then back to Henri one last time. Both of them burst into uncontrollable fits of laughter, although Logan noticed Henri only started nervously chuckling after the shopkeeper began. Beauford was slapping his stubby thigh, laughing so hard tears welled up in the corners of his eyes.

"Oh boy…oh, you *do* know how to make this *'old timer'* smile," Beauford said, forcing himself to gather his composure. He straightened his bushy white moustache with one hand and mussing the hair back into place around his earlobes. "Ain't no such thing as no scorchin', lad," he said, motioning for Henri. The delivery boy handed him a small brown parcel, while placing a small pencil in his waiting hand and moving a tiny clipboard up for the signature of receipt.

"Are you trying to tell me that you travel to the surface world?" Logan scoffed in disbelief at the incredulous thought. No one had traveled to the surface in centuries, not since the Jotnar Invasion had made life up top impossible.

"Well, hell no, lad. I ain't no *old timer*, but still, that trip's too long for these bones to take…these days, anyhow." Henri waved to Logan in the background as he zipped back out of the store, no doubt on to his next delivery. "No...I have friends what get me these things," Beauford said, sipping his tea and motioning for Logan to do the same.

"Friends huh...friends just go up to the surface, risking their lives to get you this stuff? Must be nice to be that popular, wish I had friends like that."

The gnome fell silent, reaching down to remove the cloth and get back to work adding the illegal enhancements to Logan's hand. "Don't expect you actually would want friends like that, way you treat others. Look boy, I'm only telling you this because I know people. You think I don't get all sorts of 'em in here? Be gettin' 'em all, don't ye be doubtin' it. C'mon now kid, ye got to be too smart to still be believin' in those old wives' tales about the surface," though Beauford spoke boldly, he also spoke lowly, jabbing tools into the gears, then sealing his work with the tiny jewelry torch.

"Most folk come in here just to get some o' my nice victuals, or maybe even a book lost to the ages to read. Helps 'em forget for a while ye know? Helps 'em stick their heads in the sand a bit longer." Logan wondered what sand was, but he went with it, nodding so the gnome would continue.

"I see you understand what I'm sayin' here. You can make all the empty jest in the world, but I can see the truth in your eyes, boy. You can just feel something is off 'round here, can't ye?" he closed one eye, pointing at Logan with the tip of his tiny mallet, waiting for a response.

"Absolutely," Logan lied, although he was not sure if it was to himself or the gnome. "But that still doesn't answer how you got all this merchandise."

"Well, boy, that's my business, now ain't it? I do have my ways, not too easy being tucked away in the back corner of the city, but my friends sure do provide. In fact, as you can see, my little network extends deep and far," Beauford bragged. "And why shouldn't it, even outcasts need to eat, am I right?"

"Don't seem to be much of an outcast to me. Looks more like you have it all figured out pretty good, actually," Logan said sincerely, though he doubted the gnome's claims, he had to admit the shopkeeper had a decent little setup going here. The gnome paused for a moment and smiled up at him.

"Right you be, boy, I do mighty fine for me self. However, the outcasts I refer to are the exiles of New Fal, those that been kicked over the wall. Someone's got to keep some provisions going to the poor wretches after they get booted out to the *wild lands* after all," he made the claim as if it was the most sensible thing to assume. For Logan it was anything but. "Except nothing in this world or the next is free, eh?" Beauford said.

Logan caught onto his reasoning now. It was rooted in whispered campfire tales, if you broke the laws of New Fal, the Council of Twelve would sentence you to banishment. Exile over the wall, into the wild lands, was akin to a death sentence. As a kid he never took the warnings seriously, chalking it up to more ghost stories told to frighten children into behaving. As Beauford fleshed out the details of his import export business, Logan could almost hear Elder Morgana's words echoing in his ears, *Be good or the Elders will grab you and send you into the deep dark.*

As he grew older, he still heard the stories, but with a different twist, only the vilest of criminals would be punished in such a way. One would really have to be a depraved cretin to earn exile from the kingdom. It was a rare sentencing reserved for murderers, rapists, and the like. However, this gnome in his tiny shop tucked away in the corner of the capitol, was actually claiming he exchanged supplies with outcasts from the wild lands in return for them bringing him back relics from the surface world? The whole thing seemed far-fetched to Logan, yet looking around the room at the strange items, he could just hear the ring of truth somewhere, lost in the madness of it.

"Hmmm...survival for scavenging, huh?" Logan thought aloud. "Interesting stuff old time...err...Mr. Beauford."

"I can see it in ye lad, mind as well be wearin' it on your sleeve. Got a taste for the adventure, eh? Maybe you're thinking of doing a run to Malbec?" Beauford said, hitting on Logan's intentions about leaving Fal to travel to their neighboring kingdom. Malbec was a place renown as a breeding grounds for treasure hunters. It was the very reason he

Secrets of the Elders

wanted to get the upgrades Beauford was installing, so that he could go find adventure.

"And why would I be interested in going to Malbec?" he said, with as much innocence as he could muster.

"You know why," Beauford wheezed and chuckled knowingly to himself. "Anyhow, I got a job for ye right here to get ye started. You take care of it and then we can see about havin' you make some real coin to get you on your way." Beauford said as he polished off the last spot-on Logan's hand as the metal cooled down.

"Wait, do you think I'm going to smuggle for you?" Logan asked. The little man looked disappointed at the remark, waving off the notion.

"We ain't talkin 'bout no smugglin', this here is just a simple delivery I need made," Beauford explained, washing the oil off his hands, and neatly storing his equipment.

"A delivery? You just had the damned service here a second ago, why didn't you give it to that Henri kid?" Logan asked.

"This one needs a bit of...*discretion*."

Logan straightened himself out, stretching his fingers to admire the gnome's handiwork. It was flawless in design. There was not even a scratch on the mechanical hand, no indication whatsoever of the modifications he had just paid generously for. The gnome walked over, pressing a small coin purse with a tiny scroll tied to it, into his palm.

"What is it?" Logan inquired warily.

"Drop this off at the House of Alderman and be sure to deliver it to Lady Cassandra personally. After you do so, come back and see me and I'll have some *real* work for ye."

Logan could see that was all the answer he was likely to receive. "What makes you think I'm going to do this for you? I don't even know where to find this Cassandra woman," Logan said, even though he was already putting the coin purse inside the folds of his jacket.

"You're a resourceful lad. Something tells me you'll figure it out," Beauford winked, flipping a gold coin to Logan. "In the meantime, here's a little something for your troubles."

Logan eagerly caught the money; the eccentric old bastard was right; he was definitely up for a little taste of back-alley dealings. "How do you know I won't just run off with this?" he teased.

"Well first in, I know people, which I already explained to ye. Second in, if you cross me, I'll just have some of my lads go down to Riverbell and pay a visit to your brother, Corbin, and his nice lass there, just for a bit of fun," Mr. Beauford said, wearing a sinister grin that sent a shiver up Logan's spine.

"Wait...how do you know?"

"But that ain't gonna be our relationship, right boy? I like a nice capable lad like yourself lookin' all eager and what not and am more than happy to employ you into my services and grow your *career*. Now how about instead of silly what ifs, you just go on and get that letter in the Lady's hand for me, eh? I know you gonna be just fine," he added, pouring honey over the warning to help Logan see it with clarity. The gnome was not threatening him as much as revealing the extent of his knowledge and making it clear that double-crossing would not be in the cards.

Logan's head was still spinning in circles over the conversation, as he headed toward the exit, but then a thought occurred to him.

"Wait...one other question. If the surface is not really scorched, why don't you just go back up there?" he asked.

The gnome turned to him wearing a grave expression, which was flat and unwavering. "Might be the scorching tale has holes but sure enough the Jotnar be waiting and watching boy...waiting and watching."

Mr. Beauford closed the door to his shop behind his visitor, watching through a soot covered window as the lad made his way up the alley. He wondered at life for a moment, its vast mystery never ceased to amaze him. After all these years of waiting, finally the lad was here in Fal and at the most unexpected of times. The balance of power was shifting in the kingdom of New Fal for the first time since its founding and he needed that parcel delivered to warn Lady Cassandra from turning her back on the enemies surrounding her.

However, that was the least of the plans he had for young Logan Walker. He had waited decades to meet the Walker boy and had plenty of time to devise the proper chain of events that would need to occur next. It was a simple ploy to have Todrick plant the seed in Logan's head, though Beauford did not like parting with such a sum of money, no matter how temporary. He smiled at the pouch of coins he had retrieved. No, the boy would have a greater part to play in the coming of the Fourth Age before everything was over and done. Yes…a much larger part to play indeed.

Logan stepped out into the cool evening air, still trying to figure out how the little black-market dealer knew so many personal details about his life. He supposed it was the nature of such a business to be informed.

During the evenings, the Great Crystal would dim to a dull indigo, casting a dim glow over the land. His father used to tell him stories about the nights on the surface of Acadia, saying that the sky was so bright in the daytime people had to wear blacked out glasses just to see, and at night when Themis dipped below the horizon all the stars of the universe could be seen in the heavens above. Night's topside were supposedly far darker than the lands they now lived in. He even heard people had to light candles in the evening to keep the demons away and protect their loved ones.

Somehow, that had always stuck with him. Perhaps it was how frightened he was as a child of the idea of not being able to see in that ancient dark land. Not knowing what might be waiting for him with grasping hands in the shadows. Logan felt his throat tighten up at the memory of his father.

Wow where did that come from? he wondered, shaking his head and letting the memories fall away. Gazing up at the Great Crystal, miles away in the distance, he had to smile, knowing the nights here would always be lit.

The sounds of the brothel faded in the distance as he retraced his steps back to the marketplace. Back home everyone would already be settling in and calling it a night by this time. Mainly due to the fog that would roll in off the riverbanks, making it difficult to see outside. But, even more so, it had to do with all the farmers who woke in the early hours, toiling in the fields to grow their crops.

Here in the capitol, it could not be more different, with no fog rolling through these streets, just cool crisp evening air. Yet people were still hustling and bustling whether he turned down an alley or cut across one of the main roads. He admired his new hand and slipped a glove over it as he walked along lost in a daydream, happy over the modifications he just had installed and eager to complete the job Mr. Beauford had tasked him.

Lost in his reverie, Logan almost walked into one of the peddlers. He recognized the man as the one who had given him the belt earlier in the day. The merchant's eyes were glassy and unfocused, lost in his own thoughts. It was almost as if the peddler had no expression whatsoever, as he just ambled along past Logan.

That's strange, he almost seems asleep, Logan thought, as he looked away from the man. He immediately noticed several others wearing similar expressions the further he went down the alley. Two older women in cowls quickly skittered out of his path, their gaze firmly stuck on the ground.

Just as Logan thought things were starting to get strange, the source of everyone's behavior presented itself. His heart froze, growing cold in his chest as a lump welled up in his throat. Somewhere distant, he could hear himself thinking how odd it was that his feet were locked in position. As much as he willed them to move forward, they did not seem to care.

About thirty feet up the alley, he could see the young peddler boy he had aided earlier. Even though he was too far away to tell for sure and desperately wished it was not true, something in the air electrified around him, it was palpable, telling him this was real. The boy's earlier joyful reaction to his aid flashed across his mind.

The lump of bloody, beaten flesh lying in the dirt, under tattered clothes, was unmistakably the very same peddler boy. Somehow Logan's finally moved, but it was as if someone else were controlling him. He was numb from the outside, only dimly aware that he was holding the boy's ragged form while screaming into the night for help. Of course, he knew somewhere deep inside that no measure of help could change the fact that the child was dead. But he screamed on, nonetheless.

The boy's face was crusted with so much blood, from a gaping wound where someone had caved in his skull that Logan could scarcely believe it all came from his tiny frail form. He frantically looked back and forth to the people walking by, none of which acted as if he existed. Logan called to one of the older men, who only a few hours ago cheered him on for protecting this kid. He pleaded for the peddlers to go get help, only to receive a frown while the merchant stared down at the ground, unable to meet his gaze.

Finally, two of the city watchmen came running down the alley, but they were fuzzy and unfocused. Crying was such a foreign concept to Logan. He almost thought something was wrong with his vision, realizing at the last moment that there were tears streaming down his face. He quickly wiped them away as the men slowed to a walking pace.

"Help me," Logan said, "this boy has been attacked, and he needs medical attention!" He pulled the child's limp body up from the ground, expecting one of the watchmen to aid him.

"Aw, c'mon mate...is this what you were making all that ruckus about?" the taller lawman said. Logan recognized him from next door to the Grey Crow; he was the one who had buried his face in the woman's breasts.

"I need your help to move him," Logan said, thinking these men clearly did not know what to do in an emergency. He struggled to keep the boy upright, the limp body flopping like jelly.

The shorter, pudgy lawman finally moved in to take the kid's weight off him. Except instead of helping to carry the child, he carelessly dropped the boy back to the ground, with a loud crack of bone meeting stone stinging Logan's ears.

"Effin' country bumpkin's, I ain't getting myself all bloody for some street rat." He nudged his partner, having a laugh at Logan. The taller watchman did not join in, but proceeded to scold him, clearly annoyed at being disturbed from his festivities.

"Get him to the medical center...and how would he have paid for that then, eh? The kid's already gone anyhow."

Logan knew the man was trying to calm him down in his own way, but their complete indifference to the murder of a child made his blood boil, snapping something inside the core of his reasoning.

"He would still be alive if you two sorry sacks were out here doing your job instead of loafing about with whores!" Logan blurted.

The pudgy guard flinched as if he had been struck then snarled, "And who the bloody Hel cares? Look around you idjit, no one's upset here but you." He leaned down nose to nose with Logan, raising his voice with every word. "All I see is one less rat on the streets to feed. Who are you to come down here to *my* district acting all high and mighty, anyhow?" His words were flecked with spittle and the vein in his forehead was throbbing.

"Look, you better clear off before things get ugly here," the taller man warned, circling around to Logan's side with his nightstick drawn.

"Nah, screw that Tommy, this country bumpkin's got big words to be saying," the short guard spat to his side. "This little prick wants to question our dealings, and in *our* neighborhood?"

Logan had clearly upset the man beyond reason. This was turning south quickly, moving so rapidly that he did not understand how it went from him calling for help to being cornered by armed city watchmen.

"You want to come down here, preaching to me about what I should be doing?" the angry guard spat again, waving his own nightstick around in the air as he spoke.

Logan noticed the taller man, Tommy, seemed to be feeding off his partner, a hungry look growing in his eyes. "The way it looks to me and Ralph here is *you* killed this lad to steal the earnings off his corpse. Lucky we arrived on the scene just in time to stop you from making off without paying your city taxes, eh?" Tommy said, just before he swung his weapon hard across the nape of Logan's neck. The force of the blow sent him tumbling unexpectedly to the ground. The short guard squealed his delight, like the pig he was, as he moved in to slam his own nightstick across Logan's thigh. Stars shot across his vision from the pain, while both men towered over him laughing like crows.

Logan lashed out blindly, his metal fist cracking right through Ralph's shin, splintering the bone like a dried twig. The sound of it was so loud, everyone in the area stopped to see what had happened.

Before Tommy could react to his partner's injury, Logan kicked the legs out from under him. Back on his feet, he noticed the pudgy guard pulling out a pistol. Logan stomped hard on Ralph's arm, sending the gun skittering across the alley, and gave him two quick raps on the side of the head with his natural fist. The second one knocked him out cold.

Aware that Tommy had gotten back up behind him, Logan tried to block the man's attempt to lock him in a chokehold. He struggled to rise, as the watchman clamped down around his neck. Vendors nearby ran away, screaming in fear, obviously not wanting to be blamed for any of what was happening. Logan threw his weight backward, taking Tommy down with him. He landed on the man hard enough to loosen his grip.

Logan took the advantage to slip free and wrestle his position around so that he faced his attacker, only to receive another sharp blow to the jaw from the man's nightstick. Logan saw stars again, but managed to stay in control, knocking the weapon out of reach. Grabbing onto the man's side, he dug metal fingers in between his ribs, and yanked down hard, breaking the bones. It was more than he meant to do, only wanting to twist the man's pressure point, but hearing the sound gave him a sick joy. The corrupt guard let out a blood-curdling scream and frantically tried to shimmy away from him.

"Oh c'mon, where you going, *Constable*?" Logan said. "You can't leave before I pay you my taxes, remember?" He slammed his forehead into the watchman's nose. Blood gushed out of the unconscious man's nose as Logan pulled himself up to his knees.

He reached down and flipped the guard onto his side so he would not choke on his own blood, wiping the smear of it off his own forehead. As the adrenaline began to wash through his body, he grimly took in the two men lying on the ground beside him bleeding.

Serves them right for attacking me, he thought.

Logan only realized someone had come up behind him a moment too late. He was unable to react when another loud thwack resounded in the alleyway and a blinding flash of pain cracked across the back of his neck. This time the stars flashed bright, and the ground came up to meet him, while the world faded to black.

Chapter 11

Across the city, a sleek black carriage rolled through the streets. It was wide enough to fit four passengers in its spacious quarters, and the vehicle took up most of the road. The driver busied himself whipping the large black elks, to keep it moving faster, while on either side of the carriage hung the Magistrate's personal guard, gripping leather handholds with heavy boots resting on ivory carved niches. As the carriage rolled along through the early morning, the men yelled to either side, warning pedestrians to either move or be run down like dogs.

Behind glass windows, with purple velvet embroidered curtains detailed in gold stitching, the owner sat coiled like a viper beneath his dark cobalt-blue robes. Magistrate Fafnir had a hawkish look about him, with sharp angular features. His nose was large and came to a point, matching a thin, protruding chin. The centuries had not been kind and were beginning to show, with wrinkles set in deep crow's feet around his eyes that gave them a sunken look, like his skin was too tightly stretched over his bones, yet just loose enough to hang slightly around his jowls. Fafnir preferred not to wear a hat over his bald pate. Some whispered it was because he wanted you to have to stare at the specks of discolored skin that dotted the side of his head, to throw you off and make one uneasy. He currently wore a cunning smile, as his eyes worked like daggers over the woman with which he was conspiring.

"Well, I certainly do agree with your disinclination, Mademoiselle," Fafnir said, his voice like silk across satin.

Duchess Blaunchette chittered, as she feigned embarrassment behind a hand fan. Her large quivering breasts seemed as if they might spill out of her too tight dress at any moment. A garment of this style would normally be quite flattering, but the oversized woman tended to wear her clothing a size or two smaller than she should, clinging to dreams of her long-forgotten youth. The Duchess' face was covered with a bit too much white powder, caked up around the folds of her neck and she wore her hair in long brown curls that Fafnir suspected was the work of a wig.

"Oh Magistrate, I believed you would see my point," she said, still feigning a giggle. "After all, we shan't have just any citizen thinking they can do these things."

"As always milady, you are the epitome of civil society. I will see to this at once, trouble yourself with it no further," he assured her, as his hand appeared from the folds of his robes, palm face up with his little white fingers waited like the claw of a vulture.

The Duchess cleared her throat and dropped a jingling coin purse into his grasping little talons. Quickly, the tight little bony fingers clamped around the bribe, and it disappeared into the folds once more, while he simultaneously pulled the cord next to his head, signaling the driver to stop.

"Now then Madame, if you please, I have many affairs of the kingdom to tend to this morning," Fafnir said, graciously gesturing to the door as it was being opened by one of his men.

The noblewoman shuffled sideways to the exit, balancing her weight on the guard's outstretched hand so he could help her down the steps. Once outside, the Duchess straightened out her dress and quickly peered back inside.

"Thank you again for your time, Magistrate. Your support to House Blaunchette will not soon be forgotten. We are in your debt once more," she huffed; out of breath from the labor of getting out of the carriage. "*After* this matter has been duly settled, of course."

"It honors my humble soul to receive such unworthy praise. I am but a servant to the kingdom, Madame. By tomorrow evening the offenders will be taken care of, and after that none of the first levelers will dream of trying to send their little whelps to your daughter's school again," Fafnir cooed, tilting his nose up in the air at the mention of citizens from the lower level of Fal. Before she could say more, the door was shut and the driver's whip resumed working to move the carriage along, toward the Magistrate's next destination.

Relieved to be out of sight, Fafnir dropped the façade, his face returning to its permanent scowl. "Off to Mill Road," he croaked into a tiny bell-shaped metal opening that worked as a communication device to his driver. Pulling out the purse, he counted through the coins, scribbling a tally in the little worn ledger at his side.

"Rodger, step in here."

One of the heavily armored soldiers obediently crouched through the small carriage door on his right and sat across from him, taking up nearly the entire back seat with his muscular frame.

"After our next stop, send out word to have this family *detained*," Fafnir said, handing the soldier a tiny parchment scrawled with the family's name. "They live on the eastern first level, in the smelting district. And make sure it stays quiet this time, I do not need any more badgering from Elder Reinholt."

The guard accepted the parchment, giving it a quick glance before tucking it away into the tiny pocket under his shoulder plate. "Yes sir, would you prefer section six for their detainment?" he asked, referring to one of their quieter prisons that few knew existed. It was the perfect place to make citizens disappear.

Fafnir gave a derisive snort. "Rodger...*detain them*. You are dismissed," he was annoyed to have to spell out every little thing for the man, but at the same time somewhat amused at his devious mind. Rodger gave a furtive nod and slipped back outside to his perch on the side of the carriage.

The matter taken care of, he let his thoughts wander to the future. With Elder Alain out of the way, there was a seat open on the Council of Twelve for the first time in over a century, and he intended to make sure it was his. Duchess Blaunchette had such a meager request, compared to some of the others he had taken care of over the last couple of days. Fafnir had always coveted a seat, all the way back to when he turned sixty. He had eagerly awaited the day one of the Elders would be in the right position for him to swoop in and steal their leadership, sometimes daydreaming of choking one of them to death, or slipping some poison in their meal, or *accidentally* falling down a flight of stairs. He had tried and failed at several of these schemes over the years. Never in a million years would he have dreamed such an opportunity would present itself without his direct influence. He snickered that Elder Alain had so foolishly sacrificed himself for the people of Fal! This kind of feeble-minded blind devotion to the masses was exactly the reason Fafnir needed to be on the council.

The kingdom needed a strong leader. If it had been him, he would have grabbed one of the criminals in section three and thrown *them* in the vorpal cocoon to fuel the weapon. Hel, maybe even two of them at the same time for good measure. With Alain's seat open, he was working tirelessly to secure every vote he could before the next meeting of judgment.

Apart from Elder Alain's widow, the Lady Cassandra, and that fool Count Roberro, there was no real competition for the coveted position of power. Lady Cassandra was the real threat. Like Fafnir, she was one of the original pilgrims of New Fal, fleeing into the core of Acadia after the Jotnar blight. She would be a formidable opponent, being widely respected by both the lower levelers and noble citizens alike. That meant Fafnir had to drum up whatever additional support he could muster in the House of Aristocrats, knowing that with each House he added to his fold, not only did he gain the allegiance of the aristocrats, but also their entire staff of servants. If that meant keeping some dirty little lower class Falians out of the White Tower school district for Duchess Blaunchette, that was a small price to pay, and nothing compared to what Fafnir *would* do to gain a seat on the Council.

The carriage came to a stop in front of the wood mill. While one of the soldiers headed inside, Rodger stepped to the side alley giving orders to a group of his men that were waiting outside the building, stationed there to protect the hero from Riverbell inside.

"Get to this address post haste and bring these citizens to section six for processing," Rodger ordered.

"Affirmative Captain, what are the charges?" One of the younger soldiers asked.

"No charges, no courts, this is to be a quiet one. Take them down to section three and execute them within the hour for crimes against the Kingdom." Rodger dryly ordered the execution as if he were telling them to wash his laundry. The soldiers bowed in compliance, leaving him to fulfill their task.

"Good afternoon, how can I help you, sir?" Corbin asked the soldier who had been knocking at his door.

"Corbin Walker of Riverbell?" the man roughly inquired.

"Yes...that's me, what can I do for you?"

"You'll need to come with me. Your presence is required by the royal Magistrate," he ordered, stepping aside, expecting Corbin to immediately vacate the apartment.

"I'm sorry, did you say the Magistrate? There must be some mistake. I have not..."

"Leave your abode immediately, citizen," the guard forcefully ordered, brandishing a night stick to accentuate his directive.

Not wanting to get into an altercation with a man of law, Corbin raised his hands, attempting to cool the situation by showing immediate compliance, and headed into the hallway.

"No need to get upset, I was just asking-," he said, cut off by the man's nightstick jabbing him hard in the spine.

"Move citizen."

By the time they reached the carriage, the guard had holstered his weapon and moved to open the door, ushering Corbin inside before slamming it shut behind him. Corbin was surprised to feel the vehicle already on the move, mere seconds after entering, barreling down the street away from his temporary housing.

"Corbin Walker, it is a pleasure to meet you, young man," Fafnir said. "I have heard a great many things from Elder Morgana." The old man held out his ringed hand, expecting Corbin to kiss it. He was disappointed when the young man awkwardly shook it instead but continued anyhow. "Also there have been so many tales going around already, rumors spreading through the capitol of your bold and courageous actions to warn us of the skex attack." Fafnir stopped speaking to pour Corbin a drink of water from a glass decanter set in the left side of the carriage. "Of course, I *had* hoped we would be meeting under better circumstances."

Corbin cocked his head to the side. "Well, Magistrate, sir…I appreciate your kind words, I mean, not just appreciate, but I'm honored really. But exactly which circumstances do you mean?" Corbin asked. He was never one to beat around the bush, always preferring to get right down to *brass tacks,* as Elder Morgana would say.

"Why, that would be the *circumstances* of your brother being arrested by the state, lad," Fafnir slowly explained, taking care to emphasize each word and carefully gauging the man's reaction as he spoke.

Corbin was dumbfounded, at first, he could not comprehend how his brother could possibly get into trouble lying in a healer's bed, but as Fafnir explained the previous day's events it all became clear.

Logan had left the healers without any warning and without being discharged, traveling through the city alone. Several eyewitnesses saw him stealing wares at the market, and he may have assaulted a young boy, who was in questionable medical condition. Apparently, some of the Magistrate's men had tried to detain Logan, since he was drunkenly wandering the streets and behaving erratically. Unfortunately, both of the lawmen in question were badly injured during the ordeal, and it had taken another group to stop his brother's violent outburst.

How could he do something like this? Corbin felt like a fool for thinking, after all they had been through the last couple of weeks, his older brother was finally changing his tune. He should have known better. It seemed like every time he thought things were getting better, Logan pulled a new stunt to prove him wrong. He guessed some things could just never change, but to hear Logan had gotten into a fight with lawmen, that was far more serious than his usual shenanigans.

Magistrate Fafnir tried to comfort Corbin, telling him not to blame himself. "Some people are never able to shake the past," he said with feigned ignorance.

"Shake the past…in what way do you mean, sir?" Corbin asked.

"I certainly do not mean any disrespect to our late Elder Morgana, but we did advise she take the boy to a Falian councilor years ago...when it all first happened."

"Logan is always getting in trouble, seems like no matter what we're doing he will find a way to slack off, or create a prank, but nothing ever as serious as this. I'm not sure a councilor could help him with that," Corbin said doubtfully.

"A wise woman once said, it's not the branches, but the roots that define a tree's growth. Surely, we could have prevented all this nonsense years ago, right after your mother died," Fafnir cooed, pretending to sip absently on his drink. He could have smiled like a wolf to see the puzzlement overtaking Corbin Walker. The Magistrate enjoyed causing problems where none should exist. He knew very well that Elder Morgana had kept the boy in the dark over his parent's deaths, and why.

"I do not see what this has to do with my mother, did you know her?" Corbin asked.

"It has everything to do with sweet little Melinda. If your brother had only listened to his mother and stopped trying to get her to play hide-n-seek, she would still be alive today. No one could blame poor Melinda for what happened, she was just trying to do some laundry by the river after all, but who among us could resist the playful nature of their children?" Fafnir paused to let him digest the revelation.

"I think you are mistaken sir," Corbin said, a pit opening in his stomach. "My mother died of a terrible sickness."

"Aye, there's nothing deadlier than the sickness that follows the deadly bite of a river asp," Fafnir said.

"Are you saying my mother...she was killed by a river serpent? And you believe this was because she was playing a game with my brother?" The pit in his stomach sank further down into his bowels.

Fafnir worked up a frown, "Forgive me son, I assumed you knew, but...at your age...yes I could see you would have been too young when it all occurred. I guess Elder Morgana never had the heart to tell you."

"Why would she hide this from me?" Corbin's world spun; the proverbial carpet pulled out from under his past. As he tried to make sense of Fafnir's claims his hands were shaking, spilling droplets of water from the glass onto his lap.

"Don't blame Elder Morgana, dear boy; she was an amazing woman, the ilk of which we are not likely to see again." *At least he hoped not.* "Most likely, she was trying to shelter you from the truth. Perhaps it was the wisest course. After Melinda died, your father certainly made no attempt to hide his feelings on the matter. Oh, how he loathed Logan, blaming him outright for her death. After he left, not able to bear being around your brother anymore, we pushed Elder Morgana again and again to have the boy speak with someone, to help him get through it all, but she always refused."

Corbin sat slack jawed, listening intently to this stranger's recounting of his family's past. "I...never knew," he stammered in disbelief.

"Well, you were so young, I am hardly surprised," Fafnir said, though Corbin's thoughts were turned inward, echoes of the funeral beat back into his head. He could hear his brother mourning, could see him in his mind's eye weeping by the casket, repeating over and over again how sorry he was.

"I hope I have not troubled your soul in my attempt to put things in perspective, dear boy. You see, I believe your brother is, in his heart, a good person, but until he lets go of causing his mother's death and driving your father away, things are only bound to get worse. That kind of sorrow has a way of eating away at one's soul."

If Corbin had not been so wrapped up in his own thoughts, he may have caught the gluttonous look in Fafnir's eyes. The Magistrate found it so easy to manipulate the people of Fal, that sometimes he did it just for sport.

With Corbin Walker doubting his brother, the lies of Logan's actions from the previous day were an easier pill to swallow.

"I appreciate your kind words, Magistrate," Corbin said, trying to gather his composure. "Please, tell me, what will happen to Logan next?"

"I am bringing you to him and he will be placed in your charge," Fafnir said.

"I cannot tell you what a relief that is to hear, sir," Corbin sighed. "On my honor, this will not happen again."

"You understand of course, it can only be under the agreement that you get him out of the city post haste. He is no longer welcome here. The citizens of Fal will not understand why one of their heroes has assaulted members of the watch. And I fear there are those here, who would not care of his motives, and will call for Logan's execution once the news of his criminal deeds spreads."

Fafnir could not openly exile the brothers, not after all they had done for the city, but Corbin did not need to know that. The sooner the rabble-rouser was out of his hair the better, in less than one day Logan had taken several of the magistrate's collectors off the streets, planted the seed of revolution for the Grey Alley merchants, and sent two watchmen in the healers. Fafnir needed to move quickly before word of this reached Lady Cassandra. If that meddling woman found out what happened the night before, she would be parading Logan around as a hero against *local corruption* before the week was over. Fafnir could ill afford that kind of attention right now, not when everything he worked toward was within his grasp.

The carriage came to a jerking halt, leaving them sitting in silence. A rap on the door announced they had reached their destination.

Corbin cleared his throat and spoke up, "I understand what needs to be done, sir. You have clearly gone above the call of duty to protect him and for that I offer you my sincerest gratitude. We shall be leaving on the morrow," Corbin vowed, as he stepped out into the dim daylight, before a low gray stone building where the street came to a dead end. This was a section of the capitol directly attached to the massive cavern wall, a good place providing the natural barrier needed to prevent the inmates from escaping. Three guards were already escorting Logan from the detention center. They stopped and one of them shoving him hard into the street with the butt his spear.

Logan staggered forward a few steps then looked as though he had a mind to go back and teach the guard a lesson, but before he could move to action Corbin roughly snatched his forearm. "Knock it off.

Haven't you caused enough trouble already?" Corbin snapped. Logan glowered at the guards who only laughed as they went back inside.

Logan shot his younger brother a bewildered look. "You can't be serious? I spent all night in this hell hole and that's how you greet me?" he growled, in no mood for his younger brother's righteous indignation.

"Seriously Logan, after what you did to those men, you have the *nerve* to complain about being in a cell for one night?" Corbin barked right back.

"What would you know of it? You should have seen the kid." Logan tried to explain.

Corbin curled his lip back. "Save the disgusting details for someone who cares. You went too far this time. Your actions bring great shame to our village and to our family."

Logan shook his head in disbelief, unable to meet his brother's gaze. "Who asked you to come down here, anyhow? I was completely fine without your help."

The Magistrate had climbed out of his carriage and was now standing at their side with his hands folded. "Ahem," he cleared his throat, interrupting their childish bickering and demanding their attention. "That would be me, young man."

Logan appraised him and understood several things at once. Fafnir's bone chilling tone told him the man expected nothing less than gratitude, and the cold look in his eyes made it clear that this was a dangerous man who would not be trifled with.

"This is Magistrate Fafnir," Corbin said. "He has kindly agreed to release you into my custody."

The way Corbin introduced the man, like he was some sort of royalty, disgusted Logan. Where his younger brother saw a generous benefactor, all Logan saw was a snake. "Hmmm...I see...well that's great, you're exactly the man I wanted to talk to. Do you know what your men are subjecting citizens to in there? And what about those imbeciles last night? I want to press charges against...,"

His tirade was cut when one of Fafnir's guards came up to whisper in the Magistrate's ear and Fafnir lifted a hand to silence Logan. He listened to his man with a furrowed brow. Corbin groaned, not believing how disrespectful Logan could be toward the very man who had just come to his rescue. Once the guard was finished, Fafnir mumbled some orders and addressed them again.

"I am fully aware of the entire situation that played out last night, Logan Walker. Everything is currently being dealt with and you are free to go." Logan opened his mouth to speak, but Fafnir cut him off again. "Now then, gentlemen, if there is nothing further, I will take my leave, the day is young, and there are many affairs of the state to see to yet." He turned his back to them.

Corbin let out the air in his lungs, only then realizing he had been holding his breath with worry that Logan would say the wrong thing to the great nobleman, sending himself back into the detention center. He moved to direct Logan, who was visibly agitated over being ignored, back down the street.

"Corbin, there is one other thing," Fafnir said, halfway into the carriage.

"Yes, milord?"

"There will be a gala held tonight at the House of Ciotti, in honor of Fal's victory over the wretched skex attack. We would all be honored to have the both of you attend."

"No, my liege, it is we who are honored by such a generous invitation," Corbin replied, as Logan rolled his eyes.

"Excellent, my men will send the invitation to your apartment," Fafnir said, disappearing into the carriage, which was already rolling away before the door closed.

"Oh, my liege," Logan mocked, "you are so magnanimous. What's with all the kissy kissy aristocrat talk?"

Corbin ignored him. "That was odd, a minute ago he said we had to leave the city post haste," he said, more to himself than to Logan.

Logan looked down at the coins the Magistrate's men had secretly placed in his hand. Silver to keep his mouth shut. "Not as much as you may think brother. It's this place that's odd, not that man. Actually, he fits right in around here," he grumbled under his breath, watching the carriage roll down the road and wondering what news the guard had delivered to make the magistrate offer up the invitation.

113

Chapter 12

Lady Penelope had lavishly decorated her palace for the evening's festivities. Marble columns dotted the perimeter of the large ballroom, reaching high up to the arched ceiling, circled by colorful streamers. Glistening polished tiles covered the floor, creating a mirror image of the large gathering. On either side of the area, temporary bars had been setup, tended by men in suspenders and starched white collared shirts who were busy dispensing drinks to the guests.

Logan noticed the bottles they poured from looked suspiciously like those he had seen in the backroom of the Grey Crow. Waitresses were wading through the crowd, carrying trays of delicacies. A small platform had been setup at the far end of the room, where a band played soft music, while a tall, slender woman with scarlet hair sang. The gala was alive with the sounds of chatter and clinking glasses, as the capitol's elite celebrated.

"This is a joke, we do *not* belong here," Logan said as he and Corbin made their way down the wide marble steps into the ballroom.

"Fix your tie and try to behave properly for one night," Corbin said. He had quite enough of his brother's complaining, and made it perfectly clear earlier that they would attend the gala out of respect to the Magistrate. It had been a little surprising when they returned to the apartment above the wood mill to find suits waiting inside. As soon as they were dressed, Logan made a point to tell his brother how stuffy he looked in an evening jacket.

"I think we look fine. This is the way they do things in the city," he said, even though the attire did make him feel silly.

"No, *I look great*. The ladies are going to eat me up tonight little brother. But *you* look hilarious."

One of the younger noblewomen walking by shot Logan a lusty head to toe approval, as if proving his point. He looked over at Corbin, comically wiggling his eyebrows. "What did I tell ye, eh bro? They love it," he teased.

"Logan *please*, just stay low-key tonight, that's all I'm asking." Corbin said.

"Ah, what little faith you have. I'm the king of low-key tonight. Now, if you don't mind, I'm going to mingle," Logan said, winking at his brother and quickly slipping into the crowd before he could think to protest.

Before Corbin could move to follow, Magistrate Fafnir beckoned from a nearby group. Not wanting to be rude, he headed over with due haste, entering the small gathering. "Well lad, I see you got the suit I had sent over," Fafnir beamed, happy to see the man dressed in his attire. Everyone at the gala would be discreetly talking about how he wore Fafnir's colors, stitched into the shoulders of the jacket.

"Yes, Magistrate, you have my deepest gratitude." Corbin said, offering as formal bow. "This was too kindly a gesture, milord. I will need to repay you in some way."

"Hardly necessary, after all, you are one of Fal's greatest heroes. If we can't spare a little civilized society for you, then we are all much worse off than we thought." The men and woman standing with Fafnir laughed, although the joke was lost on Corbin.

"What a dreadful experience it must have been for you, facing all those vile beasts outside the city walls," said an old aristocrat with an overly nasal voice.

Corbin was not sure what the decorum in a situation like this would be. Was he allowed to address his betters? Did the man really want a response, or would he embarrass the Magistrate by speaking out of turn?

Fafnir enjoyed watching Corbin struggle with his words. "Where are my manners? Madame and Monsieur's, may I formally introduce you to Corbin Walker of Riverbell, the hero of Fal," he said with a grand flourish of his bony arms, waving his intricately carved cane in the air.

"Corbin, lad, this is the Lady Aurelia, Lord Joseph Brussel, and his son, Sir Todrick Brussel," Fafnir said, pointing to each in turn with the tip of his cane. When he was finished, he gave Corbin a discreet nudge to respond.

115

"Pleased to meet your lordships," Corbin said nervously, producing another half bow, which Lady Aurelia found deeply amusing in a charming provincial way.

"Well, I don't want to be rude, I see you were in the middle of a discussion before I came over and interrupted," Corbin said, breaking the moment of awkward silence.

"Nonsense, my good man," Sir Joseph said, draping an arm around Corbin, and reeling him back into the gathering. "We were just in the middle of a debate, on the Great Crystal to be exact, and thought you could provide a novel perspective."

"Um, I'm not sure I'm qualified to offer any perspective," Corbin said, but the man only smiled, swirling his drink.

"Todrick here was just making a case that some of the younger citizens have turned away from the All-Father's path," Magistrate Fafnir explained.

Corbin arched an eyebrow in disbelief. Back home everyone in the village was deeply devoted to their god, the Great Crystal Baetylus. It was a way of life for his people. On every third day of the week, all would gather in the village circle to pray in supplication just at dawn. He would often find himself deep in meditation, trying to commune with the All-Father, and never a meal passed without someone thanking Baetylus for his blessings. The notion that anyone in the capitol would be straying from the path of righteousness was so alien to him, you might as well have asked him if walking upside down was better in water.

"Sir, I find that hard to believe, certainly we have not fallen that far astray from the enlightenment of Baetylus," Corbin said with the firm conviction only one of faith could possess.

"You see Todrick, Corbin is all the way from Riverbell and even *he* is still devout," Lady Aurelia smugly proclaimed, revealing he was not alone in his steadfast faith.

"He is an exception to what is happening out there in the lower levels," the younger aristocrat said curtly. Straightening his small wire frame spectacles, he snatched an hors d'oeuvre off a passing tray, and nibbled at the pastry with impatience.

Secrets of the Elders

"Hmmm...yes, ahem...Todrick may be hitting on some truth here, Fafnir," Sir Joseph said, clearly trying to move the conversation along and not dwell on his son's unseemly behavior.

"Sometimes I wonder if the poor look for reasons to disagree with us, just for the sake of being contrite," Lady Aurelia said with a superficial pout.

Corbin could not believe what he was hearing. How could these nobles actually think there were people in Acadia that did not worship the Great Crystal? The Magistrate had been watching his reactions closely and could see the pained expression of disbelief painted across his face. He wondered if the young man was in actual physical distress over the idea.

"If you will excuse us for a moment," Fafnir said, ushering Corbin away, toward the center of the room. Leaning in with both hands on his cane, he spoke a little lower. "I can see their doubt shocks you."

Corbin nodded silently in agreement.

"I have no doubt in *your* faith to our Lord above, Corbin. Would that everyone your age had it still, nay, of late there have been many whispers of a group in the capitol trying to convert others to their way of thinking. It is so sad to think that there are so many straying from the path." He let the words hang out there for others around them to hear.

"I don't know what to say Magistrate. I wish I could help in some way," Corbin lamented, really racking his brain trying to come up with a solution.

"Just your devotion to the All-Father is enough, lad. It shows me that even in the far reaches of New Fal, a little village like Riverbell can still keep the kingdom's beliefs strong." He clapped Corbin's shoulder with his bony little hand then turned him slightly to face the stage. "Speaking of which, it appears our other guest of honor has arrived."

Corbin directed his gaze to where the magistrate's cane was pointing, over the crowd of people who were all turning toward the end of the ballroom. On the stage was a man much taller than anyone he had met before, wearing a white tunic and some finely stitched matching breeches that both had detailed gold thread embroidery along the edges, running over the neckline and back. He raised his hands high in the air and gathered everyone's attention.

The speaker was bald like Fafnir, but in a cleaner more refined way, except his thick white moustache that curled slightly at its ends, which was more playful than serious. He did not ask anyone to stop speaking, nor did he need to, for as soon as Arch Councilor Zacharia lifted his arms the massive ballroom fell silent, even the clinking sounds of glassware and plates were hushed.

Corbin had never seen the Arch Councilor before, but there was no mistaking whom this great leader was. His very eyes conveyed power, the pale blue circles seeming to radiate in the candlelight of the chandeliers.

"Honored, most esteemed citizens of Fal; it warms my heart to be here with you this evening," his voice boomed across the gathering, carrying over the heads of the guests and surrounding them with his presence. "It is with both great joy and deep humility that I stand here before you. Just two short weeks ago, we faced a threat that surely could have decimated our entire civilization. During that siege upon our great city, we witnessed the very best Fal has to offer. I ask you, when we were face-to-face with death, did we cower into the night?"

The room filled with the fervent response of everyone, simultaneously proclaiming "No!"

"Did we roll over, and let the insect horde destroy everything Falians have worked so hard to build?"

"No!"

"No....no, we did not. Rather than cower in fear we faced the threat head on. On that night many of our citizens gave their lives to keep the dream of New Fal alive, and we will forever hold their sacrifice in our hearts." Arch Councilor Zacharia bowed his head, sharing the grief he felt.

"Our own Elder Alain Alderman gave his very life essence to overthrow the vile skex horde. Our dearest, Elder Morgana Ellano, leader of Riverbell, lost her life in the first insect attack, defending her people unto her dying breath." He let the words hang out there, wrapping around the crowd, settling into their thoughts.

"I would ask a moment of silence, in their memory, to think kind thoughts and offer prayer toward their afterlife in the great light of Baetylus."

The room was quiet as anything Corbin had ever witnessed, and he closed his eyes remembering sweet Elder Morgana, the woman who had taken him and Logan in, raising them like her own children. He silently thanked Baetylus for guiding her into the afterlife.

"We owe much gratitude to the gift of survival you have given us, Morgana and Alain. May you both forever be at peace," Arch Councilor Zacharia said, looking toward the ceiling.

"May you bathe in the great light," the crowd, as one, chanted.

"Today, we also come together to honor some of our living citizens. Without which many of us would not be here to tell this tale. These men need no introduction, as you have all heard the story of their perilous journey to warn us of the oncoming assault. Please join me in formally recognizing the Falian Heroes of Riverbell, Logan and Corbin Walker!"

The arch councilor waved his left hand directly at Corbin and his right hand directly to Logan. The crowd turned to face the young men, surrounding them inside circles of applause. As much as Logan was beginning to despise these aristocrats, he could see their gratitude was genuine, and could not help the cocky smile that spread across his face.

"Gentlemen, we salute your bravery. The village of Riverbell has long been an asset to our Kingdom. Many of us use their furs or crops. Their village took a heavy toll in the aftermath of the skex raid, so today we would like to introduce you to Riverbell's new leader, who has been groomed for this task under the late Elder Morgana all her life and is ready to face the challenges yet to come. Please join me in welcoming Elise Ivarone, who as of today, is to don the title *Madame* Elise." Arch Councilor Zacharia moved to the side so Elise could step forward, her pale skin almost glowing in the light of the nearby sconces.

She stood there in a fine blue silk dress that matched her eyes, with elaborately stitched golden branches and leaves reaching from the floor up to her slender waist. Her hair plaited to the sides of her head, with rich blonde braids falling in front her bare shoulders. Logan's jaw dropped and he looked around to see if his brother was seeing the same thing!

Entranced, Corbin watched her gracefully walk past Arch Councilor Zacharia. It was as if he were viewing a goddess brought to life, because for him that is exactly what she was. Elise held her chin up properly, as she had been taught by Elder Morgana, and cordially greeted the swelling crowd, a group much larger than any she had ever seen before, with as much confidence as she could muster, feeling grateful for the cumbersome dress' ability to hide her shaking legs.

The crowd ignited in applause, screaming praises for her, although Logan noticed more than one look of disdain.

"Madame Elise will be undergoing to Rite of Baetylus later this month, to become one with our All-Father and establish commune with the Council of Twelve. Long live Madame Elise!" Arch Councilor Zacharia proclaimed, while she curtsied and returned to the back of the stage.

"On the morrow our heroes will be heading back to Riverbell, where they will help in the efforts to rebuild" Zacharia addressed the gathering then directed his focus solely on Corbin.

"The people of Fal owe you a great debt of gratitude that we hope to repay through a tribute. We will be resurrecting a memorial here in the capitol for all of those that fell, including dear Elder Morgana." Corbin bowed and Zacharia addressed the greater crowd once more. "On the morrow the Walker brothers will be leaving, but they will not be alone. Some of the city's finest craftsmen will be joining them, to assist in their efforts to rebuild. We will also be sending along provisions enough to get our friends in Riverbell through this tragic event and into a brighter future." The Arch Councilor clapped his hands, prompting the audience to do the same.

"Now go, enjoy your evening! Lady Penelope has put together a grand gala for us and an even grander feast. Afterward, we will hear from Lady Cassandra and Magistrate Fafnir on why you should vote for their seat on the Council." Zacharia spread his arms out, releasing everyone back to their festivities.

Corbin absently excused himself from the Magistrate and made his way through the pressing crowd toward the woman he loved. From the base of the wooden steps to the stage, Elise was looking around the room for him. She jumped when his fingers tapped her shoulder. They shared a look, silently communicating everything they had gone through in the last couple weeks and how desperately happy they were to see each other, before melting together in an embrace that was a bit too scandalous for the presumably proper nobles surrounding them. For a moment that seemed to stretch on for hours, they held each other, his arms wrapped tightly around her waist, her lips softly pressing against his, lost in one another.

Nothing mattered more to Corbin in this world than his sweet Elise. The journey he had taken, noble though it may be, had left a void in his heart where only Elise could dwell. She had longed to hear his kind voice these last few weeks, while tending to the wounded and dead in Riverbell. The attack had not been kind on their people and the shock of her new position among them had not been an easy one to adapt to. Corbin was her strength and Elise was his.

"Ahem, decorum Madame Elise, decorum," Lady Penelope said through a clenched smile, lightly tugging the young woman's sleeve. It simply would not do to have an unwed couple locked in such a passionate embrace, and certainly not in her house of all places!

"Oh, yes of course, my apologies milady," Elise said, though she could not wipe the sparkle out of her eyes. She pulled back from his strong arms and they both began giggling like schoolchildren. Noticing the Lady's disapproving stare, she straightened her silk dress and tried to put on a serious face, while Corbin blushed and gave an uncomfortable laugh, awkwardly scratching the back of his head.

"Come dear," Lady Penelope said, "there are so many people to introduce you to tonight. And Corbin you simply must join us, as the future Mr. Ivarone of course."

Mr. Beauford watched the couple disappear into the crowd with a smile on his face. It was nice to be reminded of the good in humans. The diminutive gnome had watched the kingdom of New Fal from its earliest beginnings and had grown rather cynical in the last few decades, over what he would define as the devolution of man. He walked through the crowd with a polite tip of his brimmed green felt hat at customers here and there, many trying to rope him into their conversations, but he politely declined, promising to return later. He was looking for his new recruit, and spotted him ahead, talking with Lady Cassandra.

"I would not call that *doing their job*," Logan countered Lady Cassandra's last statement.

"You misunderstand. I do not mean the job of the guards in upholding the laws of New Fal, but it is *the* job they are being paid to perform right now, nonetheless," She countered, wearing an amused expression at his clever nature. She clearly found Logan charming.

"But..."

"No *but's* about it, young man," Cassandra said. "That is the grim reality of our capitol. What you did last night was noble enough. After all the progress we have lost in the lower levels, it is refreshing to hear of someone acting from a place of morality again."

"You agree with me then?" Logan asked with uncertainty.

"I agree with your morality, not with your actions. Think on it for a moment. Did attacking those guards do anything to help the unfortunate child who was murdered?"

"Well...I guess it did not," Logan admitted.

"Now think, if you had stopped to gather yourself for a moment, you could have used this newfound hero notoriety you've gained to bring the situation to the attention of the Council of Elder's." Lady Cassandra said, firming up her gaze to make him look her in the eyes. It was important he understand just how serious his new position in society was and what he could do with that kind of recognition.

Logan looked to this Lady, who had pulled him aside out of nowhere, with curiosity, thinking perhaps there was hope for the people of Fal after all.

"As it is, the Magistrate has already spread rumors of your *drunken temper*, attacking his *noble* city watch."

"Learning to control your emotions will be a journey worth taking," Said Beauford, jumping into the conversation. Logan swore to himself this would be the last time the little gnome snuck up on him. "Lady Cassandra, I am terribly sorry for your loss. When I heard the news of Elder Alain's death it filled me with great sorrow, noble though his efforts surely were." The gnome gave her a slow bow, pulling his wide brimmed hat behind his back, as his head dipped down close to the floor.

Logan stepped back to take in the woman's appearance. She wore black from neck to toe; even her circlet was obsidian with an Onyx set in the center. He suddenly felt like a wool-headed goat, this woman was clearly in mourning over the loss of her husband, and here he was rambling on about the city's corrupt lawmen, as if she did not have higher concerns on her mind.

"Thank you, Mr. Beauford. Your kind words mean much to me. Logan never you mind, no apologies are necessary," Cassandra said as if she had heard his thoughts spoken aloud. "In any event I want you to watch your back carefully around that one," she said, nodding across the room at the magistrate. "He is not to be trusted."

"I'm sure this has *nothing* to do with your competition for the Council seat, milady?" Logan replied.

"I see. You are a cynical one. That is good, it will serve you well. But, if you knew me better, you would know falser words have never been uttered."

"Logan, I believe we have unfinished business that beckons?" Mr. Beauford asked, wanting to pull him away before he had an opportunity to make more of an arse out of himself.

"Of course, gentlemen, I will see you at the dinner hall. I've reserved seats for the three of you nearby my table. Let us discuss this further then." Lady Cassandra said.

"It will be our honor, milady," Mr. Beauford bowed again, before cutting through the crowd.

Logan followed the gnome to the left edge of the room, down a long hallway and into an area that was away from the action of the party, safely removed from prying ears. Mr. Beauford knew that everything Lady Cassandra had to say was not just for this young man's benefit, but also for the nearby listeners whose votes she hoped to secure before the night was through. Beauford on the other hand, had no such inclination to have others privy to his dealings.

On either side of the corridor stood richly decorated columns, reaching to a flattened-out ceiling that was lower than the ballroom, with small dark alcoves dotting the hallway, filled with barely visible marble statues. Only the sconce at the end of the path was lit, where the hall split in either direction. Above which was an oversized painting of the Lady Penelope with fan in hand, the very embodiment of sophistication. The gnome stopped once they were past the middle of the corridor and turned to address Logan.

"I understand your package was compromised?" he growled.

"Compromised? No, I just delivered it to Lady Cassandra as you asked," Logan said, surprised by the accusation.

"While ye were in section six...," the gnome offered, leading him to think through the series of events.

Logan slapped his forehead. "Those bastards went through my belongings?" He was upset with himself for his lack of foresight, realizing the guards must have gone through his things while he was unconscious.

"My sources were right then. What ye just delivered was not the intended message lad. No trouble, I will deliver the proper information tonight, in person." Beauford spoke more to himself than anything, thinking aloud while he twiddled stubby fingers, lost in thought over the implications of his message being intercepted.

"That rotten bastard...I'll shove his face so far up his arse...," Logan said as he began pacing.

"This is precisely the point the Lady was trying to make," Mr. Beauford said, folding his arms across his chest. "Ye need to control your emotions, boy."

Logan was at a loss for words.

"Ye have much curiosity and skill to boast of. There can be so much good brought to the land by your family, if ye only learn to control your passion, lad," Beauford explained.

"Well, correct me if I'm wrong, but didn't I just get a standing ovation from the entire city, and wasn't I just recognized by the Arch

Councilor himself? Looks like I'm doing pretty good without your *advice*, old man," Logan said.

"I wouldna' call being sent back home on the morrow, with your tail tucked between your legs, *doing alright*. That is Fafnir's doing, he is not going to keep a meddlin' little scallywag like yerself about."

As stubborn as Logan could be, he recognized the truth of the gnome's words.

"Aye, but we won't let that stop us, eh lad? Under all that bluster, ye've got a good heart, you do. Now be a good little mule and do as the Council decreed, get back to Riverbell and help your people fix the village right and proper. When that's all done and clear I'll send for ye to come back to the capitol. There is still much for us to discuss that ye don't be knowin' just yet."

"Sounds like a plan, old timer," Logan readily agreed.

"Alright then be off with ye, it's already about time for the feast to begin," Beauford said.

"And the other half of my pay?" Logan asked, holding his hand out expectantly.

"Eh? Nice one kid, scram," the gnome laughed at his tenacity.

"Can't blame me for trying?" Logan laughed, turning around to head back into the gala, oblivious to the dark shape that silently dropped from the ceiling down the hall. The shuffle of Mr. Beauford's boots kicking against the tile, had him curiously turning to see what the gnome was doing that could make such a strange noise.

Logan's skin crawled, his body frozen in place, unable to comprehend the spectacle in front of him. The gnome was on the floor with a dagger stuck deeply into his chest. A shadow bent over him, wearing tight black wrappings around his upper body and shoulders, with ash baggy breeches flared from the top, but securely fitted around the soles of his bare feet. The assassin's skin was ebony, glistening with sweat that was dimly lit by the far sconce.

The man turned slowly to face Logan, revealing a wicked grin from ear to ear. He seemed to move like water, flowing over the floor backward, never taking his eyes from Logan. Slipping into the nearest alcove, taking with him the pilfered pouches from his victim, the man melded into the shadows. Raising a finger to his lips, he whispered "Shhh." It was like the purr of a tiger. As the assassin slipped deeper into the darkness of the recess, Logan could only see his wicked eyes and toothy smile taunting him.

Snapping out of it, Logan hurried over to Mr. Beauford, lifting his head off the floor and screaming for help. Blood poured from the gnome's open mouth, staining his bushy white moustache scarlet, and his eyes already held a dazed faraway focus. Logan reached down to the black metal of the dagger hilt and wrenched it from his friend's chest, hoping to apply pressure and stem the bleeding. The action had quite the opposite effect. Blood poured from the wound as if a river had opened in the gnome's torso, spraying past Logan's hands that desperately pressed against the gash to keep the man alive.

"Hang on...we'll get some you help."

"Loga...argh...y-you must get out of here...," Beauford gurgled, feebly attempting to push him away.

"What in blue blazes are you talking about? I'm staying right here by your side!"

"Run Logan... It's all lies. Run to the surface...argh...t-they need to know t-the truth...w-we were going to show them together," Beauford was rambling incoherently.

"You're babbling man, just take it easy," Logan said before calling out for help again. Down the hall, toward the party, he heard a woman let out a scream, signaling she was witnessing the emergency.

The gnome gathered the last of his strength to grip Logan's collar and bring him closer.

"Shut yer damn mouth and listen to me, ye knucklehead. Go to the Crow and get the pendant...argh. Get the pendant, it's in me favorite drink at the shop...bring it to me family...get it away from them...get it...get...out...of...here...," Beauford's voice became weaker, but the wild look in his eyes could not be shaken.

The woman down toward the gala was still screaming for help and a small group of aristocrats gathered near her, pointing to the men and shouting for the palace guards.

"It's all lies...you have to leave...waited so long for you...," Mr. Beauford whispered, loosening his grip and slipping away from him. Logan felt the warmth of salty tears running down his cheeks as the light faded from Mr. Beauford's eyes. This was the second time in as many days that someone he just met was murdered. He finally heard the sounds of boots running behind him, as the palace guards approached, but it was too late for them to save his friend.

"Halt murderer!" the commander of the guard ordered, threatening him with a polished two-handed trident.

"Wait, what?" Logan asked.

"Drop the weapon and move back, dog," the commander ordered, while his men slowly edged in, setting themselves up to flank him.

Logan followed the commander's eyes, down to his hands. He flinched when he saw he was still gripping the bloody dagger he had removed from the gnome's chest. He dropped it to the floor and hastily wiping the blood from his hands to no avail. The floor all around him pooled with the murdered gnome's blood, sticking the fabric of his pant legs against the tile.

"Look, you don't understand...," he said with upraised hands, trying to show he was not armed.

"Execute the murderer!" Magistrate Fafnir snarled from behind the guards.

As the men rushed in, tridents thrust forward, and Logan screamed defiantly, throwing his metallic hand in front of him to block his body. Energy crackled from the palm and burst forth in a bright light, sending the men, and crowd behind, sprawling on the floor after being blasted from the stunning shockwave.

The ringing in Fafnir's ears dulled out the groaning and shouts of the people on the floor around him. Some of his soldiers were helping him to his feet and he rubbed the dull ache from his swollen eyes. The only resident of the arched hallway remaining was a dead gnome. Logan Walker had escaped.

Chapter 13

After the concussive blast had knocked everyone to the ground, Logan wasted no time making his way toward the exit. He was already clear across the ballroom before Fafnir and his men even began to stir again. Looking over his shoulder at the chaos left behind, he missed the poor waitress in his path, who he practically flipped over. He stumbled to help her back up in his panic.

One of the soldiers saw him running toward the front doors and moved to block his path. Without giving it a second thought, Logan barreled headfirst into the man's stomach, tackling him roughly to the ground and giving him two sharp raps across the face. Women were screaming all around, hurrying to get out of the way of the lunatic barging through the party.

As he approached the outside entrance, he spotted two palace guards blocking the door. They looked anxiously past him at the crowd of panicked people.

"The palace is being attacked!" Logan shouted, pointing over his shoulder. "The Magistrate's been injured; you have to help him!"

From the guard's perspective what they saw was a scared man who was being followed by a rove of scared aristocrats, all charging out of the building. Instead of moving to detain him, one nodded and they ran inside to help their leader.

Even a good four blocks away, Logan could still hear the commotion he had left behind, as the gala's noblemen and women were filling the city street and fleeing in their carriages.

These people are crazy! What in the Hel was I ever thinking wanting to come here? he wondered, stopping to catch his breath between two buildings. He leaned heavily against the side of a building, his blood pumping hard in his ears.

He wildly tried to understand what had just happened, replaying the chaotic scene in his head. He could not understand why someone would want to kill the gnome. Maybe it was related to his black-market dealings? He shook his head. Judging by the look Fafnir wore when he was cornered, he had a hunch the weasel was behind it.

A sign across the road caught his eye, *Park Avenue...I'm close to the marketplace!* he thought excitedly, remembering how quick it had been for them to get to the palace from Corbin's temporary housing at the wood mill.

Logan moved quickly through the night streets, ducking behind trash bins or into alleyways whenever a carriage approached. He had a good lead on Fafnir and his men, thanks to one of Mr. Beauford's ingenious upgrades to his hand. The wood mill stood quietly across the street from the alleyway he hid in, everyone home for the night after a long workday.

Looking up and down the street, he could see no sign of the city watch and sprinted across the street and up the outside stairwell to the apartments. He practically ran through the shabby apartment door in his frantic flight, only dimly remembering to lock it behind him. Once inside he spied his backpack, thanking his fortune. Before heading out to the gala, he and Corbin had been sure to pack all their supplies for the trip back to Riverbell they were going to take in the morning.

Grabbing the pack, he rummaged through the contents for a change of clothing, slipping out of the blood-stained garments he wore. He was just tightening his belt when the hurried sounds of boots came from the stairwell.

Bastards already found me! he thought, snapping his head around the room looking for an escape route. He was cornered. The only way out was a window, and they were on the second floor. He could hear the soldiers grunting in the hallway now.

The window would have to do. He sprang over to it and tugged at the pane, when someone began banging on the door demanding he come out peacefully. The damn thing did not want to move! Logan cursed himself realizing the catch was still in place. He could hear the men in the hallway planning to ram the door down, just as he slid the frame up, slipping out like a fox, to hang on the windowsill. When the door burst open, he let go, landing on the awning below and sliding to the ground. He hit the ground running, leaving the angry guards behind to toss his room, thinking he was hiding somewhere inside.

Logan was another six blocks away, running for his life back toward the city gates, when his conscience began nagging in the back of his head. All he wanted was to get out of the city and get himself back home to Riverbell, wishing he had never even set eyes on this infernal place. However, Beauford's last words would not cease repeating in his head, haunting him with their plea. Logan growled aloud to himself, turning from the southern road and heading back west toward the Grey Crow. He had to fulfill the gnome's dying wish and retrieve his damnable pendant. Logan did not know why he should care one way or the other, but something deep in his core insisted it must be done.

Ah...it'll just be a quick detour before I get out of this place, he told himself. It was a thought Logan would have to keep reminding himself, as he made his way through the city. His relief was palpable when he finally caught a glimpse of the Grey Crow up ahead, sitting just as empty as the wood mill had been.

And why shouldn't it? he thought, wondering who he expected to be working there with the sole proprietor dead. Even the brothel next door stood quiet. He could hear the women inside talking and laughing over clinking plates, but none were on the balcony or out in front of the building where they could see his approach.

Logan ducked into the alleyway between the two structures, moving as far toward the end of the building as he could. He tested the windows careful to make no noise. Unfortunately, the only one left unlocked was all the way back up by the street, in plain view if any of the women should happen to look outside. Knowing he had no other choice, Logan lightly pushed upward, sliding the rickety pane along the rotting frame. Though it was old and weathered, he managed to get the thing up high enough to slip inside.

Hmmm...and Elder Morgana always said I should do something more useful than sneaking around to steal pies..., he thought, using those practiced skills now to break into the building.

Even with all the lights blown out, he could see the place had recently been ransacked. Tables were flipped over, jars smashed to pieces on the floor, some of the lanterns overhead were lying on their sides and the shelves had been fiercely searched, leaving all manner of wares and books scattered across the floor. Logan's blood froze when someone coughed from the backroom, where a dim light glowed. Working on pure instinct, he slid into a shadowy corner of the storefront, crouching behind one of the shelves and peering between the stacks to try to get a glimpse of his fellow intruders.

"What's that?" a man asked, with the voice of a high-pitched rat. "Did ye find anything?"

"Nah the kitchen's empty too…blasted gnome. Where in the devil do you s'pose he stashed it?" His companion replied in a deeper voice. Logan backed up even further into the shadows. His gut told him these men were city watchmen, and they were already here searching for Beauford's pendant!

"The Magistrate ain't gonna like this none," rat voice said, confirming his suspicion. The man grunted and something heavy hit the floor.

"Yer right about that. Let's have Joel tell him," the deep voice offered.

"Hehe, pickin' on the new guy, huh? Yeah, let's do that, it'll be a good initiation for 'em."

"Sure, if the Magistrate doesn't have him strung up for deliverin' the bad news, you mean?" the deep voice laughed.

They were still laughing over their new comrade's upcoming punishment when the pair emerged from the backroom. One of the men was wiry looking with a long-crooked nose, and wore a bowl haircut, while the other was broad-shouldered, with large muscular arms despite his oversized belly. They both wore city watch uniforms and the heavier man carried a small lantern. The skinny rat looking one nudged his companion picking something up off the floor. "The missus is going to like this, pally." Strangely enough, the guard that looked like a rat spoke in the deeper voice and the heavy man replied in the squeaky high-pitched voice.

"Nothing better than a sip of rum to get 'em in the mood, eh?" They laughed again, pilfering a couple more bottles before heading out of the building, leaving the door to bounce on its hinges a couple times before it settled down and the overhead bell stopped clanking.

Logan could make them out through the sooty windows. Once they were safely out of sight, he let out a long, drawn-out breath of air. Without time to waste, he scrambled into the backroom, crouching past the outside windows, to avoid being spotted. Clambering around in the dark, he rummaged through the rows of shelving, searching for some clue to the gnome's cryptic hiding place. All he saw were more bottles of the liquor that had been served back at the gala and the same bizarre artifacts he had grilled Beauford about only a short day ago. All the tables in the backroom were, for the most part, cleared off onto the floor, and the small kitchen area was littered with broken plates and discarded flatware.

Heading back into the storage area, he set down his pack to find a flint and lit one of the candle stubs lying on the floor. With the waxy nub in hand, he could see better and ran back over the contents of the room, hoping he had missed some essential clue.

"Damn it Beauford...where the Hel did you stash this thing?" he grumbled aloud to a nearby painting of the gnome. Beauford's eyes seemed to be following him around the room, a trick of the light and expertise of the artist.

"Hmmm." Logan moved in closer. The painting was hanging crooked, so he assumed the city watch had already searched the wall behind it. However, it was not what was behind the painting that caught his attention, as much as what was in it. Beauford sat in a red leather armchair, smoking a pipe, in some sort of library.

Slowly moving the candlelight across the picture Logan searched it until his hand stopped, the light flickering over an object that must have been what triggered his subconscious curiosity. Beside the chair was a small table with a tea set atop it, the very same tea set Beauford had used the day before!

Logan darted for the tight kitchen area, his heel sliding across the floor on a piece of broken ceramic. He thudded into one of the counters, but it did not slow his search. He worked excitedly to flip open the small cupboards one by one until he found the teapot. Setting it on the countertop, he removed the lid revealing...nothing. Logan's brows furrowed; how could the pendant not be inside? Then again, why had he thought it was inside there anyhow?

He was about to head back into the backroom, having disproved his theory, when another thought occurred to him. Lifting the teapot in front of his face Logan noticed how the base of it was taller than your average kitchen urn.

It's not inside it... it's part of it!

He dropped it to the floor and watched it smash to pieces. Lowering his candle, he noticed a glint in the dark, revealing a small piece of jewelry inside the base of the teapot. Triumphantly, he snatched the little teardrop shaped pendant on its white silver chain and moved back into the other room.

The storefront entrance dinged as the little bell above rattled. Logan's heart skipped a beat, and he blew out the candle tossing it away from him as if it were a poisonous snake.

"Not like we didn't just scour the damned place top to bottom!" the rat yelled outside. Someone outside the front of the store yelled back at him, and the door clattered against the frame.

"No use getting riled up Billy, let's just get it done," the deeper voiced man said, sounding tired and defeated.

"It's not our fault they let that Walker kid escape," Billy, the broad-shouldered man, replied. Logan ducked behind the nearest bookshelf, stunned to hear his name uttered by the man. "Besides, what makes them think the kid could have already made it this far into the city?"

His companion just grunted, moving past his hiding spot to light up the tiny kitchen. "Well, he ain't in the pantry...," the wiry guard announced. Logan tensed up. Were these men going to scour the store looking for him?

The large man absently kicked a statuette across the floor giving the area a cursory glance and grunting. "Check that side of the room," he squeaked while opening a window to look out into the alleyway.

Logan's heart was beating so hard he worried they would hear it, working to steady his nerves as the skinny watchman moved toward the shelving, slowly scanning the area with his lantern.

"What a joke...first he's got us searchin' for a journal that doesn't exist...next it's some country wahoo," the oversized man complained, beckoning his partner to follow out toward the storefront.

As the guard moved away from where Logan was crouched low to the ground, he loosened up his balled-up fists, realizing he was so tense that he had been digging the nails of his right hand into his palm.

"Wait," the deep voiced guard said, turning his lantern toward the middle of the room.

"Oh, what now?" Billy whined. "Let's just get out of here." Logan could barely make out what they were doing from behind the stacks of antiques. He had to crane his neck to see what the smaller man was pointing at in the middle of the room. When he saw his backpack, Logan's heart stood still and goose bumps crawled across his skin, silently cursing his stupidity leaving the thing lying out in the open.

Scanning the area, he saw that the men were no longer by the doorway, each taking a different side of the room with their weapons drawn. He knew this time he would not be so lucky to escape unnoticed. The lantern was moving on the opposite end of the room where a stack of crates rested, while the heavier man worked his way straight toward the shelving he was hiding behind. Logan snatched a small brass statuette of a snail and flicked it sideways out the open window, rattling across the ground out in the alleyway.

The heavier watchman stopped short just in front of the shelving, motioning for his partner to check out the noise. As the lantern moved toward the window, the heavy guard turned to face his hiding spot once more. Logan roared, shoving his shoulder hard against the tall bookcase, which toppled right over on top of the guard, burying him underneath an avalanche of dusty tomes and trinkets, followed by the shelf itself. No sooner did the bookcase hit the floor, than Logan was bolting for the exit, leaving his pack behind. The skinny guard dropped his lantern to the floor running to help lift the heavy shelving off his companion. As Logan was about to pass the doorway, a heavy fist caught him hard in the chest, knocking the air out of his lungs. He barely ducked out of the path of another roundhouse, this one coming with a five-inch barbed steel blade.

He had not even heard the other watchman searching the storefront. But if he wanted to survive, he had to adapt quickly. As the fierce looking, black-bearded man stalked in grinning at him, Logan held up his hands in surrender backing up toward the middle of the room.

"Okay you got me I'll come along willingly...," he said.

The watchman scoffed at him, wagging his pointer finger above the hilt of the dagger. "Tut tut...too late for that, briar lapin. Boss wants you dead."

The man's mocking smirk turned serious, and he lunged forward, swinging the knife. Logan stepped back, kicking a smaller crate straight up into the air; right into the path of his attacker's blade, which smashed through the wood like it was paper. Blinded by the maneuver, the guard never even had time to block as Logan broke his jaw with a staggering punch to the face, the momentum throwing him into a nearby pile of books.

Massive arms wrapped around him from behind, lifting Logan off his feet and squeezing the air out of his lungs. The large squeaky voiced man had already made it out of the rubble, wearing a slash across his forehead that seemed to have turned him into a berserker.

"Thought ye could get away from us, did ye?" he screamed in his high pitch, while his wiry little friend stalked in with a sword.

"Hold 'em still Ralph, I want to get this over with nice and neat." The little rat pulled his arm back to run their captive through.

As the man thrust the blade, Logan twisted hard toward the sky, raising his legs above his body to keep away from the sharp edge. Ralph howled as the sword ran clean through his midsection sticking out through the back of his ribs. He released Logan and gripped at his belly. Logan tumbled across the floor knocking over the man's stunned partner who was still holding the hilt of his sword. Logan kicked the man hard, twice in the head, knocking him unconscious, before the heavyset guard caught him in the ear with a deafening blow. Logan reeled from the pain as the crazed bastard threw a volley of fists into his gut. He thought the man must have demon blood to be even moving after being run through with a sword, which was still stuck in him like a pincushion.

Logan managed to duck to the side, dodging one of the man's heavy blows, which cracked into the wall instead. He howled in pain, over his broken knuckles, giving Logan just enough time to land a sure aimed fist straight into the brute's nose, breaking it under the weight of his metallic hand and followed it with a heavy roundhouse kick to the side of the head, throwing the berserker into a pile of stacked crates in the corner.

The room roared with the ear ringing blast of a fired pistol, as a bullet whizzed past his head. Logan jumped into a blind tucking roll across the room, the smell of gun powder stinging his nose. The downed bearded watchman man looked angry indeed to have missed his target, especially after said quarry had broken his jaw. Rather than retreat into the kitchen or wait while the man reloaded his single shot pistol, Logan made a mad dash forward, kicking the weapon out of his hand and battered the soldier with repeated blows until he was positively knocked unconscious.

Scanning the room to be sure none of the men were stirring, Logan retrieved his pack, flipping it over his shoulders and clipping the harness in place around his chest. While he was retrieving his laser rifle from the holster around his back, he heard a commotion of soldiers running toward the front of the building.

There would be no exiting that way for him. Hopping out the back-alley window, he turned to slide it shut just as he heard the store entrance burst open as a group of watchmen stormed the place. He pushed up against the wall of the building, keeping in the shadows as he headed toward the street. Peeking out around the corner, he caught a glimpse of a soldier that had been told to wait out front and keep watch. Inside the store, the men were destroying the place, tearing it apart to find him, while another came rushing out asking if the man had seen anyone run by. Logan was stuck, there was no way he could make it out of this alleyway undetected and there were too many guards to fight alone. He eyed the laser rifle warily. He did not want to kill anyone and doubted he could stomach such a thing.

"Psst."

He turned around to find one of the working women from the brothel beckoning him from a nearby window, while her friend ducked to get a good look at him. Logan pointed at himself and shrugged.

The woman nodded, urgently waving for him to get inside. Not one to look a gift horse in the mouth, he hopped right through just in time to avoid one of the watchmen as he rounded the corner. Logan silently thanked the women. One of them held a finger to her lips, pulling him toward the back of the apartments, past dozens of half-naked women, to where their Madame was waiting beside an armoire.

"C'mon now, boy, out through here you go," she urged while swinging the armoire doors wide to reveal a hidden stairwell that led almost straight upward.

"In the nine heavens I don't know how I could ever repay you, lady!" Logan jeered at the sight of the escape route.

"Any friend o' my little Beauford is a friend o' mine, laddie. Now add some pepper to it and get going." Her voice fell to a whisper, shoving him into the portal and slamming it closed behind. As he climbed the steep stairs, he could hear soldiers already storming her place, demanding to know if he was inside. Logan had no doubt the woman could handle the angry guards with her charms, and she was already giving them a tongue lashing. At the top of the steep passageway, he came to a porthole that opened out to an alleyway beside a great stone mansion.

For Pete's sake, I'm all the way up by the bloody Arch Councilor's palace! he thought, looking down the hill toward the lower levels.

Logan had an epiphany then, one that shook the very fiber of his being. He could see how foolish his actions had been earlier that evening, thinking he would somehow be able to return to Riverbell and escape from the weight of his accused crime. Fafnir wanted him dead, though he was not entirely certain why, and between him and home was more than half a city, filled with watchmen looking for the *murderer*.

No. Logan could never go home again. There was only one road left for him now. He would have to head north for a one-way ticket over the wall and into the wild lands. Given the alternative between that and death, he was not left with much of a choice.

Far down in the city below he could hear the commotion of guards searching for him. Logan turned north, accepting his fate with grave determination, and put the world he had known to his back.

Sounds of shouting across the ballroom caught the attention of Arch Councilor Zacharia's group. "I say, what do you think all that commotion could be, your holiness?" a thin, beady-eyed aristocrat asked, adjusting his spectacles to look over at the west wing.

Elise leaned into her fiancé; she was not accustomed to wearing dresses like this one with its tight corset and heavy petticoat, and felt off balance, craning her neck to see what the man was referring to. The Arch Councilor had been giving them a treatise on trade law, in answer to one of the merchant's questions, when they were interrupted.

"Hmmm," Zacharia muttered, fingering his curled moustache.

Corbin could see the pointed tips of tridents bobbing quickly through the crowd, heading toward the commotion, and an uneasy feeling settled over him. He grabbed Elise by the arm and pulled her behind him to see what could be happening.

Just then, a blinding light flashed across the crowd, lighting up the entire west side of the ballroom, followed by a loud boom as the floor quaked beneath the aftershock of the blast. All around them men and women were screaming, shoving past one another for the exit.

"Lady Penelope," Zacharia said, "Get Madame Elise and yourself out of the palace immediately!" Not waiting for a response, he plucked Elise from Corbin's arms and handed her off to the Lady as if she were precious cargo. "Corbin, you stick with us. Don't worry, your fiancée will be safe with Lady Penelope."

Corbin looked warily at Elise as she disappeared into the chaos with Lady Penelope and her flanking guards. She shouted for him from somewhere among the jumble of people, but he did not dare to disobey the Arch Councilor, and quickly moved to follow him.

Making their way through the throng of people was not too difficult. Anyone that saw Arch Councilor Zacharia quickly scrambled to get out of his path. Corbin stopped twice to help people to their feet, worried that they might be trampled by the near hysterical swell of aristocrats practically fighting to get out of the palace.

"Magistrate Fafnir, what is the meaning of all this?" Zacharia demanded, as the old lawman was being helped to his feet by some of his men.

"Milord," Fafnir said, clearly disoriented. "There has been an assassination tonight."

The magistrate pointed down the side hallway, to the limp body of a gnomes surrounded by a pool of blood. All around the corpse palace guards were examining the scene, under orders of their nearby commander.

"Who would have the audacity to do such a thing?" Arch Councilor Zacharia asked.

"I am the unfortunate bearer of disturbing news, milord. But it was none other than Logan Walker himself that committed the foul deed," Fafnir said, informing the arch councilor of eyewitness accounts that saw Logan stab Mr. Beauford to death.

"This is preposterous!" Corbin said. "My brother may be a lot of things, but a murderer is certainly not one of them!"

"Similar words you spoke yesterday, if I recall Corbin," Fafnir coolly replied. "It would seem there is much about your brother you do not know. My liege," he continued, directing his attention back to Zacharia, "I take full responsibility for these events, just yesterday the boy had a violent outburst not too far from the goodly gnome Beauford's shop. I should have known…should have realized more was at play. I regret to say I released him from section six, unable to believe a hero could be involved with such goings on. Now I see my folly," the Magistrate admitted, bowing his head in shame.

Corbin stood at a loss for words, his jaw hanging slackly.

"It is true, Arch Councilor, Dame Uriel saw that fiend Walker stabbing Mr. Beauford with her own eyes," the commander added, stepping into the discussion, while his men were moving the dead gnome out of the hallway. "My men and I came upon the murderer, dagger in hand, covered with the goodly gnome's blood, your holiness."

That shut up any counter argument Corbin could think to muster. He stammered, wide eyed, not knowing what to make of these claims.

"Master Beauford? But why would a hero of New Fal want to murder the goodly gnome?" Elder Agustus said, overhearing the proclamation as he walked into the fray. The room was much sparser now, most of the partygoers having evacuated the palace, leaving only council members and palace guards.

"Black market dealings, no doubt," one of the other elders commented.

"Oh, hush now," a grey-haired woman said, "it'll not do to speak ill of the dead."

"What? We all know it's the truth," the man said unabashed.

Lady Cassandra had arrived as well, furrowing her brow at the commander's claim. "I was just talking with both men only a short while ago, and they certainly did *not* seem to be holding any ill will toward each other."

"You see, there you have it," Fafnir said, "another eyewitness that they were together. Have no fear, Arch Councilor, I have dispatched my men with orders to kill the murderer on sight."

"That is preposterous!" Lady Cassandra bristled. "The boy must be brought in alive. How else can we be sure he had a hand in Beauford's murder, less he stands trial before the Council?"

"Lady Cassandra is on the right side of it, Fafnir," Zacharia said. "We have not taken complete leave of Falian law."

Just then, a soldier rushed up to whisper in the Magistrate's ear. Fafnir widened his eyes at the news.

"Further proof of his guilt!" he announced, tapping his cane on the floor with excitement. "There has been a break in at the Grey Crow. My men found Logan Walker there and tried to detain him, but alas he has escaped."

"Are you listening to this rubbish?" Cassandra asked the arch councilor, pointing at Fafnir. "Do tell us Magistrate, how was it that your men were able to get to the gnome's storefront so quickly?"

"Milady, Falian watchmen receive the finest training, honing their skills for years, and preparing for any situation. That they already arrived is only proof of their prowess and a testament to the glory of Fal," Fafnir slyly countered.

"Yet they were ousted by a young farmer?" she mocked.

"Oh, enough of this," Zacharia said. "We have serious matters to attend to at the moment; the two of you are not on the pulpit swaying votes. Corbin...is what the Magistrate said true? Was your brother arrested yesterday?"

"To my people's great shame, it is, milord," Corbin said, unable to meet the great man's gaze.

Zacharia pursed his lips and nodded to himself. "Magistrate, your men are to capture Logan Walker *alive*. I will have him brought to me personally for questioning. The council will see the truth. However, if he resists arrest, or puts any other innocents in harms way, he is to be put down."

"Your word is law, your holiness." Fafnir said, with an overly dramatic bow, before turning to give his men the new orders as the arch councilor led the group to the back of the palace.

"Sir?" the soldier who had delivered the news of the break in asked.

"Finish the job at the Grey Crow. Make sure there is no proof in the building before you burn it to the ground." Fafnir said, careful to keep his voice down.

"And the boy?"

"Make sure Logan Walker does not make it out of the capitol alive."

Like a cat pouncing from shadow to shadow, Logan moved quickly through the deserted upper-level streets of Fal. He had just narrowly avoided a passing patrol of watchmen before making it all the way to the top level of the city, heading as fast as he could muster toward the wall. He was still unsure what Fafnir's men were looking for back at the Grey Crow, or why the despicable man wanted him dead in the first place, but either way he knew he needed to get out of the kingdom, and fast, if he had any hope of surviving to see another day.

In the distance, he could hear watchdogs braying in search of his scent, confirming there was no more time for thinking, only for action. Just around the curved road, he carefully followed the movements of the men guarding the great wall, who were more concerned with watching the wild lands than the city streets. His muscles tensed, waiting for the perfect moment as he carefully timed their patrol. Mustering up enough courage, Logan slipped behind one of the guards and caught him in a headlock, squeezing with just enough pressure to cut off any airflow without breaking his windpipe. He wanted the man to be unconscious, not dead. Once he was down, Logan slid his backpack off to the side and pulled out the rope he had commandeered from the Grey Crow. His fingers worked quickly to loop it over the parapet, when another guard shouted for him to stop. The man blew hard on an elk horn to alert the watch he had found the outlaw.

Logan cursed to himself, running straight past the soldier to throw him off balance, and then stopping short, he looped back around the way he had come. The guard was baffled by his actions, until he felt the rope that had now been wrapped around his torso. Before he could look up and plead for Logan to stop, the outlaw jumped straight off the edge of the massive wall that protected the capitol from the wildlands. Logan had the rope gripped tightly in both hands, and his weight pulled the tied-up guard hard across the ground, slamming him in between the parapets merlons. With the rope hanging through the gap the guard became a human anchor, clutching desperately to the stone around him, breaking his fingernails as they scraped along the rough surface. He prayed to the All-Father not to let him fall through the embrasure, as Logan nimbly made his way down the fifty feet of rope, having to drop the last stretch through the open air when the cord ended.

Other city watchmen arrived as he made it to the ground, letting loose a barrage of bullets from muskets and revolvers at the fleeing outlaw. Thankfully, none found their mark. It did not take long before Logan was out of view, hidden among the long shadows of the wild lands.

"He won't last long out there fellas," one the men snorted. "Probably be dead before the week's end."

"Yeah? Great. *You* tell that to the Magistrate," another watchman said.

Logan smirked, hearing the guards overhead arguing over who would deliver the news of his triumphant escape, yet in his heart he felt nothing but sorrow, knowing he would never again set eyes on his homeland or speak to his brother. With one last look at the towering marble wall, that impenetrable barrier to the kingdom of New Fal, he turned toward his fate, hustling through the shadows and wondering what life would mean for him now that he was an exile.

High above the land, nestled just below the cavern ceiling of New Fal, the Great Crystal Baetylus took an interest in the little human's flight. Layers of light flickered over its multi-faceted glassy surface as the implications of this event rolled over the Falian god, stirring him from the grogginess of his recent slumber.

It was a first to see a human willingly jump the wall. Generally, they were begging not to be exiled from the kingdom below. Curious, the Crystal scanned Logan's mind, searching for some clue that would explain this rare event.

Sharply, the future danced before Baetylus, revealing that this was more than a mere moment of idle fancy. His flickering thoughts swelled into a thunderous storm of concern. What he saw had only taken the briefest of moments, but in that snippet of scrying, Baetylus understood enough to know that Logan Walker needed to be stopped. For if he was allowed to continue on this path, everything would be at risk.

Chapter 14

From floor to ceiling, the Council of Twelve chamber room was awash in white marble. The rows of seats, which were set in a semi-circle around the perimeter of the room, forming two curved tiers where the Council of Elders held court and, on occasion, invited members of the aristocracy to sit in. They were almost full today.

The Elders did not always meet in private, in fact many hearings were often held publicly, so all could witness their glorious justice system. Speakers would stand in the middle of the white room, where often a pulpit would be setup. Large metal plates were fixed to either side of the central area, with solid steel rings set in them, that prisoners could be chained to while on trial. It was not always a place for criminal trials of course, with many laws being passed, debates being addressed, or support being given to the newest *cause*.

Unfortunately, Corbin was there for none of those reasons. In fact, he was actually rather perplexed as to why the council had called upon the house of Lady Penelope to send for him in the first place. Every member of the Council of Twelve was in attendance, as well as a handful of other dignitaries he did not recognize.

Corbin knew Magistrate Fafnir and recognized Lady Cassandra from the night before, when everything went south at the gala. However, he still could not figure out why *he* was summoned. Did they really mean to punish him for his brother's accused crimes? Was he really to pay for Logan's sins in the wake of his cowardly flight from the capitol?

"Corbin Walker, you have been summoned before the Council of Twelve. We see you," Arch Councilor Zacharia said, formally opening the proceeding.

"We see you," the other ten chanted. The room had an odd way of bouncing sound back and forth against the walls, giving an illusion of other worldliness that raised the hairs on Corbin's neck. The Elders sat there, all eyes on him, waiting for some sort of response.

"I...*see you*, Councilors?" Corbin meekly said.

"That will do. Let the proceedings begin," Arch Councilor Zacharia said, gesturing to an older woman who began recording the conversation with a quill and ink.

"Corbin Walker, your brother has been charged with the heinous murder of the honorable gnome, Barthalameu Beauford of the house Ul'Brox. It has been duly dictated by this council that he must be brought in for questioning, to stand the Trial of Truth." Zacharia paused, waiting for Corbin to reply.

"Your holiness, I wish there were some way I could be of assistance, but..."

"But? But what? There can be no *but* in Justice," Zacharia said sharply. "There can be no gray area in the lines of black and white that make up our morality. This Council has given the matter great deliberation...great deliberation indeed. There are those in favor of immediate execution."

Corbin gasped. He had always been taught that every citizen would have their trial if accused of crimes.

"Be at peace, Corbin, we mean not to follow that point of view just yet," Elder Augustus said. He noticed Magistrate Fafnir sneer slightly at the man's statement.

"Nevertheless, the crimes of your brother must be answered for," Fafnir said. "Otherwise, how can anyone expect your village to remain in proper standing within New Fal? We do not intend on sending any aid toward the rebuilding of Riverbell until this matter has been properly tended to." The Magistrate received cross looks from several of the Elders for speaking out of turn.

Zacharia waited until the Magistrate settled back down before returning his attention to Corbin. "We do not intend on sending any aid toward the rebuilding of Riverbell until this matter has been properly tended to."

"Your holiness, I do not understand any of this," Corbin said. "Last *I* was informed; my brother was seen fleeing the city into the wild lands. How can we *handle* this matter without him, and why would the people of Riverbell be penalized over his actions?" Corbin made sure to address Arch Councilor Zacharia directly. As scared as he was of openly questioning the wisdom of his leaders, he demanded justification for the sudden retraction of the support his people were in dire need of receiving.

"There has been much debate over Riverbell's involvement in the recent skex attack," Zacharia said. "Rumors have been flying around the capitol that this has all been part of a larger plot fabricated by your people, fueling the insect swarm for the sole purpose of gaining notoriety that could be later used to gain influence over this Council, thus growing a power that could be used for rebellion."

Corbin could not believe his ears. Had the whole world gone mad?

"It has been decided that you will be sent into the wildlands to prove your people's innocence. If you truly believe in the glory that is New Fal and hold no ill will toward our way of life, you will bring your brother back here, where the Council will try him fairly and the truth *will* be known. If you refuse, we will have no choice but to believe the rumors are true and will move to immediately excommunicate the village of Riverbell and all of its citizens from our Kingdom."

Eyes wide in shock, Corbin took a shaky step back. "B-but...it's...I...s-surely you cannot believe we are traitors to the kingdom?" he stammered, wishing Elder Morgana was there to help them see reason.

"No. We can see your truth," Elder Augustus said. "*You* are an honorable young man, who is clearly devoted to the ideals that make up our kingdom. However, that could simply mean you were not aware of your brother's plans and does not exonerate others in your village who could likely be your brother's co-conspirators."

"It has been decided," Zacharia said. "We present you with two options today. You can either agree to go to the wildlands and bring Logan Walker back to Fal, where we will hear him and judge as our law dictates. Or refuse us and we will have no choice but to cut ties with Riverbell."

"I am the very servant of the Kingdom, milord," Corbin said. "My people have ever only acted in accordance with our laws. We are proud to be citizens of New Fal, and I fear I must be bold here. What you are saying is unfair to those families in Riverbell, who have done nothing to deserve such slanderous accusations." Corbin firmed his resolve, unable to stand by idly while false words were being spoken about the people he loved.

"And what of Mr. Beauford?" Fafnir said. "Was it fair that he was murdered?"

Zacharia shot the Magistrate a look that could freeze fire. Elder Victor cleared his throat and spoke up, "There are many viewpoints here, young man. If we cannot get to the truth, we will always lean toward the worst scenario, erring forever on the side of caution. In this way, the Kingdom stays strong, with ever-vigilant protection from that which could bring us harm. By delivering your brother back to Fal you will prove your loyalty to the citizens, and none would dare question the allegiance of your people." As the respected member of the Council spoke, other members nodded their heads in agreement.

"I fully understand and vow to do what must be done," Corbin said, holding his head up high. "I will leave for the wildlands on the morrow to find and bring my brother back."

"You will have exactly thirty days to do so," Zacharia said. "May Baetylus be with you, son of Riverbell." He closed the proceeding with a triple tap of his small wooden gavel and a pair of muscle-bound guards carrying thick tridents moved forward to usher Corbin out of the antechamber.

As soon as he stepped into the hall a young, freckled boy with curly, mussed, blonde hair made a beeline for him. "Master Corbin Walker?" he asked.

"Yes?"

"This is for you sir, please sign here," the boy said, shoving a small ledger in Corbin's hands. No sooner had he scrawled his name on the parchment, than the boy placed another scroll, this one neatly rolled up, in his hands, and zipped back down the hallway, on to his next destination.

Corbin unrolled the curious little letter, reading,

Come meet me before the 11th hour,
I want to help, come alone
84 Sycamore Lane, 2nd district

Elise stood vigil waiting for him outside the courthouse, beside the carriage Lady Penelope had leant them. She was wringing her hands together when he emerged. Once she saw him, she ran over and wrapped her arms around him.

"I was so worried!" Elise exclaimed.

"You and I both," Corbin said, hugging her tightly before gently pushing the woman at arm's length so he could look in her blue eyes. "They have commanded me to go to the wildlands and bring Logan back."

"That's madness!" Elise replied, horrified at the thought of him going outside the kingdom into the dangerous wild lands.

"I agree, but there is nothing I can do, this task must be taken care of." He spoke somberly, having accepted his fate back in the antechamber, knowing what was at stake.

"No, I'll talk to them...I'll...you cannot be expected to go out there into the wilds for something Logan did. I will make them see reason...I..."

"Dear sweet Elise, my love, if I do not go, they will excommunicate Riverbell. It will be a sign that too many will view as proof of some tale of our conspiracy for your title and to hurt the capitol."

"Has the whole world lost its senses? We loved Elder Morgana with all our hearts. Why, she practically raised you and Logan single-handed. What in the world would make them think we could possibly imagine hurting the Kingdom...and to what end?" Elise's anxiety was quickly shifting into anger. "To top it off the whole business is ludicrous. Logan is a wool-headed lout, he is a good many things at that, I mean the trouble he gets into is...well it just riles me up to think about all the stupid things he has done over the years. But a murderer? Never will I believe that your brother could hurt an innocent." Corbin knew it was this bold passion that Elder Morgana had seen in her, which marked her capability to lead an entire village.

"Agreed," Corbin said, "which is all the more reason for me to go out there and bring him back to his senses. It was foolish to run away like that. The only thing he accomplished was making his guilt ring true in the Elder's ears. At the end of the day, Logan has gotten *himself* into this mess. I have pulled him out of the fire too many times to count and I'll not be doing it again, not this time, not when he has risked the lives and freedom of every person we know. He *will* come back here and be seen by the Elders, even if I have to drag him kicking and screaming across the wildlands," Corbin said, tucking her hair behind an ear with his rough, calloused hand.

"And if he is found guilty?" she asked, staring up at him doe eyed.

"Then he will deserve the judgment given," Corbin replied evenly.

It was late into the evening when Corbin made his way around the corner of Sycamore, counting down the numbered doors. Forty-eight was just across the path, but there was no one about. He began walking up the steps to knock on the house door, when a young woman in an odd get-up stepped out from behind the bushes, whistling low for his attention.

"Follow me, Mr. Walker," she whispered, quickly ducking down a side alleyway. Corbin looked to forty-eight Sycamore then back at the girl, who was almost lost in the low hanging evening fog, before deciding to follow. Her blonde hair flowed in two bushy locks behind her neck under a wide brimmed hat that looked like something from a children's story about pirates. They moved quickly through the tight alleys, left then right then back, and all the while she kept looking back over the high collar of her black trench coat, keeping an eye on the way they had come.

Suddenly she stopped short and grabbed the rung of an iron ladder to the right that was built into the stone wall of the alleyway. Corbin followed her lead scaling the building. Once at the top, she went past the raised garden beds, into a tiny brick alcove and gave a series of raps on the wall. For a moment there was only silence then a hidden door creaked inward, revealing a candle lit room beyond. After they entered, the door closed back up by itself.

D.M. Almond

Removing her oversized trench coat, the girl politely offered to take his pack. "No thank you, I prefer to keep this on me," Corbin replied, gripping the straps a little tighter around his shoulders. He had too many supplies inside and was leery about handing them over to some stranger who just had him running through the city streets.

"Ah, you have arrived, and right on time too," Lady Cassandra said, pleased to see them, as she stepped into the room smiling.

"Your letter piqued my curiosity, milady," Corbin said with a slight bow.

The old woman's eyes were twinkling, belying a genuine warmth of spirit, as she nodded appreciatively. She did a double take at his tour guide's attire and rolled her eyes.

"Oh Jayne, would you take off that ridiculous hat?" she said. Jayne's cheeks bloomed like a rose, and she hastily removed the hat, hiding it behind her back. "You can be an odd little duck sometimes, girl," Lady Cassandra mused, clearly in a loving manner. Corbin noted that this young woman was close to the woman, more than just a servant of the house.

"Milady, I do not want to speak out of place, but why have you brought me here tonight? Surely you heard today at the Council antechamber that I have pressing matters requiring my immediate attention."

"That is *precisely* why you are here," Lady Cassandra. "I want to offer you some assistance in the matter. You have every right to decide whether you will take it or not."

"In what way? Do you have proof of Logan's innocence?" he asked hopefully.

"If I had that there would be no need for this conversation. It was I, however, who convinced the Council to extend your time to find Logan and bring him back here."

"So, you do believe Logan is innocent?" Corbin asked. "I heard you defending him the night of the gala, but I must confess to not understanding your motives. Do you know my brother?"

"No, I must admit, it was only in passing that we met. Mr. Beauford, however, was long a friend to my house and I did see the two of them together that night. It was obvious the gnome trusted your brother. Otherwise, he would never have stepped away for a private chat in the first place. They were not acting hostile toward each other in the slightest, so I've had more than a little bit of a hard time believing him guilty."

"I still don't understand," Corbin said.

"Let me cut to the chase then," Lady Cassandra said. "You were brought here tonight for the opportunity to gain great power, young man. A gift which will surely aid you in your search for Logan, as well as your survival on the other side of the wall."

"Now if you agree, I will tell you more, but you must promise to see it through to the end. If you do not wish to go any further, say so now and Jayne here will escort you back to Sycamore, where no doubt Fafnir has men searching for you as we speak."

The idea that the head of Falian lawmen would have people waiting for him was alarming. "Surely the Magistrate would not dare interfere with the council's orders?"

The women joined each other in a delighted titter at the young man's naivety, which they found both amusing and refreshing at the same time.

"The last thing that man wants is for you to bring Logan back here where the Arch Councilor can pry into his mind and see the truth of it," Lady Cassandra said.

Corbin stood there in silence, doubtful that the Magistrate could be anything other than what he seemed.

"Well Mr. Walker?" she prodded. "Are you in, or are you out?"

Elder Morgana had always said, *"You never realize just how good you have it until things change."* Or maybe she hadn't. Logan could not remember one way or the other, and did not really care anyhow, but for some reason the infernal expression kept playing through his head.

Either way the wild lands were living up to their reputation, leaving a pang in his heart for dull old Riverbell. The finality of running off into the deep dark, away from his friends, away from his brother (who might a pain in the arse, but he was *his* pain the arse) had set in. There was no going back to New Fal for him, that road would only lead to the snake, Fafnir's, version of justice, and he saw just how that played out firsthand back at the Grey Crow. This would be his home now, at least until he could figure out some other option. Logan kept telling himself he would be okay; he just needed enough time to sort things out.

The wild lands were much darker than he was accustomed, the wall of Fal obscuring much of the Great Crystal's light. Still, it did radiate enough to sustain a decent amount of plant life, though it was surely less than the lush valleys of New Fal. It had not taken long for his eyes to adjust to the change in lighting. For him the strangest part of the wild lands was how much lower and tighter the cavern became. He could see some of the giant roc-bats sleeping upside down overhead with his naked eye. Back in Riverbell you would have to climb Mount Grantuntite to get even the slightest glimpse of the flying beasts hanging around the great rows of stalactites.

No doubt the ceiling here was still plenty high, but the new distance gave him a feeling that the world had just grown smaller somehow. There were no paths out here in the wilds, no roads to guide the way, not that he was stupid enough to stay on one and be caught should Fafnir send men out to bring him back. Everywhere the landscape was riddled with unchecked growth.

Logan made his way through the night, cautiously staying close to the large stalagmites that jutted up over the landscape, like the bony fingers of buried giants. In the stories he had heard growing up, there was always talk of ravenous beasts that roamed the untamed wilds. Although they filled his childhood daydreams with fascination, now that he was actually out here, he held no desire to meet one.

A radiant pool of water lit up the area ahead, throwing an eerie dim blue glow from its surface across the rocky area. Logan crept up to the glowing pool, careful that nothing lurked in wait for him among the wide patch of grass, reeds, and a thick tree that had grown around it. Feeling confident nothing of danger was in the area, he dropped down to cup some of the water in his hands for a drink, letting the cool stuff run down his throat, satisfying the dryness in his mouth. Drops of water spilled from his hands forming ripples over the surface, each glowing like a blue halo, growing wider and wider toward the outer rim. Unbuckling his pack, he found a leather flask, which he dipped into the pool, patiently waiting until all the air bubbles disappeared.

Logan snapped his head to the east, hearing something rustle in a small outcropping of trees. Slipping the canteen back into his bag, he rolled sideways firmly tethering it back in place over his shoulder. He inched his head up through the tall reeds to try and get a better look at what was coming.

The brush rustled at the base of the trees, and a small piglet scurried toward the pool. The tension released from Logan's shoulders, immediately replaced by a growling in his stomach. This would make a fine supper and give him rations enough to last a week at least. Food was scarce from what he had seen thus far. Logan knew he needed to trap the swine while the opportunity presented itself.

The spotted piglet stopped short, as if sensing his thoughts. It sniffed the air for a moment, and Logan thought it would bolt back into the trees for sure. He wanted to squeal in delight when the piglet scurried back along its merry way to the pool of water. Logan slipped Elder Morgana's laser rifle from the holster on his back, slowly edging forward on his belly and steadying his target.

Probably only get one shot at this. Don't blow this Logan, there's no telling when you'll get another chance like this one, he thought, carefully lining up his aim on the little swine that gingerly lapped water from the tiny pond.

The piglet's ear suddenly twitched, bobbing its head in the direction it had just come, as more rustling came from the crop of trees. Logan grew excited. The piglet was enough of a reward, but another hog would be a miracle, and this one sounded much larger! A ferocious growl ripped through the air, when out of the brush leapt a cait. Propelled high in the air by muscular hind legs, the feline predator closed the distance between the outcropping and the pool with one giant leap. Its front paws landed squarely on the piglet's back. The swine squealed as the six-foot long predator's massive front claws tore into its sides, pinning the prey helplessly to the ground. The piglet thrashed about in an attempt to escape its doomed fate. The cait growled, whipping a snakelike tentacle tail over its head, to sting the prey on its side, filling the pig's blood with paralyzing venom. Within seconds, the wounded animal went limp, as the deadly stuff crippled its tiny nervous system.

Logan had grown stock-still, muscles locked in place, and his heart was beating so fast he was worried he might pass out. Nodules of light pulsed across the cait's forehead, running down the glossy blue striped skin of its back, as it feasted on the pork dinner. A high-pitched howl came from the west, causing Logan's heart to skip a beat when the cait perked its head directly in his direction to sniff the air. Throwing its muzzle back, the cait called back to another member of the pack, with a low, deep, throaty howl. The tentacle reached down like it had a mind of its own, plucking the slowly dying terrified piglet up to a fanged jaw and the cait dashed off to meet its sister and share in the bounty.

A wave of dizziness and nausea washed over Logan as the moment of danger passed. He had been only a couple steps from the dangerous predator, and it was way too close for comfort. He knew he would have to be a hundred times more careful out here in the wilds, less he wanted to be the next piglet. Wiping cold sweat from his brow, he rolled over onto his back, getting a good view of the darkness above through the boughs of the tree and imagining one of the terrifying caits was watching him from the shadowy recesses of the jagged stalactites lining the ceiling high overhead. There was no telling what lurked behind the deep shadows of these untamed lands he now roamed.

Switching gears, Logan forced himself to smile at his good fortune in narrowly avoiding the dangerous predator. However, his reverie was quickly broken by another rustling from the same crop of trees.

Does everything in the damned area live in those woods? he thought.

Rolling back onto his belly, he tried to get an eye on what was coming and was more than a little shocked to see it was not an animal at all, but a man! The stranger was running low to the ground, scanning the area, for what he assumed was some sign of the cait.

What kind of a nut job would try and hunt a monster like that? Logan wondered.

The hunter kneeled by the radiant pool of water, examining the bloody tracks left in the wake of the killing and grunted. He scanned the area to the west and north and set down his weapon, resigning himself to fill his flask. With the lid back in place and weapon in hand the man headed back the direction he had come, without so much as a sideway glance.

Looks annoyed to have lost his dinner," Logan thought, his curiosity piqued by the unexpected arrival of another human. Hopping to follow, he made sure to stick firmly to the shadows, feet graceful, gliding along through the brush. He moved with no sound at all, staying a safe distance behind the man.

Once they were in the woods, he found it to be an easy task remaining hidden behind trees and bushes. The man never had a clue he was being followed, or if he did, he was the best bluff Logan had ever witnessed. Their path led them deeper and deeper into the wild woods. They stopped at the edge of a tree line, where the ground opened to a wide chasm. The only way across was a makeshift bridge, which was nothing more than a fallen tree someone stripped and set in place.

Logan waited until the stranger was across and out of view, before creeping up to the lip of the ravine. The drop was deep enough that he could not see the bottom, disappearing into a pitch-black abyss. Falling there would be certain death. No way was he going to try a different route though, if he wanted to keep up. His mind was screaming to stay on the man, to see where the hunter came from.

Logan carefully made his way across the dead log, which rolled slightly under his weight, chips of bark rustling off into the chasm below as his feet scraped across the dead wood. Once safely across, it took him a few minutes to track the stranger's trail again. Soon enough he came to the outskirts of a camp, where he stopped to scan the ground. As he suspected, hidden beneath dead twigs and leaves was a series of taut ropes that worked around the perimeter of the camp, attached to small piles of animal bones and rusty metal. It was a good way to setup an alarm system. This way if anything nasty stumbled on the area the hunter would know. Even if it was a sloppy job at best, it was still clever.

Five large makeshift tents, made from a combination of various animal skins, twigs, and leaves, surrounded the campsite. Between the tents were a few shoddily built tables, practically overflowing with a smorgasbord of ratty supplies. Three men were having a conversation, huddled around a campfire in the center of the area. Logan worked his way in closer, hoping to better hear what they were discussing. He guessed they lived here permanently, setting up a camp such as this as a way to survive. They were a rough looking lot, wearing shabby, tattered clothing, which was filthy. Getting a good look at their unkempt facial hair, Logan appreciated the risk he had taken to retrieve his backpack, knowing he had a straight razor inside. He never felt truly awake until after he shaved in the morning. As scruffy as these men looked, they definitely looked like they could handle themselves.

"From the remains, a cait must have swiped that damn hog I were tracking," the hunter was explaining to his companions, as he set down his bow and took a seat beside the fire, which was nothing more than a tree stump.

"Hel...I wish you did bump into that cait," one of the men said. "That would have been some good grub!" The men chuckled together.

"Yeah, can you picture me trying to carry one of them back here by myself?" he threw another log into the fire, poking it in place with the end of a long metal rod, then rubbed his hands together over the flames to warm them.

The third man set a rotisserie of something that looked like plump mushrooms and a skinned rat, tail intact, over the blaze. Logan knew he was disgusted by the very concept of eating a rat, but his stomach had a different opinion altogether when he caught a whiff of the roasting meat. He was both shocked and disgusted with himself to find his mouth watering and belly growling.

"Well from the sounds of it you brought something large enough back with you anyhow," the cook said, sitting down and turning his head in Logan's direction. "You can come on out now, stranger."

The other two men jumped to their feet with weapons in hand, just as surprised as Logan by the man's cunning observation.

Standing up straight, Logan coughed loudly to clear his throat. He smiled as genuinely as one could with arrows and axes pointed toward them. With arms raised and palms facing the men, he gave a shrug. "So, I guess there's no need to announce myself?" he asked.

"Aye, and who in bloody blazes are you then, eh?" the hunter he had followed to the camp demanded, poking his axe forward with each word. Logan thought he looked pretty angry that he had been unwittingly followed.

"Just another victim of the system, friend," Logan said, hoping to alleviate the tension by relating to the men. The hunter shared a dark look with the others. This was not going to turn out well if he could not somehow convince them he meant no harm.

"Look, I wasn't trying to be sneaky, just wanted to check you out before I revealed myself. Back home, you hear a lot of weird stories about the wild lands, can't know which are true or not, and never thought I would *need* to anyhow." The more he spoke the more guilty he began to feel for sneaking up on these men. I seemed like a good idea at the time, but now he felt like a bandit. He gave the cook a weak smile.

"Settle down boys, no need to get all hostile with our guest," the cook casually called off his men. "Bruno, fetch the lad a chair, will ye?" he ordered the large man, waving Logan to have a seat by the fire. "What's your name, kid?"

"Goodly met sir, Logan Walker," he replied evenly. As annoying as it was to be called a kid, there was no reason to let himself get worked up.

"Name's Maxwell and this here be me house. That there's Bruno and our jumpy friend, who you so easily followed here, is Wart." While Wart shot Logan a dark look for making him look bad in front of his boss, Bruno plopped down another stump with the grin and glazed eyes of a dimwit.

"I apologize for the cloak and dagger," Logan said. "After what I've been through in Fal, and all the stories of dangers out here, you can imagine my trepidation."

"What's a trepidasie Max?" Bruno asked. Up close around the fire light, Logan could see them better. Maxwell was built like a small ox, but his teeth, like those of his companions, were rotting or gone entirely. Wart was appropriately named, having three yellow boils on his face, one of which harbored a long black hair. Bruno was large and pudgy, smelling like old cheese left out to rot.

"Right then, *Logan Walker*," Max said, "and I'm sure you will appreciate me companions here being a little quick to overreact, having a stranger traipse unannounced into our home?" Max forgave Logan, in a way, telling him no harm no foul, to which he smiled back at the man and gave a nod of acknowledgement.

"Do us a bit o' damage with that fancy rifle you got there, if ye had wanted, anyhow," Maxwell asked, stoking the fire with a rusty poker. "Where did a young lad like yourself come across such a fine weapon?"

"If I'm not mistaken, we didn't get sent out here by following the rules, eh Max?" Logan said, throwing him a cocky grin.

"What *did* ye do then to be sent over?" Maxwell probed.

"Me, oh I'm no different than you," Logan said, immediately sensing it may not have been the best recourse, as Maxwell bristled a bit.

"What's that supposed to mean then?" Wart asked for his boss.

"Means I'm innocent, must have been a misunderstanding with the law," Logan chuckled, not backing off.

Silence washed over the group, and the area grew uncomfortable for a moment that stretched on too long, then a low rumbling laugh grew in Maxwell's floppy belly, rising until he was slapping his knees and howling. The other pair joined in the merriment, though Bruno clearly had no idea why they were laughing.

"I like this kid!" Maxwell proclaimed, settling himself down.

He passed out chunks of the cooked rat, which the men eagerly tore into, grease dripping from their lips and running down their dirty chins. Logan tentatively pulled a small piece and sampled it, careful not to show his disgust. The last thing he wanted was to offend his new friends' hospitality. He found rat meat was tough and greasy at the same time, yet surprisingly satisfying to the hunger pangs wracking his gut. The cook gave a knowing, toothless grin, seeing this was the first time Logan had tried it.

"Ah, you'll get used to it, kid. I know the feelin', we all went through it, 'cept Bruno, he'll eat anything. Think back to a time when I was repulsed at the idea of eating whatever was available…can't really say I picture it no more," Maxwell reflected, staring into the fire, his thoughts drifting to a past Logan could only guess at.

"How long have you been out here?" Logan asked.

"Long enough," Wart grunted, his companions nodding in agreement.

The four of them sat around the fire sharing stories late into the night. Maxwell was upset by the news of Mr. Beauford's death. It seemed the gnome's claims had been true to an extent. Wild landers did find Acadian artifacts for the gnome, who would trade them for rations or supplies, but they found them out here in the wilds, not on the surface. Maxwell broke out a tiny glass bottle of clear liquor after dinner to give a toast in the gnome's memory. The four of them got to know each other by telling their tales, sharing jokes, and even singing a couple fireside odes, until Bruno was passed out in the dirt and Wart had wandered away to his tent to sleep.

"Well, it's been a good night, it has," Maxwell said. "But the time has passed for these old bones to get some rest. Ye go ahead now and take Duck's tent over yonder. He hasn't needed it for weeks since a grappler got 'em." Maxwell pointed over to an unoccupied abode, groaning as he rose.

"I sure do appreciate it!" Logan said.

"Lot's a dangers out here, kid, get some rest and we can talk more in the mornin'. Start getting you educated right proper to the way of things round here." With that, Maxwell retired to the largest tent.

As Logan headed to his shelter, he could not help thanking Baetylus for his good fortune, something rare for him to do. As he drifted to sleep, he wondered what Corbin was thinking about at that moment and wished he could somehow let his brother know he was safe.

"Hold still, country boy," Jayne teased, adjusting the strap around Corbin's bicep and pricking a small needle into his vein. The small room they had brought him into was filled with strange devices unlike anything he had ever known. Small blips played each time a line on one of the glass screens moved. The ceiling was a perfectly rounded white dome that matched the bare walls of the room. It was quite different from the rest of the house they had traipsed him through. No stately furniture sat in here, no lavish carpets or rugs decorated the floor, and the only light came from a small fire burning in the center of the round room, the flickering flames warming his naked chest.

"There, that is the last one," Jayne said, fixing another of the strange little suction cups to his skin. The things were attached to his temples, arms, chest and back.

"What is all this for again?" Corbin asked, still uneasy about what he had gotten himself into.

"For the third time, Corbin, these are not part of the ritual. This machine is to monitor your vitals throughout the process. We wouldn't want you dying on us now, would we?" Jayne teased, sharing a giggle with Cassandra. Corbin felt strangely at ease with Lady Cassandra, but these little jokes that amused her, scared him to death.

"Where did you get all of these machines?" he asked, trying to keep the conversation going so he could ignore the fact that he was nervous.

"I had them designed shortly before building the healer center. These were some of the first units used there. Of course, that was back when the place was still open to everyone in New Fal. When I retired most of this came with me."

Corbin scrunched his eyebrows together wondering how old this woman was. Lady Cassandra looked old enough to be his grandmother, but she moved with the strut of a woman half her age. Yet had not the healing center been built ages ago?

"Are we ready, my dear?" she asked her apprentice.

"Yes ma'am!" Jayne said, throwing her an emphatic thumb's up.

"Okay, Corbin...just as we discussed, fall into your regular meditation routine now. Get in good and deep, I will know when you are there, and then we will begin the ritual." Lady Cassandra guided him to a spot on the floor, where he adjusted his seating and relaxed, crossing his legs. He placed both hands palm up on his knees so Lady Cassandra could drop a tiny lotus petal in each. Corbin focused his breathing and cleared his mind, already drifting deep inside himself, using the rhythm of the machinery to lull him into a meditative trance. He had long practiced the art of tuning himself to the world under the tutelage of his sensei and was so mastered in the art that he could stroll into a village celebration and still find some focus to center himself around.

Lady Cassandra dropped her cloak, revealing tightly wound wrappings across her breasts and down to her groin, leaving arms and legs bare, as the green covering floated softly to the floor. She began swaying back and forth in a graceful dance, across the fire from Corbin. Arms moved like dancing serpents, while her fingers seemed to play through the air, plucking invisible strings. Corbin was already far too lost in himself to see the spectacle, otherwise he may have run from the room when her hands began to radiate a soft light, while she slowly chanted. Lady Cassandra's voice began to rise with each thrust of her arms, both aimed at his body across the fire. A silky substance shimmered in the air around her fingertips, leaving feint trails of purple light behind them. The chanting grew louder and louder as she fell fully into the dance, eyes now orbs of white. The light grew brighter, with more substance, and now it was as if liquid were floating in the air. Trailing patterns worked their way into an intricate glyph that circled the air in front of the entranced woman, her fingers delicately tracing the astral design repeatedly.

Lady Cassandra could see the boy's mind now, not just his thoughts, but the core of his neural network, as clear as if it were a network of rooms floating in front of her non-corporeal form. She reached deep into his psyche and began her work at forming new patterns. Corbin felt his body grow hot, sweat rolling down to the cold stone floor, and he could hear the woman speaking in some foreign language, like a dull aching in the recesses of his mind.

The glyph had widened, now stretching over the fire, where one tip intersected with his forehead and the other her weaving hands, which seemed to be dancing with a life of their own. Unraveling some of his neural patterns, Cassandra was able to find what she needed. The sorceress carefully created a bridge in his mind, opening a long dormant door. It was like throwing a switch that invited the energy of the universe to course through an opening in his body. Corbin threw his head back and howled, bright light shooting from his eyes.

"Cassandra, his heart rate had spiked!" Jayne shouted over her master's chanting.

Lady Cassandra knew how dangerous this was, but she could not stop the process. They were too far along now, and she had to tie his mind back up before pulling away. There was no way to go any faster, not that this knowledge kept her from stubbornly trying. Jayne moved to inject Corbin with a needle of adrenaline and was gently pushed back by the power of Cassandra's mind.

Wait my dear; I need only a moment more, her voice spoke in Jayne's head. She did not argue, understanding that there was much Lady Cassandra knew in the world that made little sense to her. Jayne looked down at the man, who lay sprawled across the floor. His eyes were clearly moving behind closed lids, and she wondered what he was seeing at that moment.

Splinters of his soul torn apart, Corbin screamed down into the drowning nothingness, as he felt every fiber of his being wrenched forward. He could hear his own screams for miles behind as it trailed his form. Then as suddenly as he was moving forward, he stopped. The room was still gone, leaving him floating in an ethereal void, alone and weightless, spinning head over heel.

A stabbing pinprick of light flashed into existence, far away in the center of the abyss, which he reached out for, stretching his arm all the way toward it and begging for release. Corbin's body was suddenly propelled forward again, surging like a bullet, closing the distance between him and the light, which grew larger and larger with a speed that terrified him.

In another brilliant flash, the void was replaced by a light so overwhelmingly powerful, he had to shield his eyes from its magnificence. All around him there was the sound of light dancing through water, not that this made any sense in his mind. Nevertheless, there it was, clear as day. Corbin could feel a great presence in the majestic light of this world. Body floating, he tried to peek between his fingers and see what was there with him.

"**You know me,**" The light around him pulsed, as the words shook the very world in their uttering. This was a great and powerful voice, sounding like shattering glass on his spine.

"Are you... am... I?" he stammered, cowering in fear.

"**I. AM. BAETYLUS.**"

Corbin's legs trembled like jelly, dropping him to his knees. He immediately fell prostrate, rocking back and forth in the holy presence of his god.

"**Your soul is not lost in the afterlife, my child,**" the Great Crystal said, knowing his every thought, and seeing the man believed he had died somehow during the witch's ritual.

"Oh.... oooh, All-Father, I am not worthy to be in your light," Corbin groaned pitifully, keeping his face firmly pressed to the crystal ground.

"**DO NOT THINK SUCH THINGS, MY SON. ALL ARE DESERVING OF BAETYLUS. I HAVE BROUGHT YOU HERE SO THAT WE MAY SPEAK.**"

"I am but the humblest of servants, my Lord." The concept that Baetylus had wanted to speak with him only made Corbin grovel that much deeper. His mind simply could not comprehend what was happening.

"I KNOW. MY CHILD, THERE IS NOTHING YOU CAN TELL ME, ABOUT YOURSELF, THAT I DO NOT ALREADY KNOW. BAETYLUS SEES ALL. I WATCHED WHEN YOU WERE A BABE. I WAS THERE WHEN YOU FIRST PICKED UP THE SPEAR. I HEARD YOUR WORDS WHEN YOU WERE IN ANGUISH, WHEN YOU FELL IN LOVE."

Images flashed around Corbin of himself throughout his life, as a small child, a young boy crying over his mother's grave, the first time he kissed Elise, filled with elation, all of it thrust upon him by the All-Father's will, like glass daggers piercing his psyche.

"BAETYLUS IS ALL." His god's voice grew to an unbearable booming crescendo with the proclamation.

"Blessed be thy glory," Corbin chanted instinctively.

"YOU WILL PROVE YOUR FAITH, MY SON." Another image shot at his mind. It was Logan huddled over Beauford, bloody knife in hand, shouting at the guards to stop.

"YOU MUST STOP YOUR BROTHER. YOUR PEOPLE FACE GRAVE DANGER."

"What kind of danger, oh Holy One?" Corbin begged for understanding.

More images assaulted him, faster and faster like the strikes of coiled vipers stinging his mind. Bodies lay all over the capitol, the waters of Riverbell filled with blood, Elise had maggots crawling out of her empty eye sockets. Corbin screamed out in horror, his mind reeling on the brink of madness, and Baetylus pulled back, lessening his might over the mortal. He lay there gasping for air, drool running down his chin and the taste of blood filling his mouth from where he had bit into his own lip.

After a few minutes of silence, he was able to stammer out some semblance of speaking again. "Is this our future, oh Mighty Lord from above? Is this what will happen to the people of New Fal?"

"THIS IS *BUT ONE PATH*. A FUTURE YOU CAN PREVENT FROM COMING TO FRUITION, MY SON. BE BRAVE, FOR I WILL ALWAYS BE

THERE BESIDE YOU WHEN YOU NEED ME. YOU MUST BRING YOUR BROTHER BACK TO FAL."

"I will *not* fail you, All-Father," Corbin said, staunchly determined to see his Lord's will done.

"GO NOW, READY YOURSELF. THIS JOURNEY IS ONLY BEGINNING. WE *WILL* SPEAK AGAIN, MY SON."

Corbin had so many questions for his god, his mind raced to grasp just one. He wanted to weep and beg to remain in the all-Father's light, but it was too late. The world exploded into glass shards all around him, hurling his soul into the dark void.

A stinging slap to the cheek opened Corbin's eyes, to find Jayne standing over him holding an empty needle. Behind her, in his fuzzy vision, Lady Cassandra was covering her old, tired body back up under a dark green cloak. In the distance, still echoing through his mind, the ill omen Baetylus gave rang over and over.

"Settle down now friend," Jayne said. "The dizziness will pass soon enough."

Lady Cassandra joined her and gently pushed him back to the floor, as he weakly struggled to rise.

"The All-Father...," he babbled.

Lady Cassandra perked up, hearing the Crystal god's name. *Corbin, did the All-Father speak to you?* Her voice whispered in his mind.

"What...?"

"Corbin dear, can you understand me?" Again, the words moved through his mind.

"Yes... but."

"Not with your words, boy, use your thoughts," she instructed.

"How can you hear my thoughts?" he tested the concept.

"This is my gift to you, Corbin Walker, the power within has been unlocked," she graciously answered.

"But how...?"

"Corbin dear, please try and remain focused, Cassandra said. *"Now pay close attention to what I'm about to say, we haven't much time. Did the All-Father actually speak with you?"* she brought her psyche on a

little more forcefully, attempting to stabilize the young man's quivering thoughts.

"Yes," Corbin thought. *"He did, the All-Father reached out to me."*

"Tell me everything," she demanded.

"New Fal is under great danger if Logan does not come back and face trial."

"I suspected as much. Show me." Lady Cassandra said.

"I do not understand, milady."

"Let yourself fall back into the memory. Do not try to explain it...just think through what you experienced, and I will see it unfold." His ignorance served as a reminder that mages could study for decades before unlocking abilities such as these, which she had so freely given to the man.

Corbin tried to picture his encounter with the great god, Baetylus. As he thought over the miracle, it was as if Lady Cassandra were sitting there with him, watching actors on a distant stage play out a drama.

"Ah I see it already, you are a natural, not that I had any doubt of your potential. Still though, it is impressive that you are handling telepathy so easily," she complimented him, while the vision of Baetylus' conversation with Corbin came to its end.

"Is that what I should call this miraculous gift you have bestowed upon me?" he asked.

In her response, a flood of images washed over Corbin, not as brutal as when the All-Father had shown him the future, but more like a river of time cascading over the rocks of his being.

Lady Cassandra was a Psionicist from the ancient Order of Second Sight. Long had she studied in the mystical arts, learning to access the very energy flowing through their universe, and today she had awakened a piece of him that lay dormant in mankind for over two centuries now.

Through psionic magic, he would be able to look inside the minds of those he encountered. Since the wild lands were filled with many men and women who truly belonged there, along with innocents who had been unjustly persecuted, as well as a myriad of dangerous denizens, stalking for their next meal in the shadows, the longer Logan was out there on his own, the more likely he would come to an untimely end. In the great expanse of Vanidriell, Corbin would truly benefit from this gift, being able to scan the land to find sentient life. This would give him the advantage he sorely needed to survive and track down his brother safely.

Sounds began bleeding in through their connection from around the room. He could hear Jayne's thoughts in the background, which were whimsical and warm. Downstairs a man was scrubbing the dishes, dwelling on an argument he had with his son that morning. Corbin clutched his ears, futilely trying to block out the overwhelming noises, and Lady Cassandra waved her apprentice over. Jayne placed a small, smooth metal cuff around the back of his right earlobe, which immediately muffled the whispers, leaving behind nothing more than a dull ache in his temples.

"This Svalin will help you adjust to your new sixth sense," Lady Cassandra said, while Jayne busied herself checking his eyes for dilation with a candle. "We used it in Acadia to wean the novice into their newfound skills. It is made from a special substance that helps block out any unbidden channeling of psychic aether. Remove it only while you sleep, the human body is an amazing tool, it will help you slowly adapt so you can control when and where you use telepathy."

Now that his body felt like it was back under his control, Corbin tried to stand up. "Milady, I am but a humble hunter from Riverbell. I am not worthy of these gifts, but I do thank you for them," he said with a slight bow of his head.

"Young man, the All-Father himself came to me in a vision, instructing me to awaken your potential. Who can judge you more worthy than He?"

Corbin was speechless.

"Now then there is much to teach you in a very short time."

The tent's interior was roomy, with a ceiling tall enough that a man only needed to slightly crouch stepping inside. Logan's "bed" was no more than a pile of dirty furs piled on the ground. The campfire had been put out hours ago when they retired for the evening, allowing the shadows of night to creep in and reclaim the camp. The air was surprisingly alive with the sounds of nocturnal creatures, chirping insects, hooting cave owls, and the occasional fluttering of bat wings high overhead. A couple of times Logan had awoken in a panic to the howls of caits, realizing with relief that they were faraway in the distance. Even the trees around the tent sounded alive, their leaves rustling in the cool night breeze.

When Bruno ducked under the flap, the oaf was surprisingly nimble of foot for his size, careful to make no sound, with his large stone-headed axe in hand. He stopped short, sensing Logan stir under the furs. Then, once he was confident the man was asleep, he tiptoed closer to the bed. Grimy, calloused hands gripped the hilt of his shoddy weapon, lifting it silently overhead and throwing all his weight into the blow, crashing down into the furs through the man's head, which popped like a grape. Bruno could not help hee-hawing in delight at killing the stupid man. He must have really lodged the axe into the little bastard's skull, because it refused to pull out, wedged in between the bones as if they were stone.

"Tut tut," a voice mocked him from the shadowy corner of the tent. Before Bruno could turn around, Logan threw a large stone through the air, connecting solidly with the brute's throat. Bruno clutched his crushed windpipe gasping for air, frantically trying to call out to his partners. Logan ran right in, throwing three sharp jabs into the giant bandit's side with his human hand, before shattering his pelvis under the power of his mechanical fist. The force of that last blow knocked Bruno out through the tent's opening, roughly dropping him on his back across the coarse dirt.

Maxwell was completely caught by surprise seeing his man lying on the ground. When Logan ran through the opening, he barely had time enough to get out of the way, as a hot beam scorched the air where he had been standing. Logan let off three more shots from his laser rifle, each missing their mark, as an angry Maxwell moved with far more agility than he looked to possess.

"Stay still Maxie boy," Logan said, "I want to thank you for the royal accommodations."

Maxwell let him prattle on, using his cocky demeanor to work his way in closer, making it difficult to get a good aim in the close range. He barreled into Logan, roughly backhanding him. Logan tried to roll with the sting of the man's attack, thinking to spin around behind him, but the burly bandit was not about to let him get away that easy, throwing both arms around his body in a grizzly bear hug. His rifle clattered to the ground as the air was squeezed out of his lungs by the man's powerful grip.

"Ha, ha, ha whelp, you thought to come into Maxwell's house without offering me a present?" the beast of a man cackled, his sour breath filling the air. Logan wheezed unintelligible words as Maxwell squeezed tighter, his arms locked around the foolish young man's flailing body. "Eh, what does the little piggy have to say then?"

Light flashed as energy crackled over the large man's body in burning waves. For a moment his grip locked even harder, muscles in a spasm from the electric shock that assaulted him. Then his body flopped limply to the ground.

Logan rubbed his sore ribs, looking down at the bastard. He had to take a moment to catch his breath, which was coming in ragged gasps. The metal on his hand was still smoking from the electro-shock he lit Maxwell up with and his glove was a ruined mess. Logan slammed his boot down hard onto the man's ribs, cracking a couple under his heel. Maxwell could do nothing but shriek pathetically, as he was completely unable to move, paralyzed from the attack.

"I said...you're not the first idiot to try and bear hug me. Don't know why you fools are always trying to cuddle instead of fight. Eh? What was that you were saying Maxie, my man?" Logan cupped a hand to his ear as if listening.

"Oh...that's right, you wanted a present," he said. "Sure, sure I have a present for you right here, *friend*." Logan threw all his strength into a blow from his mechanical fist, shattering the bandit's right kneecap.

Maxwell let out a bloodcurdling scream before blacking out, unable to bear the pain.

"Don't even try it, Wart," Logan growled over his shoulder. Behind him Wart had knocked an arrow with shaking hands and fear bubbling in his eyes.

"P-please don't k-kill me," Wart cried pitifully, dropping the weapon to the ground.

"Is this what you bastards do to new Wilders? Bring 'em back here, tell them some stories so you can get them nice and comfortable before you murder them for all their belongings?"

"P-please it wasn't never my idea mister, honest to death," Wart whimpered like a rat.

"Shut up and get out of my way before I shoot you dead, bandit. Show me where you keep your cache," Logan flicked the rifle to the right of the man, ordering him to move, to which Wart readily complied, scurrying across the camp and nervously checking to see if Logan was following. They walked by the spot where Bruno lay unconscious, and Logan gave him a sharp kick in the side for good measure. Wart stopped beside the largest tent, where a couple of crates were stacked.

"Go on and open it up," Logan ordered. The bandit pried the lid off with shaking hands, then stepped back looking as if he might die of fright.

The unexpected stench hit Logan's senses hard, and he almost lost the contents of his stomach when he saw the crates wretched bounty. Catching himself with a couple dry heaves, he eyed the greasy little bandit he had followed into this nightmare, trying to comprehend exactly what it was he was seeing. Wart gave him an uneasy toothless grin and shrugged. The crate was halfway full of the rotting meat of butchered humans, arms, entrails, blood, and gore. These fiends were cannibals. They were eating other wild landers!

"What the Hel is this, you sick little bastard?" Logan screamed.

"It's the bounty, Master Logan," Wart said. "This is what we... *they* trick people into the camp for. But now it's all yours, seein' as how your my new boss an all." It settled over Logan at that moment that in the lands outside of Fal it was a game of survival of the fittest.

"You knew I was following you here?" Logan asked, the doubt keenly edged in his tone.

"No, no sir, you were a happy surprise for Max. He said you were a gift from the All-Father, *dinner and weapons*, a rare delight for those exiled."

"Close that damn thing back up!" he ordered, pointing with the rifle muzzle, while his free hand only half protected his face from the stench.

Wart did as he was told, scrambling to cover the box back up and Logan slammed the butt of his rifle across the back of the man's skull, knocking his unconscious body atop the sealed box. Then he leaned over and finally let his stomach loose on the ground, as another whiff of the rotting meat filled his nose to the point he could actually taste it.

Another crate next to the unconscious cannibal began frantically thumping. At least a dozen images raced through Logan's mind of what might be inside. As he pried the lid off, he envisioned everything from a damsel in distress to a large man-eating creature was waiting for him, although none of those images quite prepared him for the naked gnome he found instead.

The little man's oversized pudgy hands were bound at the wrist by a dirty length of wire, cutting into his flesh and he was gagged with a filthy, soiled rag that had been stuffed into his mouth. Logan hurried to lift the three-foot gnome from the crate and pulled the disgusting rag out of his mouth. The gnome unleashed a flurry of curses between desperate spitting to the side, while Logan worked to remove the wire binding his wrists.

"Blech, thank you, thank you, oh thank you." He jumped up and down, getting the blood to circulate back into his stubby legs.

"Don't mention it pal, are you alright?" he asked the gnome, unsure what else to say in a situation like this.

"These weirdoes were going to eat me for dinner, like I was a roasted ham! Heard them cackling about it night before last!" he raged, running over to Wart, and kicking the cannibal's limp body repeatedly with his plump bare foot. He would have made an impressive show of it too, cursing as he was, if one blow had not missed, stubbing his large toe against the corner of the crate instead. That sent the gnome hopping up and down in circles on one foot. Logan could not help smiling at the little man's funny behavior.

"Settle down fella, everything's okay now," he said, reaching out to steady him, but pulling back not wanting to make contact.

The gnome stopped short, looking down at his flat little belly and blanching as he remembered that he was completely naked. He stammered to excuse himself and darted into Maxwell's nearby tent, returning a few minutes later wearing what Logan assumed were the clothes the vile cannibals had stripped him of when they had taken the gnome prisoner.

He was much calmer now, standing there, small chin proudly raised, and tightening the last strap of his studded metal bracers. The gnome wore black buckled boots, under brown canvas breeches, with purple suspenders over a gray tunic. He also had a small hammer latched to his belt. Logan wondered how the gnome had put on all his gear in such a short time; he even looked like he had combed his unkempt mane of silver-grey hair, taking care to pat down his overgrown sideburns and smooth out his matching bushy eyebrows. He pulled a clean rag out of his pack and handed it to the gnome, so that he could wipe the dirt off his large bulbous nose and small smooth forehead.

"Feel better, friend?" he asked.

"I surely do good sir," the gnome beamed. "Logan, was it?"

"Yes, but how do you know my name?" Logan said, checking over his shoulder to be sure the bandits were not stirring.

"Heard it last night, while you lot were chatting around the fire. Just took you for another one of these bastards at first, hard to hear locked in a wooden box you know."

"And you are...?" Logan asked.

"Names Brillfilbipp Bobblefuzz of the Dudje Bobblefuzzers, friends call me Bipp, and it has *never,* in all my years, been more of a pleasure to meet any humans' acquaintance," Bipp said, proudly offering his oversized stubby hand, which Logan heartily shook.

"Same here Brill-fil-bipp of Dudje…same here."

"As I said, friends call me Bipp, and *you sir* have certainly earned the right to claim that title!"

Cait howls rose from the west, like those Logan had heard lying in his tent, but these seemed nearby, like they were closing in on the camp.

"Must have heard all the commotion from that nice rifle of yours," Bipp said. "They have keen hearing to be sure. Best we be getting out of here right quick, eh?" Bipp waved for Logan to lead the way east, away from the camp.

He could not agree more, but before they were on their way, he had to grab some supplies of his own while the opportunity presented itself. Rummaging through the nearest tent, he grabbed everything useful he could get his hands on and a handful of gemstones that caught his eager eye, to boot. After he picked the area clean, Logan ran back to retrieve his own backpack from the tent, when another howl came from the woods outside the camp. This one was so close it must have been just over the chasm.

"Okay Bipp, time to run," Logan called, "lead the way!" He eagerly followed the gnome out of the area and into the night.

Chapter 15

Elise was lit up by the early morning light, giving her silhouette a radiant glow, as if Baetylus were trying to wrap his warmth around her. She stood in front of the massive city gates that led to the wild lands, promising Corbin she would stay safe while he was away.

"Please tell Lady Penelope I appreciated her generosity," Corbin said, referring to the supplies that had been sent down with Elise to see him off. Lady Penelope had provided a fur-lined jacket that covered his body down to the knees, and would keep him warm in the wild lands, which Lady Cassandra advised was much colder than the New Fal climate he was accustomed to. He buckled it tightly around the waist, ensuring he could still unclasp the voulge strapped to his back with ease and reach the folding compound short bow on his belt. Confident he had all the equipment needed to survive for a good month in the wilds, he moved to be with Elise.

"But what if a month comes and goes and you're still out there?" Elise said, continuing a conversation they were having before he stopped to check over the supplies.

"I swear upon the light of Baetylus, it will not come to that," Corbin said.

"But what if you get lost out there?" Elise said. She could not imagine a life without him.

"No matter what, I *will* come back for you, my love. You have believed in me all my life. Don't stop now when I need that confidence more than ever."

Elise crumpled into his arms, quietly sobbing against his chest. As far back as Corbin could remember he had known her. Elise had been a part of his days and nights, even sneaking into his dreams. They shared so many visions of their future together, having children, building a home, and all the other things that come with everlasting happiness. When he was down, she was always there ready to pick him up, and he returned the favor. They balanced each other out. No one could ask for a better life than he had already spent with her, and he would not see anyone take away her happiness.

Magistrate Fafnir had come out to watch his departure. Stepping out of his sleek black carriage, he strode over to the embracing couple. The Pale Gates were not allowed to be opened unless in the presence of either the Magistrate or a member of the Council of Twelve.

"I see we are saying our farewells?" he said, looking to the crying maiden. He slyly moved to console the woman, as the couple broke to greet him properly. "Madame Elise, you must not fret so. This whole affair will all be over before you know it, becoming just another story to tell around the dinner table."

"Good day, Magistrate Fafnir." Corbin said.

"Good day, Corbin, hope we have not kept you waiting too long, lad." Fafnir directed his focus to the gates, as if Corbin were an afterthought.

"Would that we had more time to cling to, milord. I'm afraid this still seems rather surreal to us." Corbin said.

"Now lad, have some faith," The magistrate clapped his shoulder, turning to beckon his footman to bring forth a small parcel. "In the short time I have known your person; you have represented yourself to be possessed of true honor and deep integrity," he explained, turning his back to open the hinged lid.

"That is too kind, good sir...." Corbin was surprised by the man's high opinion of him, after Lady Cassandra's warnings just hours before that the magistrate was not to be trusted.

"It is not so much a kindness as the truth," Fafnir said. "Lady Elise, do not be filled with sorrow, you waste these tears. Our hero of Riverbell will surely fulfill his task." Fafnir gave a nod to Elise then turned to face Corbin, producing a fine pair of hand tailored black leather gauntlets.

"And with your successful return we will secure the safety of your village, as well as quell these nasty rumors, proving Riverbell's true allegiance to the kingdom. Just to be sure, here is a little gift to help get you back in one piece." He offered the parcel to Corbin.

"Oh my," Elise exclaimed, covering her mouth. "Magistrate Fafnir, you truly are an amazing man."

Corbin bowed to the Magistrate before pulling the tight gloves over his fingers and buckling the connected gauntlets, which were thickly padded, around his wrists. He guessed the Magistrate had these made just for him, as they fit perfectly. He admired how the man could set his prejudices aside. The Magistrate undoubtedly hated his brother, fully believing he was a murderer, but seemed to hold no ill will toward Corbin.

"Now press tight against the palm," Fafnir said, pointing at his own hand for reference, and eagerly watching as Corbin did the same. He could feel a pressurized button inside the leather lining, which gave a light pop, releasing a two-inch steel blade from a slit in the padding that slid over the top of his hand.

"They look to be functioning excellently," Fafnir said. "*Fit like a glove* as they say, eh?"

The group laughed awkwardly for a moment, forgetting the path that lay ahead. Fafnir abruptly cut off the merriment, beckoning his men to open the gates. Behind them, the massive stone doors grated against the ground, slowly moving outward, to reveal the wild lands. Corbin and Elise were lost in a trance as the portal opened, their minds elsewhere, brooding on the dangers awaiting him.

Once the gates came to a halt, fully opened, Corbin grasped Elise's hands in his own and pulled her body close once more. They shared a long kiss, before he whispered in her ear. "Trust no one. Be the strong woman I have come to love."

With bright eyes she pulled back to stare at him in astonishment, "I will."

"By the Crystal, I swear I will be back before a month is through," Corbin promised, firm in his resolve to leave with his head held high, though every instinct in his body screamed to run back to Riverbell with her.

"I know you will," Elise said, "because if you don't, I'll come right out there into the wilds and drag you back here by the ear!" Elise squared her shoulders, trying to sound foreboding while desperately holding back her tears.

"Now, that's the Elise I know," Corbin said. He gave a curt nod to Fafnir and headed out through the Pale Gates.

The magistrate moved to stand beside Elise, and they watched Corbin leave the capitol together. He was walking with a firm determination and made no attempt to look back. Fafnir understood the man did not want to upset his fiancé any further than she already was, putting on a brave front in the face of his hopeless journey.

"He has much honor, Madame Elise. I can only hope this tragedy ends in us seeing him come back through these gates," Fafnir consoled the future leader of Riverbell.

Too scared to speak, for fear of breaking down, Elise could only stand there with a quivering lower lip, as tears streamed down her face. Fafnir coolly smiled behind her and shouted for his men to secure the city.

"Close the gates!"

Logan had a solid day's march through the wilds with Bipp, during which they had much time to catch up and get to know each other. The exile felt so at ease with the little gnome. He was not sure if that had something to do with witnessing Beauford's untimely death or if it was just that Bipp was genuinely a funny guy whom he felt comfortable being around. Whatever the reason, he found himself opening up and sharing all the details of his recent journey to Fal and subsequent flight over the wall.

In return, the gnome shared the story of how he came to be a three-day's hike from his hometown, naked in a crate, waiting to be cannibal dinner.

"We got this job out at old man Torkin's potato farm, seemed the motor went haywire on his water pump. Wasn't like it was the first time it's happened. I probably been out there once every couple of months just in the last two years. So, I grabbed me toolkit and headed over pronto! Nothing like knocking a job off early in the day so you can fit a couple rounds of scrum in, I always say."

"When I got to the farm it was plain as day that goffers had gotten into the motor, chewing the carbonator all to pieces again. Kept telling that cheapskate Torkin to get a latched cover, but he never listens. That fool would haggle over the price of air if he had to. Except Mrs. Torkin keeps him right in line, don't you doubt it."

"So anyhow, where was I...? Oh yeah, I was just finishing up tightening the rollers when I hear wings flapping real close-like. Now my first instinct was to roll under the wheelbarrow and get out of sight. And what do you think I saw right there before me very own eyes swooping out of the air?" Bipp paused for dramatic flair.

"Only one thing makes flapping sounds like that," Logan reasoned.

"Don't know about that," Bipp said, "but you guessed right. It *was* a roc-bat, and the furry flying rodent was stealing my tools!"

"Wait, what? Why would a roc-bat want a bag of tools?" Logan interrupted.

"Weren't the tools she was after," Bipp said, "it was my lunch that thieving monstrosity was vying for! So, I ran fast as these little legs could pump and snatched ahold of that bag!"

"You risked your life for some tools and a lunch?" Logan thought perhaps the gnome was a little touched in the head. Roc-bats being the size of a human, they were no easy target, and anyone that tangoed with one over a lunch must be mighty hungry indeed.

"Aw, now don't you be rude with me, even a human like yourself would have fought the critter for my Aunt Tilly's honey-soaked ham. Three years winning the town prize for that recipe she's had, damn sure worth fighting for and no way I was letting go of what was mine. Only problem, as you can imagine, is the bat did not share my enthusiasm, and had no intention of releasing its catch.

'Fore I knew what was what, we were soaring fifty feet high up in the air and wasn't she just thrashing about trying to knock me loose. Well, I did the only sensible thing, reached right down, and grabbed my trusty hammer, this thing has been in my family last seven generations you know, and gave her a right good smack in the eye. She never even saw it coming, eh?" Bipp laughed at his own joke, almost tripping over a thick root stretching across their path.

"Except then I learned a rough lesson. Hitting a creature carrying you fifty feet up in the air is maybe not the brightest idea I've ever had, which occurred to me as I was falling to the cave floor," he admitted, rubbing his bulbous nose in reflection.

"You know how they say your life flashes 'fore your eyes and all that *'see the light'* nonsense...all I can tell you was going through this head was how my honey-soaked ham was gone."

Logan could only snicker at the gnome's sentiment over his lunch, which earned him a fleeting dark look.

"Mighty Thorgar himself must have been watching over me that day. Only way I can figure I was lucky enough to land in that tar pit. That hot stuff really does the trick for your pores, I gotta admit. I was sunk in right up to my shoulders, when along came these bandits. Course I didn't know they were bandits at first, just thought they were goodly folk doing the right thing by fishing me out of that muck. Learned my mistake on that one right quick, didn't I? They didn't waste no time stripping me and binding my hands. You see those pits were pretty close to that bloody little camp them cannibals call home. So anyhow, that is how I went from fixing a pump to naked in a crate waiting to be dinner," he finished the tale, as if it all made sense.

"Wait, so if there was tar all over your clothes...then whose are those?" Logan wondered, unsure he actually wanted to hear the answer.

"Couldn't say, friend, if I had to guess, I would think these were from a guest they already had for dinner." Both men wrinkled their nose at the prospect.

Once they got past the Bipp's unlucky tale he shared more about his past with Logan. Bipp hailed from the trade port of Dudje, an entire town filled with gnomes! Apparently, they exported honey, crops from the surrounding farms, and worked the nearby mines, operating as an ore trader for the other towns in Vanidriell.

"I never even knew there were *any* towns in the wild lands," Logan said upon hearing this revelation. He was astonished to hear about a gnome civilization outside New Fal and Malbec.

"Hmmm...right, you know *wild lands* is just a name those humans in New Fal came up with, right?" Bipp said. "Folks who live out here call the land Vanidriell, its rightful name of course. We tend to keep the human rabble from Fal out of our towns. They aren't usually a good lot, but sometimes we meet one here or there that really proves us wrong. Not like the exiled criminals. Kind of like you Logan, just in the wrong place at the wrong time?"

"You really think your mayor will see it that way?" Logan asked. Bipp had kindled a flame of hope within him that the leader of Dudje would look kindly upon his rescue of the imprisoned gnome, allowing him to stay in their town as some sort of reward for the good deed. Bipp also thought it important for Logan to share the news of Beauford's death firsthand.

"Know he will. Nothing but good stock in Dudje, friend," Bipp said confidently, which put Logan even more at ease. He had not realized how fearful he felt about being homeless and doomed to a wandering life in the dangerous wild lands, without friends or family. His future was a bleak path of hermitage, until this slim chance of settling with the gnomes came along.

They were headed east at a split in the cavern, into a series of winding tunnels that grew gradually tighter. Entire sections of the tunnel seemed to loop in and wind around in a maze. If not for Bipp's uncanny sense of direction, Logan would have been lost hours ago. Then again, he could just be making it all up to not look stupid and Logan would have been none the wiser.

Shortly after crossing a trickling creek, they heard some squealing up ahead, around the bend. Bright eyed, both men looked to each other and simultaneously exclaimed, "A pig!!" They had not had much to eat since the previous day, when they caught some small fish in one of the rivers.

"Hurry 'fore she gets away!" Bipp's little legs pumped as fast as they could, but Logan quickly outpaced him laughing. Their merriment was soon cut short, when they came around the bend and almost ran headlong into a giant sauria.

This was a nasty variety of trap door lizard, the size of two people, which would jump out of a hidden alcove to spit poison in its prey's eyes then pull them back into its lair to feast. This particular sauria was about eight feet in length and half that wide, thankfully small for its species. Its back was covered with sticky spikes, and it had talons the size of Logan's head that clawed the ground. As they came ambling around the corner, it spun about to face them, leaving the pig it just captured for the newly arrived meal.

Logan shoved his small companion out of the way just in time. The sauria's face suddenly seemed to grow, as large flaps covered with spiky protrusions opened up on either side of its hissing mouth and a stream of sizzling poison spit forth, hitting the spot where the men had just been standing.

"Sweet mother of milk," Bipp said, biting his fist.

Logan had no time for words, freeing his small hand-crossbow and leveling it to let a round of double shafts fly. He aimed for the exposed sauria's side, but the sharp projectiles clattered harmlessly off the beast's scale covered shoulder. He had no time to curse the armored skin, having to throw himself in a wild roll to dodge the lizard's snapping tongue, which seemed to have an extraordinary reach. Missing Logan, the fleshy pink appendage stuck against the limestone wall behind him, saliva melting into the rock. Bipp ran forward, pounding the tongue with his tiny hammer before it could retract. The sauria let out a rattling sound of pain, snapping the tongue to safety.

"Aim for the eyes!" Bipp yelled.

Logan had already reloaded his weapon and, taking the gnome's cue, he let off a single bolt. This time he guided it straight and true to its mark, zipping dead center toward the lizard's iris. However, the sauria was not going to go down that easy. It pulled its head sharply to the side, just enough so that the bolt missed its target, again skittering harmlessly to the ground.

"Ohhhh...she's angry now," Bipp said. "Make a run for it!" Taking his own advice, he ran full tilt toward the lizard, dropping at the last minute so that his tiny body slid underneath its belly and out through its hind legs. The sauria reared back and roared, before thunderously charging at Logan to crush him against the rocks and skewer his body with its horned head. Having to react quickly, he hopped sideways against the rocky surface of the tunnel wall, moving with such agility that his feet skipped from one rock to the other until he was high enough to leap over the lizard's head. Charging too quickly to stop the sauria moved right past his gravity-defying maneuver, smashing headfirst into the tunnel wall.

Using the temporarily dazing opportunity, Logan caught up with his friend, who was standing beside the dead pig.

"It moves too fast for my crossbow," he said, trying to catch his breath and holstering his weapon.

"What else do you have in mind?" Bipp asked, hoping the man had an answer that would save them from becoming lunch.

The sauria was already recovering, shaking its horned head to straighten out the spinning tunnel. Logan's mind raced for an idea as it circled, lowering it head and clawed the ground. If it looked angry before, now the sauria was downright enraged. It let out a low growl then sprang forward, barreling down at them and opening its flaps again to spit poison.

The tunnel walls lit up when a stream of fire-like energy zipped out of Logan's laser rifle, melting through the beast's wide mouth and incinerating its insides. The sheer heat of his weapon caused the sauria's eyes to burst outward and it tumbled in mid charge to the ground. Still rolling forward it came to rest only inches from their feet, while they stared on in shock, with Logan still aiming his rifle in disbelief. Both men cheered in celebration, and Bipp even ran over to waggle his hindquarters at the beaten monster.

"Plenty of food for us now, huh?" Logan bragged, eagerly gesturing at the horned lizard.

"Can't be eating that, no sir. Filled with poison he is, right flowing through the blood." Bipp shook his head, then pointed happily over to the hog, turning Logan's frown back into a smile.

"The pig's another story, that's good meat there as sure as my Aunt Tilly is a butcher!" Bipp slapped his hands together, licking his lips hungrily.

The pair high-fived each other at the bounty in front of them, like two school kids. The pig had to be a good two hundred pounds of tender meat and the tunnel here forked past a clearing where the ceiling raised high again, back up into the darkness, meaning there should be no problem lighting a fire to set up camp. Things were really looking up for the companions. Logan's smile withered when the sound of wings beating through the air came from overhead. He spun around to see what was coming when a giant roc-bat swooped down to snatch their prize!

"Drats...there goes my ham again...," Bipp grumbled, looking sad enough to cry as the bat plucked the pig up into the air.

Logan felt his insides boiling. Nothing out here in the wild lands was fair. "Not on my watch," he said through gritted teeth, determined to take control of the situation.

He lifted his metal fist high, aiming at the fleeing bat. A small latch popped open on top of his hand, whirring as the little spring mechanism popped up, revealing a tiny pill shaped metal capsule.

"What in the seven blazes is that thing?" Bipp asked, the engineer in him fully piqued.

"Not sure...let's find out!" Logan mischievously replied, as he released the pill. It zipped through the air into the shadows above, where the bat had just flown out of view, leaving behind a small spiraling stream of smoke. They waited for a few silent moments, both holding their breath in anticipation, but nothing happened.

Bipp scratched his head. "Well, at least we tried, and that's all you can do sometimes, right?" he said trying to sound optimistic, though the pitiful whining pitch in his voice belied his true feelings.

"I guess...," Logan said, about to admit defeat when the capsule tapped its target, letting off a massive fiery explosion overhead that rocked the cave, violently shaking the walls all around them. In the bright fiery ball of the blast, Logan could see the ceiling was far closer than he had judged, not that he had a clue what the weapon would do in the first place anyhow.

They had to run as fast as they could, sprinting in opposite directions as, first the dead bat, and next their pig came crashing down to the ground, quickly followed by an enormous stalactite, which was knocked loose from the ceiling. As the gargantuan rock hit the ground it shattered into hundreds of rocks, some small but most large. One of the smaller pieces flew sideways, catching Logan squarely in the back, throwing him face first to the cavern floor.

He decided it was probably a good idea to stay put until the storm of rocks abated, which was not for several minutes. As the cloud of dust settled, he could dimly make out a wall of boulders the direction he had come. It may have stretched up a good twenty feet or more.

"Logan!" Bipp yelled from the other side. "Logan! Please tell me you're alright, friend!"

"I hear you Bipp!" he had to shout, so the gnome could hear him through the thick pile of boulders that stood as a barrier between them, dividing the travelers.

"Thank the gods man...I thought I lost you for sure there!" Bipp said. "Can you make it over the rockslide?"

Logan tried to see the top of the rockslide through the settling dust. "I don't think so and I left my rope back in Fal anyhow."

Bipp waggled his fingers nervously in front of his face thinking of a solution. "You had better head northeast then. These tunnels meet back up after a while. Your way is a little trickier though, lots of twisting channels to traverse. Going to have to keep heading north then east in that order as the paths split!" Bipp instructed, unable to see Logan nodding his head.

"Got it. Don't worry about me, I'll meet you on the other side!" Logan shouted back.

"Be safe, friend!" Bipp said.

The gnome backed up from the wall and prepared to head into the northern tunnel when he spied a big fat pig leg sticking out of the rubble beside him. He stopped and flicked out his small dagger licking his lips. "Looks like I got me some ham after all."

Chapter 16

Waking from his slumber, Corbin decided it was time to find his brother's trail again. Lady Cassandra had not had much opportunity to train him in the use of the psionic arts, but what little time they did have was spent focusing on his core skill. Eager to learn, they had worked straight through the night. He was exhausted by the time he met Elise at the Pale Gates and had no time to rest when he first left Fal.

Outside the wall, Corbin did not need to rely on telepathic tricks to find his brother's trail. For that, he required only a short run to the area where Logan had last been spotted, where he easily found the site where the city watchmen had shot at his brother. The soil was scorched in black splotches where the soldiers had missed him.

Logan's flight from Fal was easy enough to track, as he did not seem to be bothered with covering up his tracks. This did not surprise Corbin in the least. His older brother had always been brash and cocky. Then again, he probably assumed no one would even bother chasing after him into the wilds. Following the boot marks, broken twigs, and bent plants for some time, Corbin finally came to a small ethereal pond, where he completely lost the trail.

This was as good a place as any for him to rest, so he climbed up a nearby tree trunk, and strapped the leather buckle of his belt around both his wrist and a nearby branch, this way if he began slipping while resting, he would be tugged awake.

That was a couple hour ago, and the rest had done him well. Now it was time to get on the move again, to close the distance Logan might have gained with his two-day head start. Balancing with the arches of his feet on separate branches and stretching out his back without moving them, he gave a light push down, followed by another, springing up from the limber branches high into the air, and spinning into a backward somersault to land gingerly on his toes in the tall grass below.

For some reason Logan's trail had gone cold after stopping at this pond. All physical evidence of his movements ended abruptly after he lay in the grass by Corbin's feet. Touching the Svalin on his ear, Corbin tried to fall into himself, as Lady Cassandra taught him the night before. It was not unlike the meditation his sensei, Rimball, had spent years mentoring, yet with a heightened sense of awareness to the world around. Sometimes when Corbin fell into a deep meditation, one that he completely drifted in over hours, it was as if his physical body were distant, removed from his physical being.

This was something other than that. It was more like his corporeal form was a tuning fork, sensitive to the psychic energy radiating from the world around, the aether. Probing in the darkness for a point of light that revealed some sentient semblance of a living creature, the energy rippled over the landscape in waves. Lady Cassandra compared it to the way a bat sent out sounds, hearing them bounce off objects to tell it where to go. She said that would be a good way for him to begin, being a novice in the skills of psionicism.

"Watch Out!"

The words jolted Corbin to his core, as if someone had just shocked his nerves with energy. Acting on instinct alone, he threw his body into a defensive crouch, rolling in a sideways spin and springing to his feet with his polearm waving in front of his body to block the unknown threat. If he had not moved with such alacrity, the massive cait that pounced the spot where he had been would surely have killed him with ease. Instead, its muzzle was snapping at air, as the beast confusingly thought he had slipped into the dirt below.

Corbin used his momentary advantage to stab the monstrous smooth skinned feline hard in its flank. The voulge was much heavier than he was used to wielding. Lady Cassandra had gifted it to him, saying that fighting in the wilds with a spear was akin to suicide. *"You need a nice solid piece of Falian steel in your hands to survive out there,"* she had said. The weapon was considerably heavier than his spear, made up of a solid steel shaft the size of his body, with a long-curved blade at the top. Unaccustomed to the weight of the new weapon resulted in his strike being no more than a flesh wound.

The upper hand was gone, and the cait roared its defiance, baring razor sharp tusks that dripped with saliva and double rows of matching incisors that ran all the way to the back of the predator's jaw. Its muscular body tensed, and talons lashed out fiercely for his midsection. Corbin used the voulge as a pole vault, bringing his body recklessly close to the curved blade on his way up, before another backflip brought him out of reach. No sooner did his toes touch the ground than the beast moved in again for another slash, but this time he was prepared, deftly dodging on the balls of his feet to the side and jabbing in, to sting the back of the monster's paw.

Without waiting for it to retaliate, he raced away. The cait quickly moved to pursue, lashing out as it ran after him, coming dangerously close to nipping his calves. Corbin pushed himself even harder, knowing that to slow for even a fraction of a second could mean his death. Lured into his trap, the cait slammed hard into the trunk of the tree that Corbin ran straight up, flipping onto the beast's back and straddling it like a horse. From this vantage point, he meant to dig the voulge down deep into the monster's neck.

"Behind you!"

This time the warning came with a flickering image, in his mind's eye, of the monster's tentacle-like tail stinging him. Understanding Baetylus' warning, Corbin spun around, still straddling the beast as it quickly adapted to having a rider. In an angry frenzy from being duped by its prey again, the cait whipped twin tails at his head. He blocked the oncoming assault with his weapon, weaving left then right.

The cait bucked hard to throw him off its back, but Corbin's legs were gripping it like a vice. Again, the tentacles came in for a sting, this time changing tactics to grab for his weapon, wrapping snakelike appendages around the voulge and yanking back hard. Corbin did not let go of his weapon, as he knew to do so would mean game over, and instead used the momentum to throw himself into the air. Letting go with one hand, he flicked open the wrist blades Fafnir had given him, and tore right through the stinging tails, sheering them both clean off the beast's body.

How it howled then, with bright green blood gushing out of the gaping wounds. Out of its mind in pain the feral beast fell on its back, desperately rubbing against the dirt as if it could somehow wipe away the pain. Standing firmly on the ground where he landed, Corbin hurled the voulge like a javelin. The blade dug deeply into the dangerous creature's exposed belly, where it tore a hole large enough for the monster's insides to spill out across the soil. The cait howled for its sisters, letting off an agonizing death rattle.

Confident that the stalking predator was slain, Corbin bent down to hold his knees and catch his breath. Adrenaline was still coursing through his body, leaving him shaky and anxious from the deadly encounter. Falling to his knees, Corbin gave a prayer of thanks to his god for warning of the danger.

"The wilds are a dangerous land, my son," Baetylus said in his mind, his voice as strong and clear as if the words had been spoken aloud. **"To survive out here you must remain ever vigilant. There is much yet to be done."**

"Blessed All-Father, your gifts are many," Corbin intoned, feeling the Great Crystal's presence slipping away, leaving him alone, cold and sweating in the dirt. Opening his eyes, Corbin could see a faint wisp of blue smoke trailing into the outcropping of trees past the radiant pool of water. Baetylus was giving him yet another gift, pointing in the direction of his wayward brother.

Quickly retrieving his weapon, Corbin searched the area and found there were indeed tracks around those trees to follow, but they were not Logan's. They were too light for his brother and the gait was wider. Someone had come through here recently, maybe not Logan, but someone the All-Father wanted him to find just the same. He followed them. The tracks were sure, straight and true, this man had known exactly where he was going. Soon enough Corbin crossed the chasm, using the makeshift log bridge. He caught the scent of burning wood on the breeze, so that coming around the bend to find a camp was not as surprising.

Three men were going about their business; one of them stripping the meat off a cait that hung to the side of his tent. The other was working to get bandages tied around his companion's arm, while he himself wore stripped rags, wrapped tightly about a bloody stump that used to be a leg.

Secrets of the Elders

"Ho there," Corbin announced himself, stepping into the camp with arms raised so as to not frighten the wounded men. The largest of them stopped his work butchering the cait, switching to a defensive posture with a dagger in hand.

"Rest easy wilders, I mean you no harm," Corbin said firmly.

"Ah, a guest!" Maxwell invited him into the camp with all the usual rigmarole, seating him by the fire. He explained how the camp had been ambushed by two caits, one of them taking his foot for a snack. Corbin offered his assistance, tending to the Maxwell's gored appendage with some of the provisions he brought for the journey.

"Is it normal for them to attack you here in the camp?" Corbin wondered. It did not seem like the men would be able to last long enough to build such a home if monsters like the cait were a common occurrence.

"The wild lands offer many dangers, wanderer, you can never tell just what might happen from day to day," Maxwell said. He slurred a little as he spoke, slightly deranged from the poppy milk he had been sipping to numb the pain.

Still, it was interesting to Corbin how the man evaded his questions. He noticed some of the wounds seemed to look different than he would have expected to come from the wild predators.

"Use your gift," Baetylus whispered in his mind.

Sitting back beside the fire, Corbin made a show of rubbing his hands to warm them, as he slipped into the psionic plane. He stared deep into the embers, relishing in the warmth dancing over his skin. Focusing his concentration, his mind probed Wart, who had taken over the work of gutting the captured cait. Corbin circled around the man's psyche searching for an opening. Dipping into the swirling thoughts, he caught a glimpse of the cait attack on the camp, followed by Bruno charging in to save his leader. A myriad of visions floated in the fog of the man's recent thoughts, before one starkly demanded his attention. It was an image of Logan fighting these men! Corbin instantly recoiled, loosening his grip on the man's thoughts. Maxwell noticed the flinch and sat up, nodding to Bruno who was stalking behind him.

"What troubles you, friend?" Maxwell asked. "You look like ye just seen a ghost then, eh?"

Corbin did not respond, shaking his head before speaking. "Think I nodded off for a second there, it *has* been a very long day." A lie followed by a truth.

The man watched him with an excited gleam in his eyes that Corbin had not noticed before. His eyes darted around the camp taking in the big picture. One of the tables was covered with many things, and also stained in blood, and the crates by the side of the main tent were also stained red as well. These men were remarkably fed for wilders. He could smell the stink of Bruno edging in close behind him and hear him drawing a long-curved blade.

"True enough," Maxwell cooed. "It *has* been a long day. You just warm up beside our fire and make yourself at home, wanderer." Corbin was careful not to betray his suspicion when Maxwell slowly reached for something behind him.

Corbin nodded and smiled back at the man then suddenly punched his hand hard into the air behind him, his gauntlet blade flicking like the tongue of a snake, running straight through Bruno's throat. In the same fluid movement, he spun to stand behind the dead man, using his body as a shield against Maxwell's fired crossbow bolt. Tugging his arm to pulling the wrist blade out, he heaved Bruno's limp body on top of Maxwell, burying the crippled man under two-hundred pounds of lifeless weight.

Wart came in hard, screaming in a high-pitched snarl, and cutting his skinning knife through the air in wide lunges that Corbin easily danced around. Bringing his voulge across his back, he severed the man's hand from his body and before he could even scream out in pain, spun back around, cleaving Wart's boil-covered head with one mighty swipe.

Maxwell had freed himself from under Bruno's dead weight and was scrambling away from the scene on his hands and knees, toward his tent. Corbin ran over to stomp his foot down hard on the man's back, pinning him in place.

"Argh!" Maxwell howled, wetting himself in the dirt.

"What did you do with my brother, dog?"

"Didn't do nothing...," Maxwell was cut off by Corbin's heel grinding deeper, twisting his lies into another scream of agony.

"I know he was here," Corbin snarled at the disgusting cannibal. "Don't even try lying to me. Where is my brother? Tell me now!"

"Okay...okay... Just, please...just stop. I'll tell you everything," Maxwell rasped.

"Now," Corbin demanded.

"He came here and attacked us in the night, never even saw him enter the camp. Was a little thievin' gnome with him too. Argh... oh please stop, it's the god's truth.... We offered him a place to stay, and he took 'vantage of our generosity..."

"Do you even hear yourself?" Corbin asked, truly dumbfounded at the extent of the man's corruption. "Do you honestly think I would fall for these fabrications?"

"By the Crystal's light, it's the honest truth. That's why we tried to kill ye, could see you were his brother. Ye look just like each other." A seed of doubt wriggled around in Corbin's mind. Did he even really know his brother? The All-Father himself had shown him an image of Logan killing the man in New Fal and warned that he was putting the entire kingdom in danger.

Maxwell could feel his growing trepidation. "Ye're brother's an outlaw now. Ye can't say this is a surprise, eh?"

Corbin slammed the pommel of his polearm down on the man's spine, shutting him up. Reaching back, he unlatched the Svalin from around his earlobe, releasing a tidal wave of thoughts that assaulted his mind. Images fluttered like crows past his psyche.

As he had suspected, these men killed many victims in the wild lands. They were cannibals that preyed off newly exiled Falians. He saw them try to kill Logan, in vain, and watched as his brother bested them and escaped to the north with a freed gnome.

Reaching up, he latched the Svalin back in place, warding off the onslaught of psychic energy. Pain lingered as a dull ache against his throbbing forehead. Maxwell had scurried away from him while he was in the trance and sat propped up beside his tent, aiming a crossbow directly at Corbin's head.

"Don't know what kind a demon magic ye trying to pull here wanderer. I felt you in my head! Recommend it's time you leave 'fore I have to put you down." Maxwell's hands trembled as Corbin stalked toward him fearlessly. "I'm tellin' ye boy, it best be time ye leave well enough alone!" he insisted louder, phlegm frothing from the corner of his dried lips.

Corbin took another step. With a click the released bolt skimmed past his cheek, grazing it just enough to leave a thin red line. He grimaced at the cannibal leader and buried the head of his voulge deep into the man's chest.

"May the All-Father have mercy on your sinful soul," Corbin said, as the light faded from the man's eyes.

He stood in silence for a while, the night breeze whipping his long hair across his face. His eyes scanned the camp, taking in the carnage he had just unleashed. Corbin had never killed another man, never even imagined himself capable of such a thing. Yet he had dispatched these wretches without a second thought. The weight of the world, of the past couple weeks…of it all, came crashing down heavily on his soul.

Weakly falling to his knees, Corbin Walker wept into the night.

Logan felt as though he had been walking in circles for days now. In reality, he knew it could only have been a couple hours since he and Bipp were forced to part ways. But paranoia was kicking in hard. He was not sure if it was the lack of oxygen in these smaller tunnels, or just the cramped feeling of rock closing in around him that set his mind racing. Tunnels like this did not exist in the expanse of New Fal, where the cavern soared high enough to fit entire mountain ranges and valleys.

After about an hour of walking, the rocky burrows began to close in so low he could reach up and feel the cold, damp ceiling. With each turn onto a new path, he hoped the tunnel would open back up, but instead the walls were closing in tighter and tighter the deeper he traveled.

At every fork he took out a lodestone, dangling it on a string, and went either north or east. Except for one split. That one went both directions, so he decided north trumped. He hoped.

That was hours ago and now he had to admit to himself that he might actually be lost, but stubbornly pressed on, refusing to be defeated by some dark tunnels. He used the idea of Dudje to spurn him forward. He was really looking forward to seeing Bipp's hometown, and maybe even trying some of the scrum the gnome kept going on about.

Isn't this just my luck? he wondered. *Finally go and do something Morgana could be proud of and where does it get me? Exiled from the kingdom...* Logan snorted to himself. It would be the last time he made that mistake...literally, since he could never go back. Pangs of sorrow racked him, thinking on Riverbell, lost forever to him.

Just as well, the village has its fill of honor from Corbin anyhow. He chuckled aloud. Not that his little brother's good nature was a bad thing, quite the opposite, it was just that sometimes he could be a little blind in his willingness to "*do the right thing.*" And that had always irked Logan.

Ahead the channel split into four sections, one was too tiny for him to get in, so he did not bother considering it. The other three were all regular size, so he pulled the lodestone out and let it dangle. It circled slowly in the air before leaning in the direction of north, pointing him toward the path to his right.

As Logan made his way deeper into the new corridor, the walls really pressed in. There was only about enough room left to raise his arms slightly, but that soon ended as the tunnel pinched to a narrow gap. Logan stopped to ponder his insanity at going any further. Surely, he should backtrack the way he came and start over? Side stepping through the tight opening, he squirmed ahead one slow step at a time, the walls so close together that his cheek rubbed against the jagged stone. Panic gripped the deeper he went. His legs became wobbly and if the walls weren't so tight, he may have fallen over.

Before long he was barely able to inch along, forcing himself to keep moving out of the fear that should he stop, he would never have the courage to go again. Visions of his childhood gripped him, remembering the time he was stuck on the highest branch of a ract tree, unable to come down until his father climbed up and got him.

Logan whispered to himself, "Just keep on moving. Don't think about the walls, just keep pushing forward."

The tunnel floor gradually became soft, like the fur rug in front of Morgana's fireplace. The feel of it settled his nerves a bit, taking the tension out of his legs. The crippling fear abated, and he began to shuffle along at a steady pace again. Soon the walls opening back up into a regular sized tunnel. The ceiling was still low enough to touch, but that sure as hell did not bother him anymore. The walls here were covered with a layer of light purple moss that drifted to a dull gray carpet over the floor of the passageway.

Never one to resist his own curiosity, Logan tentatively fingered some of the furry stuff. The moss was soft like velvet and let off an pungent aroma similar to the lavender Miss Iva grew in her garden. The scent of it lingered intoxicatingly over his hand and the wall sparkled where his finger had been. A circle of shimmering light worked its way from the spot, like the ripple of a pond, across the wall and spreading down the tunnel. One of the ripples hit a bump and split off into another and then another, radiating all the way down the corridor in shimmering luminescent circles. They were even on the ceiling and the walls, delightfully dancing in concentric patterns all around him!

The beauty of it all put Logan at ease with the world. He felt gleeful to walk along paths such as these. There was so much happiness to be found in life that he had never imagined before. Smiling, he playfully flicked the purple moss again while he worked his way through the tunnel, merrily whistling and thinking how much he looked forward to telling Bipp about this wonderful place. Life was so awe-inspiring and blessed. How could anyone's heart not be filled with love after seeing the beauty of Vanidriell? He wondered why he had ever been miserable in Riverbell, as it was probably the most perfect place to live in all of New Fal.

Even as Logan lay down to take a nap in the cozy, soft, loving embrace of the poisonous moss, and the reality that the bumps on the floor were actually the decomposed carcasses of other creatures that had made the same mistake of wandering into this tunnel, and even after he realized he would surely die here in the plant's dangerous trap of spores, even then...Logan Walker could still not help but smile and snuggle in for his nap.

Since Corbin left the cannibals' campsite, his brother's trail became simple to follow again. The gnome that accompanied his brother was not exactly the sneakiest of individuals, based on the sloppy trail he left in his wake. Again, he could see that neither of the men were even mildly concerned with covering their tracks. And why should they be? How could they possibly imagine they were being tracked? The sheer indifference Logan possessed filled Corbin with a wave of anger.

It was not long before he came across the corpse of the slain sauria lizard and the towering pile of rubble beside it. Corbin was trying to determine what kind of creature stuck out from under part of the rock. *Did someone cut a section of this things leg off?* he wondered, as he rubbed fingers across the dried wound, and then smelled the tips, determining it to be a pig.

The scene around him did not make much sense. It seemed there was a battle. The dead sauria was a clear testament to that. But how had these boulders buried a pig which looked freshly killed, and what was a hog doing in these tunnels beyond the forest anyhow? Corbin decided none of that mattered, picking back up on the gnome's trail. The only thing that was important was to find Logan as soon as possible. Every day he journeyed took him further from New Fal, and more importantly Elise.

"*Corbin. Behind you,*" a gentle voice whispered, tickling the hairs of his neck.

Corbin was startled when he turned around to find a man who had certainly not been there before standing beside the pile of rubble. He was older than most of the folk Corbin had met, with wrinkles lining his face that somehow revealed an underlying wisdom and a caring nature. A big bushy white beard hung from his face reaching all the way down to the midsection of his long white robes, which swayed back and forth, though no wind existed in this part of the tunnels.

The stranger leaned forward on a tall knotty oak staff and stared deep into Corbin's soul with twinkling silver eyes and a familiar smile. Corbin knew he should be on his guard, but something about the figure stopped him from brandishing his weapon.

"Who are you?" he tentatively asked.

"*You know who I am, Corbin Walker,*" the stranger confidently replied.

He did know. It made no sense, but he did. This was the god of his people. He was staring at the corporeal form of Baetylus himself! Immediately Corbin fell to the ground in an act of worship, groveling before his great master.

"Rise, my son," he kindly commanded, this time out loud, drifting across the dirt to tower over Corbin, and gently motioning for him to stand up. Rising he could see the figure was an elaborate apparition, faintly translucent, revealing the rocky wall through the visage. When it moved, Baetylus blinked in and out of the air slightly.

"Great All-Father, how is this possible?"

"Anything I wish is possible," Baetylus stated, an edge of annoyance lingering from the boy's question.

"Surely, I meant no disrespect toward you, oh Magnificent One," Corbin groveled.

"The gift you now possess allows me to speak directly to you. It is a rare thing for man to be bestowed such wonders. I have decided to directly help you bring Logan back to New Fal, lest many people will die in the kingdom of man due to the careless actions of one."

"As has been explained All-Father, but why do you come to me in this guise?" Corbin asked.

"When last we spoke it caused your mortal shell great pain. This was not my wish. Your human body is frail indeed, so I come to you in a way that is easier for your simple mind to comprehend," Baetylus said plainly, not meaning to insult the mortal, but speaking matter of fact.

"How truly blessed and honored I am," Corbin said.

"I will not be with you long, for your mind cannot handle it. Perhaps in time, but not quite yet. Follow me, my son." The visage drifted back to the rocky wall of tumbled boulders and pointed at its center. "Your brother is here."

Baetylus noticed the look of distress that washed over his servant and corrected. "Not *under* the stones, *past* them." To illustrate his point, he pushed his arm into the barrier, disappearing up to the elbow in the stone. Corbin exhaled a heavy sigh of relief. He felt unworthy to commune with his Lord after such a misunderstanding.

"Move the boulders out of the path and I will show you the way," Baetylus ordered.

Corbin set his voulge down and began trying to pry a massive rock from the barrier.

"Not like that...," Baetylus said. "Use your mind."

"Uh...what?"

"Move the rubble out of your way with your mind," Baetylus said as if it were common sense.

"Great Lord, please forgive me. I am but your ignorant servant. How would I move these mighty boulders just by thinking of it?"

"Fall into yourself and find the channel of power that attunes you to the universe," Baetylus said.

Hands resting at his sides, Corbin closed his eyes and did as he was instructed. After long minutes, focusing deeply on the inhale and exhale of the air around him, he felt a tingling sensation around the periphery of his being. He searched for it and felt as if a door was open wide, letting a flood of teeming psionic energy encircle his aura.

"Good, you are a natural,". Baetylus calmly encouraged him. "Now let the power flow into your soul."

Corbin opened a hole in the fabric of his mind, letting the pent energy funnel inside, slowly building up in intensity. It was like filling a barrel with rainwater, except instead of rain there was a living river of thought, filling fuller and fuller until his head felt ready to explode.

"Now release that store of energy against the barrier of rocks," Baetylus commanded.

Corbin could not stem the flow flooding into him, building up to a breaking point against his psyche. He scrambled futilely against the current that overwhelmed his will, desperately clambering for the energy to stop flowing. In a panic, he released it.

Shards of light spit forth from the center of Corbin's forehead, exploding in the air just short of his face. The rock wall was completely unfazed, while he on the other hand flew backward through the air, propelled by the sheer force of releasing the pent-up energy. He landed squarely atop the dead sauria. The tunnel walls were spinning as he sat up, trying to catch his breath and Baetylus' visage watched by the rocks, wearing a look that was either of amusement or annoyance, although he guessed it was a little of each.

"Perhaps we should just have you climb *over* the barrier instead," Baetylus offered.

"Agreed." Corbin rubbed his arm where it had hit the rough scales of the sauria's back.

Producing a grappling hook, Corbin swung the rope around in a circle, throwing it up and over the top of the rockslide, before pulling back to catch a firm hold. Testing the grip with his weight, he decided it was safe enough and carefully scaled the barrier. Baetylus suddenly appeared next to him, flickering in and out of existence higher and higher up the face of the rockslide, each time leaving a feint blue glow to mark where he had been.

"Follow my path to make it over more quickly," the god ordered. Corbin altered his ascent as instructed, finding the All-Father's path much easier to traverse, and quickly made his way over the other side.

"I must leave you now, my son," Baetylus said, regretting he could not stay.

"Please All-Father, stay with me…guide me just a little while longer," Corbin whined, longing to remain in his glory.

"It cannot be done without damaging your mind. Fear not, my child for I will light the way for you. Once you make it to the black gap, wet some cloth and wrap your face to stay safe. If you do not heed these words, it will be the end of your journey on this plane."

"I will, Great Baetylus," Corbin said. "Thank you for the gift of your wisdom!"

The white bearded visage faded, revealing a blank stone wall behind it. It was easy for Corbin to make his way through the winding tunnels. At every intersection Baetylus had left a feint glow on the ground to mark the way, speeding his progress considerably. Corbin did not even bother slowing his pace, blindly running down the paths marked by the All-Father. Soon enough the tunnels squeezed in, getting tighter and tighter, and he spied the dark gap ahead.

Pulling out a spare tunic, Corbin drenched it with the water from his flask, tying it around his head and covering his face, as was warned. Only his eyes remained uncovered as he slipped through the tight opening and into the purple moss-covered area.

He recognized the plant at once. It was called Morpheus' Embrace, known to release a poisonous spore that would make one delirious, knocking the unsuspecting victim out. The tunnel was virtually lined with the nasty stuff, which was pretty enough, but deadly to be around. The poisonous moss would intoxicate the unsuspecting victim into an induced state of delirium, with a strong desire to rest. Once asleep, its victims would never awaken, starving to death, and decomposing to feed the vile spreading plant.

Scanning the area, he could see a multitude of dead animals that had walked into the trap, only stripped carcasses remaining as bumps along the tunnel floor covered with a blanket of the stuff.

Suddenly Corbin's heart leapt with joy, spying his brother asleep around the bend. Logan was cozied up to the carpet of moss, like a babe resting in his mother's arms. He was a lot heavier than when they were kids, but Corbin could still carry him. With a grunt, he tossed Logan over his shoulder and pushed himself upright.

A wave of relief washed over him, knowing that he had found his brother. Now all the misunderstandings could be set right. Arch Councilor Zacharia would see Logan's truth, Riverbell would be safe once more, and life could return to normal.

Chapter 17

"Riverbell will burn to the ground." Fafnir cruelly promised through the thick iron bars of Lady Cassandra's cell. Not for the first time, she wondered how she could have ever underestimated the crooked lawman's reach, and his audacity. When soldiers stormed her house, she had demanded to know the meaning of their intrusion, only to be met with shackles. Somehow, the greedy little weasel had learned of her gift to Corbin Walker, no doubt through spies he must have among her own household staff.

"The council will *never* approve such a thing," Cassandra scoffed. "You have really crossed the line this time, Fafnir. There is no way the rest of the Elders will tolerate you locking a widow of the twelve in your filthy little dungeon."

"As if you matter to them, silly old witch. *I* am the law, and *you* have violated the decree of our beloved council," Fafnir cackled, shrugging off her empty threats.

"You know very well...," Cassandra began.

He cut her off, with a whack of his cane against the bars. "Save your drivel for the council. The law is the law, magical practice is forbidden," Fafnir said, referring to the ritual she had performed on Corbin Walker, which *was* forbidden over a century and a half ago.

Magic was no longer to be practiced, although many of the Falians still did, and was *never* to be taught to the younglings. Only the original pilgrims, of which a mere handful remained, could still grasp the possibilities the universe had to offer. It was deemed that the naïve younger Falians could bring danger to their sanctuary of New Fal if they were to delve into the magical arts, repeating the mistakes of the past.

"Don't lecture me about the laws my own husband helped write, you impertinent, hypocritical fool," Cassandra snapped. "Who in the blazes does not use a little magic in their life?"

"Ah, that may be true, but none of us would go so far as to invoke the power and produce an apprentice." Fafnir rubbed his pointer fingers together mocking her. "Naughty naughty..."

"I swear on the seven you will never get away with this!" Cassandra slammed the bars in frustration.

The gate opened with a rusty groan, and a hooded man stepped into the single celled room. Magistrate Fafnir cordially bowed, like a sniveling rat, to the new arrival. Elder Viktor removed his hood as he came into Cassandra's view, stopping in front of her cell.

"Thank goodness you are here Viktor. This scoundrel thinks he can win a seat by throwing his competition in a cell!" Cassandra said, trying to remain stoic, though she was secretly relieved to see her husband's longtime friend come to rescue her.

The man pulled Fafnir in close to him, huddled in whispers she could barely make out, before turning to face her. "Shut your mouth witch," Viktor said coldly. "How dare you presume to utter my name? That is *Elder* Viktor to you." Viktor sneered in a way she had never seen before. How could he be speaking to her this way, after all the years of friendship shared between their families, after all the hardship they endured together molding New Fal into a thriving human civilization?

"Fafnir, is their some more bloody witchcraft afoot here? Do my eyes deceive me, or has the righteous old bat finally found herself at a loss for words?" Viktor taunted.

"I do believe you are correct, most esteemed one," Fafnir said, bobbing his bald head like a vulture.

"This must be some mean-spirited joke, Viktor? Surely this cannot be real?" Cassandra gasped.

"Again, she does it? That is *Elder Viktor,* you imbecile. All these years having to listen to your fool of a husband preaching and preaching to us. Now I'm finally rid of the self-righteous, sanctimonious bastard and you really thought I would want to hear his echoes from your mouth in the Council of Twelve day in and day out?" Viktor did not expect an answer, but cruelly enjoying the look on her face.

Cassandra felt the world closing in around her. How had she missed this man's hatred for her all these years? Had there been no signs? He stood at her wedding. He was there from the time their children were baptized in the light to the time they were given funeral rights. To think all these years he had hated Alan, it was something she could not find the ability to comprehend. The idea of it pulled the strength from her legs, causing her to feebly walk backward and sit on her musty cot, all the while staring back at him in disbelief.

"Arch Councilor Zacharia will never let this happen to me," she stammered weakly.

Viktor laughed, as if she had told the funniest joke, slapping Fafnir's arm to see if he heard the same. The Magistrate leaned in with a sinister grin that cut through the shadows. "The Arch Councilor will obey the law," Fafnir promised. "You know he will see the truth and you will not see an inch of mercy from that man."

"By this time next week, you'll be hanging out there in the square," Elder Viktor promised.

The men were still laughing, making jokes to each other about her plight, as they left. For the first time in Lady Cassandra Alderman's very long life, she found herself deeply alone, and *very* afraid of the future.

An aroma of roasting meat lulled Logan away from the dream he was enjoying. As a child, he was running through fields of golden grass, laughing while he playfully hid from his mother.

"Where did my little bean go? Hmmm... now where could he be?" She teased, knowing he could hear her, and also exactly where he was hidden. He bent over, trying to hold back his giggles with tiny hands.

Stirring on his side in the dirt, he still wore a smile, as the feel of it swirled on the edge of his thoughts. The mouthwatering aroma of food stirred Logan from his slumber. Something was roasting in the nearby crackling fire.

Mother must have dinner almost ready, he thought. The feel of rope binding his wrists snapped him out of the fantasy, like the sharp backhand of reality. Logan's mother was dead, and he did *not* know where he was, or why he was tied up. Trying to remain as still as possible, he craned his neck to look around from under the wool blanket someone had laid over him.

A fire *was* crackling not too far from him, and something *did* smell wonderful as it cooked. At least that part was not a dream. He could make out that he was no longer in the tight tunnels, the cavern seemed to open high above again, feeling more familiar, like the area back home, except a little more devoid of plant life.

"I see you're awake," a familiar voice noted. Firm hands shifted his bound body into a sitting position facing the fire and then his captor walked to the opposite side, turning the skewered meat over the flames as they danced across his face.

"Was it all a bad dream?" Logan asked, hoping the entire surreal experience was something his mind had conjured up.

"I'm afraid not, big brother, though I wish that were the case," Corbin replied, with an unfamiliar edge of spite lacing his tone.

"I suppose it couldn't be. If it were a dream, Elise would be the one here cooking for me," Logan joked, still unsure what to make of the situation.

"I'm here to bring you back home," Corbin said, devoid of emotion.

"That's great for you, but I'm not going," Logan said as casually as he could, shifting his arms to try and get some blood circulating into his hands.

"Well, I could always put you back where I found you in the Morpheus Embrace," Corbin offered, though they both knew it to be an empty threat.

"Oh, you're a regular riot today… Why am I tied up?"

"Sorry," Corbin said, though he was not sorry in the least. "I cannot risk you running off. There's too much at stake. Besides what were you thinking leaving the palace in the first place?"

"What was I thinking? Oh, just that dying was not a position I would like to be in. Hmmm…or maybe, I was thinking I would not even be in this mess if my fool of a brother didn't drag me to Fal in the first place. *Oh Logan, we must go warn them.* Why, so they could throw me over the wall?" Logan snapped.

"What did you expect them to do, throw you a parade for stabbing that poor gnome to death?" Corbin yelled back, determined not to back down from him for once.

"You really are something, you know that? Always flapping your gums when you don't have a clue what you're talking about!" Logan gritted his teeth, wishing he could snap the rope and give the little brat a once over.

"Oh yeah, it's always everyone else's fault but your own, same old nonsense. The world's out to get my big brother, he *never* deserves it," Corbin said sarcastically, while turning the spit over the fire again.

"I never deserve to get caught, if that's what you mean," Logan mumbled under his breath.

"What did you say?" Corbin demanded.

"I said, you can take that spear of yours and stick it up your...," Logan began.

"They are going to excommunicate Riverbell from New Fal," Corbin flatly cut him off.

Logan's mouth hung open for a moment then he clamped it shut and stared in disbelief at his brother. "That's just...that's...insane. Why would they?" His typical bravado was momentarily stemmed trying to wrap his mind around the concept.

"The council is saying you killed that gnome because he found out about some conspiracy of Riverbell to overthrow the government. Some are saying the attack on the capitol was actually riled up by *our* people, and if *you* do not go back, the kingdom will cut ties with Riverbell, permanently."

"Those dirty bastards," Logan growled.

"Yep, there you go again, blaming everyone else but yourself," Corbin shook his head, disgusted and annoyed.

"Corbin, you don't understand. This all must be that sneaky snake Fafnir's doing. We need to...," Logan tried to tell his brother all he had witnessed, but again was sharply cut off by Corbin's indignant attitude.

"We? There is no *we* anymore, there is just me. Me and my people of Riverbell. All my life you have never once had a single nice thing to say about our goodly village. It's always been about juvenile dreams of making a name for yourself in the capitol...for a *'real life'*. In just two days you sat at the center of two murders. That's one for one. Tell me something big brother, how is the *real life* treating you?" Corbin's words stung like thorns, and Logan wilted under the look of hatred in his eyes.

"Corbin, if you just listen to me, I can explain...," Logan said softly.

"No. I'm done listening to your false words. I've been listening to them all my life. It's nothing but a pack of lies, all of it...just excuses to justify why you are so selfish. You are going to sit there and blame goodly Magistrate Fafnir for all your problems? An honorable lord, probably the next to sit with the Twelve, is somehow the reason you stabbed that gnome to death? Fafnir, who has been *nothing* but kind to our people in this time of need, bringing gifts and encouragement to Elise and me. This is where you dare to lay blame?"

Logan had never seen Corbin like this before. Something had changed in him. He was normally a calm, reserved man, but now he was really getting worked up and sounded like an entirely different person altogether.

"Listen to reason, man," Logan said.

"Just shut your mouth. In the morning I'm bringing you back to New Fal, and just in time too, with only eight days to spare."

"So that's it then, going to toss your brother to the wolves just like that? My life is that insignificant to you, eh?" Logan said somberly, seeing even now, reuniting with his brother out here in the wild lands, that he was still truly going to be alone for the rest of his life.

"Oh please...when we get back to Fal you will be seen in front of the entire Council. Arch Councilor Zacharia has promised to see the truth and Riverbell will be freed from suspicion." Corbin waved away the notion of somehow abandoning his brother by bringing him to justice.

"You will excuse me if I do not share your blind faith in the system," Logan snorted derisively.

"Well, either way you *are* going back," Corbin flatly stated, biting off a hunk of the cooked meat.

"Yeah, probably not...," Logan said.

"Didn't I just tell you to shut your mouth?" Corbin snapped back, just as a tiny frying pan let out a gong, batting across the back of his skull. Corbin spit his food out into the fire, eye's bulging from their sockets as his body slumped sideways.

Bipp hopped up, down, and side to side, doing a happy dance, turning to shake his rump, which to Corbin looked like six gnome arses waggling at him as the cavern blurred.

"Geez, did you have to hit him so hard?" Logan asked, concerned even though he could not help laughing.

"That's a strange thing to be worried about when you're being rescued, ain't it?" Bipp said, smoothing back his wild mane of silver hair, curious to understand the ways of humans.

"He's my brother." Logan explained, turning about so the gnome could untie his hands.

"Oh...strange family customs your people have," Bipp said as he pulled the tight knots loose.

"It's a long story. Grab my pack. We have to get out of here quickly," Logan urged, rubbing the sore burning skin around his wrists.

Bipp ran back around the fire, hopping over Corbin's prone groaning body. Snatching the pack, he gave the man another loud thwack on the head for good measure.

"Would ya stop that already?" Logan scolded.

"Yeah, yeah, geez, that's some gratitude you're giving me," Bipp whined, handing him the pack.

"I am eternally grateful to you Bipp, I guess now we are even, eh?" Logan said and then turned to his brother. "*Go home Corbin.* Forget about me. Tell the Council I died in a rockslide or something." He nodded his farewell and the companions headed away from the campfire. "How in the blazes did you find me anyhow?" he asked Bipp.

"Well, that's a long story, you see...," the gnome began recounting his tale.

Corbin tried to watch in a daze, as the two moved off into the distance, bickering with each other like an old married couple. "I guess the gnome can be sneaky after all...," he muttered to himself, just before losing consciousness.

"Thank you for your support milady," Jayne bowed respectfully to Elder Esther Bran.

"You tell Lady Cassandra I'll be bringing the others by on the 'morrow. Fafnir will not get his way this time!" Elder Esther vowed as her butler opened the door to let the young woman out of the estate.

Following another bow, Jayne stepped out into the cool night air. Shivering, she pulled her trench coat tighter around her waist. Her boots clapped loudly against the cobblestone, ringing in the empty night streets and spreading the swirling low hung fog away from her.

It had only been six hours since Lady Cassandra sent the telepathic command. Yet in that time Jayne had raced around the city, speaking with three other council members, who were still loyal to the memory of Alain, bless his soul. Madame Esther marked the fourth and that should be more than enough support to help sway the Council's decision, freeing Cassandra from the awful dungeon cell. On top of that, it had only taken the slightest suggestion from Jayne to have the labor leaders from three of the lower levels rouse up a mob. She imagined right now, on the other side of the city, they were causing quite a fuss, demanding the Lady Cassandra's release in protest outside of section six. Magistrate Fafnir was going to have his hands full tonight.

A water pail rolled loudly into the street from the back of a waste cart she had just walked past, startling her from her thoughts. Peering down the empty lane, she could see no one was about. Every doorway seemed vacant, and she reasoned that no one would be out for a stroll at this time of night. Jayne often carried a nightstick as protection, though Lady Cassandra insisted it was unnecessary. She flicked her wrist, uncoiling the weapon now and crept slowly toward the large trash bin. Edging in, she leaned forward, twisting to see just beyond the low squat container.

Many different scenarios were playing out in her mind as she anticipated the moment when her stalker would jump out. She would punch him in the throat then knee him in the groin, or just use her nightstick to shatter his kneecap, or maybe she would feign a swing of her nightstick and instead head butt him before calling for the night watchman. All these thoughts and more ran through Jayne's head as she circled the trash bin, but none of them occurred. She did something else. She yelped. For some reason she found the sight of a small mangy alley cat hissing and running between her legs far more frightening than any stalker could have ever been.

Jayne silently cursed herself for letting the stray animal scare her so, and put her weapon away, hoping no one saw the embarrassing exchange through a curtained window. At least the boost of adrenaline warmed her, providing the extra boost she needed to hurry back to Cassandra's house. The place was so empty and cold without her mentor. When the lawmen had come to take her away, they had left the house in such disarray. The staff was busy getting things back in order, when Jayne had found Cassandra's handmaid, Rosa, on the rooftop garden, weeping over the flowers her master had grown with so much love.

"F-first Master Alain, n-now the Lady…what are we to do?" Rosa had sobbed. Jayne comforted her, telling the woman that everything would be fine, and intending to make that a reality. After everything Lady Cassandra had done for her, taking her in off the streets, educating her, giving her a life of meaning, there was no way Jayne was going to sit by while the corrupt Fafnir…

Her thoughts were cut off again, and this time she was sure it was no cat behind her. Something had been shuffling softly against the stone and when she stopped short, it went just a second longer. Jayne started walking again, her boots clicking on the cobblestone and once more, the soft shuffling began. She realized without a doubt that someone was following her! Jayne walked a little faster then stopped with a spin to catch the stalker. As she did so, a shadow slithered into the corner of a nearby building.

A cold dread fell over her. Something about the way her follower moved told her this was not something to face alone. Not that she was one to frighten easily. After all she had seen on the streets what more there was to fear really? But this was different, she could almost feel the raw danger permeating off this person, setting off alarms in her head. Jayne could almost smell it in the air like a burning casket had just paraded by. As if in answer to her thoughts, the stalker maliciously grinned at her with gleaming teeth that cut through the shadows like a blade.

All her energy was thrown into a pure flight of terror, moving on the verge of hysteria to escape the pursuer. Jayne raced down the street, fearing to look back, terrified of what was in those shadows watching her. Her legs pumped harder and harder, furiously pushing through the night. Jayne felt that if she slowed, even in the slightest, the shadow would be there to take her.

Her heart surged with hope, rounding the corner into the alleyway behind Cassandra's house. Just up ahead the ladder came into view, singing to her of sanctuary. As she closed the space to it arms reached out from the side alleyway to wrap around her. Jayne let out a shrill scream and batted her fists at the man, struggling to free herself.

"Whoa...calm down, Jaynee!" John announced, quickly pulling back with palms outstretched. He had never seen Jayne react like that in all the times he had snuck up on her over the years. He calmly showed her his palms again, eyeing the nightstick she had flicked open to its full length.

"John Gates, by the Crystal, you scared me half to death," Jayne said. John was a pain in the arse. He was charming enough at times, but the constant mooning over her was tiring. He would have been the last person she wanted to see even an hour ago, as she obviously did not have time for silly flirtatious games this evening, but at that moment, the sight of him was nothing short of a godsend. Jayne hugged him in relief, using the maneuver to look over his shoulder down the lane.

"Someone was chasing me," Jayne whispered in his ear, not wanting the pursuer to know what she was saying.

John spun around, looking down the narrow path with zero tact. "I don't see anyone..."

"Right, well let's not stay out here and wait for him to show up," Jayne said, beckoning him to follow her up the ladder.

"Is this one of those weird roleplaying things you are into?" John asked, happily getting an eyeful of her perfectly rounded behind.

"Just get inside, and stop checking me out," Jayne giggled, shoving him inside the house. Once the door was secure, firmly clicking back in place, she slipped off her trench coat. She narrowed her eyes at him. "Anyway, what were you doing out there at this time of night?"

"Rosa said you went out, and I figured I'd wait until you came back" John explained, which was normal for the man. He had been trying to court her for some time.

"John, I really do not have time for silly flights of fancy right now. Things are dire, and I have to be..."

"I already heard all about Lady C. Are all the rumors true? Has she been locked away?" He was acting uncharacteristically serious. Normally life was a joke to the rich boy.

Jayne nodded. "I've been out gathering support for her all day and night. Tomorrow we are all going down to section six to hash out the broader details with Lady Cassandra. Fafnir won't know what hit him by the time we get through." Jayne said, excited by all the backing she had mustered.

"Good, that's exactly what I wanted to talk to you about. You see, I have a plan, and it's going to be the icing on the cake." John was eager to tell her his idea. Jayne smiled at the young man, he could be a pompous arrogant spoiled aristocrat, but at this moment she saw him in a whole new light, one she could actually relate to, and instantly decided she liked him better this way.

Listening to his plan, Jayne smiled confidently. It was a good one, and tomorrow it was going to knock the socks off Lady Cassandra.

CHAPTER 18

Over the hill, nestled in a deep valley ahead, the town of Dudje came into view. It was a wondrous sight to behold, gnome craftsmanship being what it is. Logan figured that there had to be hundreds of homes nestled in the town, and according to Bipp, each household contained dozens of family members living together.

Nearby to the west where the cavern ended, water foamed high up the face of a wall. A majestic waterfall roared there, forming the Green Serpent River at its base, which cut directly through the valley before snaking northeast. The gnomes had carved a massive face around the deep hole from which the water flowed, giving the illusion of a mighty crowned gnome roaring while frothing water pouring from his lips. The waterfall was some distance away from Dudje, but from this vantage point, he could see it clearly and it made the air misty, smelling like sea foam and sandalwood. At the falls base, there was a large wooden water wheel slowly spinning in the flowing river.

Bipp explained that his people captured energy from the moving water, which they then funneled along the town in lines that were attached to the various buildings. Twinkling lights ran up and down the oddly winding streets, giving the place an amazing presence in the underworld. All along the river, barges made their way in and out of the trade port, transporting goods to a network of other gnome settlements.

The hill dropped into a steep decline, and the path became a series of carved steps. This was safer than the shale they had been traversing, which was slick from the spray of the waterfall, yet still tricky for a big-footed human to manage, the steps being carved for gnomish-sized travelers and all. The path came right down to the edge of the riverbank, before it cut sharply right, away from the water and into a wide hand carved tunnel, boring under the next hill.

Dudje could only be accessed from the south by this route, and they had wisely built it in a such a way as to provide a natural barrier to their settlement. They made their way quickly through the burrow and on the other side the ceiling opened back up to the cavern. The walls widened slightly to the sides and Logan was alarmed to see that overhead sat four armored soldiers, spears pointed down at them. From the top of the town wall in front of them, a blue-bearded guard shouted down.

"Whatcha be wanting wanderers?"

Bipp raised his finger ready to answer when one of the soldiers overhead jubilantly interrupted him. "Blimey, it's none other than Brillfilbipp Bobblefuzz hisself, back from the dead!"

The rampart overhead filled with a gleeful commotion at the news. Two of the soldiers even dropped their spears and broke into a merry jig, twirling around each other with one arm locked in the others elbow. The third clapped his thick hands excitedly, carelessly dropping his spear to join in. The tip of it dug firmly into the ground between Logan's feet. The gatekeeper roared with laughter, throwing the switch and opening the massive stone gates outward.

Bipp looked to Logan, down to the spear by his feet, then back up and gave a nervous chuckle. "Sorry about that… The boys can get a little excitable at times."

Logan just shrugged. No sooner had they passed through the gates than a small crowd of nearby gnomes came scurrying over to greet Bipp. Walking through the streets, they were swarmed by the little people, each making sure to greet Bipp, welcoming him home with pats on the back and questions followed by more questions. The children were the worse of the lot, but several women also assaulted Bipp with unexpected kisses, some more passionately than others. It would seem he had become quite the lady's man, especially now that his story had spread through the town.

It went a little like this; Farmer Torkin ran back into town to alert the watch that Bipp fought off a ten-foot roc-bat that was trying to steal their crops. He was said to have battled the creature, like a classic hero of gnomish myth, when another twice its size swooped out of the air to carry him away. Apparently, Bipp bravely fought the bat hundreds of feet in the air shouting, "For Thorgar's glory!" before disappearing into the wilds, forever lost to his people.

213

Bipp laughed heartily at the ridiculous tale, which was currently being retold by the town barber. Logan noted that though his friend did not confirm the story to be true, he also did not go out of his way to deny it. He looked to be having so much fun with all the attention that Logan could hardly fault him for it, especially after all the white lies *he* had told over the years.

While the gnomes of Dudje were surely excited and merry to have Bipp back among them, there were also many distrustful looks thrown Logan's way. Even after Bipp's retelling of his capture and rescue from the cannibal's camp, most of the cheers were oddly aimed the gnome's direction, celebrating the fictional daring-do-whether tale they preferred of his escaping.

Not that Logan really minded, as entranced as he was by the architecture of this town. Once they were past the gates, the road was paved with cobblestones, periodically breaking into elaborately carved slate steps with metal railings that were fashioned in the shapes of slithering snakes and dragons, their scales serving a dual purpose of aesthetics and a textured gripping. The entire town was built upon stone hills, with roads winding up and down, curving around higher and higher to the tops of small, rounded peaks.

All along the charming roads were strange structures. They were unlike the wooden cabins he grew up in or the buildings in Fal, which were carved from the very rock of the original mountain his ancestors had settled. Instead, the buildings of Dudje were made of brick and something Bipp called plaster. The sides of some held large iron wheels attached to old pipes entering and leaving the structures, creating a network that attached them all together. When he asked Bipp what they were for, he whispered, *"the plumbing."* Logan found that somewhat gross to think about.

Why would anyone want to relieve themselves in their own home?

Even more interesting, the houses were built on top of each other, like stacked piles of books set at odd angles. One shop sold radishes from a squat rectangular building to the side of which, iron rung steps spiraled to a home cropping out from the rooftop that was tall and narrow. Most of the area was covered with a type of sphagnum moss, which was apparently fantastic for growing flowers and attracted plenty of small cave finches of all colors.

Another spectacle he had never seen before were the colorfully spotted mushrooms that dotted the landscape of neighborhoods and shops. Some had wooden swings hanging from them, or small gnomish children kicking a ball on top. The town was truly awe inspiring with its merry residents and brightly lit streets.

The deeper they made it into Dudje, the less the town folk swarmed them, until they were finally left walking side by side with only a handful of Bipp's friends, and one woman who stared at him with a sparkle in her eyes. During their travels, he told Logan much of Clara, whom he had been chasing after for years now. Logan guessed the heroic tales Farmer Torkin had spun swayed her to see what she had been missing all these years.

"We are almost at the town hall!" Bipp proudly exclaimed. The news sent butterflies fluttering in Logan's stomach. There was a lot at stake here for him. If the meeting with Mayor Fimbas went well then, he would have a home again. But there was that lingering doubt that his request would be denied.

The rounded building that was the town hall stuck out of the scenery like the top of some buried Elder's bald head. It was considerably larger than the stacks of homes surrounding it. The place was carved from a single massive block of stone and looked like it could withstand the ages right up until the end of time. The gray structure was flecked with mushroom-capped domes, and jutting guard towers rested all around it. At the top of a long series of steps, two statues of massive basilisks sat on either side of the entrance, as if left by the gods to guard the place for eternity.

Bipp's retinue quieted to a respectful murmur once inside the hall. High above Logan's head a grand fresco decorated the rounded ceiling, and the interior of the structure was lined with finely carved cherry wood walls. Another set of wooden doors, again tall as the ceiling, sat closed in front of them, at the end of a bright crimson carpet where the hallway curved around the center of the building's inner circle, dotted with alcoves, each showcasing marble statues of different ancient kings and heroes of myth.

A group of heavily armored gnomes blocked the group's path, spears pressed together to form a barricade. Their leader folded his thick hairy arms over a chest of chainmail with animal skins poking out from the sleeves and glowered at them under a conical helmet that covered the top of his large head.

"Falians ain't allowed in the mayor's chambers, Bipp. You should know better," The scruffy looking gnome informed Bipp, from beneath his wildly unkempt salt and pepper beard, and frayed eyebrows.

"Rest easy Grubblefrop, this here is a good friend of mine," Bipp said merrily enough. "Saved me from some cannibals looking to make themselves a gnome sammich."

"I don't care if'n King Ul'krin himself stepped out of the grave and escorted the man here, only Mayor Fimbas himself can give the order for entry to the *human*. And ye got a better chance of seeing me dance a jig than that happening," Grubble growled, the scars on his face twitching. Bipp moved to protest, but the gnome scowled at him with black pupils and shot Logan a dark look, as if his very presence offended the warrior. Bipp's face grew red, and he looked as if steam might shoot out of his ears.

"It's okay, Bipp," Logan said. "I'll wait right here while you go on in and talk with the Mayor."

Bipp cooled off quickly, winking at Logan to signal his show of anger was only a ploy. "Fine Grubblefrop, but my friend is staying right here in the hall."

"Aye, all the better for me to keep an eye on the human anyhow."

As Bipp approached the massive doors, Logan was amused to see a smaller four-foot portal swing inward from the center. When it shut, not even the faintest hint of an outline remained.

Hours trickled past slowly in the great curved hallway, and Logan could only pace back and forth, patiently waiting for his friend to come out. The entire time the warriors watched him warily, with Grubble not even trying to hide his look of disdain. Echoes of conversation from inside the chamber could be heard, but the words themselves were too muffled to make out.

When the bell gonged from the roof of the building, announcing the time for second supper had arrived, the soldiers took turns pulling out small parcels to eat. They supped on candied mushrooms, potato stews, and other richly smelling foods, while the rest kept their vigil over Logan, daring him to try some human trickery. Finally, the small wooden door opened outward once more, catching one of the guards by surprise and knocking him face first into his companion's stew.

"Send in the human," boomed a voice from the inner chamber, leaving Grubblefrop with an expression of sheer bewilderment. The blood drained from his face, and he began frantically looking from the open doorway to Logan.

A cocky smiled spread across Logan's face as he strutted past the rude little warriors, "Guess you owe me that jig, huh?"

Inside, the antechamber was much smaller than he could have anticipated, the ceiling dropped down and this round room was dotted with doorways to other offices. Book-lined shelving circled half the room, and the floor was covered with a large cherry red rug woven with patterns of flowers and mushrooms.

A large gnome, being roughly four feet, which for his race was big indeed, sat behind a long desk built from walnut wood, a very rare material in Vanidriell. He sat perched in a tall, stately chair, which was lined with a matching cherry red, plush fabric, wearing a golden circlet around his head. The headdress was set with a flawless polished emerald that matched his thick mossy-green hair and muttonchops. Strange thin swirling lines danced in patterns on his smooth forehead and cheeks. They were neither painted on nor scars. Bipp's smiling face popped around one of the seats facing the desk, and he happily motioned for Logan to come sit beside him.

"Thank you for seeing me, Mayor Fimbas," Logan said, trying to sound as respectful as possible, but the gnome bristled up at him.

"We do not speak until the mayor allows us," Bipp whispered, explaining the man's ire.

"Did not think to teach the Falian the proper decorum of court, Brillfilbipp?" the mayor said in a gruff voice, to which the little gnome could only reply with a shrug and an innocent smile.

"Falian, I have heard much of your deeds to rescue our goodly engineer, Brillfilbipp Bobblefuzz. For this you have the gratitude of Dudje." Although he was brimming inside to hear the praise, Logan held his composure and bowed his head, trying to convey he was humbled by the man's words.

"Bipp here has brought the matter of your living arrangements to the attention of this office, petitioning to allow you a place among our people," the mayor said, prompting Bipp to punch his friend's forearm and wiggle his eyebrows in delight.

"That request has been denied," Fimbas stated flatly. Logan felt like someone had punched him in the gut and his stomach churned sickly at the news. Bipp looked much the same. "You may speak now."

"I don't understand, Mayor," Logan said. "From what I saw walking through town it looks like there is more than enough room here for me, and surely Bipp can attest to my honorable intentions. Is it a matter of earning my keep? There has to be plenty I could do for you around here?" Logan's mind raced for an idea that would sway the mayor's decision.

"The bottom line here is that we do not know you," Mayor Fimbas said. "All we do know is that you are a *Falian*."

Logan furrowed his brow.

"Ah, I see our little engineer has not told you? Please you must pardon his mistake. It is easy for us to forget just how short human lives are. You see, Falians are forbidden in the town of Dudje, as they are in most of the settlements of Vanidriell."

Logan was flabbergasted by that news. "To be honest, Mayor, just a few weeks ago I had no idea any other settlements even existed in the wild lan...er...in *Vanidriell*. All my life we have only ever heard of New Fal and our neighboring kingdom, Malbec."

"Typical Falian arrogance... To teach that anything outside their stolen kingdom is nothing more than *wild lands*. I do not fault you this ignorance lad, it was bred into you," Fimbas casually laid the insult at his feet.

"Please Mayor...I do not know what the people of New Fal did to earn such hatred," Logan said. "But being an outcast of the kingdom myself, it is only with good intentions that I come before you."

"This was mentioned earlier. Tell me more about becoming an exile," Fimbas prompted. While Logan retold the story of his journey to Fal, warning the city and fighting off the insect horde, the mayor looked quite bored. Though when he came to the part about meeting Mr. Beauford, the man perked up and his face grew heavy indeed to learn that the goodly gnome was murdered, listening intently to the tale of the ebony skinned assassin. Once Logan's tale was over the mayor sat there in silence, slowly turning the rings on his chubby fingers.

"That is quite the yarn you have knitted, Logan Walker of Riverbell. How do I know you are telling the truth of it?"

"I could ask the same of you in a different way, why did you invite me into your chamber without taking away any of my weapons, knowing I could easily jump across this desk and murder you? The answer is simple, because you trust in Bipp, who trusts in me, a mutual feeling that we have both earned. You bring me in here to toy with me, knowing you are not going to let me stay, yet teasing me with hope. What reason could I possibly have to lie?" Bipp widened his eyes both at his friend's bold words, well intentioned as they were, and at Mayor Fimbas who was rumbling with laughter.

"That very question reveals your youth, and the deep disconnect between human and gnome thinking. I can see you truly believe the idea of lying over this would be absurd which gives me a glimmer of optimism that perhaps there is still hope for the humans of New Fal after all. Then again most likely not, since they chased *you* out, eh? As for being defenseless, are you really foolish enough to believe I would allow such a thing?"

The gnome directed his attention around the ceiling where dozens of miniature crossbows were being held steady through circular portholes, all pointed at Logan's seat.

"Mayor, I did not mean to...," Logan said.

219

"Don't worry lad, I know you were not threatening me, and I see the truth in you. Something my great Uncle Beauford no doubt saw as well. Otherwise, why would he have taken you under his wing in such a short time?" As uneasy as he was to learn that dozens of crossbows were pointed at him, Logan was dumbfounded to hear this.

"Mayor Fimbas, I had no idea you were related to Mr. Beauford. Sir...there was one other task he charged me with before dying...," Logan said, unsure how to proceed.

He reached into his vest to pull out the pendant he had been keeping safely tucked away beside his heart, and presented it across the desk to the mayor, who grew wide eyed and sucked in his breath. Fimbas gently took the teardrop shaped jewel, dangling it before his eyes in awe. Overhead the gnomes began whispering excitedly. "I swore to Beauford that I would get this to his family and am humbled to know that task has been completed."

The mayor eyed him as if he had forgotten the man was in the room. Putting the pendant in his own jacket pocket, the gnome tapped a finger to his lips, studying Logan. "It is very interesting though, your tale. What I am sure you are not aware of is the fact that my Great Uncle was not only a wealthy merchant in New Fal, but also, and long before he settled with the humans, a famous Seer among our folk."

"What is a seer, sir?" Logan asked.

"Not a seersir," Fimbas said. "A *Seer*, it's like a prophet, means he often divined the future."

"Kind of like a fortune teller?" Logan asked.

"Not in the same way you mean it, with scarves and cards and such. No, this is less a telling and more of a glimpse. Beauford was never known for being overly open to strangers. Him taking you into his employment, not even knowing you, that rings of something from ages ago," Fimbas thought aloud, trying to grasp a memory that made sense in this context.

"Are you saying he saw Logan in a divination?" Bipp asked, sparking the bridge in the mayor's mind.

The mayor tossed Bipp a cross look at him for interrupting his train of thought, even though it had helped form the connection he was trying to grasp. Snapping his fingers, Fimbas stood up and circled the desk, motioning for the pair to follow. Grumbling across the room, he thumbed across a shelf of dusty tomes until he found what he was looking for. Flipping through the worn volume, titled *Divinization's of the Fourth Age by Beauford Bomble,* the Mayor found the entry he was looking for and tapped on the page.

"Yes, yes, here it is, I remember coming across this when I was a wee lad," He read on.

'In the waning month of Farl,

Triumphant, our engineer will reappear.

The Walker brings the talisman back to blood,

Swayed by the path of truth,

Following the emerald snake north,

Thus, will mark the dawn,

And so, begins the Fourth Age of Acadia.'

"What does it mean?" Logan asked.

"Only Uncle Beauford himself would know the answer to that question," Fimbas said. "And he ain't around no more, eh? Whatever he saw, he found it important enough to warn you to go searching for the truth and set you on a path that would lead to my very doorstep with his dying breath."

"What else does it say?" Bipp asked eagerly.

"Nothing more, some information about crops, marriages, births, etc. Wasn't like my Great Uncle walked around spitting out major events day in day out. But he did reference *the Walker*. Now that I hold this in my hands, it's starting to come back to me. This tome was one of his last journals, before he suddenly packed up and left Dudje to set up his shop on New Fal."

"At the time, everyone thought he had lost his wits and figured the scrying had finally turned him mad. Not my da, though. He always said if Great Uncle Beauford did something, you could bet there was a good enough reason behind it...and now I think that motive's finally starting to become clear," Fimbas paused to stroke his chin thoughtfully. "Of course, this could all be nothing more than a faint glimpse into your future."

"But by the looks on both your faces I'm guessing it's a little more important than that?" Logan said.

"The seer said *Fourth Age of Acadia*, Logan," Bipp said.

"Yeah, what's such a big deal? We all know it's the year 396 and the fourth century is upon us," Logan said.

"What Bipp here means to point out, and your human mind is not perceiving, is the mention of *Acadia*," Fimbas said. "Now, I don't know about you Falians, but we gnomes of Vanidriell stopped referring to Acadia ages ago, when we first came down here. The only time any of us even say it is when we are talking about..."

The hairs on Logan's neck rose and goose bumps trickled across his forearms as the realization hit him. "...the surface world," he finished for the mayor.

"Exactly," Fimbas clapped the book closed and placed it back on the shelf. Moving to a nearby table, he stretched out a tall scroll across it, holding down the edges with a paperweight and a fantasy book he had been reading about a lonely troll. Logan could see it was a map of Vanidriell, but it was unlike any he had ever known of, showing dozens of gnome settlements. The mayor traced a path with his thick ringed forefinger, starting at Dudje.

"This is where we are now, and if I'm correct, which is usually the case, you need to follow the Winding Trail east until you hit the Green Serpent River again. Then work your way northward keeping on the river's course, until you reach...." The mayor stopped at a fork in the river, and silently followed it right, to the town of Mushroom Hollow. Shaking his head he started over, following left instead where it flowed a short distance before disappearing into a marked sink hole. When he came to the spot he tapped, grumbling under his breath at Logan's destination.

"Sweet mother of pearl," Bipp gaped, staring wide eyed at where the mayor's forefinger rested.

"Watch your mouth, youngen," Fimbas said.

Logan pointed around that section of the map "What is that area there?"

"It makes sense to hear the words now... Beauford must have seen you traveling to the ruins of Ul'kor." As the name was spoken both gnomes crossed their fingers twice over their hearts, muttering an incantation. "Tis the ancient site of Gnome civilization in the underworld, a massive kingdom only whispered of over campfires, human. Aye, if there were ever a place of truth, 'twould be there for sure," Fimbas reckoned.

"Not sure I like the sound of this place," Logan said.

"Wouldn't be blamin' you for that," Fimbas said. "Even the most stalwart gnomish treasure hunters know better than to try their luck at Ul'kor. That place was the site of a great evil, a huge war waged on our very doorstep; pushed we gnome's deeper into the underworld and scattered us across the land."

"What could have happened there to drive out a whole city of gnomes?" Logan said.

"Not just our race were driven out, was humans and bullywogs that lived there too. None know what it was that happened there, all the gnomes from back then have long since passed into the glorious halls of Valhalla. And don't you think none of 'em were talkin' too much about it when we was youngsters, neither. The mere mention would get ye done over real good, and that was if ye were lucky." Fimbas bristled, repaying one such time in his mind.

"Well, it sounds like something that happened ages ago," Logan said. "Why haven't your people ever just reclaimed the land?"

"Would that we could. Whatever it was scattered us, to build new homes all across Vanidriell. Once they were built, not many wanted to go back for the cursed place. Meant having to rebuild all over again, and what's the point. It's too far up anyhow, thin air up in those parts. Besides, the few foolish enough to try their luck never returned, except one mighty warrior of legend, and that was my own da. He used to tell stories about how he got close enough to see that the area is now completely overrun with cobolds and their wicked pets."

"What's a cobold?" Logan asked.

Mayor Fimbas looked as if he wanted to spit on his own floor. "Vile creatures, a little smaller than a gnome, but covered in fur and scales. They're flesh eaters and filthy dogs at that."

Most people would hear this and run in the opposite direction. Most people would understand the weight of fear that played in the mighty gnome leader's words. After all, legends always came from some measure of truth. The problem was that Logan Walker was not most people. He was the boy who dreamed of adventuring in the forests of Malbec, searching for lost treasures and coming back to town a hero with women fawning over him. He could not help the devious look that spread over his face as the possibility of those very adventures were now being laid out before him.

"Looks like I need some supplies, Bipp," he said. "I'm going to Ul'kor!"

"Count me in!" Bipp said, hopping in the air and slap his hand in excitement. They laughed together for a moment, forgetting their manners in the presence of the mayor, who sobered them up under a withering glare.

"This is by no means some trivial task you are choosing to embark upon," Fimbas warned. "Just because Uncle Beauford saw it does not mean it needs to be."

"I understand that Mayor...I do," Logan said, showing a little humility for once. "We do not mean to take this lightly. It's just, if this is what Beauford wanted...what he saw, then I feel it's my duty to see it through. There's something deeper here than I can understand, and I need to figure out what that is."

Mayor Fimbas bowed his head and turned to Bipp, "Brillfilbipp, if you insist on accompanying this human to Ul'kor, I must demand sending some sort of protection for you." No sooner did the mayor call for his guards to get Grubble, then the gnomes above clambered in the ceiling passageway and the chamber door was swinging back open. The old, grouchy gnome warrior tentatively approached his mayor.

"Grubblefrop Gilviri, you who have long served the Town of Dudje faithfully, I have a request for you," Mayor Fimbas began.

"Sure, you be sayin' request, but from the tone of it, it's soundin' more likely to be an order, milord," the bedraggled gnome replied.

Fimbas smirked. "Quite the same thing last I recall. I need you to accompany loyal Brillfilbipp here to the ruins of Ul'kor."

At this, the veteran's eyes widened to the size of saucers, bushy eyebrows arching in surprise, "Tis madness...surely ye cannot be meaning..."

"I can and I am. The only madness here would be for us to let young Bipp go on a journey of such magnitude without the likes of Grubblefrop Gilviri, the only warrior alive what could handle such an undertaking. Surely you can dispense a handful of cobolds, even at yer old age, eh? Besides, it's long past time you got out and carved a couple more notches into yer belt. You don't think I don't be knowing how bored you are sitting in front of me doors all day?"

"It is my honor to serve as Captain of the Town Guard yer lordship," Grubble replied halfheartedly.

"Bah, drop the humility. I can already see by the look in yer eyes you're lusting for adventure." Logan noted that there was certainly a different look about the warrior, although he was not sure it was one of excitement. "Now you go get ready for the road, its leaving first thing in the morning for the lot of you. And make sure our engineer here gets back safely, or at least mostly in one piece."

"It will be done, milord," Grubble said and gave an obnoxiously mocking bow before the trio headed out to get some sleep for the evening. They would be setting out first thing in the morning, and Logan wanted to be well rested.

Lady Cassandra pushed her mind, probing the vast distance of the wild lands, riding on currents of psychic energy to return to her body after trying to find Corbin. She had set out to speak with him and was just about to establish a connection, when he had been knocked unconscious by Bipp's frying pan. Any conversation they were able to have after that would likely be forgotten or written off as an after effect of the blow.

A commotion in the passageway outside instinctively brought her reeling sharply back into her corporeal form. As she reentered her body, she could hear the guard apologizing that he could not let anyone in under Magistrate Fafnir's personal orders.

"I don't care if the All-Father himself came down here, tugged on your ear, and gave you the orders. Fafnir has no rule over the Twelve; you will obey as you are told, citizen."

Cassandra smiled to herself. Elder Esther was not one to be bullied, and certainly never by a dungeon guard.

The rusty iron wrought gate creaked open. Every time the thing moved it hurt her ears. Visitors filled up an area in front of the barred cell and Lady Cassandra stood, mussing her robes into a more presentable shape. She was embarrassed that her friends would see her in such a state and could not help feeling self-conscious about the fact that she had not bathed in two days, smelling her unwashed skin beneath the dirty clothes.

"Greetings, Elder Esther," she said, kneeling respectfully.

"Oh, do rise, Lady Cassandra," Elder Esther retorted like a whip. "After all these years, everything we have all been through together, you bow to no one."

"I thank you for your gracious words, Elder," Cassandra said, bowing slightly again. After almost two centuries it was hard to break old habits.

The other three Council members and two lords greeted her with proper decorum. "We are calling in favors from all corners of the city, milady," Sir Robert said. "Soon enough we will have you out of this dreadful place."

"And into that empty Council seat as well," Elder Esther added. They had been working all morning gathering support for her cause. There were many who would not stand for her being locked up under such ridiculous charges. Teaching magic was outlawed, true enough, they themselves were the ones to write that law into existence.

"But that was meant for destructive magic, as Fafnir knows well enough. To haul you down here for sharing the art of telepathy, after all these years, it's nothing short of ludicrous," Elder Marcus said. Everyone knew he took on a new apprentice every fifty cycles. Just as Lady Cassandra had taken Jayne in, seeing her potential from the moment they met, and training her to be a disciple of the psionic arts.

"If we are not keeping the teachings alive, how will our successors survive when we are all gone?" Lady Cassandra pointed out.

"That's right, but this Fafnir does not think the same way. He expects us to live on forever, just because we have already made it all these years," Esther said, referring to one of the popular rumors about the Magistrate, although Cassandra was not so sure it was correct. There seemed to be something else behind his nefarious motives to gain power. He had shifted somehow in the last quarter century, but she was not sure why.

They spoke for a bit longer, swearing allegiance to her cause, before departing. None of them felt good about leaving her there alone, in a cell treated like a common criminal. Jayne and John lingered behind, so that they could speak privately. Jayne had looked angry since she arrived, the sight of her mentor locked away in this musty cell was clearly making her blood boil.

"Jayne, what is it, dear?" Lady Cassandra said, tenderly soothing her apprentice.

"I mustered the clergy members and got the support of the labor leaders. Tonight, they are going to gather out in front of this dungeon again and demand your release," Jayne said. She was excited by the prospect of all those voices uniting to her Ladyship's cause.

"Hmmm...that could be dangerous for them," Cassandra said.

"That pig Fafnir would never dare make an open move against so many innocent people," Jayne said. "They all know it too; I think in a lot of ways this protest was a long time in coming."

"Best tell them to keep it peaceful and stay safe," Cassandra advised, absently rubbing her palm up and down the rusty bars of her cell.

"No doubt the magistrate will try to lure them into violence," John agreed, moving closer to the pair.

"What else is there," Cassandra asked. "Surely the two of you did not stay behind to tell me about the protest?"

Jayne silently motioned to John, signaling him to check the gate and make sure the guard was not listening in. Once he nodded, keeping watch so she could speak, Jayne moved in closer to the cell and began to explain in low whispers.

"John has a plan to help get you out of here," Jayne said. "You see, he overheard his uncle talking to one of Fafnir's henchmen. It seems Fafnir was the one who ordered the execution on Mr. Beauford, because he was trying to get some documents off the goodly gnome." Lady Cassandra was less surprised by the revelations than Jayne would have expected.

"That's all well and good, but there is no way to prove its truth," Cassandra said. "John's uncle is not likely to step forth and Fafnir's assassin is even less likely. All we have is hearsay."

"Wait there's more," Jayne said. "It appears the assassin Fafnir sent ran off to Malbec with the loot and documents. He was drunkenly bragging about it at the Lion's Tooth Tavern and Fafnir has dispatched men to kill him. John and I are going to intercept them and warn the Constable who is holding the vagrant. If we move quickly enough, we should be able to get those documents before Fafnir does. And the best part is that the assassin has already agreed to hand them over, at a price of course."

"With those in hand, not only will we prove Fafnir has become corrupted, but also that Riverbell is completely innocent of the accusations he has been spreading around the aristocracy," Cassandra said, growing excited. They had the Magistrate right where they wanted him.

"And Arch Councilor Zacharia will see through these weak charges set against you. He might even commend you for helping the hero,

Corbin Walker, bring home his innocent brother!" Jayne clapped her hands together. John spun his finger, signaling the guard was back.

"John, Jayne, you must both get to Malbec with due haste," Cassandra implored.

"We are leaving as soon as we walk out of the building milady. Rest assured I'll be sure Jayne will get what she needs." John bowed to Lady Cassandra, who noticed Jayne was slightly blushing at his new chivalrous behavior.

"Be safe my dear girl, and may the light of the Crystal guide you," Cassandra said. Things had certainly shifted in their favor. "Maybe I don't need to contact Corbin after all," she thought, rolling an egg-sized Onyx in her palm.

From the street outside section six, Magistrate Fafnir watched the last two visitors exit the building, through the window of his carriage. His lip curled at the thought of the sanctimonious little pigs plotting against him. Outside section six, close to forty men and women were gathering for an evening of protests. Some were already shouting for Lady Cassandra's release. His men had asked if he wanted the rabble rousers arrested, but he scoffed, "No let the little street urchins have their moment in the light." Then paused to add "But *do* record all their names, so we can *keep an eye on them* after this is all through."

Fafnir put on a brave front for his men, but the old man was secretly bothered by the recent turn of events. He had not anticipated the outpouring of support Lady Cassandra's arrest incited. This would not be good for his plans. Zacharia would be displeased to hear of the people's unhappiness. If he caught wind of the protest, the Arch Councilor was sure to follow the will of the people. The old goat was getting soft. You did not bend over for this rabble of commoners. They were nothing but lower-level trash. If Fafnir were the High Elder, he would make an example of the entire lot, crushing them beneath his heel like ants. And who among them would dare step out of line after that?

A rap came lightly on the side of his carriage. His guest had arrived. Fafnir bid her enter, and she slipped in, hood hanging low to hide her face.

"Oooh, how provincial of you," he teased over her weak disguise. "What do you have to report?"

"Everything has been taken care of, milord," the woman said. "You were right, she was easy to ploy."

"That is always the way of these country bumpkins, too stupid to get out of their own way. It's no wonder Elder Morgana went to live with them." To Fafnir the farmers of Riverbell were nothing more than fodder for his plans. "You have done well. If you deliver as agreed the trade rights of Riverbell will be yours to own," he promised, feeling a little better knowing at least this part of his plan had not fallen through.

The woman bowed her head then slipped out of the compartment back into the street, leaving him to brood in private. Looking back outside at the rabble, causing a commotion, Fafnir could not help worrying that it was not enough…. not nearly sufficient to overcome the support Lady Cassandra was gathering. Perhaps he had made a mistake betting against her? Maybe he had pushed the scales too far in the wrong direction…? Scowling, he called for his guard.

"Yes Magistrate?" the guard said.

"I've changed my mind. Get some men together in plain clothes, *no uniforms*. Then go hurt a couple of those dogs for their disobedience," Fafnir said, cruelly pointing a crooked finger at the protesters.

Chapter 19

Corbin needed to figure out a way into the amazing town below. He had spent some time during the late hours studying the layout of the place in wonder. Everything else outside of New Fal was supposed to be a wild and untamed dangerous expanse that could not support civilization. Yet, here was a thriving trade port despite those claims and the place was anything but wild, clearly shipping goods in both directions on the green foamy river below. It was a complete contradiction to what he knew about the world.

After the initial shock from that revelation wore off, Corbin scouted the area to find some way to slip inside undetected. The entrance was far too exposed for him to show up at the gates. They would spot him in a heartbeat. Logan would have too much warning if that happened, and Corbin was uncertain whether the gnomes would be welcoming toward him anyhow, considering his brother was traveling with one of their people. The layout of the town was impressive. The only way in was through a tunnel carved under the hill below, but that was guarded by five heavily armored gnomes.

Circling the outskirts of the settlement, there was literally no other accessible point of entry. The place was surrounded by the very hillside itself and climbing up them would leave him completely exposed to the dutiful guards.

This did not deter Corbin; it was more of a challenge that he was ready to conquer. If he had learned one thing in his short life, it was that there is always a way through the defenses of his prey. You just have to remain patient and keep looking. Once he spied the miners coming from the area at the base of the waterfall, he knew he had found the chink in Dudje's armor. Surely, it was not a big enough weakness to cause any real harm to the town, but still enough for him to sneak inside.

Miners came out every hour in groups, wheeling heavy barrows filled with a grayish-silver ore. They loaded these onto waiting barges that transported the heavy load into Dudje through a massive portcullis.

Scouting it, he knew the opportunity had to be seized swiftly. As he ran down the hill toward the riverbank, Corbin was careful to keep his footsteps silent, and used the cover of large mushrooms and thorny bushes to hide his descent. He waited, carefully timing it just right, until the miners were not looking in his direction, joking with one another while delivering another load to the barge.

Then, slick as a snake, he fully immersed himself into the icy river water, with only a thin reed sticking out of the surface, giving him something to suck in the air with. Corbin slowly waded through the foamy green liquid, wrist blade extended in case he ran into something hungry, until he bumped the side of the barge.

Hugging the moving boat, he made his way around to the side of the hull while it edged along the river. He had to duck back under as it came closer to the portcullis, to avoid being spotted by the armored guards overhead. He could make out their murky shapes on the rampart above from beneath the water, marching back and forth to keep watch.

Once inside the town, the barge drifted sluggishly down a long gnome-made canal, where boats were docked on either side, fixed to their owners back steps. Dozens of diminutive gnomes went about their business along the cobblestone streets that ran parallel to the slow-moving river, carrying baskets of vegetables, or walking with their children on the way to meet a relative. It was just regular everyday business for the peaceful folk, very much like his home of Riverbell. Except his village never had anything as impressive as the electric lights dotting the various houses in town.

Corbin wondered what kind of lightning stone they possessed, to generate so much power. With no time for gawking at the twinkling lights, he set his mind to the task at-hand, remaining hidden and looking for some clue as to the whereabouts of Logan. Outside the city, this had seemed hopeful. However, now that he was here, looking at the tightly packed buildings, and obvious lack of any other humans, it seemed unlikely he would be able to get very far before being spotted.

Secrets of the Elders

The barge motor came to a low rumble as it drifted into dock, prompting him to stay on the move. Corbin popped back under the water. Like a fish, he knifed his way across the river to an empty docked boat. With barely a splash, he pulled himself out of the green river and up the side of the cargo vessel. It was large enough that he could hide unseen behind some sealed crates to dry.

Pulling off his breeches, he rang them out as well as possible then switched for a dry pair in his sealed pack. Cool evening air was rolling off the river and he sighed to feel the warm fabric against his skin. Corbin was changing his top, when he dropped the wet tunic and peeked around the crates. There were voices coming from the doorway at the end of the short wooden dock.

He cursed himself for being a fool. There was no escape route to slip back into the water without someone catching him. If he went over the hull, the five gnomes unloading ore would have an eyeful, and he did not dare attempt to run across the deck, which would completely expose him to the three now making their way down the small dock.

His only option was to become a shadow, shifting deeper into the barricade of crates. As quietly as he could, he slipped back into the soaked tunic. Suddenly the riverboat growled, as one of the gnomes had begun paddling his legs hard to get the kinetic motor activated. Corbin knew it was time to make a run for it. He readied to jump out onto the dock, praying the sailors would not see their intruder, when a woman shouted from the doorway to her husband who was on the boat.

"You forgot your breakfast, you lug head," she exclaimed, running the food down to him.

"Aw, I just wanted to see you come a running sweetness," the gnome said. His friend thought that was funny, but she only scowled.

"Just you try to get back before dinner time. And don't go getting drunk, neither."

The gnome blew her kisses and promised not to. Then the boat was off, ripping into the still water with some vigor. Corbin decided there was nothing to it. He would have to cut his losses and figure out a better time of day to sneak back into the town. Not that he had much choice as they approached the second portcullis. He scrambled to conceal himself snuggly between the shadows of two stacks of crates, thankfully invisible to the guards overhead, as they came out the other side of town. The river sure did not cut through too much of the place, he wondered, unlike Riverbell, which more or less ran parallel to the Naga River.

He had little hope of slipping off the boat, which was small enough that he could smell the gnome's sugary scrum when it was uncorked. Corbin decided to wait until the sailors had enough of the drink to make them sloppy, and there was more distance away from the armored town guards. With nothing else to do, he hunkered in for a short rest.

The drunker the sailors got the more stories they told. One was recounting a tale of his fishing trip from the previous week, which would sound like a boring topic unless you were a gnome who had been pulled under water by not the fish but the bait you used. Corbin liked these gnomes. They were a funny pair and he felt guilty for stowing away on their vessel.

But it was time he made his move.

As if someone had heard his thoughts, the motor suddenly switched off, and one of the gnomes began hushing his companions. "Shhh…, come on now, quiet you two. Do ye here that?"

Corbin's heart was thumping in his ears. Did they hear him readying to jump off the boat? One of the gnomes tried to laugh it off, telling his friend he had too much to drink, when he snapped at them. "Listen…there it is again."

Corbin held his breath, wondering how good their little gnome ears could possibly be. Did they hear him breathing? He had no wish to hurt these gnomes and was prepared to make a mad dash for it before it came to that.

"Ah, I hear it now!" the joking gnome agreed.

Corbin could hear it now too. With some relief he listened intently, knowing it was not him they heard, but someone singing up ahead on the shore.

Secrets of the Elders

"Ho there! Where ye off to so early, Grubble?" the sharp-eared gnome called out to someone on the riverbank.

"Never ye mind, Pike, ye nosey blabbermouth," a gruff voice hollered back, with a hint of jest.

"Who's he with?" Pike asked his friend. "'Fraid I'm too drunk to see straight?"

"You're seeing right enough. That there's the engineer Bipp, and a...*a human?*" he said low enough so Grubble could not hear them. The problem of course is that what a gnome considers low while he is drunk on scrum is actually quite loud to the sober minded.

"Bah, don't ye worry what we be doin' with a Falian," Grubble called back. "On official government business we are. 'Sides I have to keep little Bipp here safe on the road, boys!"

He was clearly annoyed at being caught and trying to play it aloof. The trio had slipped out early in the morning to keep their expedition quiet, but now that Pike saw them every sailor and merchant down the Green Serpent would be aware before nightfall.

"Best be keepin' him safe or I'll have to have that lout Gil fix old Ness here next time she breaks down!" Pike joked, slapping the side of his boat.

"Better off using those oars, bwahahaha," Grubble said.

Corbin peaked over the edge of the boat. There close by the edge of the river on the trail stood a pair of gnomes, with his brother. Baetylus was mighty indeed, watching out for him like this. He silently thanked the god for his good fortune then stood fully upright.

Logan was watching the drunken sailors when he saw Corbin rise, with a finger pointed directly at him. Bipp and Grubble were completely surprised, jumping back away from the water's edge. This completely confused the oblivious sailors, who could not see Corbin behind the crates from their vantage point.

"Run!" was the only thing Logan could think to yell, pulling his good friend Bipp back up the trail. The trio made a mad dash at full speed, as Corbin dived into the river with a loud splash.

The gnomes looked at each other in confusion, with Pike shrugging before firing up the engine and going back to their drink. "That was weird."

The current had more force to it here, but Corbin made it across well enough. Once he was out of the drink, he hit the ground running. All the years Logan was up to his pranks and loafing about, finding anyway he could to get out of chores, Corbin was honing his hunting skills and mastering his martial arts. The distance between them was shortening, with great speed.

Baetylus' form appeared ten yards ahead in the tall grass to the right, pale and ghostly. The god's voice was much lower now in Corbin's head, dampened by the distance to his crystalline shell, *"Cut across here. Stop your brother!"*

Without a second thought, Corbin ran through the thicket, jumping over a downed rotting log and back onto the trail where it wound around a corner. He landed directly in front of the fleeing group. The look of triumph on his face was quickly wiped off when the gnomes spread to either side of the path, each holding a rope taut in their strong stubby hands. The chord hit his shins, flipping Corbin over face first into the dirt, while his brother jumped over his prone body.

"Quickly now, get up! They are getting away!" the All-Father's voice echoed far away.

Brushing the dust from his eyes, Corbin hopped back to his feet in time to hear a heavy splash, followed by another. Coming around the corner, he saw Logan standing atop a large boulder over a steep precipice where the river dropped to the east.

"Logan stop!" Corbin called, halting in his tracks, worried his brother would do something reckless. "Get down from there, it's dangerous! You have to come back with me," he pleaded, holding out his arms, "think of Riverbell."

Logan looked down at him, wondering why his brother had followed him this far? Why couldn't he just go back and leave him alone? "Go home Corbin, just tell them I'm dead," he said for the second in time in as many days, thinking his brother must not have understood him the first time due to Bipp's frying pan greeting.

"You know I can't do that!" Corbin shouted. "For once in your life, stop being selfish. You have to come back and make things right, now get down here!"

Logan just stared lovingly at him and smiled. He wished he could be the person his brother wanted him to be. With a shrug, he jumped backward off the ledge into the rushing water. Corbin was simultaneously filled with both dread for his brother's safety and rage at his callousness. Already in action, he did not need to hear the All-Father's echoes, spurning him to pursue. There was just enough time to take in a gulp of air before he leapt down off the small cliff into the rushing green river below.

The current pulled him much harder this time, as the river churned in a steep downward slope, building momentum the further it went. The world became a flurry of waving arms, desperately fighting to keep above the chill water. His body was yanked underneath over and over again. Each time, he clawed to get his head back above the surface, gasping for precious oxygen, with only a momentary glimpse of what lay ahead.

Narrowly he missed an outcropping of rocks through sheer luck. Logan was slightly further ahead of him, doing the same, while each of the gnomes fought the rapids on some sort of thin metallic floating devices. Another mouthful of the icy water filled his lungs. Corbin dimly wondered how something so cold could burn his insides as the current pulled harder against his body.

Some primal instinct in him knew that if he did not let go and accept the pull of the current, he would never win this battle against nature. Letting his body fall limp, he was tugged forcefully down to the riverbed below. Throwing his weight into it, he zipped past Logan's struggling form. By now his lungs felt ready to burst, sorely needing oxygen. He knew it was time to make a wild scramble back to the surface. As his head shot up out of the water, Logan was within arm's reach, yet he could not grasp him, choking to get the river water out of his lungs and bring in air.

Rapidly approaching, downstream, was a gnomish built barricade of wooden stakes, bound together in a crisscross pattern. This was to signal inexperienced sailors to stay away from that area of the Green Serpent, as it led to cursed lands. Grubble was already pulling Bipp out of their lightweight craft by the barricade. Logan was groping wildly for a handhold on one of the tuberous roots sticking into the river from the leafless trees that lined its muddy banks. Corbin thought that was a good idea and tried to do the same. He had a grip on one, steadying his body against the current, but it snapped in half, and he went back under. Logan was already out of the rapids and reaching down to yank his little brother from the drink.

He heaved Corbin onto the bank of the river and held his knees trying to catch his breathe. Corbin vomited up the water still slushing around in his lungs. As his chest heaved to catch warm air, Logan patted his back, forcing more of the stuff out.

Corbin swatted his arm away in disgust, a look of revulsion etched on his face. To Logan it was as if he wore a mask. One that looked like his younger brother yet was so twisted with hatred he could be a stranger. He even wondered for the tiniest fraction of seconds if this was not an imposter after all.

"You maniac, you almost got us killed!" Corbin screamed, rising from the mud.

Logan could not believe his ears. "You got some nerve, I told you to go home. What were you thinking following me out here? This isn't one of your hunts Corbin... I'm not a boar, I'm your family."

Baetylus voice was a mere whisper in the back of his mind, urging him to reason with Logan, find some way to get him to come back before it was too late. Corbin rubbed his temples, unable to think clearly. "You do not even care about Riverbell. You could care less that right now Elise's life is in danger!"

Logan stopped, "Elise is...but why would they hurt little Elise?"

Years of pent-up frustration bubbled to the surface of Corbin's mind, "It never ends with you, does it? Nothing matters in your sick version of reality, except what you need. No wonder dad left; how could he possibly want to stay around someone as pathetic as you?" Corbin was shouting now, his heart filled with rage and veins pumping adrenaline. The pained look on Logan's face did not even register. All he saw was a selfish smile on his disgusting selfish face, a face he wanted to crush.

Baetylus coldly whispered into that rage, *"Destroy him."*

It was the third jab to Logan's stomach that told him his own sibling was attacking him! Corbin was fast as a serpent, giving no warning as he furiously pressed in with a flurry of fists. Throwing a blind backhand that connected with his brother's jaw gave Logan just enough time to mount a defense, throwing his forearms up to block the next round of blows.

Unlatching his hammer, Bipp moved forward to come to his friend's aid, but was blocked by Grubble's thick hairy forearm. The warrior nodded at the skirmish. "Not our place, this be family business." Bipp understood, but it did not make him feel any better. There was something deeply wrong watching the two men fight. "Cheer up, maybe we'll get lucky and the Falian will kill yer friend. Then we can get home early." Bipp gave the chuckling warrior a disapproving glare, but he hardly seemed to care.

Logan ducked under another roundhouse, snapping his leg out into his brother's thigh, knocking him off balance. He moved in for a follow up, quickly redirecting to avoid a crashing blow from the unsheathed voulge.

"Have you lost your mind?" Logan screamed at the lunacy of his brother pulling the deadly weapon on him.

Corbin did not reply, instead swimming in his blind rage. He swung the voulge directly for Logan's midsection, barely missing with each swipe coming dangerously closer. Logan kicked hard into the ground, flinging dirt into his brother's face.

Rubbing the stinging stuff out, he was blind against Logan's uppercut. Corbin was practiced in the martial arts, as good a fighter as any ever met in New Fal. But he was no match for Logan's sheer strength. The uppercut lifted him right off his feet, which Logan deftly followed by slamming both fists into his chest. By the time Corbin hit the ground, it was a good five feet from where he had been standing. When he lifted his head, he found Logan running in to continue the assault.

Corbin waited until the distance was closed, then cartwheeled his legs into a spinning ground kick, throwing Logan off balance, and following up with three more jabs to his pelvis, knocking the air out of him. Logan did not have time to block Corbin's choking grip on his throat, while his left hand continued to pound into his gut, slapping away feeble attempts to block.

"Well, that's too much," Bipp said. "We gotta jump in Grubble."

The older gnome was about to agree, when he stopped Bipp again. "Shhh…do ye hear that?"

Logan was not sure who he was looking at. Surely this could not be the kind, generous, loving brother he had grown up with? This person was a stranger to him, his face dripping with hatred, his eyes filled with a maniacal gleam. Logan tried to gurgle out a protest for his brother to stop, but the words could not escape through the maniac's strangling grip. The world began to fade around the corners.

It was surreal the way the anger melted away, as if a mask fell off revealing Corbin wearing of horrified look of recognition around his eyes. Suddenly Logan was thrown to the side, just as a small arrow zipped past where his head had been.

"Cobolds!" Grubble howled out, the word meant as a battle cry, swinging a readied double-headed battle-axe to face the enemy.

Bipp was already by Logan's side, helping him to his feet as Corbin protected the two of them, swinging his voulge in a defensive circle, knocking two more arrows out of the air. The cobolds were screaming and hooting like animals as they crashed in around the group. The feral little creatures resembled a twisted version of the gnomes, except with tufts of fur covering the backside of their arms and legs, and their faces more like a cross between a dog and snake with slits for eyes and rows of needle-sharp fangs. They were slightly smaller than the gnomes and wore the skins of animals they had hunted, some with matching bone jewelry.

Grubble roared back at the screaming monsters, whipping his axe down hard enough to cleave the closest one nearly in half, from the shoulder down to the waist. Logan caught a flurry of movement behind him. He spun around just in time to block one of the creature's swinging daggers with his metal hand. Bipp jumped out from his side and caved in the humanoid's skull with a heavy blow from his hammer.

The ferocious onslaught rushed in from all sides. Corbin no sooner parried a swinging club than he was working to block another stinging dagger. Moving his weapon back to block the blunt weapon, he deftly reversed course leading with the voulge blade. The maneuver worked, severing the dagger wielder's forearm clean off. Corbin flinched when a crossbow bolt whizzed by and embedded deeply into the other monster's forehead. Looking back, he saw Logan reloading his weapon as three more of the feral creatures rushed through the bushes behind them.

Bipp flung some shimmering dust in their faces, blinding them long enough for Corbin to flip over his brother's head and land behind the humanoids. Bipp bludgeoned the nearest one, while the other two did not have time to react, rubbing the stinging stuff out of their eyes. Corbin threw his weight into a wide swing of the voulge, beheading both mongrels in one blow.

Logan let a double shot of bolts fly, taking out a cobold who was just about to slam a club into Grubble's skull from behind. A pile of the vanquished monsters littered the ground like bloody torn ragdolls around the veteran warrior.

And just like that, the battle was over as fast as it had begun, leaving only the dim echo of clashing weapons. The silence was almost staggering in the wake of the sheer violence they had just been thrust into. The group looked around at each other in wonder, taking in the dead humanoids littering the riverbank. There had to be ten cobolds at least. Someone walking onto the scene would have thought them a band of madmen, as Grubble began laughing at their fortune.

Bipp shared his mirth, and Corbin felt it too. They had just been confronted by an entire band of cobolds and come through the other side unscathed.

But not Logan.

He swayed slightly as he hovered over the bodies of the creatures he had just slain. Bipp's laugh faltered as he followed Corbin's gaze to his brother. Logan was staring at his crossbow, his face was drained of color with beads of cold sweat on his brow, and he looked like he was ready to be sick. He took a deep steadying gulp of air and Bipp walked over to him.

"We killed them...," Logan said, looking down at the gnome. "Murdered every last one of them."

Bipp set a hand on his shaky forearm, steadying the crossbow, "We didn't have a choice," Bipp said, feeling his pain.

"I never...they were alive and now they're dead," Logan whispered.

"Suck it up goldilocks," Grubble said, wiping the blood off his axe head. "Ain't like you can reason with the dogs."

Logan's head twitched in an unsure nod, "Yes...of course. It was necessary."

Waves of guilt washed over Corbin, watching his brother's reaction. The sick feeling that had assaulted him at the cannibal's camp came back. He knew exactly how Logan felt. How could he ever have believed that his brother was capable of murdering Mr. Beauford?

With a very real look of concern, that only siblings could share, Corbin grabbed his big brother by the arm and turned him around to face him. Logan's eyes unglazed a bit and he stared back at him. A wall of silence went up in the group, the gnomes stopping to watch the exchange.

Logan stared firmly into Corbin's eyes, "You have to believe me. I did not murder him."

What Logan could not know, was that at that moment something deep inside him flared Corbin's psionic talent, driving deep into his brother's mind and flooding him, not only with images of all Logan had been through since they arrived in Fal, but also with his emotions. He felt his older brother's anguish when he held the young peddler boy's dead body, and the overwhelming guilt for not being there to protect the boy from the ruffians who did this. He felt enraged by the watchmen's callous words, and the heart gripping terror watching the ebony skinned assassin's toothy grin slinking into the shadows, followed by deep anguish when the light faded from Mr. Beauford's eyes.

Such an overwhelming surge of emotions rained over Corbin's mind that tears began to stream from the corners of his eyes. He understood it all now, everything his brother had experienced in Fal, and the fear he felt, fleeing over the wall, thinking how he would never see his brother and Elise again.

Corbin pulled his brother in for a hug. He did not need to express that he believed him. That is the funny thing about brothers. If they only try, they can always understand each other, without words being necessary.

Grubble clapped the back of Bipp's neck. "Are ye gonna cry now too?" He mocked the little teary-eyed gnome, though Bipp noted there was a small squeak in the warrior's voice as well. "Been spendin' too much time with the human lad."

The men broke to gather themselves and Logan walked the area, retrieving any bolts still in useable condition.

Meanwhile, Bipp approached Corbin, thumbs tucked into his pants pockets. "So, uh...yeah...sorry about that whole frying pan business. Seemed like a good idea at the time. I mean, you *did* have him hogtied fit for a barbeque." Bipp kicked the dirt as he apologized.

"No worries, good gnome, I understand," Corbin said. "My brother is lucky to have made such a good friend out here." With that out of the way the men all respectfully introduced themselves to one another.

Logan finished surveying the area and walked back over to the group. "Corbin, *I will go back with you*, there is no way I can let Elise live in danger." A flood of relief washed over Corbin that was so intense he thought he might pass out.

"That is so great, I promise you that Arch Councilor Zacharia and the Elders will see the truth in you, as do I. We can settle this misunderstanding, and everyone will be safe."

"I believe in you, I really do," Logan said. "However, I will only return with you once we see this journey through to the end. I can't just abandon this, there is too much I need to know. You see Mr. Beauford warned me...," he walked Corbin through the story of how he came to be there, searching for the truth that Mr. Beauford only hinted at.

"Hmmm...I am as intrigued as you," Corbin said thoughtfully. "What was so important that Fafnir had to kill Mr. Beauford? It would do us well to uncover this, it could help us to prove your innocence and shed light on the Magistrate's corruption."

"To discover the truth, *it is all lies*," Logan said. "Curious last words...right? You must admit, since leaving Fal, we've certainly been confronted by lies. For example, why not tell us the truth of the gnome settlements out here, why lie about the wild lands?"

"Yes, it is a bit puzzling," Corbin said.

"And after reading the seer script in Mayor Fimbas library you can see why I need to do this?" Logan asked. He stopped and cocked his head as something occurred to him. "Wait, how in the heck did you track me all this way anyhow? You've always been a good scout, but no one is *that* good."

"It's a long story, I'll tell it to you on the way to Ul'kor," Corbin said. "I know how much this means to you, and it sounds like we're almost there as it is. We should be able to get in and out with enough time left to make it back to New Fal before the remaining twelve days are over. I promise you this brother; I will not sway you from this path."

Baetylus urged Corbin to reconsider, quietly protesting the dangers of going any further into the wilds. But he silently disagreed, trusting in his brother's destiny.

"If you two are done kissin' and makin' up," Grubble said, "best we be gettin' out of here before another raidin' party discovers our presence. Have no doubt that some of the little rats may have heard all the commotion and went to get reinforcements."

The group agreed it would be better to vacate the area right away. They made short work of tossing the dead cobolds into the river, hoping it would at least buy them some time. Deciding the path was too exposed, they slipped into the dense overgrowth, heading north, toward the ruins of Ul'kor.

"So...tell me this long story of yours," Logan whispered to his brother.

"Smells like a dog's arse out here," Grubble complained in a hushed voice, pinching his large nose in disgust.

"Kinda mentioned that already...," Bipp groaned, starting to lose his patience with the old warriors' constant grumbling. Grubble was undoubtedly an amazing fighter, infamous all throughout Dudje for his exploits. However, Bipp was starting to wonder if he could get away with another frying pan trick shot to the grouchy gnome's head.

Logan hushed both of them while Corbin was trying to focus on falling back into his trance.

They had been making their way, carefully and quietly, through the outer ruins for a couple hours now. The place was overgrown by all manner of plants, as if the land of Vanidriell had long ago reclaimed the very rock used to build the outskirts of Ul'kor. Here, the cavern ceiling sharply rose to a staggering height, even taller than the kingdom of New Fal. Deserted buildings were found all around the ruins, though they were not as tightly packed as Dudje. And the landscape was much flatter, but otherwise the buildings were much the same, being stacked on top of each other. Thick vines ran up the crumbling walls and dark green lichen blanketed the area along with crooked leafless trees and tall reedy weeds. The whole area smelled like a rotting garbage pile.

They were unsure if it was from some great battle, or if it was simply the work of time that had left the outer city in such ruins. Walls were toppled, stones shattered where they lay, and buildings were crumbling everywhere they looked. The entire place looked like one giant cemetery, except the monoliths and mausoleums used to be shops and homes.

Corbin had been using his power to guide them safely through the ruined landscape, which was littered with filthy cobold dens or packs of the creatures sitting around campfires. Baetylus hovered next to him, unseen by his companions, instructing in the use of his psionic abilities. The Crystal god was much more vivid now that Corbin had taken the Svalin earpiece off, un-shielding his mind.

At first, the idea of exposing himself to the massive amount of latent psychic energy flowing from the multitude of sentient beings in the immediate area unnerved him. The All-Father was easily able to calm him, talking Corbin through dampening out the sounds by lacing layers of energy around his mind, acting as a one-way psychic shield.

Narrowing his focus down to the immediate area, Corbin was able to adapt well to his god's wisdom, probing into the darkest recesses of the surrounding structures, and around the multitude of blind corners. The seething minds of cobolds stood out like glowing beacons against the lifeless expanse surrounding them. In this way, he was able to pick a path through the outer city of Ul'kor, each time avoiding a run in with the abandoned city's savage inhabitants.

"Do not let the gnomes prattle disturb your concentration, my son," Baetylus cautioned, bright white robes flowing even though there was no breeze. *"Focus your mind. We must get you out of the open and into shelter."*

Corbin was pleased when the All-Father offered to help. He had thought his god would be angry for going against his wishes to assist Logan. Instead, he proved how magnanimous he truly was by forgiving the disobedience, understanding that the bonds between siblings were sacred. He had vowed to his Lord that they would return as soon as Logan finished fulfilling his murdered friends' dying request, well within the timeline set by the elders.

A pack of cobolds was sleeping in the bowels of a nearby structure that had been tipped on its side decades before. "We need to go down this alley and come out around that building to the east," Corbin whispered to his companions.

"Aye, aye Captain," Grubble said, mocking him with an overzealous salute before striding down the alleyway and muttering to himself about the ridiculousness of taking orders from humans.

"Don't let it bother you," Logan said. "He seems to be in a perpetual state of grumpiness."

Bipp hopped straight up and skittered to catch up to them. Sneaking quietly past the abandoned buildings, the party white knuckled their weapons, ready for a skirmish at a moment's notice. The battle by Green Serpent River had taught them these cobolds, diminutive though they might be, were not to be taken lightly. The buildings began to become sparser, until soon there were none. Instead, the landscape became a long flattened out stretch of overgrown grass leading to a wide chasm. Between the thick clumps of weeds on the ground were massive stone tiles made by the ancient gnomes.

"Wow, this is the real Ul'kor, huh fellas?" Logan said, as they all stared up in awe at the massive spire towering beyond the chasm. The aerie was easily twice the size of the city of Fal, rising high up into the air above, almost reaching as far as the ceiling itself. All manner of buildings and turrets were carved majestically around the spire's rocky unpolished face.

Silhouettes of domed roofs could be dimly seen on top of the mighty column, signaling where the true city of Ul'kor rested. A wide stone bridge, overgrown with weeds and tangled vines, led the way to the Hall of Ul'kor, seat of the builders, at the base of the spire. Past the bridge, the entrance loomed high, coming to an arched point. Sets of statues depicting gnome mages stood on the either side of the bridge every twenty feet or so, staring down at travelers entering the city.

A gruff slap in the arse snapped Logan out of his reverie. "C'mon fancy pants let's get yer show on the road already." Grubble led the group across the area, with the brothers having to duck low in the tall grass to keep out of sight.

Baetylus' visage drifted over the grass without disturbing any of the tall reeds. Closer to the bridge now, they could see the moss had grown over the dead remains of gnome and human bodies, leaving behind nothing but the skeletal remains covered in rusty armor and overgrown with plants.

"These remains have to be centuries old," Corbin reasoned based on what Bipp had told him of Ul'kor lore.

"Leave it to the filthy cobold mongrels not to bury our kin," Grubble said, spitting on the ground in disgust. Every honorable soldier deserved a proper burial.

As they made their way across the bridge, Bipp craned his neck to the side, squinting to try and make out what might be past the dark entrance to the aerie. His mam's voice kept playing in his head; scolding him to be a good boy otherwise he would have to go live in the ruins with the demons. Even then he knew it would never happen. It was just something they said to make youngens behave, but it sure felt like a possibility now. As they passed the last set of statues, dull gray marble eyes seemed to follow the party and he worked hard not to stare up at them.

The main corridor was lined with a series of carved brownstone totem poles, with all manner of animals and faces stacked on top of each other, supporting the heavy weight of the city above. Some of the faces had worn away ages ago, while others lay on the ground staring up at them. Now Bipp could feel *their* eyes watching him as they crept through the hall. When Logan grabbed his shoulder, meaning to signal a halt, the gnome almost squealed like a lass. Biting his fist, he was just ready to scold the man, but his friend held a finger to his lips and nodded toward his brother.

Corbin silently beckoned for them to follow him up a side stairwell, sensing a handful of cobolds further down on this level, and secretly having Baetylus guide him upward. Grubble led the way, carefully scouting around the rounded stairwell to make sure nothing lay in wait. The way was blocked by a large rockslide at the next floor. The Falians had to help the gnomes climb over and they continued their progress up the steps, until they came to another doorway.

Stopping for a moment Corbin reached out again, sweeping the area for sentient life, and then waved them on once more. He was becoming very skilled with the use of his power, to the point where it almost felt second nature.

Everyone came to a halt as a stone clattered across the floor from the shadows. Grubble reacted swiftly, leaping into the dark corner and swinging his double-headed axe down, while the rest of the group instinctively fell into a triangle formation, backs all facing each other, ready for the fight. When none came, they were confused.

"Grubble...?" Bipp whispered.

The old warrior chuckled, coming out of the shadows holding a foot long rat at arm length. "Mmmm...stews for dinner tonight, boys."

Corbin wrinkled his nose. "Sounds like something those cobolds would like."

Grubble gave him a dark look. It was clear he did not like being compared to a cobold. "That's a stupid human thing to say, not that I expect much more from ye. A cobold wouldn't even be able to guess what to do proper with a nice meal like this."

"It's actually better than it looks," Logan said.

"Blech," Corbin said sticking his tongue out, "when did you try rat?"

"Jerk named Maxwell fed me some," Logan said, noticing his brother turn cold hearing the cannibal's name.

"You sure it was rat and not human?" Corbin asked gravely.

Logan was about to protest, but at that moment he realized there really was no way to tell. His heart skipped a beat. Maybe he did eat human or even gnome for that matter! Then he remembered watching the rat roasting over the fire, and laughed away the vile notion, shaking his head and striding confidently forward.

Something snapped loose and Logan's body flung in the air upside down, dangling on a rope wrapped around the ankle of his left boot. To the side a large piece of metal clambered to the floor from the wall where it was leaning, letting off a loud crash that echoed down the hallway, an alarm to announce prey had been caught.

"Blasted idjit, ye set off a damned trap!" Grubble complained as Bipp jumped up and down looking every which way in panic.

Logan knew their lives were at risk if he did not act swiftly. Pulling his upper body toward the rope, he grabbed it with one arm and pulled the weight of his torso toward the middle, unwinding his ankle and falling to the floor.

Grubble was slapping the head of his axe against his calloused palm, waiting for the oncoming assault. Corbin, on the other hand, had different ideas and snatched the rat from the warrior's belt, quickly looping the rope around its dead neck. Before the gnome could protest, Logan was pushing him and Bipp into a doorway down the hall, safely out of sight. As Corbin shoved the old door closed, he could only hope its scraping rusty joints would be unheard by the rambunctious cobolds making their way down the corridor. The humanoids were hooting and hollering in excitement to see what their trap had caught today.

"Oh yums, what izz it, maybe a juicy little lizard?" one of the dirty beasts asked, drool dripping from its fanged mouth.

"Looks like rat fer lunch, boys!" One of the monsters held up the catch proudly.

"Give it here, I wants a taste," another demanded, reaching for the morsel and receiving a backhand across the face from the trap-master.

"Back off ya pissants," the trap-master growled. "This will make a fine stew, maybe with some dried morels." The group eagerly nodded and licked their lips.

Bipp and Logan had to bite their tongues at the look on Grubble's face. They did not wait for the furry monsters to reset the trap, instead heading deeper into the dark room they had ducked inside, toward a rear entrance. They found the network of chambers on this side of the hall were all interconnected, running parallel to the corridor by open arched doorways. The furnishings had long past rotted, and the contents of the many rooms were in complete disarray after some ancient rounds of pillaging. The rooms were swimming in cobwebs and dust, and smelled of some foul, sour, odor the companions could not place.

They had to creep in the cover of rubble, as one of the rooms was missing a wall to the hallway. Of course, in this one exposed area, two female cobolds sat around a small fire in the hall, waiting for their trappers to come back with a meal.

"Smells like they caught themselves a plump juicy gnome!" one of the monsters declared, sniffing the air.

"Think its ghosts you be smelling again," the other disagreed.

The companions had no intention of sticking around long enough for either monster to find out which was right. They were already safely three rooms away by the time the trappers returned. Here the network of chambers came to a dead end, forcing them back out into the hallway, completely exposed.

"They are far enough down the other end," Corbin reasoned, reaching out to probe their path.

"Bipp what does that look like to ye? My eyes aren't what they used to be," Grubble asked, pointing above the slightly open wooden doors at the end of the hall. They were rotting and a stone plaque rested above them, etched with words neither brother recognized.

"Looks like old Gnomish script, hmmm...let's see." Bipp squinted to read the ancient script in the dark, scratching his head and lost in thought.

"This is what you have been searching for," Baetylus said, his ghostly form appearing beside Corbin.

"It says *king's audience,*" Bipp translated.

"What does that mean?" Logan asked.

"Means shut yer stupid pie hole and follow us, *human.*" Grubble slipped through the crack into the chamber beyond. Bipp shrugged apologetically and followed the warrior.

Through the other side, Logan bent down to whisper in his friend's ear. "What is his problem with us anyhow?"

"He doesn't trust you," Bipp said quietly. "Well not just *you*, he doesn't trust *any* humans. Not likely to find many gnomes that do."

"I can see that, but what I don't understand is why," Corbin said, joining the conversation.

"Cause yer *not to be trusted*," Grubble answered for him. "Beyond me why you think we would believe in ye bastards after everything ye done to our people." The brothers were both confused, they did not know about any feuds between the human and gnome races.

"Hmm, I think we may know more about Falian history than you," Bipp said, crawling over a collapsed pillar that had been smashed into large chunks across the corridor. By their silence, he judged he was correct.

"Ages past we gnomes came down into Vanidriell to leave the lands of man. Seems your folk were too much to handle up on the surface world, and there was a craving to get back to our roots anyhow. Anyway, centuries passed in peace, and my ancestors built a great kingdom here, devoted to the pursuit of knowledge and honing of craft.

Then, one day along comes the children of man again, seeking refuge in our lands. It seemed the surface world was being taken over by marauders who were bent on humanity's xenocide." Corbin hushed Bipp for a moment, searching the dark stairwell ahead for enemies. After a thorough probe, he motioned for them to continue. Both brothers were intrigued to hear a gnome perspective of their history.

"Where was I?" Bipp said. "Right...the refugees. So of course, our goodly ancestors took your people in. We even made homes for the humans and showed them lands they could live in and survive. We taught them how to farm the soil of Vanidriell and helped build towns for them to live in cohabitation with us." Grubble growled listening to the engineer's retelling of the well-known gnome history.

"Humans be a greedy lot though. No offense, I like the two of you well enough, not trying to be insensitive or nothing, you just are. It was not long before humans were setting up laws of their own, forcing goodly gnomes out of their homelands and robbing our people of their birthright. Your original council of twelve stole what we had been ready to freely give, backstabbing our kin and becoming violent. As you can imagine most gnomes would not be caught dead talking to the lot of you." Bipp shrugged, he really did like the two of them and was not about to be concerned with old grudges. He would rule his life based on the evidence set before him, a philosophy which most likely led to his becoming an engineer.

Grubble on the other hand, despite finding he did not actually mind the Walker brothers, would never bend his mind to accepting humans as anything other than untrustworthy fiends.

"That is just awful Bipp, I am so sorry." Logan gave a heartfelt apology, one that Corbin was touched to hear, since his brother was not one to show sympathy, being more likely to turn any situation into a joke. "So, is that why your nose is so big?" he added, proving Corbin wrong yet again. The little gnome giggled at his friends teasing until Grubble stopped dead in his tracks and turned to point a hairy finger at them.

"Ye think it's funny do ye?" Grubble scolded. "Yer people come down here and ruin everything for us good folk, and ye laugh about it?"

He clearly forgot himself, raising his voice and turning puffy cheeked as he spoke.

"No Grubble," Corbin said. "My brother did not mean to offend you, and we certainly don't think what happened back then was a matter of comedy either."

"Damn straight it's not," Grubble said. "Look around ye, does this look like something to laugh about?" Grubble spat on the ground in disgust, catching some of the flecks in his beard.

"Now Grubble...we don't know this was human work," Bipp said.

"Who else could have done this? Everything they done touched of ours turned to rot. Mark my words, the little *secret* old man Beauford was tellin' ye to find, it's just proof of the human evil that done cursed great Ul'kor." The gnome was speaking a little too loudly now for Corbin's comfort.

"Look you better calm down," Corbin said, "any louder and the whole city is going to know we are here."

"Well shut yer yap then," Grubble said, turning his back on them and stomping up the stairs.

The companions marched on for half a day, making their way up through the cursed crumbling deserted spire. Sometimes it was hours between cobold sightings, while at others the area was practically overflowing with the stinking humanoids, slowing their progress to a crawl.

At times like that they would find themselves slinking through shadows and behind any cover they could find. Somehow, either through sheer luck or high skill, or perhaps a little of both, they made it through their stinking ranks without a single fight.

The air began to pick up a different scent to Logan, less musty, and he had a hope that they were climbing out of the dank place. He let out a long sigh when they ducked through the last stairwell, out into the cool cavern air, surrounded by ancient towering structures. The perimeter of the upper city was surrounded by low-lying stone rails, built to stop the unwary from falling off the edge of the aerie. Gripping a cold moss-covered railing; Logan peered over the edge. Far below, the bridge they had crossed now looked like a miniature version of itself, silhouetted by the pitch black of the chasm underneath.

The two gnomes took in the scene with heart swelling awe and a profound pride, knowing they were the first of their people to behold the city in centuries. Colorful stained-glass domed towers riddled the tightly packed buildings, with all manner of gargoyles carved around their tops. One structure was large and squat, held aloft by spiraled columns that were so thick it would take five gnomes hand to hand to wrap their arms around them. Parts of its roof had caved in long ago and were now overgrown with thorny vines. The ceiling of the immense cavern was lined with a carpet of glowing blue moss, which blanketed the entire city in a faint eerie glow.

"We are going to need to rest for a short while at least," Corbin said.

"Ach, I hate to admit it, but the man's right," Grubble said. "Let's see where we can find some shelter."

Bipp gave an involuntary shudder as they made their way down the abandoned cobblestone road. He could not stop watching the empty window holes on either side of the ancient street. It felt as though there were eyes hiding behind each shadow, following him, even though Corbin assured there were no cobolds inhabiting the area.

"That should do for a bit," Grubble said, pointing down a long narrow alleyway, at an empty doorway. "Run yer little trick and see if it's safe."

"There is no one there. It's nothing like the rest of the city, not even any rats." Corbin's throat seemed to go dry as he spoke.

"Just say it like it is, fancy pants," Grubble grumbled in annoyance, heading down the alleyway. Despite Corbin's reassurances, Bipp could not help checking the windows and edge of the rooftop as they passed through the cramped alley, thinking that any second something foul was going to jump out and snatch him away. At the end of the alley sat a small, rounded courtyard, with a large crumbling marble fountain, long dried out and stained around its edges with brown smears. At its center rested a broken statue of a winged goddess reaching for the sky.

"I ain't going in there," Bipp croaked as they approached the open doorway of an ancient bathhouse.

"Bah, ye been hanging around with the human here too long if yer being afraid of a little bit of shadows." Grubble was cross to think a good gnome like Bipp would let some unlit room get the better of him. Gnomes had been living in the dark caverns of Vanidriell since the beginning of the Third Age. Anyhow, light was for surface dwellers.

"It'll be okay Bipp," Logan said. "Corbin says there's no one around. We should be safe here, for a while at least." Logan's coaxing worked and he led his friend into the shelter. There was a little discussion over whether they should start a fire to warm up. However, Corbin and Grubble both reasoned it would not be worth the risk, with the chance of cobolds spotting the flames and smoke outweighing the idea of warm toes.

"I'll take first watch while you guys get some rest," Logan offered, and they all settled in for some much-needed sleep.

Chapter 20

Lady Cassandra could hear the temple bells tolling in the distance, announcing the ninth hour to all of Fal. She could see nothing but the inside of the black hood they had placed over her head, while a prison guard prodded her from behind with the butt of his trident to keep her moving.

Stepping outside, Cassandra could hear the angry mob gathering for her public trial. People parted from their path, being ushered to either side by the barking soldiers in front of her. She stumbled on a rock and almost lost her balance. Someone shouted for the soldiers to let her go when the bottom of the hood flapped open, revealing nothing but the legs and worn boots of those pressing in around her. Someone was fervently speaking to the crowd up ahead, but she did not recognize the voice. Cassandra decided to reach out into the psychic Aether, to mirror what the attendees were seeing.

At the base of the crudely built trial platform, Elise Ivarone stood before a crowd of peasants, preaching of Lady Cassandra's innocence. The people of Fal were engrossed by her every word, genuinely interested to hear what the new Madame of Riverbell had to say. But why would this girl be trying to help her? Surely, they had not formed any sort of relationship in the small time she had been in the capitol. In fact, the women did not even know each other. She wondered if it could be rooted in her decision to help the Elise's fiancé with his task.

Curious, Cassandra's mind brushed against the girl's thoughts, sipping on the swirling waters of her memory. A scene unfolded like a foggy dream, of Lady Penelope convincing Elise that it would befit her new station to show support for the wrongfully accused noblewoman. Cassandra could see the way the girl ate up Penelope's suggestions.

She could not help the lingering smile under the hood. It never hurt to find new allies, no matter how many she already possessed. Even the callous Lady Penelope saw a need to be on her side. Of course, it must for no other reason than to align her house with the power of the winner. The woman never did bet on a loser.

Who was Cassandra to argue? Today Fafnir would eat his leering smile, him and Viktor, and then she would make sure they were paid back in full for this transgression. That weasel might think this little game he played out was all in fair sport, but Cassandra would make certain he got what was coming to him.

Her eyes stung as the hood was unceremoniously yanked from her head. Cassandra was now standing on the wooden stage that would serve as her trial grounds. She could not imagine how Fafnir convinced the Council to try her publicly. Her mouth went dry when she saw the noose tied at the front of the platform. In the back of her mind, she wondered if it was even half as rough as the stuff they bound her wrists with, and just as soon, recognized what an odd thing it was to ponder.

Most members of the Council were already seated on the stage. Thoughts of the noose quickly faded, replaced by a sense of calm as she looked over at Elder Marcus and his comforting smile. Cassandra raised her chin up high, waiting for the Arch Councilor to arrive, and well past ready to get on with this charade.

Magistrate Fafnir made his way through the crowd with the Arch Councilor at his side. No soldiers were necessary where Zacharia was concerned, the citizens, noble and peasant alike, moved respectfully out of his path.

Elise was still lost in the throes of her speech to the mob when the two men arrived. She even looked their way as Penelope had instructed, so the Arch Councilor could see what a capable leader she would be for New Fal.

"What in Acadia is that girl doing?" Zacharia asked the Magistrate.

"It would appear, milord, she has been rousing up the people all afternoon. There has been much talk against the council's decision to try the witch Cassandra today." Fafnir slithered like a snake in the Elder's ear.

"Hmm, perhaps we misjudged the citizens of Riverbell after all." Zacharia brooded, watching the young woman he had granted sanctuary riling up the crowd. "I will speak to the other members of the council on what they have heard."

Ready for this moment, Fafnir signaled his men, who were dressed in plain clothes disguised as peasants. Hidden throughout the crowd, the lackeys sprung to action, throwing rotten vegetables and fruits at the girl. After a couple hits, Elise scrambled to get out of the line of fire, sending a ripple of laughter through the crowd. She stopped short and caught one of the apples midair. Unseen by those surrounding him, the magistrate gave the slightest of twitches with his cane, sending a burst of magic into the unsuspecting girl. Cassandra could see the look of utter disbelief on Elise's face, as one of her hands moved of its own volition, flinging the grimy apple directly at Arch Councilor Zacharia, where it bounced harmlessly across his chest, leaving a smear of rotten fruit on his robe.

The crowd fell silent while the Arch Councilor's expression grew dark indeed, and Elise stammered to explain. Cassandra could see it all unfold plain as day, from her vantage point, but no one else seemed to notice. No one except for Lady Penelope, who wore a smug grin.

"So, this was her ruse all along?" Cassandra thought.

"Seize that woman," Fafnir shouted right on cue to his soldiers, who were quick to obey. Grabbing Elise, they pulled her forcefully up onto the back of the stage, where two guards held her on her knees at spear point. Arch Councilor Zacharia took his seat and rang the small bell to commence the proceedings.

"Esteemed members of the Council, may I interject before we proceed with the right of truth?" Fafnir boldly asked over the crowd, dramatically waving his arms in the air to gather everyone's attention below.

"Showboat all you want weasel," Cassandra thought. *"It won't help you."* There were far too many allies for this kind of nonsense. Zacharia bowed his head, allowing the man to proceed.

Fafnir bowed low to the Elders then turned to address the crowd. "Good citizens of Fal, we have come together today to witness the trial of Lady Cassandra Alderman, accused this day of breaking the hallowed laws of our fair kingdom." The citizens in the mob began shouting that this was absurd, calling the Magistrate a liar and telling him where he could stick his charges.

Elder Viktor rose to his feet, slamming his staff on the ground to quiet the hecklers. "Silence! You *will* respect the laws of trial, or you will be removed." The crowd fell silent. Heckling Fafnir was one thing, but no one dared speak out against a member of the Twelve.

Fafnir bowed to the man in gratitude. "As I was saying, we have come here to witness the trial of Lady Cassandra Alderman. But before we begin, as the Magistrate of our grand kingdom, I feel it is my job…nay, my duty as a seeker of justice, to bring new evidence to light."

Cassandra could not possibly comprehend what trickery the rat was pulling, but her stomach felt queasy, nonetheless. A murmur ran through the crowd, getting louder as it headed toward the stage. Citizens were stepping aside to let someone through, but Cassandra could not make out whom it was. Her stomach felt hollow, and her heart grew cold at the sight.

"Behold the traitor, Jayne Aldermankin, the Lady Cassandra's very own handmaiden," Fafnir said. "Caught this very morning by the good Sir John Pinkle, as she tried to flee our city carrying secret stolen scrolls of magic and plans of Fal's defenses to Malbec."

John roughly pulled the young woman through the crowd toward the stage. Jayne looked haggard. Her skin was layered in dirt and her clothing torn. He pulled her up the stage by a rope tied around her throat. Cassandra could see the girl had been severely beaten and judging by the glazed look in her eyes drugged as well.

John stopped at the top of the steps to give a good shove with the heel of his boot against the dazed woman's hindquarters, toppling her hard into the wooden planks of the platform. Sobbing, Jayne pitifully tried to pull herself up, but she was too weak to manage it. Armed soldiers roughly yanked her to a standing position.

"Those are scrolls from the Council sanctum!" Elder Viktor exclaimed, feigning astonishment and pointing at the items John was handing to the Magistrate. Fafnir held them up for all to see.

Arch Councilor Zacharia was on his feet, absolutely outraged at the theft. "Where did you get these scrolls, young lady?"

"I'm afraid she cannot answer you, milord," Fafnir said. "Good John here had to ward himself from the witch's infernal sorcery but fear not we know the conspiracy in full after an extensive investigation." Fafnir gripped Jayne's jaw, opening her mouth to show the council they had removed her tongue, seemingly to protect themselves from hexes. Gasps ran through the crowd and one woman screamed that she a witch. Fafnir shoved Jayne back to the planks as others joined in, screaming out for her execution.

That tightening feeling in Cassandra's stomach moved to her chest and tears streaked from her eyes to see Jayne's abuse. She pulled the girl into her arms and tried to comfort her. She could feel Jayne's heart beating hard enough to pop through the ragged shirt and smell the rank stink of fear on the girl.

"Tell us of this conspiracy, Magistrate," Elder Viktor commanded.

"Jayne thought to ploy good John here. It has long been common knowledge that he has sought her hand in marriage. She thought to play on those feelings, and that was her folly. Had she not underestimated this man's honor, his loyalty to Fal, we may never have found out until it was too late. For Jayne wanted his help to get her back to Malbec, where her conspirators even now await the return of Lady Cassandra, *their leader*! It has all been a ruse, to gain power over the council, to take over our land and overthrow the great kingdom of New Fal!" Fafnir incited the crowd nearly to riot with his words, while Arch Councilor Zacharia had to slam his gavel repeatedly to silence the bloodthirsty mob.

"We have seen enough," Zacharia said. "The trial will not progress. The evidence of truth has been presented. All of those in favor for a vote of innocence?"

Only Elder Marcus raised his hand. The world fell away from Cassandra, as he looked round himself in bewilderment at the rest of the Council.

"All of those in favor for a vote of guilt?" Every single other member of the Twelve raised their hands, some even happy to do so. People she had counted on, that she trusted, people that had made promises to support her, rose their hands while meekly looking away. Unable to meet her gaze as they cowardly went along with the will of the people.

"So be it," Zacharia said. "On this day, the Lady Cassandra Alderman will be hanged to the death for the crime of unlawful magical instruction and the proof of treason against the kingdom. Her handmaiden Jayne Aldermankin has also been seen guilty and will be hanged to the death."

Jayne's panic racked her body in convulsions, as Arch Councilor Zacharia pronounced their death sentence. "Furthermore, given the evidence of both women being at the center of this conspiracy, all members of the Alderman House will be taken into custody and summarily executed before dawn."

Cassandra felt her body grow numb. She felt far removed from her physical being, distant from these dark events. It was as if she were floating above the stage, wondering at the spectacle below where nothing seemed real. A soldier fiercely tore Jayne away from her, pulling the mewling girl toward a second noose they had setup. Fafnir shoved Elise hard to the ground by Cassandra's feet.

"And what of the treacherous Elise Ivarone of Riverbell, Arch Councilor?" he asked with murderous intent gleaming in his eyes.

Zacharia studied the girl for a moment, thinking through the best course to take. "Take her back to the dungeons where we will try her in private on the next eve."

Cassandra reached down to help Elise to her feet, slipping a smooth stone into her palm and whispering into her ear, "Protect this for me until Corbin's return. Have no fear child, all is not lost."

Fafnir signaled a soldier to separate the women and sidled in, eager to lead her to the awaiting noose. He looped it over her neck with a deep look of satisfaction. She had indeed underestimated him for the last time.

"Nothing to say again, *Lady* Cassandra?" Fafnir slithered in her ear making a show of slowly tightening the noose. "This is turning into quite the habit."

Cassandra spit in his face. It was the first time in almost two hundred years she behaved so crudely. Fafnir carefully wiped the spittle from his cheek then backhanded her sharply across the face. Instead of crying out, she began to laugh at him.

"What is so funny?" he snarled, pulling the noose snug around the soft skin of her wrinkled neck.

"I stopped them," she managed between the bubbling laughter.

"Stopped who," Fafnir growled, "what are you prattling on about woman? Have you taken leave of your senses so quickly? Please, do not take the pleasure out of this for me."

"Back in the Citadel...over two centuries ago...it was me. I was the one who stopped the Council from killing you." Fafnir pulled back from the woman, searching her eyes for some hint of madness. She grinned ruefully at him, and he held his breath.

"What...?" he stammered.

"You half-blood filth, they were right all along. One way or another, you can never trust a jotnar." She smiled, vindictively revealing the bastard's half-blood lineage.

The Magistrate stumbled backward away from her, almost tripping on his own robes. She followed him with unwavering eyes then turned, bravely facing the crowd with her head held high. A loud click sounded as the executioner pulled the heavy wooden lever, opening trap doors beneath the women.

Jayne struggled hard against the noose, as it dug deeply into her gurgling neck. Lady Cassandra, however, was eerily calm, thinking only on how the rope did indeed scratch just as badly as it had on her wrists.

In the center of the mob, she could make out Alain's spirit, standing with arms outstretched. He was waiting for her to join him in the light of the Crystal. She followed him, deep into the bright, mystical light of the after world, and far away from the bloodthirsty cheers of the crowd below.

Logan's boot scuffed against a pebble, skittering across the floor and waking Bipp from his deep slumber. He had been dreaming of a time when Ul'kor was filled with other gnomes, alive and thriving as the cultural center of Vanidriell. As it faded and he realized it was not real, he felt a pang of sadness that it had all been lost to the ages. His friend scuffed a boot across the tiles again. Bipp dimly wondered why Logan was pacing around in the back of the room.

"He's probably having a hard time staying awake," he thought. Bipp's rubbed the sleep out of his eyes and stared across the room to his companions. *"That's funny,"* he thought, *"how is Logan making all that noise when he's sitting slumped against the wall across from me?"* The thought of it was like being doused with a bucket of icy water. His heart, along with the tufts of silver hair covering his ears grew stiff. Again, the sound of something scraping against stone came. Bipp was fully out of his daze now, realizing with whimpering horror it was coming from right behind where he lay. He held his breath, not daring to reveal he was aware something was in the room with them. Slowly he reached for the hammer resting next to his boots. His fingers froze in place when he felt hot sticky breathing on his neck. Unable to contain himself any longer, Bipp howled, waking up the entire camp. Cold claws clamped around his ankle and yanked his body across the stone floor, toward a shadowy corner in the back of the room.

Logan jumped up, cursing himself for nodding off. He saw Bipp being dragged across the floor and lunged to grab ahold of his wrist. Whatever had him was fiercely stronger than a cobold, wrenching the screaming gnome into an opening at the base of a ruined wall. Corbin charged past him, into the shadows already swinging his polearm past Bipp's feet. The blade chopped into something hard, taking a chunk out, but not severing the grasping claws. Grubble grabbed the pleading little gnome's other wrist and threw his weight backward, pulling Bipp further away from the shadows, giving Logan just enough leverage to free his hand and blindly let out an electric blast from his metal fist.

The area lit up with a flash. For the briefest of moments they all got a glimpse of the horrible creature that had their friend. It was a flicker of long gangly arms, covered with rotting gray flesh, bloody drooping eyes filled with an unquenchable hunger, and sharp bonelike spikes running along a horribly disfigured spine. The creature gurgled as the electricity knocked it painfully back. Dropping to all fours, the nightmare scurried backward into the hole and disappeared.

Flipping onto his back, Bipp scrambled away from the opening still thrashing his arms out to hit the terrible thing that was no longer there.

"What in the bloody hell was that?" Logan asked his brother "I thought you said there was nothing in here?"

"There wasn't when I scanned the area," Corbin said, sounding unsure of himself. "I'm sorry...this is all new to me."

"It's not yer fault twinkle toes," Grubble said. "That there was a bonestalker, mindless remnant of some unlucky bastard. No one's home in there." Grubble rapped on his temple for reference. "The cursed things will follow their prey for days, waiting until the time is right to come in and snatch ye when ye be safe in bed." He spat on the floor in revulsion.

"Take me for what?" Bipp's said, his face drained of all color.

"Suck yer brains out, naturally," Grubble casually replied, gathering up his boots to get dressed.

"And...we're done resting." Logan said. As he went to move, he staggered sideways. Corbin reached out to steady him, but he shook his head and used the wall for support.

"Where does your fist get the energy to do that?" Corbin asked.

Logan shrugged and popped the cap on his waterskin, knocking back a long steady gulp.

"Well, you better be careful using it," Corbin said. "It looks like it takes a heavy toll on you."

"Can we just get out of here?" Logan said.

Nobody needed to be told a third time, all of them more than eager to put some distance between the bathhouse. With weapons drawn, the companions fell into a defensive formation, Corbin taking the lead. Logan and Bipp each watched the buildings to their sides, and Grubble stalked behind to defend their rear. After about an hour of marching without being pursued, they relaxed a little.

"We're almost all the way across the city," Corbin pointed out. "If we go any further, we'll be out of the ruins entirely."

"That can't be right, we haven't found what we came here for yet," Logan complained.

"Okay, where do we go next then, what's your plan?" Corbin asked expectantly.

"I don't know, I kinda thought it would just sorta come to me once we got here...," Logan admitted, hearing how ridiculous it sounded when spoken aloud. He shook his head in embarrassment.

Baetylus appeared in front of Corbin, blocking his view of Logan. He pointed his staff to a nearby domed building. *"This is where you will find what you seek."*

Corbin sensed many cobolds living in the structure. *"All-Father, how can we possibly hope to remain undetected while we search this place?"* Corbin said, using his mind to speak, not wanting his friends to hear the fear laced in his words.

"You are the righteous chosen of Baetylus. Fear not the petty weak-minded humanoids, they will be of little challenge for you, my champion." Corbin nodded his head, feeling more confident to have his god's trust.

"We should head there, to that domed building," Corbin said. "That is where I sense the answers Fimbas sent you to seek are most likely to be waiting."

Grubble shook his head and pointed his axe to the largest building instead, eyeing it at the end of his blade with one eye closed. It towered over everything around, built in tiers of sharp angled stone carved into rectangular buildings, connected as one large towering gnothic structure. Something was protruding from the roof, but at their low vantage it could not be seen clearly.

"I don't know why but, the All-Father is pointing us in that direction," Corbin insisted.

"Don't give a flippin' flyin' crap storm what yer voices be sayin'...," Grubble said. "Makes the most sense to check out the King's Castle first." Corbin could see there was no deterring the gnome from his course.

"I agree with Grubble," Logan said thoughtfully. "We should check it out. I mean just look at the place, it's practically begging for us to come inside and take a peek." He sounded excited at the prospect.

265

"Clearly there is no stopping your curiosity," Corbin said. "Let's head there first, but afterwards to the other, agreed?" Logan and Bipp nodded, but Grubble just shrugged.

The castle's gates were crushed inward, shards of stones littering the ground. One of the doors was still miraculously hanging on a lone hinge. Logan could only guess what could have been strong enough to do that much damage and hoped he never had to find out. All around the ground were strewn rusted remains of armor and dried bones of gnomes and humans.

"Didn't I tell ye Bipp, there's yer proof, it was the human traitors that brought this curse down on Ul'kor." Grubble slapped the engineer's chest, pointing at the mess.

The interior of the castle was overgrown with weeds as well, but there was still something majestic about the place, as if all the damage in Acadia could not wipe away the pride that had been masterfully crafted into the stoic building.

They traveled through the ruins for some time, with Bipp showing the way, translating ancient writings that marked directions. The gnomes of old were very pragmatic in their construction. Ahead of them the hallway ended in double doors before veering sharply to the left.

"There's the king's court up ahead!" Bipp exclaimed scurrying onward in excitement. Grubble lunged forward, yanking the engineer back by his collar.

"Watch yer step ye idjit," he warned, slapping the back of Bipp's head and pointing to the walls. They were lined with fist-sized portholes.

"Looks like a defense system, probably setup to stop invaders," Corbin guessed.

"Course it is, standard gnome build-out. Ye just have to step in the right order." Grubble explained, referring to the large square floor tiles.

"Hard to see what the patterns are," Logan said. "How are we going to get across?" He was anxious to get inside. They were so close to uncovering Mr. Beauford's mystery, he could feel it in his bones.

"I could always throw you across to test it out...," Grubble offered. "Bah...I'm just kidding. First thing is don't be steppin' where them dead rats are," Grubble said, referring to the cobold corpses that lay about the wide hall, marking wrong paths. "Secondly, these dogs must have figured out the right path. Ye can see where some of them are much less dusty, must be used more often."

Corbin looked closely at the tiles, most of which were virtually covered in a thick layer of dirt and dust. The gnome's reasoning was sound. Some of the tiles were clearly used more often, evidenced by the tracks in the dust. Using this logic Logan recklessly skipped from one to the next, safely making his way across the trapped hall. Once on the other side he turned to give his companions the thumbs up signaling for them to follow.

They were about halfway across to meet him, when footsteps announced a visitor, freezing them all in place like statues. Logan slipped into a dark corner beside a fallen section of the hall wall just in time to conceal himself from a cobold who drunkenly staggered into view from the side corridor. The filthy humanoid stopped to urinate on the ten-foot oak doors, completely oblivious to the trio standing still in various locked poses down the hall behind it. Burping, the monster finished with a wiggle, then turned around to stretch. He cocked his head and looked at the group curiously, trying to make sense of what he was seeing. Then the little dimwitted humanoid sobered up, straightening out his back like a board. He opened his mouth to shout. Logan jumped out of the corner to stop the monster, but Corbin's voulge flew through the air, hurled like a spear, and beat him to the punch, cleanly pinning the vile creature's head to the massive door.

Grubble looked back to the man with a leering smile. "That was a pretty decent bit of slice 'n dice." He nodded appreciatively, bringing a smile to Corbin. Adding, "For a human..." as he pulled the weapon from the door and tossed it to him.

Logan was trying in vain to pry the sealed doors free, but they would not budge. "How do we get these blasted things open?" he gasped, exerting all his force in the attempt. Grubble grunted, shoving him to the side, and moved in to add his strength, but still the door would still move.

"Not likely to get them open that way," Bipp said, showing them a mechanism on the wall that he said would activate the doors lock. "These ruins here would be the way in, just have to figure them out."

"How long should that take?" Logan asked, disappointed at being slowed down yet again.

"Hmmm..., could be some time lads. This is some ancient language for sure, going to have to figure out the right order." He scratched the tip of his nose thoughtfully, playing out different combinations in his head.

Logan came up behind him and laughed when he saw the ruins etched in the wall. Each set of markings was carved into a cylindrical stone that rotated up and down forming the proper combination across. "This would have been operated by the king's guard, a failsafe against intruders," Bipp murmured, still tapping his nose. Moving in front of him, Logan rolled the pieces into different positions and stepped back.

"Could be dangerous to put in a random sequence, in fact it's guaranteed to be," Bipp warned, stopping him from throwing the switch.

"It's not random, I saw this somewhere... Think it was an old book I read in Elder Morgana's library?" he said, directing the question to Corbin.

Looking at the symbols Corbin felt a heavy sense of deja vu. "Wasn't *in* a book she had. This exact ruin was carved into the wood above the bookcases in her bedroom!"

"Some old bat had our ancient kingdom's ruins carved into her bookshelves?" Grubble asked skeptically.

"It would make sense in a library," Bipp remarked thoughtfully. "The four of these together means to say, '*Knowledge is truth, Power is blind'.*"

With that, he stepped forward to push in the large stone switch, activating the mechanism. Soundlessly the doors opened inward. As they stepped inside Bipp whistled at the majestic throne room beyond, which was vast. The king's court was so large it could fit half an army and still have a little wiggle room. And the place was pristinely preserved, the strains of time only leaving a stale odor to the air, though the walls were covered with dust and cobwebs. They could see a great battle had been fought in this room, as the corpses of humans, gnomes, and cobolds could attest to.

"Well would you look at that?" Bipp wondered, pointing up at where the stained-glass ceiling was holding the largest stalactite any of them had ever seen up close.

"It must have crashed down from the roof of the cavern somehow," Logan said.

"I can't believe the glass did not shatter entirely from the weight of this thing," Corbin replied in awe.

"Gnome craftsmanship is a thing of beauty, lad," Grubble said, proudly admiring the ceiling.

The masterfully set stained glass around the hulking rock, though splintered, was still intact. They could see the blue glowing moss far over ahead, which made the colorful images iridescent, and bent against the stained glass to light the room up. Across the room, an empty, ornately carved throne of gold, with red satin lining, sat at the top of a short flight of stairs with a smaller twin beside it.

"Look up there at the carvings," Logan said, referring to a series of chiseled marble cameos surrounding the perimeter of the ceiling.

Grubble muttered that he could care less about some artwork. What he really wanted to see was the throne, up close and personal. The warrior made it halfway across the room before smacking hard into an invisible wall, his big nose flopping sideways and his salt-n-pepper beard flattening against the unseen barrier. The companions were startled by the ringing sound the impact made, echoing sharply across the room.

"What in the blazes?" Grubble snapped. There was nothing in front of him but air.

Bipp ran up to check it out, slapping a palm on the invisible thing. Each hit rang dully in the chamber. "Some sort of magical barrier, never heard of nothing like this before..." Bipp looked up from where the wall would be to see if there was anything overhead.

"Some more evil human witchcraft, no doubt," Grubble mumbled, rubbing his jaw.

"What do these mean?" Corbin asked, pointing to the cameos above.

"It's like a story retelling important events that occurred during the time of King Thorgar and his forebears," Bipp explained, having read about Acadian temples that did something similar with their windows.

Corbin nodded. It made sense, the scenes did seem to depict the gnomes coming to Vanidriell and building the great city of Ul'kor, practicing their craft at creating many other ancient artifacts. Story after story played out on the ivory marble carvings. The gnomes explored the land, searching high and low, until one day they came across the Great Crystal god Baetylus, who graced them with his wisdom and warmth. From that day forth, they were devoted to his glory, reveling in the love and promise of an everlasting afterlife. The ghostly visage of the All-Father shimmered into view nearby Corbin, smiling lovingly at him.

"I... I can't believe this... I never imagined...," Logan said, dropping his rifle to his side, deeply awestruck by the revelation. His skin grew pale.

"It truly is magnificent is it not?" Corbin wondered aloud, while the All-Father laughed warmly beside him. "Bipp, I had no idea your people followed the teachings of Baetylus. Why didn't you join me any of the times I was in prayer?"

Grubble scrunched his face and looking at him. Bipp furrowed his brow, as if he just asked him the question in a foreign language.

"Corbin...what in the Hel are you talking about?" Logan asked incredulously, while emphatically gesturing at the scenes. "Don't you understand what this means?"

Baetylus silently nodded his head, looking up at the reliefs in pride. "Of course," Corbin said. "I'm being foolish, this place is centuries old, and your people have forgotten most of the teachings learned here." He shook his head. "What was I thinking? But now that you see…now that *we* know, together we can be heralds to a new age in Vanidriell. Your people can become one with the Great god Baetylus once more, and the broken bonds between our races can finally be restored."

Logan looked to the gnomes then back at him flabbergasted. "I think he's had mental break, lads," Grubble said, with a sincere look of concern.

Logan took a couple long strides over and backhanded Corbin squarely in the jaw, shocking him to his senses. "Snap out of it, Corbin, this is serious!" he yelled, grabbing his brother's head, and forcibly directing his gaze back up at the cameos.

This time it was as if they were fuzzy or unfocused somehow. Corbin squinted and rubbed his eyes to make them out better, they *were* high up after all. The gnomes came into Vanidriell ages ago; they built great cities, starting with Ul'kor. They practiced deep ancient magic, tapping into the secrets of the universe and pushed the boundaries of their sciences, propelling technology vastly with the insight of mankind who later joined them.

There was a carving of Arch Councilor Zacharia himself and the rest of the council of Twelve making a pact with the gnomes!

"But how can that be," Corbin stammered. "These ruins are ancient; how could the Elders have been here?"

"Keep looking," Logan said.

Together the gnomes and humans created their crowning achievement, the Great Crystal Baetylus, a tool to bring life to the wilds and spread their kingdom even further into the desolate caverns of Vanidriell. With this mighty construct, they could sustain plant and animal life in previously uninhabitable regions of Vanidriell. However, over time, the Council turned their back on the gnome's warnings and shut themselves away from the rest of the land.

Corbin shoved his brother away, staggering back in disbelief. This had to be a mistake, or some trick! Baetylus was still laughing, but there was a different lilt to it, like the keen gloating of a crocodile that was enjoying the feast.

"All-Father, this can't be true," Corbin pleaded, turning to Baetylus. "How can you be a creation of the gnomes?"

"Oooh...the lad has surely had a mental break," Grubble said "He's even talking to himself now."

Baetylus' cackling swelled and it was as if a veil was pulled from Corbin's eyes. For the first time he noticed the thin lines of energy flowing from his body, feeding the symbiotic monstrosity before him. His hands twitched and he stepped back from the Crystal god shaking his head in denial. The air about the room swelled in a spiral around the white robed man, whipping the companions clothing and hair toward him as his form grew brighter.

"Great Thorgar...," Bipp shouted as the visage became visible to the entire group. "Where did *he* come from?"

"Foolish puny mammal," Baetylus' voice roared in Corbin's mind. "You should have done as you were told! I warned you to get your brother back to Fal! I told you not to come here!"

With both hands, Grubble heaved his mighty battle-axe at the deity, but he flickered, and it passed harmlessly through.

"You should have listened to your God, *boy*," Baetylus boomed like the center of an inferno, his face morphing into a hideous otherworldly snarl. As the winds grew stronger the false god's mouth grew longer and longer, lips stretching to the floor and sucking in the air around them. Bipp fell on his back, being pulled in toward the sick gullet.

"Don't do this, my Lord!" Corbin pleaded.

"It is too late. Now you DIIIIIIEEEEEE!!!!" the Crystal roared with peels of twisted laughter as it crushed Corbin's mind under the sheer power of its being with one massive blast, as easy as snuffing a candle. The visage exploded in the center of the room throwing their bodies hard into the wall behind. Corbin did not even have time to ponder his fate, as a wave of psionic energy tore through his exposed mind.

"By all the gods of Mytar," Grubble groaned, pulling himself back to his feet. "What in blazes was that?"

Logan was sobbing, begging his brother to wake up as he crawled across the room to his limp body. Even the notoriously grouchy Grubble felt the strings of his heart pulled to hear the young man's pain.

Bipp just stood there, balancing himself against the wall on shaking legs, hopelessly watching his friend. Logan desperately felt for a pulse that he knew would not be there and wailed in utter despair, confirming that Corbin Walker was dead.

Baetylus cackling form slithered through the night, searching for the sleeping mind of the cobold shaman, Burgoth. The filthy little monster rested at the feet of her master, the resident king of the Ul'kor ruins. She was happily dreaming of whipping her minions as they begged at her own hairy feet for mercy. It was a little thing for the Great Crystal to interrupt the dream, much simpler than the suggestions he fed humans. With a thought, the whips morphed into snakes, turning to bite at her face. Burgoth threw the weapon into the fire. Eating her worshiper's whole instead. The snakes slithered away from the flames down a long winding corridor. Chasing them the shaman could see their shadows sprawled across the walls. The silhouettes were in the shape of two gnomes and one human, all carrying sacks overflowing with shiny sparkly trinkets!

Burgoth snarled awake, bolting upright to call out for her apprentice as she roused the king from his own dreams of a gnome invasion. "Master, we haves some intruders," her snake-like tongue flickered with the dire implications. "They are in the old false King's chambers trying to steal our treasures."

The king shoved her away, rolling out of bed and roaring for his men to raise the alarm and alert the city. They had intruders to hunt down.

Grubble was anxiously pacing in front of the massive doors to the King's court, which he had pushed securely closed, slapping his battle-axe against his palm.

All around the city echoes of screeching cobolds could be heard. He told Bipp the dogs were coming, and it was only a matter of time before they were surrounded. Grubble had a heavy suspicion that the bloody Crystal had alerted their presence somehow. Logan was no use to them, mourning over his brother in a nearly catatonic state. He just kept rocking back and forth holding the dead man's head to his chest.

Meanwhile Bipp was frantically searching the room for an alternate route. They could not head back out the gates of the castle. That would be akin to suicide with nowhere to hide from the hundreds of cobolds no doubt gathering in that direction. Standing their ground and facing the horde was a death sentence. Even as good a warrior as Grubble was, the odds were overwhelmingly stacked against them. Bipp kept finding himself back at the invisible wall, kicking and cursing the damnable thing for blocking their exit.

What gnome worth his salt would build a great hall like this for a king without an escape route? Even a backwater trade port like Dudje had escape tunnels built under the mayor's home. Sure, they were the same routes used to transport waste, but hey, what worked works.

Bipp stopped and snapped his fingers. That gave him an idea! He held a hand up while mentally circling the room. Another snap and he pointed to a specific tile. Running over to it, he giggled when he saw what he was looking for. Eight ruins woven together to make a larger picture, etched onto the solid marble. Waggling his stubby fingers, Bipp read them to figure out the right sequence then pushed down a couple into the floor. Each one clicked in place forming the insignia for the city engineers and the tile popped straight up from the floor, bobbing on a spring below.

Bipp whistled for Grubble to come over and together they turned the large tile counterclockwise, lifting it to reveal a tunnel. "These are the utility shafts!" Bipp said, excited at discovering ancient Ul'kor engineering. Outside the doors the sound of cobolds could be heard right in the hallway. They were screaming to kill the thieving gnomes.

"Get the human," Grubble said, thumbing over his shoulder.

"Logan, we have to go *now*," Bipp called as he ran over to his friend. Logan looked over with glassy eyes and tears leaking down his face.

"He's dead," Logan mumbled absently.

"C'mon now," Grubble said, "Ye've got to snap out if it man. We've got to be getting out of here!" He grabbed Logan and shook him forcibly. From the hallway, they could hear the cries of unlucky cobolds followed by iron spears rattling against the stone walls. Bipp guessed that some of the approaching monsters had triggered the traps.

"I can't leave him here all alone," Logan said.

"Ain't said nothing 'bout leaving no warrior behind," Grubble said gruffly. He reached down and flung Corbin's body over his shoulder like a sack of potatoes. Bipp tugged on Logan's sleeve, insisting he follow them. The doors to the king's court rattled as something massive battered them. "At least the bastards don't know the combination to release the locking mechanism." Grubble said.

The door rattled again; this time accompanied by a splintering noise. "Not sure it's going to matter much," Bipp said.

Grubble hopped straight down into the hatch, disappearing from view with Corbin's corpse. Bipp motioned for Logan to follow then jumped in behind him. Once they were all in the cramped tunnel, Logan helped Bipp move the large marble tile back in place overheard, turning it clockwise and pulling down to seal it. They were just in time as they heard the doors burst inward, chunks of wood rattling over the floor overhead, followed by the sounds of dozens of cobolds pouring into the room screaming for blood.

Chapter 21

Elise sat alone in her drafty prison cell, mulling over the loss of Lady Cassandra. She was trying to understand why this all happened, and how it could be better for the kingdom. Trying to rationalize the insanity of it all, to somehow put it in the perspective of the Elders, who must surely always have the best interest of the people in mind.

Her mind kept wandering back to Corbin. What would he do if he saw her locked away in a cell like some criminal? She imagined what he might say to the Elders to free her, how he might handle her accusers and make sense of the situation. She had really messed this one up, not seeing through Lady Penelope's ruse to set her up. But why? What had she done to deserve the noblewoman's ire?

Elise wished he was there more than anything else in the whole world, to help her understand what was happening, and hold her tight. Whenever she thought about Corbin, she found it hard to breathe. It had already been twenty-one days since he left, and the Council made it clear that she would be the next execution should he not return with Logan by the week's end. Again, her mind wandered to what he would say to the Elders when he returned, how he would react to the news of her treatment by Fafnir. She could almost hear his voice in the back of her mind.

"Elise..."

"Yes, my love," she whispered, imagining she was speaking to him.

"Elise..."

She spun her head about in shock. The word became an actual whisper in her cell! What trickery could this be? Was she losing her mind? Had the insanity that gripped the capitol found its way into her own heart?

"Corbin?" she tentatively asked, thinking she must be mad indeed.

"Elise." The word tickled her neck, sending chills down her spine.

Corbin's mind had wandered the wastes of Vanidriell in search of his love. He refused to go into the light, stubbornly committed to warn her of the dangerous truth first.

"Elise, my darling." Waves of emotion rocked her, simultaneously resonating his deep affection and profound sorrow. "I am...I am *dead*."

Elise sobbed, hearing the words she had dreaded since he first stepped outside the city.

"Do not cry, my dear," Corbin said softly. "You must listen. I do not know how much time I have." Elise nodded, choking on her anguish to hear his words. "It was Baetylus. He murdered me...the Great Crystal is a lie."

Elise gasped, her senses reeling at the proclamation. "But...I do not understand. What you mean? Why would the All-Father *murder* you, who have long been a devoted follower to his teachings?"

Feeling that words could not adequately express his message, and not knowing how long he had left, Corbin reached into her mind, using the psionic energy that he was wrapped in to communicate to her through images.

Elise sucked in her breath and snapped her eyes open wide. Her head cocked back toward the ceiling as eyes rolled back in her head. Corbin's memories played across her vision. She watched the All-Father reaching out to teach Corbin, to guide him along the path and save the people of Riverbell. She saw his long trek through the wild lands, his encounters with Logan, his journey into the ruins of Ul'kor.

When Corbin's soul was forced from his corporeal form, snuffed by Baetylus' overwhelming psionic mastery, he had locked minds with the Crystal, if only for an instant. That fraction of an instant was all that he needed to see the truth of its past. The Crystal was created by the goodly gnome clerics of Ul'kor, as a way to bring the astral powers to Vanidriell. Their intentions were noble and pure, to help create life in some of the uninhabitable caverns, to make plants grow, and help animals survive. The Crystal was their crowning achievement and the king of Ul'kor praised the Cleric's for its creation in a lavish ceremony.

From the time Baetylus was born, it could sense the beings around it. It tried to communicate with them, but none would talk back. So, it sat alone, in the light, able to hear the world around but never participate. Over time, the Crystal gave itself the name Baetylus and longed to live life like those it served. It watched as humans fled to

Vanidriell from a power on the surface they could not match. It felt pure sorrow when the gnomes gifted it to them, in order to create a new homeland, and was forced to stand vigil leagues away as monstrous humanoids took over the city from which it was created.

Ah, but the *humans*, they were so very different from the gnomes. Baetylus found it could actually communicate with them. Not directly, but by swaying their thoughts. Soon after New Fal was established, the Crystal began to play with the new species like toys. Baetylus rejoiced for the first time since it came into the world. The Crystal's happiness was short lived however, as it found it could interact with the humans, but still could not speak directly to them.

Baetylus was simply not strong enough.

Craving an end to its unyielding solitude, Baetylus devised a plan. It began to feed off the life energy of all animals in New Fal to gain strength. The more sentient creatures offered a tastier morsel to its newfound hunger and as it fed off their energy, the Crystal grew larger and more powerful. To its annoyance, the gnomes began to become wary of their creation, warning the humans to stop their new religion, which was spreading through the land in worship of the construct. Baetylus would not tolerate the devious little gnomes' disruptions. Why shouldn't he be allowed to grow and communicate as they did?

Corbin watched in horror through Baetylus' mind as he turned the humans on their peaceful friends, forcing any gnome who had influence out of the very lands they had created and expanded to help the surface refugees.

"This is horrific," Elise gasped, shaking out of the trance.

"Baetylus is not a god," Corbin said. "It is more like a leech, and the people of New Fal are its prisoners as much as food its unquenchable appetite."

The room swooned and Elise had to lean her back against the wall where she sat to not fall over.

"There's one other thing you must see," Corbin said. A memory shot into Elise's mind like a hot knife, rocking her once more. Corbin did not mean to hurt her, but his control over the psionic realm was more powerful than he realized. In her mind's eye she saw the cameo from the King's Hall. Carved into the ivory marble was none other than Arch Councilor Zacharia, receiving the Crystal from the gnomes.

"How can that be?" she gasped.

"I do not know," Corbin said. "Only that the Elders have clearly kept our people living in many lies."

Elise was overcome by the information. It was all a little too much for her to grasp. To think Corbin was dead, yet somehow speaking to her, and that the All-Father was a false god. She pushed against her temples squeezing them in frustration, straining against this assault on her core beliefs.

"You *must* get our people to Malbec," Corbin warned, "away from the Crystal's influence."

"How can that be possible? Won't Baetylus just force us to stop? How can I defy the will of a god?"

"It is *not* a god," Corbin snapped. "You must stop thinking of it that way. The Crystal can push the human mind with suggestions, but it cannot make you do anything you do not want to." An image of him wildly assaulting his brother ran across her mind, followed by profound shame. "The only reason I could see him so clearly was the power Lady Cassandra unlocked from within."

As he sent the thought to her, Corbin could see a violent flash of Elise's memory laid open in the ethereal flow. The event's she had endured played before him.

"I am so sorry Elise," he said. "Lady Cassandra was a wonderful human being. It pains me to think she died as punishment for trying to help us…"

Elise was a river of emotion, comforting his distraught soul.

"Strange as well," he wondered out loud, "I thought for sure I sensed her presence here with you when I arrived."

Thinking how that could be, an idea occurred to Elise. Pulling the stone Lady Cassandra had given her out of her dress, she held it up as if Corbin could see which he could through her mind, but not with eyes on the physical plane.

To Elise the stone was a simple smooth obsidian, but to Corbin it was a fantastic glowing onyx, brilliantly illuminating the spiritual plane.

He was taken aback to see the images swirling deep inside the magical stone, and moved in closer, hoping to make them out better. Far away, inside the heart of the mystical stone, another world existed. It was a beautiful land, softly lit by a glowing orb high in the azure blue sky, with lush fields and gently trickling creeks. Beside the brook sat a younger Lady Cassandra, smiling contentedly with her bare feet splashing in the cool water. She looked over her shoulder, sensing Corbin as he connected minds with Elise so she too could view the amazing spectacle.

"Lady Cassandra...is that you?" he asked. Her lips moved to respond, but they could hear no words. Then the stone warmed in Elise's hands and the sorceresses' words flowed from his fiancée's mouth.

"Poor children, I am here with both of you," Cassandra spoke through her in a light voice.

"But I watched them execute you?" Elise asked in her own voice.

"Alas, this is true. The woman you knew as Lady Cassandra has been murdered by the vile traitor Fafnir. Long has the wretched half-blood jotun coveted power, and finally to our misfortune he has gained it. Woe be the future of New Fal with him sitting on the Council of Twelve." Cassandra lamented.

"But, if you are not Lady Cassandra, who are you?" Corbin inquired perplexed.

"I *am* Cassandra, a reflection of her at least. Long ago, I was wise enough to store a sliver of my soul inside the Onyx you now possess. When I died a piece of me split off and remained here, stored with what is left of my power in the living realm."

"I did not know such a thing was possible," Corbin said.

"I see the world you live in so much more clearly now. What fools were we, not to heed the warnings of the goodly gnomes. We can only dare to hope that it is not too late for the people of New Fal. The two of you must act as their saviors... You must be their voice of reason, freeing the bonds that chain our society to the corrupted abomination."

"But milady," Elise said, "how can we do anything? Corbin has been murdered and I am trapped here in a dungeon far away from my people."

"Dead? Oh no, my dear...Corbin is not dead. He is very much alive, just not inside his body at the moment," Cassandra said. "His love for you, so absolute, bound his spirit to Acadia long enough for his soul to gather in this protective cocoon of psionic energy," she explained, referring to the thick living blankets of blue energy that were swirling around his spiritual form, invisible to Elise's naked eye.

Corbin's mind danced around the form of Elise, rejoicing in this truth and thrilled at the newfound possibility of hope Cassandra presented.

"Corbin Walker, you will need to return to your corporeal form alone, if you can still find it, for I cannot help you with that. The longer you are out of your mortal coil the more damage may be caused, not to your mind or soul, but to the Acadian shell that is your body."

Corbin knew the implications were dire, conveyed by her mental projections. If he could not return quickly enough, his body would cease to be habitable. "But what of Elise and my people in Riverbell?" he asked.

"Fear not, for I have a plan," Cassandra said. "The universe has opened up to me in a different way, never had I such vision in life. Your journey lies past the ruins of Ul'kor, to the surface. I sense it is there that you will find a great mage, named Isaac, who will have the answers we seek. I will help Elise escape, buying time until you can free the people of New Fal from the shackles they unwittingly live under."

"Lady Cassandra, wasn't the surface destroyed in the great wars?" Elise asked, not understanding how someone named Isaac could be living up there.

Corbin understood. He had guessed it while exploring the Ul'kor ruins but did not want to fully accept the reality. "It's all been a lie, Elise. The wildlands, all those gnomes' towns out there, everything they told us about our history."

Cassandra confirmed his suspicion with a solemn nod.

"It was necessary to protect the survival of mankind. Unfortunately, there is not nearly enough time for us to go over our long-embattled history right now. The top priority is for you to get back to your mortal shell. I will give you a boost, but you must hurry and be on your way."

Corbin knew she was right; he could feel it as if the longer he drifted in this form the less substantial he was becoming. But the idea of parting from Elise was unbearable and he ached just to remain by her side.

"Please Corbin," Elise said in her own voice, "you must do as she says."

Corbin wrapped himself around her. "I *will* come back for you," he swore to the woman he loved more than life itself.

"I have faith in you," Elise said. "Now go, track down this Isaac. Find out how he can help us and come back to me." Corbin could feel her belief in him. In her heart of hearts, she knew that the man who dared to defy death just to speak with her one last time would find a way home again. It still pained Elise to feel his presence fade away and she began to cry, left alone once more in the cold dank cell.

"You are *not alone*, my dear," Cassandra said. "Now hold the Onyx to your forehead so I can channel my magic through your avadhuti, into the physical plane."

Elise did as she was instructed, closing her eyes as the warm stone touched the soft skin of her forehead. Clouds of purple energy swirled from within the rock, moving in tendrils outward, covering her body with the magical will of Cassandra. Weaving with mystical mastery, Cassandra opened a rift in the physical plane around them that dropped Elise through a void.

Landing on her feet in the dust she almost dropped the magical artifact. As Elise looked around, she was dumbfounded at the heavy expenditure of power Cassandra had unleashed. Where only moments before she had been sitting in a New Fal dungeon cell, now she was miles away in the village square of Riverbell! There was no time to stand in awe, however. An astonished farmer named Barth stood stock still, rubbing his eyes in disbelief at her sudden appearance.

"Don't just stand there Barth! Alert the entire village. We are in danger, and we have to escape right NOW!" she barked at the man, determined to set her people on the journey that would take them safely away from this cursed kingdom.

Chapter 22

The cramped utility tunnels were pitch-black. Even the Vanidriell dwellers, who were accustomed to darkness having grown up in caves all their lives, had a hard time seeing further than an arm's length ahead. They had stopped to rest hours ago and the time for moving on was well past, but neither gnome had the heart to tell Logan that. His brother's lifeless body was laid respectfully on the stone floor, covered with a wool blanket from his pack.

The trio left the cobold horde far behind, fleeing as fast as they could through the cramped tunnels beneath Ul'kor palace. For a while, they could still hear the humanoids running up and down the corridors above, bitterly searching for any sign of the intruders. Bipp reasoned the monsters were too ignorant to figure out they were in the maintenance shafts beneath the building. Only an engineer would think to check inside them, and he doubted there were too many plumbers in the mix of rabble up above.

No one had spoken for some time now, dwelling on the loss of their newest companion. The stuffy air felt palpable with sorrow, so thick that even Grubble felt on the verge of it, although this could have been more out of frustration than anything else. Logan was not sure how long the tears had been running down his numb cheeks. He felt cold and alone, though his good friend Bipp sat close at-hand.

"Corbin...I'm so sorry for your loss," Bipp croaked. "My heart bleeds for you." He was not sure if the man was listening, or if he had slipped back into some sort of catatonic state, but felt it was well past time to break the awkward silence.

Logan looked over at him with cloudy green eyes, unaware what his friend had just said, "It's all so crazy...he can't be dead."

"I'm sorry lad," Grubble said filled with remorse, "but the lad's cold as a wet stone in the wind."

Logan pressed the palms of his hands against his closed eyelids, shaking his head. "All these years...all this time I had...and I wasted it."

"Aw c'mon Logan," Bipp said. "You can't say such things."

"You don't understand," Logan said. "When I was growing up all I could ever think about was how to get him to leave me alone... just give me some peace and quiet, but every time I turned around, *there* was my little brother following me around again." Logan found the words sticking in his throat. "I spent years walking around and acting like a jerk...wasted, just wasted all that time I could have spent with him."

The gnomes did not know what to say. Bipp looked to the ground while Logan rubbed his eyes again. "I just wish...," he mumbled barely audible to them, "I just wish I could go back and do it all over again. This time I'd never take him for granted. I'd never blow off his stupid requests... I'd even force myself to not let his self-righteous personality get under my skin...I'd..."

Corbin's body twitched beneath the blanket, breaking the conversation as Logan quickly shuffled away from.

"Just the rigor mortis creepin' in, fellas," Grubble muttered, having seen it more times than he would wish upon anyone. The pair looked at him, surprised by the uncharacteristically intelligent observation. This was probably the smartest thing to come out of the old gnome's mouth since they had joined up. Usually, it was *bloody* this and *blazes* that, followed by some spitting.

The body twitched again, proving him wrong by sitting upright! Now Grubble was the one frightened, quickly putting distance between himself and the apparent zombie. Corbin's head slowly turned under the blanket, to look directly at them. As the man moaned, Bipp was the first to react, hopping forward and clunking him across the head with his small frying pan.

"Ouch!" Corbin yelled gripping his forehead.

"Fer Crystal's sake, Bipp, what the Hel are you doing?" Logan shouted, snatching the pan from his friend's hand before he could strike again.

Bipp shrugged. "Thought he was a zombie, sorry..." he rubbed his nose, uncomfortably embarrassed, but still not quite sure he was incorrect.

"Who the heck believes in zombies?" Logan said, helping his brother sit back up. "What are you, ten?" A small lump was beginning to swell on Corbin's head where the pan had connected.

"Yeah, what are ye thinkin?" Grubble added half-heartedly. "Zombies? Pish posh."

"Ugh...," Corbin groaned. "Hey guys...I'm back." His mouth was dry as sawdust, and his head was throbbing.

"How in the blazes *are* ye still alive?" Grubble asked, while Logan noticed he still had not put away his axe.

"It's a long story... I'll tell it when we get out of this place." Corbin tried to stand, but his legs were too weak, so Logan braced his body. The humans had to crouch low anyhow, the maintenance shafts being built to accommodate gnome workers. A crashing sound echoed through the tunnels, deafening in the closed quarters.

"Hey this is great! Now Logan can tell ye all those things he's been meaning to say!" Bipp exclaimed merrily, while emphatically nodding his head.

"Eh...what was it you needed to say?" Corbin weakly asked his big brother.

Logan bit his lip. "*What?* Oh nothing, the little fella probably bumped his head or something... Who knows what he's even talking about half the time?"

Corbin was too disoriented to take note of the exchange, shrugging and turning his head away to stop the tunnel from spinning. Logan silently scowled at Bipp who just shrugged innocently.

"You got some timing I'll tell ye, Falian," Grubble said, gathering his supplies from the floor. "Sounds like the rats done found our hidey hole!" He slapped Bipp's pack to his chest.

"Probably the work of Baetylus...," Corbin reasoned, rubbing the tight muscles in his legs to get blood flowing again.

"The All-Father?" Logan said. "So that *thing* was actually him back in the king's hall? Why would..."

"Honestly, we don't have time for all that. Right now we have to focus on getting out of here alive."

"I second that one," Grubble said and turned to head down the shaft.

"Wait," Corbin gathered the group in close. "It does not matter where we go, the Crystal will track us down and guide the cobolds to our location. But not if I have anything to say about it." He clasped the Svalin back in place over his ear lobe, thinking what a fool he had been to blindly follow the deity. No wonder Baetylus had been so insistent to have him take off the mind-shielding device. The magical ward in itself would not be enough however, so Corbin fell into his trance. The throbbing ache of his head made it difficult to find a focus. During the short time he was out of body, Corbin had kept his mind together by sheer force of will and working the psionic energy, unraveling new mysteries in the psychic aether that would have taken the layman years to comprehend.

Now that he was alive again, the aether flowed into new patterns much stronger than before, intricately bending to his will. The area around his chest lit up from a bubble of psychic energy that stretched outward until it covered the entire group. Grubble looked like he was ready to flee but forced himself to stand his ground. The bubble split off forming around each of them like a cocoon, smoothing out against their contours, and disappearing into their skin. The tunnels were filling with the sounds of bloodthirsty cobolds entering from far off, by the King's chamber.

"What is this stuff?" Logan asked in awe as it disappeared.

"I do not fully understand yet, but you can think of it like a blanket to protect us from Baetylus' filthy probing suggestions. To him we just became invisible." Corbin felt weak and tired from expending so much energy, his body already feeling stiff and aching from the near-death experience.

"Great stuff...let's get going," Grubble said grouchily and raced down the hall, tired of waiting around for magic tricks.

The brothers followed him, with Logan bracing Corbin's weight and helping him make his way. Bipp was staring at his forearms, wondering where the magical shield went, and whether he should be worried if Corbin got a sudden craving for meat. Realizing he was alone, he hopped up and chased after the group into the darkness.

Logan was the last of them to climb out of the maintenance shaft. He wanted to make sure the gnomes had a boost to get out through the floor. The cobolds could still be heard from somewhere distant in the network of tunnels below. At first there had been enraged screams at losing their trail, but that had faded as time dragged on with no sign of the intruders. Corbin said they must have been having a Hel of a time trying to find the group without the mental suggestions of Baetylus.

Grubble judged that they should be on the far side of the palace at this point, the opposite direction to home unfortunately, but far enough away from the cobold horde to regroup and come up with a better plan to get out of Ul'kor.

"What part of the castle is this?" Logan asked Bipp, looking around at the strange place. The walls were dyed a turquoise color that, even covered with dust, stood out in stark contrast to the drab walls from earlier.

"Only poffers fancy enough to care about coloring walls is the clerics' guild in Hodric's Hill," Grubble said. "If you ask me, we can do without all the flim flam of different colors. It's too distracting."

"Be about right, if you see the ruins carved overhead," Bipp said, pointing straight up at the ceiling of the curved hallway. A large, rounded stone was set overhead, with another old gnomish ruin carved into it.

"It's some sort of protection spell, right?" Corbin asked the scholarly little engineer.

Bipp nodded. He was impressed to hear someone else in the group knew something of ancient symbolism. "Cleric magic to be precise. This is probably from the infamous Crow's Guild."

Around the corner, the hallway came to an abrupt dead end, splitting to either side and forming new paths. "Which way do we go?" Corbin asked.

Bipp inspected the keystones above the entranceways. "Says Wisdom and Botanicals...," Bipp translated, pointing at each in turn.

"Elder Morgana always said, *when in doubt choose the wisest path*," Logan joked, deciding for them and prompting Corbin to search for signs of life ahead. He scrunched his forehead finding something peculiar. Corbin turned about and pointed down the Botanical hallway instead.

"There's something down there, but it's not sentient...," Corbin said. "I can't explain what it is I'm sensing. Almost like a pulsing..."

"Should we check it out?" Bipp said.

"Alrighty then...Botanicals it is," Logan said, turning about face to the other hallway. The path snaked back and forth, which was odd, as there were not many rooms off it that they had seen thus far. Each room was barren, some held nothing more than a mortar and pestle or even an alembic for alchemy, but most were pillaged long ago by the invading horde.

Corbin let them know they were getting closer as the alien feeling grew stronger. They had to stop short around the last bend when the path ended prematurely. This time there were no other paths splitting off. Instead, it looked as if the entire corridor had been sealed away with a large stone plug that had been set tightly into the space.

"This is it!" Corbin said. "This is the source of the pulsing." He tapped the hot stone, unsure what to make of the strange carvings covering it.

Bipp studied the area carefully, his concentration intense. "Probably more human trouble by the looks of it," Grubble complained kicking the dusty floor while he paced.

"Hmmm...this is very interesting. These inscriptions are not just written in High Gnomish, but are also from the magical dialect, so they are not only ancient but were also used by only the most advanced Clerics of Ul'kor." Bipp thought out loud.

"Huh, so ye can't translate it then?" Grubble grunted contemptuously.

"Didn't say that. Did you guys hear me say that? That's not what I said. Spent half my twelfth year at Pomk University learning High Gnomish, happens to be one of my specialties...hehehe." Bipp held his hands at his waist beaming, but the group did not seem moved by his scholarly knowledge. "Right...anyhow says here, more or less, that this area's been sealed off," he added.

Logan slapped his own face in frustration, which the little gnome found puzzling. "Bipp, we *know* it's sealed off... What we don't know is why."

The gnome looked up at him and nodded his head, turning back to the strange blockade. "Hmmm...says something about the Ul'kor rift and some such about an evil that..."

"Fer Thorgar's sake lad, just read the whole flippin' thing out loud to us from the beginnin'!" Grubble snarled. He was clearly past the point of annoyance and even unlatched his battle-axe for extra incentive. Bipp gulped and read from the beginning.

> *'Through this portal lies the heart of our Kingdom,*
> *Sealed forever, protecting Vanidriell,*
> *from the Traitorous fiend Hublin.*
> *Goodly gnome turned to the path of Evil,*
> *Power he sought, our kingdom he split.*
> *Never release these cursed grounds,*
> *Less you free Shadows upon the land once more.*

The message was clear and foreboding. None of them intended to try to get past this seal.

"So, all this time...," Grubble whispered, "it was a gnome what caused the fall of Ul'kor?" He sounded as if he could hardly believe his own realization.

"Well, Grubble," Logan said, "at least now we know it wasn't human trouble after all, eh?"

The little warrior growled and punched the stone seal several times in a rage. A crack of light blinded them, and they found Grubble on his back.

"I wouldn't mess with that thing if I were you," Logan said.

Grubble got to his feet and glowered up at him, before spitting on the ground at the seal's foot. With that, he turned and stomped back down the hall, muttering and cursing the whole way.

"What has gotten into him?" Logan innocently asked.

"Seriously, Logan?" Corbin asked. "Sometimes I don't know what to do with you." He shook his head and chased after the warrior.

"What?" Logan asked again, still not understanding why Grubble would be so upset. He looked to Bipp and shrugged.

"Ye have to understand this is a shock to us," Bipp said. "All our lives we knew Ul'kor was cursed. But not to be hurting your feelings, general consensus has always been that it was something the humans did to our people. For us to find out now, after all these years thinking otherwise, that it was one of our own what did this to our race...well it's a lot to take in." Bipp knew Logan did not mean any real offense and reasoned that sometimes the young man was just too dumb to know any better.

Corbin bolted back around the corner looking frazzled. "I don't know where he went off to! One minute he was there and the next he was gone!"

"Did you search for him with your mind thingy?" Bipp asked.

"When I put that shield on us, it blocked him from me as well. If I take it down that exposes us all to Baetylus again, and he'll know I still live to boot."

"That's not good," Logan said.

"Most likely he just needs time to stew," Bipp said. "As I said it's a lot to take in."

Logan nodded his head. "Okay, but it's going to be dangerous to stay in one place, especially cornered in this dead end."

"Look, let's retrace our path to the other halls," Bipp said. "He couldn't have gone too far."

Logan and Corbin agreed. They wanted to be rational about their approach to finding Grubble. All the way back they saw no sign of him. Bipp began nervously fidgeting his thumbs, worried that their companion had been captured. They traveled as far back as where the path first split and decided to follow the alternate route until they came to an exit, bringing them back outside into the night air.

"There is no way we could have missed him in there," Logan insisted, looking back at the castle walls.

An arrow hissed through the air, clipping the wall just beside him. Weapons were immediately drawn, and the trio fell into a triangle formation ready for the fight.

"Oh, sweet mother of pearl," Bipp croaked, astonished at the horde surrounding them. There had to be at least thirty of the little monsters blissfully unaware as they searched the courtyard for the intruder's whereabouts. The archer who had spotted them and thought to make a name for itself cursed its luck at missing the unsuspecting target.

"Well boys, it's been fun, but I think it's time to RUUUUUNNN!" Logan yelled. Bipp hopped up, his little feet pumping in midair, and landed barreling full speed ahead. The archer called out to alert his clan, jumping and pointing at the fleeing intruders.

They ran straight for the edge of the spire, where a massive stone bridge, lined with gnome statues of guardians and wide enough across to fit five carriages side by side, arched across the yawning chasm. A band of cobolds ran to block their escape as the horde behind sprang into action, clambering over one another to get to the intruders and howling in glee.

Logan called for his companions not to slow their pace, running hard into the group blocking their way to the bridge. He did not waste time with hand-to-hand combat, taking one of the beasts out with a laser blast to the chest and slamming the butt of his rifle hard across another's forehead.

Corbin spun his voulge around low, knocking three of the monsters to the ground, while Bipp barreled into another headfirst, hurling the screaming creature over the edge of the cliff. As gruesome as their onslaught was, the cobolds quickly recovered. The little hairy humanoids were stabbing, bashing, and slashing at them with all manner of crude weapons. As soon as one fell another was there to take its place, rushing in from the side.

"There are too many of them!" Logan shouted before blasting another pointblank in the chest, while looking over his shoulder at the incoming army of humanoids.

"We have to get past them to the bridge," Corbin yelled, "it's our only hope!" He danced backward, avoiding a dagger and swung his weapon in for a fatal blow. The horde was close enough now, where they could rain a barrage of tiny arrows down upon them, callously taking down a couple of their own kindred in the process. One pierced right into Logan's thigh. Howling, he missed an opportunity to block, catching a dagger across his forearm. Corbin saw his brother go down, but there were too many of the little monsters around him and the horde was closing in quickly.

The eager furry cobolds jumped up and down, stomping on Logan where he hit the dirt, as he tried in vain to protect his head with a blocking arm. One of the laughing monster's head went flying past its friends as a roar announced Grubble's arrival on the other side of the blocking clan. Corbin took full advantage of the moment, slashing brutally against the pressing beasts. Both worked furiously to cut a swath through their enemies while Bipp helped Logan to his feet, who had begun blindly firing rounds off with his plasma rifle hoping the take down some of the incoming attackers.

Their path clear, the companions took flight over the massive stone bridge. If Bipp had taken a second to look down over the edge, the engineer in him may not have been able to get across, realizing how high they were on a centuries old, unkempt, stone overpass. Logan took up the rear blasting deadly shots into the wall of snarling pursuers. The horde broke once on the bridge, with lone cobolds splitting off in different directions, and a couple even slipped under the suspended platform, scurrying on all fours.

"Did you know they could do that?" Logan asked Bipp in bewilderment.

"They're cobolds!" Bipp replied, as if that were answer enough.

Grubble shouldered one of the beasts hard, shoving its flailing body off the bridge. "Less talk more killin'!" he growled.

Corbin ran from side to side, cutting down the humanoids as they scrambled from beneath the bridge trying to get behind the companions and box them in. Logan felt an icy chill as more and more of the monsters flooded toward the overpass from inside the city. There seemed to be no end to their numbers, there had to be hundreds of them! As if that were not bad enough, something large was making its way through their ranks, flinging cobolds in the air to clear its way. Logan took another newcomer down then decided he did not want to be on the welcoming committee for whatever was coming.

He turned and sprinted further onto the bridge. Over his shoulder, he spied the hulking form of a gigantic shiny black rhino beetle as it rammed through the blocking horde. The ground of the bridge shook as it stomped heavily onto it. On its back rode the cobold King, swinging an eight-foot flail with a spiked ball at the end. Grubble barely had time to move out of the way before the weapon smashed past his shoulder. The chain still caught him, throwing the gnome spiraling in the air across the wide bridge.

Logan stopped short, and let off a blast, just missing the gloating riders spinning weapon. The king directed his attention toward him, confidently gritting his thick fangs before charging the armored beetle straight in his direction. Pulling on chains that were bored right into the armored hulk's head, the king forced his pet to thrash the three-foot horn at the tip of its face as it came on. Logan rolled across the area like a ball, having to drop his rifle, which was mangled to a pulp under the sheer weight of the mount's stomping legs. Skittering to a halt, the chieftain turned around, pulling hard on the reigns with one arm, while swinging his mighty flail with the other.

Corbin sprinted in, using his voulge to pole vault high over the mounted cobold leader. As he passed overhead, he swung down in an arc, cutting the laughter from the monster along with half his ear. Corbin cursed his aim. It was a prime opportunity lost. Bipp had no time to watch the spectacle, holding off circling cobolds while Grubble recovered his senses.

The king roared and brutally charged, in another attempt to crush Logan. He was in a murderous rage, having been cut by the other sneaky human. To avoid being crushed, Logan desperately threw himself over the edge of the bridge. His metal fingers dug deeply into the crumbling stone and stopped his fall, until he was dangling dangerously on its side. As the rhino beetle barreled past where he had been, it crashed right through a towering gnome statue, shattering it in a shower of rocks and dust that rained down all around Logan's cringing form. The king peered back over to Corbin, coldly laughing over his victory.

A shocked cobold stared Logan in the face. He was hanging right in front of where it crawled across the underside of the bridge. Logan seized the moment of surprise to disarm it with a smile then yanked down hard with his one free hand around its filthy neck, dropping the screaming monster down the dizzying heights, into the yawning abyss below.

Above, Grubble had come to his feet and was viciously cutting down cobolds left and right. The chieftain reigned in his beast, seeing his men go down, and slammed the swinging flail across the warrior's back, ripping pieces of his armor off in chunks. Grubble roared, thrown by the weapon's momentum into the air again. He let his axe fly from his powerful grip, spinning through the air, head over hilt to land sure and true into the horned mount's cheek. The beetle's high-pitched screech of pain was so loud everyone on the bridge had to stop for a moment and cover their ears. Then it barreled in to eat the little gnome, oblivious of its master's commands.

Corbin threw himself swiftly across the ground, redirecting and cushioning Grubble as he hit the bridge. Another statue was shattered on the other side of the ancient bridge and the rider's flail dug a chunk out of the stone at their heels.

"You okay?" Corbin asked the wounded gnome.

"Fit as a fiddle," Grubble growled, wincing and unlatching a sickle from his belt.

Logan took Bipp's offered hand to help him back onto the bridge. When he tried to release the clutching metal fingers, a heavy piece of stone came with them. The king was just getting ready to crush his brother's exposed flank with the deadly swinging flail! Logan acted quickly. He almost fell forward throwing the chunk of bridge as hard as he could muster.

He could not help laughing as his aim hit the cobold leader square in the side of his head, almost wrenching him off his saddle and disarming the flail from his grasp. The head of the weapon went flying into a nearby group of cheering cobolds who were gored by the deadly spikes. Logan called for his companions to retreat, running past the stunned king to the far side of the bridge.

"He's turning about!" A wide-eyed Bipp warned. His brother stopped in the middle of the bridge, spreading out his feet for support, and harnessed his voulge behind his back.

"Corbin, are you out of your mind?" Logan screamed.

Corbin blocked him out and channeled the psychic aether around him, letting it build up inside him until it felt likely he would burst. The monstrous horned beetle was nearly upon him. Opening his eyes, he screamed for Elise and let the pent-up energy shoot out like a lance, burning and tearing into the beast's mind. The beetle stopped its charge, screeching again and standing upright on hind quarters, while the other four legs scrambled in midair.

Logan let out a massive electric blast from his fist, cooking the exposed underbelly and ripping the rhino beetle's insides apart. The vicious king tried to escape his mount as it flipped onto its back, but he was not nearly fast enough. It fell over him, crushing half his body under its weight. The bridge shook violently as the hulking beast crashed down on its back. No sooner did it lay still, than Grubble made his way over and was pulling his battle-axe from where it was stuck in the vanquished beetle's armored face.

The cobold horde fell silent, watching in horror as their great and mighty leader was bested by the foul greedy humans and gnomes. Grubble stalked around the armored hulk, all the while contemptuously eyeing the monstrous horde. Their chieftain was squirming, desperate to get out from beneath where his legs were pinned. He fell stock-still seeing the angry gnome stalk over to him. Grubble spat on the ground toward the king's clan. Without taking his eyes off their ranks he lifted his battle axe high overhead and slammed it down with a furious cry. The blade cleaved the king's head off with the one mighty swing. Grubble bent down and picked up his prize, lifting it high into the air for all to see, then spat again and threw it far across the bridge into the mob of humanoids.

"Go back to Hel, where ye came from!" Grubble shouted to the monstrous horde then strode back toward his companions, ignoring his serious battle wounds in his moment of triumph.

"They're not following," Logan said.

"They're confused with no one to tell them what to do," Corbin reasoned.

A bolt flew from the crowd, piercing hard into the center of Grubble's back. The gnome warrior staggered forward a few steps, and opening his eyes wide, sucking in air.

Burgoth, the shaman, grinned cruelly from inside the horde, to see that her shot found the mark. Grubble stood still, staring at his companions while the air behind him filled up with a cloud of raining arrows, one after the other thudding into the proud warrior's back. He stubbornly marched back toward them, flinching with each stab.

Corbin and Bipp ran out to pull the gnome across the rest of the bridge. Shaman Burgoth snarled, "Slay the defilers!" The cobolds hooted and squealed, racing across the bridge toward them. Corbin made it to the other side, pulling Grubble off the bridge, and Logan aimed his fist high into the air, shouting for his brother to hurry.

Corbin shot him a puzzled look.

"I've got an idea," was the only explanation he gave as the small compartment on top of his mechanical fist opened. A tiny pill shape zipped into the air high overhead. There was a smoky spiral in its wake and Logan turned his head, shielding his eyes and motioning for Corbin to do the same.

There was a loud explosion that rocked the entire cavern. The moss ceiling lit up with a wave of fire. Corbin finally understood the wall of rocks he had found beside the sauria while tracking Logan, as gigantic stalactites dislodged from the ceiling, pummeling the bridge to pieces, and smashing their enemy to a pulp.

The cobolds howled fearfully, scattering in every direction, some jumping right off the bridge in their mindless terror. Within seconds the bridge, which had withstood centuries of time, was obliterated by the falling ceiling, and the vicious cobold horde was sent fleeing back into the cursed ruins of Ul'kor.

Logan did not have time to savor their victory as Bipp's sobbing drew his attention. Grubble lay still in the dirt on his side, blood leaking out of him faster than they could possibly hope to stem. Corbin was speaking quietly to the old gnome, trying to keep him aware while he broke off the arrows one by one. The warrior grabbed his forearm with a grip strong as a vice to stop the pointless effort.

"Never ye mind that now lad...it's to the halls of Valhalla for me," Grubble said, accepting his fate. He was proud to die a warrior's death. Corbin offered a heartfelt apology trying to voice how sorry he was that they had let him down.

"Ye did nothing of the sort...," Grubble said, his voice like grinding stones. "Yer some of the good ones don't ye be doubtin' it... I'm proud to have fought beside ye. Truer warriors have never been seen."

"For humans, eh?" Logan stammered through the pain clenching around his throat, forcing the gnome to laugh painfully.

"Aye, even fer humans...best man-folk I ever done met, lad," Grubble admitted as he closed his eyes for the last time in Vanidriell. Many years of his long life stretched out before him, all the dreams, all the moments of happiness and sadness, the taste of butterscotch, the meaninglessness of anger, all of it passed through an empty void that whispered his name.

Grubble's aching chest stopped moving and his grip loosened on Corbin's wrist as a look of content washed over him. Corbin could dimly make out the proud warrior's soul leaving his body for the afterlife, wondering aloud if his beloved wife Annit would be waiting for him, and he silently wished the gnome good speed on his journey.

Chapter 23

At first time passed by slowly, the days dragging on as each of them took turns carrying Grubble's rotting body. After a two-day march, they found an area with soil soft enough to bury the warrior respectfully. None spoke as they laid him to rest. Bipp topped the grave with a cairn of stones.

"He deserves a hero's parade in Dudje," Bipp said, choking on his words. "Not this pitiful grave far away from home."

Logan placed a hand on the gnome's shoulder to comfort him. "Aye, he was an amazing man, who died a warrior's death that surely the gods themselves could smile upon. We were better for knowing him." Corbin was not sure how much belief he held in the gods anymore, but he found his brother's humility touching. Bowing their heads, they stood silent vigil for a few hours before forcing themselves to resume their march.

As they walked, Corbin filled them in on everything that he had witnessed while in death. At first Bipp doubted it had all actually happened, thinking perhaps it more likely some deep dream Corbin had lost in on the brink of death. On the other hand, the gnome saw how readily Logan was to accept his younger brother's word. Either way, the decision was made for them. The way back to Dudje was lost, the bridge to Ul'kor destroyed, and the surface was supposedly close by, based on Corbin's testament. They were determined now to find the man named Isaac who would help them free the people of New Fal. Three more days dragged by in the wide lifeless tunnels.

"Bah, I think we've been sent on a wild goose chase by your ghost lady," Bipp said, breaking the silence.

"We're running out of rations too," Logan said, shaking his head. Bipp's stomach growled loudly at the mention of food. They had run dangerously low on provisions and were forced to ration them.

"Could be a wild shot," Corbin said, "but then what do you make of that?"

They had just reached the top of a sloping tunnel, pointing ahead. Before them, the cramped area widened out into a taller cavern, at the end of which was a dead end of sorts. The companions all drew their weapons as they approached, carefully surveying their surroundings.

"There's something you don't see every day, eh?" Bipp wondered in awe, referring to a large, shiny column that came down from the ceiling to the floor.

"What do you think it is?" Logan asked his brother as they made their way closer to the strange pillar. At its base a doorway lay open in ruins, exploded from the outside in, crushing the small room behind it into a twisted, crumpled mess. Corbin stuck his head through the opening to gaze up into a shaft of darkness.

"Looks like some sort of manmade tunnel." His words echoed up the metal tube.

"Aye, like an elevator but smaller," Bipp reasoned, comparing it to the pulley system used to transport workers and ore in the gnome mines back home. They clambered over the wreckage inside the shaft to search for footholds he said should be there. The iron rungs stretched all the way up and disappearing into the shadows above. Corbin stopped his brother from climbing, to tie a rope around each of their waists, connecting them in a lifeline.

"We have no idea how far up this thing is going to go, best to play it safe," he reasoned.

Logan had to be extra careful gripping the rusty metal rungs, less he crush one with his mechanical grip. Up and up they went, climbing for what felt like eternity. Bipp's shorter arms grew tired quicker than his companions did, so the men had to take turns carrying him on their backs. Just when Logan's muscles were burning beyond belief, aching for rest, he caught a glimpse of something to their right.

"Look there," he said. "I think it's a door." He pointed to a feint rectangular outline set in the shaft next to them. Bipp nodded excitedly, scrambling up his back and stepping on his head to get back on the ladder.

"If this is like the 'vators back in the mines, we should find an...*ah*, yup here it is!" Bipp worked a rusty door the size of his hand open. Inside it, he struggled to turn a metal valve. At first it did not want to budge, but then with a sharp groaning it slowly turned counterclockwise. The outline moved inward, revealing a double set of doors that shifted slowly to either side, opening a portal.

Light flooded the shaft from the chamber beyond, stinging their eyes, which had grown accustomed to the bleak darkness. One by one, the companions pulled themselves through the opening, until they all lay about in pile, heavily breathing and rubbing sore muscles. Logan began laughing, happy to be out of the never-ending tube. Looking around them, he could see the dim light was coming from a small recess in the wall. Standing up he gauged the room they were in was not built of stone or wood. The walls' material was alien to him, yet comforting in some primal way.

"Yuck these floors are all sticky," Bipp said, slapping the ground with his bare hand and pulled it away with a slight sucking sound.

Strands of thick webbing covered the ground in interlacing patterns. At the far end of the room lay piles of rounded clumps of the stuff. Corbin found that the sole doorway out was stuck in place and refused to budge.

"I don't have a good feeling about this place," Bipp said. "This room is giving me the willies."

"Feel like sitting ducks in here," Corbin agreed. "Let me boost you up to that opening so you can try and get this door open from the other side?" he asked Bipp, pointing above their heads where a section of the ceiling had been torn away revealing a crawl space over the doorframe.

The gnome climbed up over his shoulders and, once inside, turned to give an encouraging thumb up. "Okay, I won't go too far, just enough to see where this leads. Be back in a jiffy, fellas." With that he scurried away on all fours.

"Corbin, come check these out," Logan called over his shoulder, inspecting two large hanging sacs. They were covered with more of the sticky strands. He pulled a dagger out and cut a long slit down one. A putrid odor of rotting fruit hit him in the face, leaving them both gagging hard to get the foul taste out of their mouths. Inside the sac was a grisly form. Some sort of oddly contorted humanoid that had been sucked dry of its fluids, leaving only a mummified husk of skin and bones.

"I think this was a person," Logan said, looking at the humanoid's strange clothing.

His heart jumped two feet from his chest when the sacs twin shifted slightly. He hoped his little brother did not notice the reaction. "Try that one, something is inside," Logan said, brandishing his revolver and steadying it on the sac. Corbin looked to him, gave a nod, and slit the sac wide open. This time a fresh body fell forward out of the thing. Logan reflexively reached out to catch it from hitting the floor and sharply realized how disgusting it must be, flinging the thing away from himself.

They were both astonished to find it was a female human!

"How in the Hel did she get up here?" Logan said. "Where did she come from?"

The woman lay sprawled across the floor, eyes closed, her skin a pale gray sickly color and long raven-black hair strewn across the sticky strands of webbing. Corbin tried to mouth a response, but he was unable to find adequate words to describe his thoughts and before he could muster anything intelligible, they heard Bipp's screaming.

Running over to the hole, Logan shouted for the gnome. Bipp answered by jumping out of the void, screaming and pointing over his shoulder while dashing to the far side of the room. The brothers did not need more information than that and quickly joined him with weapons ready.

Four sets of glowing yellow eyes appeared in the recess, hungrily staring at them, followed by long furry arachnid legs reaching around the opening. A giant spider dropped to the floor in front of them, as another joined it overhead. They were the size of large dogs, and Corbin's skin crawled to behold them. Logan shouldered his awestruck brother out of the way just in time to avoid a hissing stream of green venom.

"I'm getting good at that," Logan said to Bipp.

Another hairy beast skittered across the ceiling, its eight legs driving the predator with lightning speed. Logan let off two short shots, each bullet tearing off one of the monster's legs, while his brother fended off the stalker to their front. The spider hissed in pain, dropping from the ceiling belly side up. Bipp ran in for the kill, slamming his hammer hard into the thing's abdomen, but a thrashing leg caught him, throwing the gnome onto remnants of a hanging sack, where he solidly stuck and frantically tried to wiggle free.

The spider was not dead yet and it flipped back over with thick yellow blood oozing across the floor beneath it. A strand of webbing caught Logan's pistol hand, yanking him forward, toward a set of hungry snapping fangs.

Bipp dropped from the sac, landing on top of the beast's furry back as Logan struggled against its pull. Multiple eyes shifted to look at the gnome and the spider bucked, flinging him over Logan to land between Corbin and its sister. Logan could see his brother had the other beast in hand, four of its legs already dismembered. His captor pulled hard on the strand again, reeling him in closer to dripping fangs while its back legs anchored against the floor.

"Want a taste, do you?" Logan grunted, struggling to break free. "I'll give you a taste, tell me what you think." Logan gripped the sticky strand with his metal hand, letting electricity course through it into the monster's open mouth. The spider chittered a high-pitch noise that made his stomach feel sick. The sides of its body burst open from the inside, and the cooked beast fell limply to the floor.

Logan tried to break free from the webbing, so he could help his brother but there was no hope. Corbin circled the spider, rolling to the side each time it frantically spit venom at him. He could not help smiling at his brother's skill, to have such a dangerous monster cornered like that. Corbin feinted right, the spider's eyes and body following him, then shifted sharply to the left stabbing the beast's face with his voulge. The spider let out a death rattle with convulsing legs as it too fell limp.

Bipp jumped up and down celebrating, kicking the spider where it lay in front of the door, taunting the unmoving body.

"Corbin, I could use that blade of yours," Logan said, gesturing to his hand where it was stuck in the webbing.

"There goes your other gun, guess you are going to have to learn how to fight like a man now, huh?" Corbin teased, cutting the strands free.

Logan backhanded his brother hard, throwing him to the floor with the force of the surprise attack. Corbin was shocked to look up and see his brother's hand glowing hot white.

"Bipp duck!" Logan screamed, as another spider slid down from the hole overhead on a strand of webbing, fangs dripping with venom. The gnome hopped out of the way and a blast rang in their ears, hotly sizzling through the spider, which was slammed flat over the sealed door. When the beam subsided, there was nothing left of the sneaky predator but a gaping hole in the metal door, surrounded by the burnt outline of spider legs.

"Blazing dogs above, you saved my skin!" Bipp exclaimed.

"That's twice now you owe me," Logan groaned from the floor, where he weakly sat on his knees. The depletion of energy was too much for him to handle after days without eating. Logan shot his brother an apologetic look for hitting him so hard, but Corbin shrugged it off and went back to cutting him free from the strands.

"Why didn't you just *blast* your way free from this stuff?" Corbin asked.

Now it was Logan's turn to shrug, "It takes too much out of me. I'm pretty sure the blast is powered by my own life force...or nutrients or something. I don't know, I never got to ask Mr. Beauford."

"Ooooh, who is the lovely lass, then?" Bipp hooted standing over the woman they had freed from the spider's feeding sac. Logan noticed her skin was not as gray anymore, color returning to her face. He rubbed his freed wrist as Corbin moved over to her, placing two fingers under her jaw and searching for a pulse.

"She is still alive, but barely, who knows what those *things* were doing to her."

"Looks like they were slowly feasting on her insides," Logan said. "This other guy's been sucked dry."

"Um...fellas?" Bipp called from the blasted doorway. "You gotta see this." He was staring through the hole into a blue glowing room. They joined him on either side, gazing through the portal where an enormous chamber lay beyond. It was at least fifty times the size of the one they were in and stretched so far back it seemed to go on forever. All along the walls, row upon row of man-sized glass cylinders were stacked. Each one was full of a frozen glowing blue liquid that housed a sleeping human hooked to some sort of breathing apparatus.

"What in the blue blazes?" Bipp stammered.

The brothers could only look to each other, then back at the woman behind them.

"Well boys, looks like we found Isaac," Logan said.

Corbin nodded his head in agreement. "Yeah, but which one is he?"

"Let's wake the lass and find out, shall we?" Bipp asked.

The brothers nodded at the same time, staring out into the rows of sleeping humans, and wondering what dark secrets might await.

Epilogue

Baetylus watched on through the eyes of the shaman Burgoth. It was disappointed to see the Walker brothers escape, but at least they would not be able to come back to New Fal and ruin everything the Crystal had spent generations putting into place.

Corbin Walker was a tricky one. It had vastly underestimated the power of that man's mind and had a sneaking suspicion he had garnered help somewhere else. It was a shame all these deaths were not closer, where it could feed off their dying souls. So much power to be harvested with such a massacre. And after the meddlesome boys had ruined its plans to have the skex swarm feast off the citizens of Fal. That had brought on a feeling that the Crystal had never felt before, something of annoyance. Baetylus did not like wasting its time, and it had taken several months of focus, constantly sending its will into the dimwitted insects, to muster them up and send in the wave of attacks. He lamented the missed opportunity for reaping, that would have greatly boosted his strength.

"Ahhh...," the Crystal sighed, leaving the distant ruins of Ul'kor behind and directing its attention back on the human city of Fal below. Here its latest pawn lay in bed, tossing about in a feverish sleep. Baetylus cackled over Fafnir's anguish as visions of a taunting Lady Cassandra plagued his dreams. The Magistrate was running down an endless street while citizens were throwing rotten vegetables at him and screaming for his execution. Around a bend, Arch Councilor Zacharia pointed an accusatory finger at him, "*Half-blood.*"

How weak and fragile the human condition, yet how delightful for Baetylus to toy with.

Dipping inside the dream, he appeared before the Magistrate as the visage of an old man in white flowing robes. Baetylus sent out a mental suggestion to the Magistrate that everything was safe now, calming his churning mind. Fafnir gathered his dream self, looking around at the fading shadows of his tormentors, and understanding that his Lord had come calling again. He was a little embarrassed with the realization that he had been caught having a nightmare, not wanting his god to see this moment of weakness.

"Fear not my son. It is natural for mankind to dwell on baser fears" Baetylus said.

"All-Father," Fafnir bowed low, "to what do I owe this great honor, my Lord?"

"The dangerous Walker brothers are gone from this realm. They will no longer pose a threat to our people," Baetylus said.

Fafnir felt a wave of relief to have the despicable problem dealt with. He had feared Logan's return and had worked out several scenarios to hide the truth of his involvement in Beauford's assassination, but once Arch Councilor Zacharia opened your mind there was not much hiding of the truth. To know the man would never be able to return just secured his seat on the Council.

"I see your greed for personal glory has not lessened," Baetylus coolly observed.

"My humble apologies, Lord. Everything I do is truly for the betterment of my people," Fafnir groveled.

"Humph, I almost think you believe your righteous lies," Baetylus said. "And what of the Ivarone girl, I do not see her anymore?"

"She has gone missing, my Lord," Fafnir said, "though we are still trying to figure out how." He quickly added, "We will catch her soon enough, however."

"It would be wise that you do. And be sure to lay waste to Riverbell. I will damn their souls to the abyss for this betrayal." Fafnir could almost hear the hunger in his god's voice, though he had no idea it was for the souls it would soon feast upon.

"I already have men traveling there to execute every last one of them as we speak, Great One," Fafnir said.

Baetylus got what it had come for and switched the nightmare back on for Fafnir, turning up the intensity for fun through a minor mental suggestion. It had dwelled so long in this one's mind that it was mere child's play to influence the man, who had already forgotten his conversation with the Crystal and was running terrified down the streets while his tormentors cut his bare blue skin with whips, yelling for the death of the half-blood jotnar traitor.

Baetylus coiled inside its crystalline shell above the kingdom of New Fal, smugly savoring another day to come with its playthings. Soon the corrupt sentience would gather enough power to walk among the weak-minded mortals below and claim its birthright. However, until then, at least it had the upcoming harvesting of souls from Riverbell to look forward to. The idea of it had him cackling so loudly into the psychic aether that all the babies in Fal woke with cries in the night.

Secrets of the Elders

D.M. Almond

FOLLOW THE ADVENTURES of the Walker Brothers and their companions, in book two of the series, LAND of the GIANTS.

Become an Acadian today to receive free exclusive short stories at http://www.dmalmond.com and to keep up to date on everything Acadia.

If you enjoyed the novel even half as much as David enjoyed writing it, there can be no finer gift than a review! Reviews are vital to an author's ability to be seen by others. Please share your thoughts on Amazon's review section http://www.amazon.com/dp/B00KSFZSU4

Acknowledgments

Without your input, this project would have been impossible. I appreciate all the time and energy each of you put into this. Special recognition for Jeni, who really went above and beyond.

Richard Skelany - Beware of falling asleep beside mushrooms little Necroscope.

Serophin – No one runs backward through a window with more flair.

Denier Spade – When will you rage?

Robert Fox – Keep to the shadows my friend.

Jeni Hamilton – I promise never to add S's to my backward and toward again!

D.M. Almond

D. M. Almond is secretly a Muppet, waiting for Kermit to call him back to the show. In the meantime, he spends his nights shackled to a keyboard, tapping away at the keys in some unyielding search for Acadia, a place he hopes you have enjoyed visiting. David does not take himself seriously and neither should you.

Made in United States
North Haven, CT
01 March 2022